**Selected praise for
Michelle Sagara's**

CAST IN SHADOW

"Intense, fast-paced, intriguing, compelling
and hard to put down, *Cast in Shadow* is
unforgettable."
—*In the Library Reviews*

"Michelle Sagara has created one of the most
intriguing worlds I have ever read."
—*Fallen Angel Reviews*

"Deep, dense and passionate..."
—*Romantic Science Fiction and Fantasy*

"No one provides an emotional payoff
like Michelle Sagara. Combine that with
a fast-paced police procedural, deadly magics,
five very different races and a wickedly
dry sense of humor—well, it doesn't
get any better than this."
—Bestselling author Tanya Huff

CAST IN SHADOW

MICHELLE SAGARA

LUNA™
www.LUNA-Books.com

LUNA™

CAST IN SHADOW

ISBN 0-373-80254-4

Copyright © 2005 by Michelle Sagara

www.LUNA-Books.com

Printed in U.S.A.

Acknowledgments

Terry Pearson, Tanya Huff and Rhiannon Rasmussen all read the initial proposal and outline while I fretted, because I'm good at that. The fretting. They even wanted to read *more*, and did. Also, my editor, Mary-Theresa Hussey, for giving the book a home, and for asking the right questions to keep it on track. Consider them the away team for this book.

The home team: My husband, Thomas West (whose last name I also write under), my children, my parents and my son's godfather, John Chew, and his wife, Kristen; my brother Gary and his wife, Ayami. The Tuesday night and Thursday night crew.

Thanks.

This is for Chris Szego, who read it first, and gave me exactly the encouragement I needed at exactly the right time.

CHAPTER 1

Black circles under the eyes were not, Kaylin decided, a very attractive statement. Neither was hair matted with old sweat, or eyes red with lack of sleep. She accepted the fact that on this particular morning, mirrors were *not* going to be her friend. Luckily, she didn't have many of them in the small quarters she called home. She got out of bed slowly, studiously avoided the short hall that led from her bolted doors to the kitchen, the closets and the large space she lived in otherwise, and lifted clothing from beneath a rumpled pile, examining it carefully.

It sort of looked clean.

She pulled the linen tunic over her head, cursed as her hair caught in the strings that secured it and yanked, hard. Shadows fell over the ledge of her single window, stretching across the floor at an ominous angle. She was going to be late. Again.

Pants were less tricky; she only had a few, and chose the black leather ones. They were, at the moment, the only ones she owned that weren't cut, torn or bloody.

She'd have to ask Iron Jaw for a better clothing allowance. Or more time to spend the pittance she *did* have.

The mirror in the hall began to glow, and she cursed under her breath. She'd clearly have to ask him on a *different* morning.

"Coming," she muttered.

The mirror flashed, light hanging in the room like an extended, time-slowed bolt of lightning. Iron Jaw was in a lousy mood, and it wasn't even lunch. He *hated* to use the mirrors.

She buttoned up her pants, pulled on her boots and sidled her way toward the mirror, hoping that the light was the effect of lack of sleep. Not much hope there, really.

"Kaylin, where the *hell* have you been?"

No, the mirror this morning was definitely not her friend. She pulled her hair up, curled it in a tight bun and shoved the nearest stick she could find through its center. Then she picked up the belt on the table just to the left of that mirror and donned it, adjusting dagger hilts so they didn't butt against her lower ribs.

"Kaylin Neya, you'd better answer soon. I know you're there."

Putting on her best we-both-know-it's-fake smile, she walked over to the mirror and said, sweetly, "Good morning, Marcus."

He growled.

Not a particularly encouraging sign, given that Marcus was Leontine, and had a bad habit of ripping the throats out of people who were stupid enough to annoy him. His lower fangs were in evidence as he snarled. But his eyes, cat eyes, were wide and unblinking in the golden fur that adorned his face, and his fur was not—yet—standing on end. His hands, however, were behind his back, and his broad chest was adorned with the full flowing robes of the Hawks.

Official dress. In the morning. Gods, she was going to be in trouble.

"Morning was two hours ago," he snapped.

"You're in fancy dress," she said, changing the subject about as clumsily as she ever did.

"And you look like shit. What the hell were you doing last night?"

"None of your business."

"Good answer," he growled. "Why don't you try it on the Hawklord?"

She groaned. "What day is it?"

"The fourth," he replied.

Fourth? She counted back, and realized that she'd lost a day. Again. "I'm missing something, aren't I?"

"Brains," he snapped. "And survival instinct. The Hawklord's been waiting for you for three hours."

"Tell him I'm dead."

"You will be if you don't get your ass in here." He muttered something else, a series of growls that she knew, from experience, meant something disparaging about humans. She let it pass.

"I'll be there in half an hour."

"Dressed like that? You'll be out in thirty-five. On your ass."

She put her palm on the mirror's surface, cutting him off and scattering his image. Then she went to her closet and began to really *move*.

Bathed, cleaned, groomed and in the full dress uniform of the Hawks—which still involved the only intact pants she owned—Kaylin approached the front of the forbidding stone halls ruled by the three Lords of Law: The Lord of Wolves, the Lord of Swords and the Lord of Hawks. At least that's what they were called on official documents and in polite company, of which Kaylin knew surprisingly little.

The Swords were the city's peacekeepers, something ill-suited to Kaylin; the Wolves were its hunters, and often, its killers. And the Hawks? The city's eyes. Ears. The people who actually *solved* crimes.

Then again, she would think that; Kaylin had been a Hawk for the entire time she'd been involved on the right side of the law, and didn't speak about the years that preceded it much.

By writ of the Emperor of Karaazon, the Halls of Law were the only standing structures allowed to approach the height of the Imperial palace, and the three towers, set against a wide stretch of expensive ground in the shape of a triangle, flew the flags of the Lords of Law: the Hawk, the Wolf and the Sword. From her vantage, they could hardly be seen; she was too close. But from the rest of the city? They never rested.

Neither, she thought, did the people who served them. She was damn tired.

The front doors were always manned, and she recognized Tanner and Clint as they lowered their pole-arms, barring her way. It was the Hawk's month for guard duty; they shared rotation of that honor with the Swords. The Wolves, lazy bastards, weren't considered fit for dress duty. Or ritual entries.

She hated ritual.

Clint and Tanner didn't love it much better than she did.

"Kaylin, where the hell have you been?" Tanner asked. It was the refrain that punctuated too much of her daily existence.

"Getting cleaned up, if you must know."

Tanner was, at six and a half feet, tall even for a human. His helm was strictly a dress helm, and it gleamed bronze in the afternoon sunlight, running from the capped height of his head down the line of his nose, as if it were a bird's mask. To either side of the metal, his eyes were a dark, deep brown.

Clint shook his head, and the glinting helm's light left an after-image in her vision. But he smiled. He was about two inches shorter than Tanner, and his skin was the dark ebony of the Southern stretch. She loved the sound of his voice, and he knew it.

It wasn't the only thing she loved about him.

"You've got to give up the moonlighting," he told her.

"When the pay here doesn't suck."

He laughed out loud, his halberd shaking as he began to lift it. "You really didn't get much sleep, did you? Iron Jaw has ears like a Barrani—he'll have your hide on his wall as a dartboard."

She rolled her eyes. "Can I go now?"

"Your doom," he said, his voice still sweet with the sound of amused laughter. But his expression gained a moment's gravity as he leaned forward and lowered that voice into a fold of deep velvet. "Sesti told me."

"Sesti told you what?"

"What you were doing the past two days."

"Tell her to piss off next time you see her."

He laughed again. She could spend all day making him laugh, just for the thrill of the deep rich tones of that voice. But if she did it today? It would be her last day. She smiled. "That won't be until his naming day." Aerian men were forbidden the birthing caves—unless those caves held the dead or the dying. Even then, they could come to claim their wives, no more. Kaylin had never understood this.

"When are you off duty?" she asked him.

"About two hours."

"You haven't been home yet?"

"Not yet."

"Sesti had a boy. Healthy, but his feathers were a *mess*. Took us three hours to clean 'em down."

"Always does," he said with an affectionate shrug. "Go on. Iron Jaw's been biting anyone who gets in reach."

She nodded, walked past and then turning, reached out to touch the soft, ash gray of Clint's wings. They snapped up and out beneath her fingers.

"You haven't changed in seven years," he told her, turning. "Don't *touch* the flight feathers."

If the exterior of the Halls of Law was forbidding, the interior was hardly less so. The front doors opened into a hall that not even cathedrals could boast. It rose three storeys, and across its vaulted ceilings, frescoes had been painted—Hawk, Wolf and Sword, trailing light and shadow in a grim depiction of various hunts. Sunlight streamed in from a window that was at least as tall, and certainly more impressive; the colors of the paint were protected from sunlight, and always on display, a reminder to newcomers of what the Halls meant to those who displeased their rulers.

But this hall was not meant to intimidate; it was built with a practical purpose in mind—which wasn't true of many of the Imperial buildings. The Aerians that served the Lords of Law did not walk easily in the confined, cramped space of regular human halls. Clint, armed and armored, could easily take to the air in the confines of the rising stone walls, and high, high above her, the perch of the Aerie loomed; she had seen him reach it many, many times. Aerians circled above her, against the backdrop of colored fresco, and as always, she envied them their ability to truly fly.

The closest she'd ever gotten involved a long drop that had almost ended her life. She wasn't eager to repeat it.

And if the Hawklord had really been waiting for three—close to four—hours now, she didn't give much for her chances. She began to run.

To the east of the Aerian hall, as it was colloquially called—and never in the hearing of one of the three Lords—stood another tall set of doors, adorned by another set of guards.

She recognized them both: Teela and Tain. They were sometimes called the twins by anyone who had no experience with the subtle temper and cruelty of the Barrani; they were seldom called that twice by the same person. Delicately built, they stood slightly taller than Clint, slightly shorter than Tanner.

Some people found the Barrani beautiful; Kaylin wasn't so certain, herself. They looked ethereal, delicate and just ever-so-slightly too perfect. Which made her feel solid, plain and grubby. Not exactly a way to win friends and influence people.

They wore the gray and gold of the Hawks in a band across their foreheads; their hair—gorgeous, long, black as the proverbial raven's wing—had been pulled back and shoved neatly beneath it. Human hair—at least in the ranks of the Hawks—was not allowed that length; it got in the way of pretty much anything. But the Barrani? No such restrictions were placed on them.

Of course, having seen them in a fight, Kaylin was painfully aware that those restrictions would have been pointless.

Teela whistled. At six foot nothing, she wore armor that suited her fighting style—which is to say, none at all. But she carried a large stick. "You're late," she said.

Kaylin had to look up to meet her emerald eyes. And emerald? They really were. Hard, sharp and a little brittle around the too perfect edges. That and a stunning, endless shade of deep, blue green. "That's news?"

"No. That's the sound of me winning the betting pool."

"Good. I was rooting for you—and now I want my cut."

"You'll get it," she said with a grin, "if you survive old Iron Jaw."

"I'm not worried about Iron Jaw. Tain, tell Teela to *shut up* and get the hell out of the way."

"What, do I *look* stupid?"

"Usually."

"Not that stupid." He grinned; the row of his perfect teeth had been chipped in one fight or another. When Kaylin had first been inducted into the Hawks, Tain was the only Barrani she could always recognize when he stood among a group of his own people because he *had* a visible flaw. His only flaw. "Oh, I should warn you—"

"Save it for later."

He shrugged, lazy and slow. "Remember, Kaylin, I did try."

She was already past them, and she spent what little breath she had left cursing the fact that the damn halls were so long.

Old Iron Jaw's desk was huddled in the center of about a dozen similar desks, and distinguishable only by the presence of the Leontine who occupied it. Well, by that and the long furrows he'd dug there over the years when his claws did their automatic extension and raked through the surface of dense, heavy wood. This happened when he was annoyed, and the person who had annoyed him had the good fortune not to be close enough to bear the brunt of those claws instead.

For good reason, no one with brains got close to an angry Leontine. Iron Jaw—called Sergeant Marcus Kassan to his considerable face—was one of the very few who had managed to make it into the Hawks—Leontines were a tad on the possessive side, they didn't share space well, and they responded to an order as if it were a suicide wish and they were magic wands.

Iron Jaw, among his own people, would be called the Leontine word for kitten—and its only equivalent in human speech was, as far as Kaylin could translate, Eunuch. No one used it in the Hawks.

He growled when he saw her. It was a low, extended growl and he didn't bother to open his mouth to make it.

She lifted her chin, exposing her neck in the universal gesture of submission. It was only half-fake. In spite of his legendary temper, his surliness and his habit of making the word martinet a hideous understatement, she *liked* him. Unlike most of the Barrani, whose lives were built on so many secrets and lies they were confounded by something as inelegant and boring as truth, Iron Jaw was exactly what he appeared to be.

And at the moment, that was pissed off.

He leaped over his desk, his shoulders hunching with a grace that belied his size, and landed in front of it, four inches from where Kaylin stood her ground. His eyes were wide and his breath—well, it was cat's breath. Never a pleasant thing.

But she knew better than to run from a Leontine, even this one. He let his claws touch her throat and close around the very thin membrane of her skin.

"Kaylin," he growled. "You are making me look incompetent."

"Sorry," she said, breathing very, very carefully.

"Where were you?"

"Getting dressed."

The claws closed slightly.

There was no way around it; she told him the truth. "I was with Clint's wife, Sesti. Sesti of the Camaraan clan," she added, feeling an edged claw bite skin. Knowing that she bled, but only slightly. "She had a difficult birthing, and I promised the midwives' guild—"

He snarled. But he let his hands drop. "You are not a midwife—"

"I am—"

"You're a *Hawk*." But his fangs had receded behind the generous black curl of what might loosely be called lips were they on someone else's face. "You used your power."

She said nothing for a minute. "I couldn't do that. It's forbidden by the Hawklord." Which was more or less true. Well, more true. Kaylin was, as she was loath to admit, a tad special for an untrained human. She could do things that other human Hawks couldn't. Hell, that other humans couldn't. The Hawks knew about her, of course.

And the Hawklord? Better than any of them, he had his reasons for mistrusting the use of that power. But what the Hawklord didn't see, didn't hurt. As long as he didn't hear about it.

"Well. Sesti will owe you. Which means Clint will pay." Marcus wouldn't tell the Hawklord. Not for something like this. Leontines had a strong understanding of debt, obligation and family. After a moment, his perpetual lack of blinking made her eyes water. "How was the birth?"

"The baby's fine. The mother's exhausted."

"Was it a close thing?"

She shuddered. She'd been late once or twice when the midwives had called her—but that was in the early years, and when she'd clearly seen the cost, she had *never* been late again. They would have called it a miracle, in the Hawks, if she could make them believe it. "Close enough. But they'll both pull through."

He shrugged, and leaned back against the desk. It actually groaned. "More, I'm certain, than can be said of you. The Hawklord is waiting. In his tower."

Could things be *any* worse?

She made the climb up the stairs unescorted, although guards flanked the closed doors on every landing. They nodded, and one or two that knew her well enough either shook their heads or smiled. They were almost all human or Aerian; the Barrani were trusted, but only to a point. On a good day, she might take the time to ask them what the Hawklord wanted.

This wasn't a good day.

She made the landing of the last set of stairs, stopped to catch her breath and shake her legs out and then straightened her shoulders, adjusting her sloppy belt. It was two notches too big, again. And she hadn't had time to punch a few extra holes.

Her hair was a flyaway mess, and her cheeks, she knew, would be a little too red for dignity—but she often had to choose between dignity and living another hour. She paused at the unattended door, and placed her palm against the golden symbol of the hawk that adorned its lower center. It was a *tall* door.

Magic trickled up her hand like a painful, frosty flicker. She hated it, and gritted her teeth as it passed through her skin. Of all the things she had had to learn to accept with grace, this was the hardest: to leave her palm there while magic roved and quested, seeking answers.

It was apparently satisfied; the doors began to swing open.

They opened into a round, domed room: the height of the Tower, and the face it showed to all but the most trusted of the Hawklord's advisors. Given what she knew about the Hawklord, that that number was higher than zero should have come as a big surprise.

She bowed before the doors had fully opened. Because she wore the uniform of a Hawk, a bow was required. Had she worn any other uniform, she'd probably have had to throw in a long grovel as well as a bit of scraping.

"Kaylin Neya," the Hawklord said coldly.

She rose instantly.

Met his eyes. They were like gray stone, like the walls of the round room; they gave no impression of life, and they hinted at nothing but surface. His face, pale as ivory, heightened their unusual color; his hair, gray, fell beyond his back. He was not Barrani, but he might as well have been; he was tall, proud and very cold.

But his wings crested the rise of drawn hood, and they were white, their pinions folded. Hawklord. It was not because he was Aerian that he was Lord here.

"Hawklord," she said.

His face grew more stonelike.

"Lord Grammayre," she added.

"I have been waiting for half of a day, Kaylin. Would you care to offer an explanation for the waste of my time to the Emperor?"

Her shoulders fell about four inches, but she managed to keep her head up. "No, sir."

He frowned, and then turned toward the distant curve of the shadowed room. In it, she saw a small well of light. And around that light, a man.

Some instinct made her reach for her daggers; they were utterly silent as they slid out of their sheaths. That had been a costly gift from a mage on Elani Street who'd had a little bit of difficulty with a loan shark.

"I have, however, no intention of embarrassing the Hawks

by allowing you to speak on their behalf. I have a mission for you," he added, "and because of its nature, I wish you to take backup."

Great. She looked down at her boots, and the low edges of the one pair of pants she now owned that wasn't warzone material. "Lord Grammayre—"

"That was not, of course, a request." He held out a hand in command, but not to her. "I would like to introduce you to one of your partners. You may recognize him; you may not. He has been seconded from the Wolves. Severn?"

She almost didn't hear the words; they made no *sense*.

Because across the round room—a room that now seemed to have no ceiling, her vision had grown so focused—a man stepped into the sun's light.

A man she recognized, although she hadn't seen him for years. For seven years.

In utter silence, she threw the first dagger, and hit the ground running.

He was *fast*.

But he'd always been fast. His own long knife was in the air before she'd run half the distance that separated them; her thrown dagger glanced off it with a sonorous clang. Everything in the Hawk's tower reverberated; there could be no hidden fights, here.

"Hello, *Kaylin*."

She snarled. Words were lost; what remained was motion, movement, intent. She held the second dagger in her hand as she unsheathed the third; heard the Hawklord's cold command at her back as if it were simple breeze in the open streets.

The open streets of the fiefs, almost a decade past.

His smile exposed teeth, the narrowing of eyes, the sudden tensing of shoulder and chest as he gathered motion, hoarding it.

Left hand out, she loosed a second dagger, and he parried it, but only barely. The third, she had at his chest before he could bring his knife down.

Too easy, she thought desperately. Too damn easy.

She looked up at his lazy smile and brought her dagger in.

Light blinded her. Light, it seemed, from the sound of his sudden curse, blinded him; they were driven apart by the invisible hands of the Hawklord's power, and they were held fast, their feet inches above the ground.

Her eyes grew accustomed, by slow degree, to the darkness of the domed room.

"I see," the Hawklord said quietly, "that you know Severn. Severn, you failed to mention this in your interview."

Severn had always recovered quickly. "I didn't recognize the name," he said, voice even, smile still draped across his face. He moved slowly, very slowly, and sheathed his long knife, waiting.

And she looked up at his face. He wasn't as tall as Tanner, and he wasn't as broad; he had the catlike grace of a young Leontine, and his hair was a burnished copper, something that reddened in caught light. But his eyes were the blue she remembered, cold blue, and if he had new scars—and he did—they hadn't changed his face enough to remove it from her memory.

"Kaylin?"

She said nothing for a long, long time. And given the tone of the Hawklord's voice, it wasn't a wise expenditure of that time.

"I know him," she said at last.

"That has already been established." The Hawk's lips turned up in a cold smile. "You seldom attempt to kill a man for no reason in this tower. But not," he added, "never."

She ignored the comment. "He's no Wolf," she told the man who ruled the Hawks in all their guises. "I don't care what he told you—he doesn't serve the Wolflord."

He chose to ignore her use of the Lord of Wolves, her more colloquial title. "Ah. And who does he serve, Kaylin?"

"One of the seven," she said, spitting to the side.

"The seven?"

She was dead tired of his word games. "The fieflords," she said.

"Ah. Severn?"

"I was a Wolf," he replied, as if this bored him. As if everything did. He ran a hand through his hair; it was just shy of regulation length. "I served the Lord of Wolves." Each word emphasized and correct.

"You're lying."

"Ask the Lord of Hawks," he told her, with a shrug. "He's got the paperwork."

"No," the Hawklord replied quietly, "I don't."

Severn was silent, assessing the tone of the Hawklord's

words. After a moment, he shrugged again; the folds of his robes shifted, and Kaylin heard the distinct sound of cloth rubbing against leather. He was not entirely unarmored here.

Too bad.

"I was a Shadow Wolf," he said at last.

"For how long?" She refused to be shocked. Refused to let his admission slow her down.

"Years," he replied. Just that.

She didn't believe him. "He's lying."

"I didn't say how many," he added softly. As if it were a game.

"He is not lying," the Hawklord told her. "Believe that when the unusual request for transfer between the Towers arrives, we check very carefully. When the man who requests the transfer is of the Shadows, our investigations are more thorough."

"Thorough how?"

"We called in the Tha'alani."

She froze. She had faced Tha'alani before, but only once, and she had been thirteen years old at the time. She had sworn, then, that she would die before she let one touch her again. The Tha'alani were an obscenity; they touched not flesh—although that in and of itself caused her problems—but thought, mind, heart, all the hidden things.

All the things that had to stay hidden if they were to be protected.

They were sometimes called Truthseekers. But it was a paltry word. Kaylin privately preferred rapist as the more accurate term.

"He subjected himself to the Tha'alani willingly," the Hawklord added.

"And the Tha'alani said he was telling the truth."

"Indeed."

"And what truth? What could he say that would make him worthy of the Hawks?"

But the Hawklord's patience had ebbed. "Enough to satisfy the Lord of Hawks," he told her. "Will you question me?"

No. Not if she wanted to be a Hawk. "Why? Why him?"

"Because, Kaylin, he is one of two men who understand the fiefs as well as you do."

She froze.

"The other will be with us shortly."

After about ten minutes, the Hawklord let them go. Mostly. The barrier that held Kaylin's arms to her side slowly thinned; she could move as if she were under water. Given that she was likely to try to kill Severn again the minute she got the chance, she tried hard not to resent the Hawklord's caution.

"Feel all better now that that's out of your system?" Severn asked quietly.

She wanted to cut the lips off his face; it would ruin his smirk. "No."

"No?"

"You're not dead."

He laughed and shook his head. "You haven't changed a bit, have you Elianne?"

"Tell him to let us go and you can find that out for yourself."

"I doubt the Lord of Hawks would take the orders of a former Shadow Wolf. Although given your tardiness and his apparent acceptance of it, he's a damn site more tolerant than the Lord of Wolves was."

"Try."

He laughed again. "Not yet, little—what did he call you? Kaylin? Not yet."

The Lord of Hawks watched them with the keen sight of their namesake.

"You want to send us into the fiefs," she said at last, trying to keep the accusation out of her voice.

"Yes. It's been seven years, Kaylin. Long enough."

"Long enough for what? Three of the fieflords are outcaste *Barrani*—I could live and die in the time it took them to blink!"

The Hawklord turned his full attention upon her. "I think I have been overly tolerant," he said at last, and in a tone of voice she hadn't heard since she'd first arrived in this tower. "You are either Hawk or you are not. Decide."

Her silence was enough of an answer, but only barely. "The third is coming now."

The door, which had probably closed the moment Kaylin had fully stepped across its threshold, swung open again.

A man walked into the room. He wore no armor that she could hear beneath the full flow of his perfect robes. Her hearing had always been good. "Lord Grammayre," he said, bowing low.

"Tiamaris," the Hawklord replied. "I would like to introduce you to Kaylin and Severn. You will work with them."

The man rose. His hair was a dark, dark black—Barrani black—but his build was all wrong for Barrani. He was a shade taller than Teela, and about twice her width. Three times, maybe. His hands were empty; he carried no obvious weapon. Wore no open medallion. The hand that he lifted in ritual greeting, palm out, was smooth and unadorned.

Kaylin and Severn could not likewise lift hand—but their background in the fiefs hadn't made the gesture automatic. Lord Grammayre was under no such disadvantage; he lifted his ringed hand in greeting, and lowered his chin slightly.

"Tiamaris has some knowledge of the fiefs," he told them both. Tiamaris lowered his perfectly raised hand, and turned to face them.

Something about the man's eyes were all wrong; it took Kaylin a moment to realize what it was. They were orange. A deep, bright orange that hinted at red and gold. Her own eyes almost fell out of their sockets.

"You have the privilege," Lord Grammayre told her quietly, "of meeting the only member of the Dragon caste to ever apply to serve in the Halls of Law."

Severn recovered first. He laughed. "It's true, then," he said, to no one in particular.

That rankled. "Like you'd know true if it bit you on the ass."

"You really are a mongrel unit."

"No, Severn," the Hawklord replied softly. Too softly. Had it been anyone else speaking, Kaylin might have dared a warning kick.

She hoped Severn hung himself instead.

Severn fell silent.

"The Hawks have always been open to those who seek service under the banner of the Emperor's Law. Where service is offered it is accepted, by whoever offers it. Tiamaris has chosen to make that offer, and it has been accepted, by the Three Towers. And the Emperor. If the Wolves choose different criteria upon which to accept applicants, that is the business of the Lord of Wolves; if the Swords choose to retain only the mortal races, that is likewise the concern of *their* lord.

"I would, of course, be pleased to explain your mission. But I have spent precious hours in this tower, and I have other duties to which I must attend. The Lords of Law meet within the half hour." He reached into the folds of his robes and pulled out a large gem.

Even Kaylin could see it glow.

He held it a moment in his open palm. "This contains all of the information the Hawks have been able to gather about your mission. Some of it was placed within the gem by the Tha'alani, some was placed there by Wolves and Swords. You will study it," he added quietly, "and it will tell you all you require.

"If you have questions, contain them. You will have to find answers on your own. You will speak to no one of what you see within the gem. It is spellbound, and it will enforce that command."

He hesitated a moment, and then, lifting his hand, he gestured. Kaylin fell an inch to the ground and stumbled, righting herself.

"Kaylin."

She turned. Saw that he held out both his open hand and the large gem it contained—to her. For just a minute she considered the wisdom of a different occupation.

But her past would follow her out the doors; here it was hidden. Without a word, she held out a hand, and he dropped the crystal into the shaking curve of her palm. Blue light seared her vision; her fingers closed instinctively.

She was surprised when she didn't throw it away.

"Interesting," the Hawklord said softly. She thought he might say more, but the meeting with the Lords of Law clearly demanded his full attention. "You are dismissed," he said quietly. "You may speak with Marcus. Tell him that you are to be equipped in any reasonable manner. Remind him that the equipment is not to be logged.

"That is all."

CHAPTER 2

Judging by the quality of the silence, which had gone from absolute to cryptlike, Iron Jaw still hadn't recovered his good humor, such as it was. The people who usually occupied the desks in line of sight seemed to have developed an extended case of lunch. Kaylin's stomach really wanted to join them. Either that, or to lose the breakfast she hadn't had. She couldn't quite decide which.

Severn. Here. Her hands were fists, which, given that one of them was clutching something with sharp edges, was unfortunate. If it hadn't been years since she'd badly wanted to kill someone—and face it, she wasn't angelae—it *had* been years since she'd tried. Her timing, as always, was impeccable.

Marcus looked up from his paperwork. She wondered which poor sacrificial soul had delivered it. She didn't envy them.

"Well?" He growled.

She shrugged. Not really safe, given his mood—but she was in a mood of her own. "We need a safe room," she told him, waving the crystal she still clutched.

His brows rose, or rather, the fur above his eyes did. When it settled, he looked annoyed. Nothing new, there. "West room," he said, curtly. "And those two?"

"Ask the Hawklord."

His lip curled back over his teeth, and she decided that his mood trumped hers. "Severn," she said curtly. "Formerly of the Wolves."

"Here?"

"I said formerly."

"And the other?"

"Tiamaris. He's a ..."

The low growl deepened. The Leontine slid around the desk, paperwork forgotten.

Tiamaris stood his ground. Stood it with such complete confidence, Kaylin wondered if anything ever shook him.

"That's a caste name, isn't it?" the Leontine asked.

"That is none of your concern, Sergeant Kassan," Tiamaris replied. His voice gave nothing away. Kaylin was impressed. Not that he knew Marcus's rank—anyone who knew the uniform could see that—but that he knew his pride name.

Marcus drew closer, and as he did, he gained height—or at least his fur did. It was a Leontine trait, when the Leontine felt threatened. That usually only happened in the presence of his wives or his kits.

Severn sat on an empty desk and folded arms across his chest, smirking. Kaylin almost joined him. Almost.

But she didn't want to be where he was; she had decided that a long time ago. Wouldn't think about it here, because if by some miracle Marcus didn't go feral, she might, and she didn't want to be the cause of an office death. Not when the Hawklord had made clear what the price of that death would be.

"Tiamaris, you said?" Marcus's growl could sometimes be mistaken for a purr. Kaylin kept a flinch in check as she realized Iron Jaw was actually speaking Barrani. It was the formal language of the Lords of Law, and as he was allergic to most forms of formal, he seldom used it.

Tiamaris raised a dark brow. They were almost of a height. Marcus continued to close; Tiamaris continued to mime a statue. Inches fell away.

Men. "Actually, Marcus, *I* said it," Kaylin lifted the crystal as if it were an Imperial writ.

To her surprise, Marcus actually turned to look at her. But if his gaze was fastened on the crystal she held, his words were for Tiamaris. "This is *my* office," he said quietly, each word textured by the full growl of a Leontine in his prime. "These are my Hawks. If you…choose to work here, you accept that."

"I choose to serve at the pleasure of the Lord of Hawks," was the neutral reply. It, too, was in Barrani. Kaylin realized that she had not heard Tiamaris speak in any other language since he'd entered the tower.

Kaylin tried again. "We're to be kitted out," she began. "And the Hawklord—"

"He told me." He turned his gaze back to Tiamaris. "This isn't finished," he said quietly.

"No," Tiamaris concurred, in an agreeable tone of voice that implied anything but. "It's barely begun. Sergeant?"

"Take the West room," he replied, eyes lidding slowly. Kaylin knew, then, that Tiamaris was close to death. Would have been, had he not been a Dragon. "Kaylin, show them."

She took a deep breath. Thought about telling them all that she wasn't their babysitter. Thought better of it a full second before her mouth opened on the words. "Right." She offered a very sloppy salute, palm out but not exactly flat. It was also, she realized, as Iron Jaw stared at it, the *wrong* hand.

"You two, follow."

"Whatever you say," Severn told her, sliding off the desk. "Lead on, Kaylin."

The West room was one of four such rooms, and they were all just as poetically named. The Leontines didn't really go in for fancy names. Near as Kaylin could tell, the Leontine word for food translated roughly as "corpse." Some accommodations had to be made in culinary discussions.

When Marcus had first taken the job, the safe rooms—like all of the rest of the rooms in the labyrinthine Halls of Law ruled by the Hawklord—had been named after upstanding citizens, people with a lot of money or distant relatives of the living Emperor. Marcus had pretty much pissed in every possible corner in the Hawks' domain, and after he'd finished doing *that,* he'd fixed a few more things. Starting with the names.

Still, in all, West was better than some seven syllable name that she wouldn't be able to pronounce without a dictionary. Now if he'd only do something about the damn wards on the doors....

Before she touched the door, she turned to Tiamaris. "Don't antagonize him," she said quietly.

"Was I?"

She didn't know enough about Dragons to be certain he had done so on purpose. But she knew enough about men. "Marcus crawled his way up the ladder over a pile of corpses," she replied. "And we need him where he is. Don't push him."

For the first time that day, Tiamaris smiled.

Kaylin decided that she preferred it when he didn't. His teeth weren't exactly like normal teeth; they didn't have the pronounced canines of the Leontine, but they seemed to glitter. His eyes certainly did.

She pushed the door open and walked into the room.

"Severn," she said, the name sliding off her tongue before she could halt it, "sit down. Tiamaris?"

"Kaylin?"

"We can't proceed until the door is closed—the gem is keyed."

"Ah." He crossed the threshold into the small, windowless room. It looked like a prison cell. On the wrong days, it was. And the prisoners it contained? She shuddered.

The door slid shut behind him. Severn sat, lounging

across a chair as if he were in his personal rooms. Tiamaris sat stiffly, as if he weren't used to bending in the middle.

And Kaylin stood between them, between the proverbial rock and a hard place. She looked at Severn. Looked at the familiar scars that she'd never forgotten, and looked at the newer ones.

She wanted to kill him.

And he knew it. His smile stilled, until it was a mask, a presentation. Behind it, his blue eyes were hooded, watchful. His hands had fallen beneath the level of the plain, wooden table that was the only flat surface that wasn't the floor.

"Are you really a Hawk?" He asked casually.

"Are you really a Wolf?"

They stared at each other for a beat too long.

"Kaylin," Tiamaris said quietly. "I believe you have business to attend to."

"I'm a Hawk," she replied.

"Why?"

"Why?" Her hand closed around the crystal. "Yeah," she said to Tiamaris. "Business. As usual."

There had been a time when she would have answered any question Severn had asked. Any question. But she wasn't that girl, now. She had no desire to share any of her life with him. Instead, she looked at the crystal. Some hesitance must have showed, because Tiamaris raised a brow.

"You are familiar with these, yes?"

"I've seen them," she said coldly.

"But you've never used one."

She shoved nonexistent hair out of her eyes, as if she were stalling. Her earlier years in the streets of the fiefs had proved that lies were valuable. Her formative years with the Hawks had shown her that they were also usually transparent, if they were hers. At last, she said, "No. Never."

"If you would allow me—"

"No."

Another brow rose. "No?"

The word sounded like a threat.

"No," she said, finding her feet. "The Hawklord gave it to me. You try to use it, and if it's keyed, we'll be picking you out of our hair for weeks."

His smile was not a comfort. He held out his hand. "I have the advantage," he told her softly, "of knowing *how* to unlock a crystal."

After a pause, in which she acknowledged privately that she *was* stalling, she said, "Why is he sending a Dragon into the fiefs?"

Tiamaris shrugged. "You must ask him. I fear he will not answer, however." His eyes narrowed, gold giving way to the fire of red. "I confess I am equally curious. Why has he chosen to send an untried girl there?"

"I'm not untried," she snapped. "I've been with the Hawks for seven years."

"You've been with the Hawks," he replied, "since you were thirteen. By caste reckoning, you were a child, then. You reached your age of majority two years ago. In accordance with the rules of Law, you have been a Hawk for two years."

"Caste reckoning," she snapped, "is *for* the castes. I grew up in the fiefs. Age means something else, there."

"So," Tiamaris said, splaying a hand across the table's surface. "That was true."

She looked at him again. *How much do you know about me?* Which wasn't really the important question. *And why?* Which was. "You've been a Hawk for a day, if I'm any judge."

"Two," he replied.

"It takes longer than two days to make a Hawk."

He shrugged. "It takes only the word of the Hawklord."

He was, of course, right. She cursed the Lord of the Hawks in the seven languages she knew. Which wasn't saying much; she could only speak four passably, but she was enough of a Hawk that she'd picked up the important words in the other three, and none of them were suitable for children or politics.

Languages were her *only* academic gift. She'd failed almost every other class she'd been forced to take. Lord Grammayre had been about as tolerant as a disappointed parent could be, and she'd endured more lectures about applying herself than she cared to remember. At least a third of them had been delivered in Aerian, he'd been that annoyed; it was his habit to speak formal Barrani when addressing the Hawks, although when frustrated he could descend into Elantran, the human tongue.

"The crystal," Tiamaris said.

She'd bought about all the time she could afford. Grinding her teeth—which caused Severn to laugh—she put her left palm over it; caught between her palms, the crystal began to pulse. She felt its beat and almost dropped it as it began to warm; warmth gave way to heat, and heat to something that was just shy of fire.

She'd touched fire before; been touched by it. Someplace, she still bore the scars. But she'd be damned if she let a little pain get in her way. Not in front of these two.

The crystal was beating. She felt it, and almost recognized the cadence of its insistent drumming. After a moment, she realized why; it had slowed, timing itself to the rhythm of her heart.

Which was too damn loud anyway.

"Here we go," she said softly.

Kaylin.

The Hawklord's voice was unmistakable. She relaxed, hearing it; it was calm and almost pleasant. An Aerian voice.

Kaylin, witness.

The fiefs opened up in her line of sight; she lost track of the room. She could see the boundaries that marked the criminal territories colloquially called the fiefs; they occupied the western half of the riverside, swallowing all but the Port Authority by the old docks. The view was top side, high; someone had flown this stretch. Someone had carried the unlocked crystal, linked to it, feeding it images, vision, the certainty of knowledge.

Grammayre? She couldn't be certain.

The Lords of Law were the fist of the Emperor; they

owed their allegiance and existence to his whim. This was a truth that she had faced almost daily for seven years. The Hawks, the Wolves and the Swords were not soldiers; they were no part of the Imperial army.

But they were allowed arms and armor, by law; in their individual ways, they kept the laws of the city of Elantra. And if that wasn't a war, she didn't want to see one. No one loved the guards who served the Lords of Law, but almost no one crossed them. Not outside of the fiefs.

Within the fiefs?

Old pain crossed her features, distorting them. She closed her eyes. Her vision however, was caught in crystal; she watched as the fiefs drew closer, undeniable now. Saw the boundaries beyond which the Lords of Law had little sway, held little power, and all of that power theoretical.

The armies would have more, but the Emperor seldom allowed the armies to crusade within *his* city.

And so the fiefs continued to exist.

In the fiefs, the slavery that had been abolished for a generation and a half still existed in all but name. Whole grand houses, opulent, golden manses, opened their doors to visitors, and within those doors, the rich could purchase anything. A moment's illegal escape, in the smoke-wreathed rooms of the opiates. A moment's pleasure, in the private parlors of the prostitutes. And a death, here or there, if one's tastes shaded to the sadistic.

Sordid, storybook, the fiefs made their money off those who would never dream of living within their borders.

And the fieflords ruled. They had their own laws, their

own armies, their own lieges—everything but open warfare. Open war in the city *would* bring the army down upon them all. This was understood, and it was perhaps the only thing that kept the fieflords in check. But in Kaylin's experience, it wasn't near enough. People lived and died at their whim. Money ruled the fiefs; money and power.

But the people who lived in them, who lived in the old buildings, the crumbling tenements, the small, squalid houses, had neither. They made what living they could, and they dreamed of a time when they might cross the boundaries that divided the one city from the other, seeking freedom or safety in the streets beyond.

They might as well have lived in a different country.

"Kaylin?" Tinny, robbed of the threat and grandeur of a Dragon's natural voice, she heard Tiamaris.

"Can you see it?"

Silence. A beat. "No," he said quietly. "The gem is, as you claimed, keyed to you. It appears you are to be our conduit to the investigation." He didn't sound pleased, and she knew she was being petty when she felt a moment's satisfaction.

But the satisfaction was very short-lived; the view dipped and veered, rolling in the sky. Clint had once taken her up in the air. She'd been with the Hawks for a handful of weeks, and she was thin with the hunger that dogged most children in the fiefs; he'd caught her under the arms, and she'd clung to him, determined to fly with him.

But she had found the distance from Clint to ground overwhelming. She couldn't follow what she saw; couldn't do anything but shut her eyes and shiver. Wind against her face, like it was now, was a reminder of what she wasn't: Aerian, and meant for the skies.

But he'd held her tight, and his voice, in her ear, became an anchor. He teased a sense of security slowly out of her fear, her frozen stiffness, and she had at last opened those eyes and looked. He took her to his home, to the heights of the Aeries in the cliffs that bordered the southern face of the city.

His home was not the home she had fled.

Not the home that the crystal's flight was returning her to.

The first fief passed beneath her shadow. She saw the tallest of the buildings it contained, and saw the gallows and the hanging cage that lay occupied beside it. Someone had angered the servants of the fieflord here, and they meant it to be known; the cage's occupant—man? Woman? She couldn't tell from this distance—was clearly still alive.

The voyager didn't pause here; he merely observed.

From a distance, she was encouraged to do the same. But she had seen those cages from the ground; had watched a friend die in one, had discovered, on that day, what it meant to be truly powerless.

She struggled with the crystal, but she was overmastered here. The Hawks—her place in the Hawks—had given her the illusion of power. And the Hawklord was going to strip her of it before he let her leave. To remind her—as she had not reminded herself—that she was still powerless, still young.

This is the domain of the outcaste Barrani fieflord known as Nightshade, his voice said. *We do not, of course, know his real name. It is hidden by spells far stronger than those we can comfortably use. Not even the Barrani castelords dare to challenge Nightshade in his own Dominion.*

She closed her eyes. It didn't help.

You know this fief.

She knew it. Severn knew it. They had lived, and almost died, in its streets. And Severn had done much, much worse there. The desire to kill him was paralyzing. It was wed to a bitter desire for justice—and justice was a fool's dream in the fiefs.

There are deaths here which you must investigate. More information is forthcoming.

The crystal shifted in her hands, becoming almost too hot to hold. She held it anyway as her view suddenly banked and shifted.

She was on the ground. The smell of the streets, overpowering in its terrible familiarity, filled her senses. She staggered, stumbled, stood; she looked down to see that her tunic—an unfamiliar tunic, a man's garb—was red with blood.

She felt no pain, but she knew that *this* memory was courtesy of the Tha'alani, and she hated it. It was different in all ways from the distant observation of the Hawklord; it was full of terror, of pain, of the inability to acknowledge or deny either.

She stumbled in the streets, and her arms ached; she was carrying something. No, *he* was, whoever he was. He stumbled along the busy streets; the sun was high. Some people watched him from a distance, open curiosity mixed with dread in their unfamiliar—blessedly so—faces. None approached. None offered him aid with the burden he bore. And when his strength at last gave out, when his knees bent, when his arms unlocked in a shudder that spoke of effort, of time, she saw why; saw it from his eyes.

A body rolled down his lap, bloody, devoid of life.

He screamed, then. A name, over and over, as if the name were a summons, as if it contained the power to command life to return.

But watching now as a Hawk, watching as someone trained to know death and its causes, Kaylin knew that it was futile.

The boy—ten years of age, maybe twelve—had been disemboweled. His arms hung slack by his sides, and she could see, from wrist to elbow, the black tattoos that had been painted there, indelible, in flesh.

She had seen them before. She knew that it wasn't only his arms that bore those marks; his inner thighs would bear them, too.

She screamed.

And Severn screamed in quick succession as she inexplicably lost contact with the gem.

Her hands were blistered; her skin was broken along the lines of the rigid crystal. And so were Severn's. He dropped the crystal instantly and it hit the table with a thunk, fastening itself to the wooden surface.

She thought it should roll.

It was a stupid thought.

"What are you doing?" She shouted at Severn, the words ground through clenched teeth, the pain in her hands making her stupid.

"Prying the gem away from you," he snapped back, composure momentarily forgotten.

"Why?"

He shrugged. The shrug, which started at his shoulder, ended in a shudder. "You didn't like what you were looking at," he added quietly.

"And it matters?"

"Yes."

"Why?"

He didn't answer.

"That was brave," Tiamaris said, speaking for the first time. "And very, very foolish. The Hawklord must have gone to some expense to create this crystal. It is…obviously unusual. Kaylin?"

She shook her head. Actually, she just shook. She wanted to touch the gem again, and she wanted to destroy it. Torn between the two—the one an imperative and the other an impossibility—she was frozen.

Tiamaris said quietly, "I owe you a debt." The words were grave. His eyes had edged from red to gold, and the gold was liquid light.

"Debt?"

"I would have taken the gem. It would have been…unwise. It appears that the Hawklord trusts you, Kaylin. And it would appear," he added, with just the hint of a dark smile, "that that trust does not extend to his newest recruits."

But Severn refused to be drawn into the conversation; he was staring at Kaylin. His own hands had started to swell and blister.

"Did you see it?" she asked him, all enmity momentarily forgotten. He was Severn, she was Elianne, and the streets of the fiefs had become that most impossible of things: more terrifying than either had ever thought possible.

He shook his head. "No," he said, devoid now of arrogance or ease. "But I know what you saw."

"How?"

"I've only heard you scream that way once in your life," he replied. He lifted a hand, as if to touch her, and she shied away instantly, her hand falling to her dagger hilt. To one of many.

He accepted her rejection as if it hadn't happened. "I was there, back then," he added quietly. "I saw it too. It's happening again, isn't it?"

She closed her eyes. After a moment, eyes still closed, she rolled up her sleeves, exposing the length of arm from wrist to elbow.

There, in black lines, in an elegant and menacing swirl, were tattoos that were almost twin to the ones upon the dead boy's arms.

She was surprised when someone touched her wrist, and her eyes jerked open.

But Tiamaris held the wrist in a grip that could probably crush bone with little effort. Funny, how human his hands looked. How human they *weren't*.

She tried to pull away. He didn't appear to notice.

But his eyes flickered as she drew a dagger out of its sheath with her free hand. She'd moved slowly, and the daggers made no sound—but he was instantly aware of them.

"I wouldn't, if I were you. Lord Grammayre is not known for his tolerance of fighting among his own."

"Let go," she whispered.

He didn't appear to have heard her. "Do you know what these markings mean?" He asked. His inner eye membrane had risen, lending opacity to the sudden fire of his eyes.

"Death," she whispered.

"Yes," he replied. He studied them with care, and after a moment, she realized he was *reading* them. "They mean death. But that is not all they mean, Kaylin of the Hawks."

"This isn't—this isn't Dragon."

"No. It is far older than Dragon, as you so quaintly call our tongue."

"Barrani?"

His lip curled in open disdain.

"I'll take that as a no." She hesitated. These patterns had been with her since she had gained the age of ten, a significant age in the fiefs. Not many children survived that long when they'd lost their parents.

"Where did you get these?"

"In Nightshade," she whispered.

"Who put them upon you? Who marked you thus?"

It was Severn who answered. "No one."

"Impossible."

"I saw them," Severn replied. "I saw them...grow. We all did. They started one morning in Winter."

"On what day?"

"The shortest one."

Tiamaris said nothing. She wanted him to continue to say nothing, but he opened his mouth anyway. "I saw the bodies," he said at last. "And the tattoos of the dead did not just, as you say, 'start.' They were put there, and at some cost."

"Not hers," Severn said quietly.

Tiamaris frowned. "There is something here," he said at last, "that even I cannot read."

"Do you—do you know someone who can?"

"Only one," Tiamaris replied, "and it would not be safe for you to ask him."

"Why?"

"He would probably take both arms."

Severn said, "He could try." And his long dagger was suddenly in his hand.

Kaylin looked at it. Looked at Severn. Understood nothing at all. "How do you know how to read this?" she whispered.

"I am considered a scholar," was his cautious reply. "I dabble in the antiquities."

Which meant magery. She didn't bother to ask.

"Let me go," she said wearily, adding command to the words.

To her surprise, Tiamaris withdrew his grip. "You are

interesting, Kaylin, as the Hawklord surmised. But I am surprised, now."

"At what?"

"That the Hawklord let you live."

Kaylin said nothing.

Again, for reasons that made no sense, Severn said, "Why?" His hands had once again fallen beneath the surface of the table.

"Your story…is strange. And you must understand that the deaths in the fiefs some years ago were also investigated."

The deaths. Seven years ago. She shuddered.

For the first time since she'd met Tiamaris, his expression went bleak. The way distant, snow-covered cliffs were.

"You were there, back then," she said softly.

"I was there."

"And you weren't a Hawk."

"No."

She lifted a shaking head. Looked down at her arms. "What does it mean?"

"I don't know," he replied, even now, eyes upon her face. "But in the end, the killings stopped. Does the Hawklord know of these?"

She nodded. She almost matched his bleakness. "He knows almost everything about me."

"And he does not suspect that you were involved in the incidents."

Her eyes rounded. She was too stunned to be angry; that might come later.

"You don't understand, and clearly Grammayre did not

see fit to inform you. As I will be working with you, I will. The first death must have occurred—and Lord Grammayre would be acquainted with the approximate time—on the day you say these appeared. On the same solstice."

The silence was, as they say, deafening. And into the silence, the shadow of accusation crept.

"She had nothing to do with the deaths of the others," Severn snapped. "They were all—"

Kaylin said, "Shut up, Severn."

To her surprise, Severn did.

"I believe you" was the quiet reply. "Having met her, I believe you." Tiamaris looked across the table at Kaylin; the table seemed to have grown very, very long. From that distance, he said, "You said that it had started again. Tell me what you think has started."

She swallowed. Her mouth was very dry. "The deaths," she whispered at last. "In Nightshade. I thought—when the first body appeared—I was *so certain* I would die next. Because of the marks. We all were."

"All?"

Her lips thinned. She didn't answer the question. It wasn't any of his damn business. A different life.

"What happened?"

She shook her head. Inhaled and rose, placing tender palms against the hard surface of scarred wood. "I didn't die. I don't know why," she said at last. "But I do know where we're going."

"To Nightshade," Severn said quietly.

"To Nightshade." She started toward the door. Stopped.

She turned back to look at Severn, who had not risen to join her. "It's not finished," she told him softly.

He said nothing, but after a moment, added, "I know. Elianne—"

"I'm Kaylin," she whispered. "Don't forget it."

"I won't. Will you?"

She shook her head, and instead of murderous rage, she felt something different, something more dangerous. "I won't forget what you did, in Nightshade."

He said nothing at all.

"I need to get something to eat. Meet me in the front hall in an hour. No, two. Be ready."

"For the fiefs?" He laughed bitterly.

Tiamaris, however, nodded.

She left the room, walking quietly and with a stately dignity that she seldom possessed. Only when she was certain she'd left them both behind did she stop to empty the negligible contents of her stomach.

Marcus was there, of course. As if he'd been waiting. He probably had. He placed velvet paw-pads upon her shoulder, and squeezed; she felt the full pads of his palms press into her tunic. Warmth, there.

"Kaylin."

"I don't want to go back," she whispered, in a voice she hated. It was a thirteen-year-old's voice. A child's voice.

"Don't tell me where you're going. If I'm not mistaken, you're bound." He glanced at her blistered palm and his breath came out in a huff that sounded similar to a growl.

It was a comforting sound, or it was meant to be. If you knew a Leontine. She knew this one.

"But I can guess," he added grimly. "Come. The quartermaster has given me what you requisitioned."

"I didn't—"

"The Hawklord understands where you're going," Marcus said quietly. "And he was prepared. He was not, I think, prepared for losing the half day. He's docked your pay."

"Bastard," she whispered, but with no heat.

His hand ran over her rounded back. As if she were his, part of his pride. "I brought you this," he said, when she at last straightened, her stomach still unsettled.

She knew what he held.

It looked like a bracer, but shorter, and it was golden in sheen. Three gems adorned it, and to the untrained eye, they were valuable: ruby, sapphire and diamond.

But Kaylin knew they were more than that. "I won't lose control," she started.

His eyes were as narrow as they ever got. "It wasn't a request, Kaylin. I know where you're going."

"He told you?"

His nose wrinkled as he looked at the mess around her feet. And on it.

"Oh."

"Put it on," he told her, in a voice that brooked no refusal. A sergeant's voice.

"Marcus—"

"Put it on, Kaylin. And if I were you, I wouldn't remove it for a while."

She took the bracer from his hands and stared at it. It had no apparent hinge, but that, too, was illusion. She touched the gems in a sequence that her fingers had never forgotten: blue, blue, red, blue, white, white. She felt magic's familiar and painful prickle at the same time as she heard the unmistakable click of a cage door being opened.

"Did he tell you to make me do this?" she asked bitterly.

"No, Kaylin. I think he trusts you to know your own limits."

"Do you?"

"Yes," he said softly. But he waited while she slid the manacle over her left arm. "In as much as you can know them, I do."

"What does that mean?"

"You know what it means."

And she did. "I—I haven't lost control since—"

"You weren't in the fiefs, then." He paused for just a moment, and then added, "Kaylin, your power—no one understands it. Not even the Hawklord. He's kept it hidden. I've kept it hidden. He is the only one of the Lords of Law who knows what *can* happen when you lose it. And he's the only one who should."

She closed her eyes. "The Hawklord—"

"Trusts you. More than that, he shows some affection for you. I have come to understand his wisdom. Even if you can't be on time to save your life or my reputation." He turned away, then. "Leave the mess. I'll have someone else clean it up."

She still didn't move.

And heard his growling sigh. He turned back. "What you did with Sesti, what you did with one of my own pride-wives, is not something that either the Hawklord or I could have predicted *could* be done."

"Sesti was—"

"Kaylin. You wouldn't have gone to Sesti if you thought she'd survive the birthing on her own. You would never have risked the exposure. You've been damn careful. You've had to be. But you saved her, you saved her son. You saved *mine*. I wouldn't make you wear this if you were going someplace where I thought you'd have to—"

She lifted her hand. "It's on, Marcus," she said, weary now.

The last thing she wanted to think about was power.

Because she'd discovered over the years that it always, always had a price, and someone had to pay it.

CHAPTER 3

"You're an hour late," Severn snapped.

"You had something better to do?" She ran a hand across her eyes and winced; it was her blistered hand.

"Than being stared at by a bunch of paper-pushing Hawks?" He spit to the side.

"We didn't ask you to transfer," she snapped back. Not that she was fond of being stared at, either—but she was used to it, by now. Besides, it meant that Marcus's fur had settled enough that the rest of the office had decided it was safe to come back to work.

"In the event that it comes as a surprise," Tiamaris said, in his deep, neutral tone, "Kaylin is not known for her punctuality. She is known, in fact, for her lack—even by those outside of the Hawklord's command."

Used to it or not, no one liked to be reminded that they were a public embarrassment. Kaylin flushed.

"Here," Severn said, and tossed her a vest. It was made of heavy, molded leather, and it was—surprise, surprise— her size. It was the only armor she wore. "Your quarter-master *moves*. You're sure you're just a Hawk?"

"What else would I be?"

His expression shifted into an unpleasantly serious one. "A Shadow Hawk," he said quietly.

"I don't live in the shadows," she murmured uneasily.

"Since when?"

When she offered no answer at all, he added, "Put the armor on, Kaylin."

She grimaced.

Another habit that had come from the fiefs; you didn't want *anything* weighing you down, because if you had to bolt, you were doing it at top speed, and usually with a bunch of armed thugs giving chase. Severn *had* changed; he wore leathers without comment. They suited him.

He also wore a long, glittering chain, thin links looped several times around his waist like a fashion statement. She doubted it was decorative.

But she had her own decorations.

Neither of them wore the surcoats that clearly marked the Hawks—or any of the city guards. No point, in the fiefs, unless you wanted to be target practice.

"You've got expensive taste," he said, staring at the edge of the manacle that peered out from beneath her tunic. The gold was unmistakable. "I guess you get better pay than the Wolves do. We don't even get a chance to loot the fallen."

Tiamaris eyed them both with disdain.

"Where's your armor?" she asked the Dragon. Anything to change the subject.

"I don't require any."

She raised a brow. She'd heard that a dozen times, usually from young would-be recruits. But then again, none of them had ever been a Dragon.

"We're not covert," she snapped.

"No one is, in the fiefs." His shrug was elegant. It made boredom look powerful.

Severn had a long knife, a couple of obvious daggers.

She had the rest of her kit, her throwing knives, the ring that all Hawks wore. She twisted the last almost unconsciously.

"Why were you late this time?" Severn asked quietly.

She started to tell him to mind his own business, and managed to stop herself. She was about to go into the fief of Nightshade with him. She wanted to kill him. And she knew what the Hawks demanded. Balancing these, she said, "I went back for the rest of the information in the damn crystal."

"Without us?"

She nodded grimly.

"How bad?"

"It's bad," she said quietly. Really, really bad. But she didn't share easily. "There were two deaths. Two boys."

His expression didn't change. He'd schooled it about as well as she now schooled hers. "When?"

"Three days apart."

Tiamaris's brows rose. "Three *days?*"

She nodded quietly.

"Kaylin—I'm not sure how aware you were of what happened the last time…you were a child."

"I was aware of it," she whispered. "Because I was a child in the fiefs."

"There were exactly thirteen deaths a year for almost three years. We could time them by moon phase," Tiamaris added. "The Dark moon. At no time in the previous incident did the deaths occur at such short intervals."

She nodded almost blankly.

"Where did the new deaths take place?" Severn's voice was harsh.

"Nightshade," she said bitterly, shaking herself. "The fieflord must have been in a good mood. We didn't lose anyone while we were investigating the deaths."

Severn whistled.

"Timing or no, it was the same," she added hollowly. "As last time. The examiner's reports were also in crystal."

"And the Hawks' mages?"

She nodded. "Their reports are there as well. Or rather, their précis on the findings. It's all bullshit."

"What kind of bullshit?"

"The unintelligible kind. You take magic exams in the Wolves?"

He shrugged. "Take them, or pass them?"

In spite of herself, she laughed. "Me, too." And then she forced her lips down, thinning them. Remembering Severn's last act.

He knew, too. He looked at her, his gaze steady. "Elia—Kaylin," he corrected himself, "it wasn't—"

But she lifted a hand. She didn't want to hear it.

Severn took a step closer, and her hand fell to a dagger. He ignored it. Her hand tightened.

Rescue came from an unexpected quarter.

"If you're both ready," Tiamaris said, glancing at the very high windows in the change rooms, "we're late."

"For what?"

"There are only so many hours of daylight, and not even I want to be in the fiefs at night."

The Halls of Law receded slowly.

Tiamaris was tall; his stride, long. Kaylin had to scamper to keep up, and she hated that.

She might have been taller had she not hit her meager growth spurts in the winters. That had been in the fiefs, and food had been scarce. Now that food wasn't? She hadn't gained an inch. She was never going to be tall. And Tiamaris? He'd probably never gone hungry in his life.

No, be fair. She had no idea what a Dragon's life was like. She only knew her own. And she knew that Severn, damn him, had no problem matching the dragon step for step. Severn? He'd gone hungry as well. Bone hungry, thin, gaunt with it. They'd weathered those seasons together.

She was veering dangerously close to the land of what-if, and she gave herself a harsh, mental slap. She'd bandaged her hand, but she clenched it nervously, looking at Severn's back. He'd grabbed the crystal. He'd tried to save her the pain. Why?

She could almost imagine that he'd really changed. Had

emerged from the fiefs, become something different. She hated the thought. And why? Hadn't she? Wasn't that exactly what she'd done?

Glancing up, she saw the flag of the Hawks on its tower height, and she stopped a moment, hoping to hear its heavy canvas flap in the wind. But she was earthbound. Funny, how it was the unreachable things that had always provided her anchor.

No, she thought, almost free of the shadows cast by the Towers. She hadn't changed anything but her name. And now she was going back home.

Because she served the Hawklord, and the Hawklord commanded it.

The richest of the merchants liked to nest in the shadows of the Halls; they lined the streets, their expensive windows adorned by equally expensive dress guards and clientele. There were jewelers here—and what good, she thought bitterly, did they do? You couldn't eat the damn things they produced, and they didn't stop you from freezing to death in the winter—and clothiers, a fancy word for tailor. There were swordsmiths, fletchers, herbalists and the occasional maker of books. When she'd first heard of those, she'd snuck in with a pocketful of change to see what betting odds were being offered, and on who. Oh, that had kept the company in laughs for a week.

What was absent were brothels, which lined the richer parts of the fiefs. Here, in the lee of the Halls, there were no girls on window duty, beckoning the drunk and the young, idle rich; she'd found the lack hard to get used to.

She had known some of the girls who worked in the brothels, but not well; they were keen-eyed and sharp, and they often recruited the unwary. Not that Kaylin had ever been lovely enough to be in danger of *that* particular fate.

But she didn't pity them. Not those girls. There were others, on darker streets, where windows were forbidden because they hinted at freedom. She'd seen them as well. Seen what was left.

Not all of the buildings that stood around the triangular formation of the Halls of Law were stores; the guilds made their homes here as well. And not all of the guilds were adverse to the presence of the Hawks. Kaylin frequented the weavers' guild, and the midwives' guild, almost as a matter of course. But she stayed away from the merchant guild, because it reeked of money and power, and she recognized that from a mile away. She thought that many of the men who had purchased membership in the merchant's guild also purchased other services in the fiefs, but it was something that wasn't talked about. Much.

And when she'd first arrived? Well, she hadn't talked much either.

"Kaylin?" Tiamaris touched her arm and she jumped, turning on him. His brow rose, breaking the sudden panic.

"Don't touch me," she snapped.

"You really haven't changed much, have you?" Severn said, eyes lidded. She couldn't read his expression, but the scorn in his voice was unmistakable.

Takes one to know one was not a retort she could be proud of, so she didn't make it. Near thing, damn him.

"What is it?" She kept the irritation out of her voice by dint of will.

"You've slowed."

"Sorry. I was thinking."

"They forbid that, in the Wolves."

In spite of herself, she smiled. Severn had always made her smile. Always, until he hadn't. He saw the change in her expression, and he fell silent.

They walked.

The streets opened up; horses were the mainstay of the merchants and the farmers who traveled up Nestor street. Nestor followed the river that split the city, crossing the widest of its many bridges. It was home to many lesser guilds, to lesser merchants and to the one or two charitable buildings that she thought worth the effort. The foundling halls, for one. She frequented those as well, but was more careful about it. Today she didn't even acknowledge it with a glance. Because Severn was with her.

Foot traffic stayed to either side of the road, and merchants were not above taking advantage of this. Her stomach growled as she passed an open baker's stall.

Severn laughed. "Not much at all," he said, shaking his head.

They were eating as they crossed the bridge over the Ablayne River; Kaylin stopped to look at the waters that ran beneath it. She wanted to turn back. *Hawklord,* she thought, as if he were a god who might actually listen, *I'll go. I'll go back to the fiefs. Just give me any other partner. Even Marcus.*

Severn stopped beside her, and that was answer enough. She drew away, dropping crumbs into the water. Something would eat them; she didn't much care what.

The streets on the wrong side of the river would still be wide enough for wagons for blocks yet, but the traffic was thinner. In the day, the outer edges of the fiefs seemed like any other part of the city. If you stayed there, you'd probably be safe; patrols passed by, a stone's throw from safety.

"Did that crystal of yours tell us where the hell we're going?" Severn asked her.

"Which hell?" Actually, all things considered, it was an almost appropriate question. "Yeah," she said. "Brecht's old place."

"Brecht? He's still alive?"

"Apparently." She shrugged. "Might even be sober."

Severn snorted. And shrugged. His hands, however, stayed inches away from his long knife. One of these days— say, when one of the hells froze over—she'd ask if she could take a look at it. From the brief glimpse she'd had, it was good work. "So much for dangerous. Why Brecht?"

"He found the second body."

Severn winced. "He's not sober," he said.

An hour had passed.

They'd wandered from the outer edges of the fief into the heart of Nightshade, which had the distinction of being the closest of the fiefs to the high city's clean, lawful streets. Because of its tentative geography, it *also* had the distinction of having more of an obvious armed force than the fiefs tended to put on display.

Kaylin and Severn knew how to avoid those patrols. Even after seven years, it came as second nature.

Tiamaris was grim and quiet, and he followed where they led—usually into the shadowed lee of an alley, or the overhang of a rickety stall—when one of these patrols walked by.

And patrol? It was entirely the wrong word. It reeked of discipline and order, and in Nightshade, they were almost swear words. They certainly weren't accurate.

"Why exactly are we hiding?" Tiamaris asked, the seventh time they rounded a sudden corner and retreated quickly.

They looked at each other almost guiltily, and then looked at Tiamaris. Severn's laconic shrug was both of their answers.

"You're a Dragon?" Kaylin said, hazarding a guess that was a pretty piss-poor excuse. She knew that maybe one in a hundred of the petty fief thugs would recognize a Dragon for what he was, and he'd probably do it a few seconds before he died. Or after; in the fiefs some people were so stupid they didn't know when they were dead.

Tiamaris raised a dark brow; his eyes were golden. He didn't feel threatened here. And because he didn't, he probably wouldn't be. That was they way it worked.

"Fine," she said. She unbent from her silent crouch and looked askance at Severn. His lazy smile spread across his face, whitening the scar just above his chin. It was the last scar she'd seen him take, and it had been bleeding, then.

"I should probably tell you both," she added, keeping apology out of her voice with effort, "that the Hawklord has strictly forbidden all unnecessary death in the fiefs while we're investigating."

"Define unnecessary." Severn's face was a mask. Wolf's mask. She could well believe he'd found a home in the Shadow Wolves. The Shadows—Hawk, Wolf and Sword—usually said goodbye to their members in a time-honored way: they buried the bodies someplace where no one would find them. She couldn't understand why he'd left them. Or why they'd let him go.

Didn't, if she were truthful, want to.

She shrugged. "Ask the Hawklord. It was his command."

"Interesting," Tiamaris said quietly.

"Interesting how?"

"Rule of law in the fiefs is defined by the fiefs. Even the Lords of Law accede that this is the truth."

She shrugged.

His frown tightened. "Are you always impulsive?"

She shrugged again. "I'm always late, if that helps." And then, because his condescending tone annoyed her, she added, "You think he doesn't want to annoy the fieflord."

"I think he feels it imperative that we don't."

"And that implies that we're here with the fieflord's permission."

"Not, legally, a permission that is his to grant, but yes, that is what I think."

She turned the words over, thinking them through. After a moment, she glanced at Severn. He nodded. "I'm thinking," she said slowly, "that I really don't like this."

Severn smiled. "I'm thinking that it's time for a bet."

"You haven't changed either," she said. The smile that crept over her face was a treacherous smile. She couldn't—quite—douse it. *Think,* she told herself grimly. But thought led to the past, and the past—it led to darker places than she could afford to go today.

She pulled back. "What bet?"

"Well," he said, nodding to the east, "there are four armed men coming this way."

She nodded.

"And we're not ducking."

Nodded again.

"They'll probably take it as a challenge."

Three times, lucky. "And so?"

"So we'll probably have to fight."

Tiamaris said, in his crisp, bored Barrani, "I think that unlikely."

"Don't interfere, and we will."

"And what will that prove?" Kaylin asked, ignoring Tia-maris.

"Nothing."

"And the bet?"

"We fight."

"Some bet."

"And whoever pulls a real weapon first—you or me—loses."

"What's the debt?"

"I win, you let me explain."

"No."

"Then don't lose, Kaylin. Here they come." His smile was a thin stretch of lip over teeth. It made her feel every one of the five years that had always separated them.

"Fine."

Tiamaris rolled his eyes. "You are *children*," he said, just shy of open contempt. The words were Barrani—she wondered if the Dragon condescended to speak any other language when dealing with mere mortals—but the tone wasn't. Quite. He folded arms across his broad chest and leaned back against the faded wood and brick of an old building.

The men closed in. They were armed; they carried naked blades. One sword, she thought, a short one, and three knives that were as long as Severn's weapon.

"Hey, hey," one said. He was a tall man, and his face was knife-thin, his eyes dark. "You're visitors, I see. You've probably forgotten to pay the toll."

Severn said nothing.

"You pay us, we'll let you pass."

Kaylin added more nothing.

The man smiled. "You don't pay, and we'll double the tolls, and extract them from your purses. Oh, wait, you don't seem to have them." He shrugged. Without turning, he said something in mangled Barrani. Kaylin understood it and tensed.

But her hand didn't fall to her daggers, her throwing

knives or her small club. Instead, she widened her stance and waited, watching them carefully. They wore some armor; it was piecework, and it wasn't very good. But they weren't slugs; they *moved*.

Two to one odds gave them some confidence; it was clear that Tiamaris had no intention of interfering, and he became just another part of the landscape. In the fiefs, this was not uncommon. In fact, given it was the fiefs, there were probably people up windowside, in the relative safety of their tiny homes, crouching and making bets with their roommates. Betting was the pastime of choice in the fiefs, especially when it involved someone else's messy death.

"How well did they train you, in the Wolves?" Kaylin asked.

"Watch and see."

"Like hell."

He laughed.

She might have added something, but there was no more time for words.

She should have let Severn take the leader, because they were both the same height, and the advantage of height was not her friend. There was an advantage in lack of height, but it usually involved doing one's best to look harmless and pathetic, and she'd given up that route when she'd left the fiefs to find the Hawklord.

Being a woman? Meant nothing, to the fieflord's thugs. Hell, she'd seen women in their ranks who were far more vicious than the men when they wanted to be.

The city ladies made femininity a triumph of style, and honed their tongues instead of their daggers. Kaylin knew that seven years in the city had failed to make a mark when she swung in before Severn could.

The leader wasn't stupid, but he *was* overconfident; she wasn't armed, and she wasn't dressed like a flashy guard. He swung the dagger wide, choosing its edge as a threat, and not its point.

Damage, not death; not yet.

His loss. She let him swing, raising the bracer that caged her; the knife's edge sheared through linen threads, and bounced up at an angle, leaving his ribs exposed. She was inches from his side before he could bring the long knife down, and she raised her leg to deflect his awkward kick.

She swung in, one-two, breath coming out like short, sharp punctuation as she applied the whole of her considerable training to a single point. She felt bone snap; heard him grunt. He was good; she gave him that. He did no more than grunt.

But he didn't have much opportunity; her fist rose, opening at the last minute into flat palm as it clipped the underside of his chin, snapping his head up. She hit him in the Adam's apple, and he stumbled backward.

Severn's snap-kick sent him into the two men who were coming up behind him. He didn't hit them dead on; they'd already started to separate. But he did hit their right and left arms, putting them off balance.

Rules in the fiefs were pretty simple. Honorable fights were for stories, idiots or dead people.

Kaylin was already on the move, going for the man with

the long knife on the left; Severn had the man with the short sword in his sights. She had the impression of height, width, dark hair; she could see a flash of red as the man with the sword swore, again in mangled Barrani. No doubt at all who these men served.

The man she now faced, off balance, was heavier than his leader. He wasn't any better armored, and he was cautious—but overbalanced and cautious were a poor combination. She let gravity take its toll on her opponent. He was fighting it, but that meant he was fighting on two fronts. She launched into a roundhouse kick, grounded her foot, spun on it, and finished with a back kick. Nothing broke this time, but the man staggered, dropping his weapon as he clutched his stomach.

The fourth man came in on her right.

He'd had enough time to survey the fight, and just enough time to pick his target; she obviously appeared to be the weaker of the two. It annoyed her. Marcus would have had her hide—although he considered humans to have so little hide it was almost not worth taking—had she let the annoyance get the better of her.

She did the next best thing; she kicked his knee. Hard. She caught him on the side of the leg, and he grunted; he swung his long knife in, and she twisted her arm up in an instinctive, almost impossible position, to deflect it. Thankful for cages, for just a minute. There wasn't a weapon in the city that could go through that bracer. The blow drove her arm into her chest, and she threw her weight onto her back leg, snapping a kick with her front one.

He grabbed for her leg. He was too slow; it brought his chest in close enough that she could hit him. She did, throwing her fists forward and butting the underside of his chin with her head.

She heard his jaw snap shut.

And then he went flying as Severn caught the side of his head with an extended side swing. He wasn't even breathing hard.

And he wasn't carrying a weapon. Then again, neither was she. She straightened up. "Two and a half," she said calmly.

"Two."

"Yours was an assist. I had him."

Tiamaris, however, had had something different: enough. "If you insist," he said in cold and perfect Barrani, something to be feared in the fiefs, "you can play these games until sunset. But if you've finished proving some vague human dominance theory, we have work to do."

Killjoy. She caught his expression, however, and slammed her teeth down over the word.

"Training in the Hawks isn't bad," Severn said, as he fell in step beside her, shortening his stride.

"Wolves obviously know what they're doing," she replied, grudging the words. "We're even here."

He nodded. "Why are you in such a hurry?" He asked Tiamaris's back. "Brecht won't be sober."

He wasn't. And he wasn't clean either. Not that it made that much difference; Brecht ran a bar, and the smells that lingered in the daytime were already overpowering enough.

"Is he even alive?" Severn asked, from the vantage of the open door. There were no lights, and the windows were all shuttered. Brecht had always been damn proud of the fact that he *had* windows. Well, one of them, anyway. The ones near the door were pretty much boards, these days.

"He's alive," Kaylin replied, grimacing. "He's not conscious, but he is alive." She stood over the ungainly heap that Brecht usually became when he'd emptied too many bottles. Counted the empties beside him, and whistled. "I don't think we're going to be able to wake him up."

"Hang on," Severn said. "I'll be back in a second."

"Where you going?"

"The old well."

She laughed. "Don't forget a bucket. This isn't the city market."

"Good point."

Brecht sputtered a lot when the water hit his face. He had to; he had been in the middle of a very noisy inhale. His eyes were red and round when they opened, and he grabbed an empty, cracking it on the hardwood of his personal chair. It shattered in about the right way, leaving him with a suitable weapon. Not that he was in any shape to wield one.

Kaylin stood in front of him, and held out both palms, indicating that she meant him no harm. Or, judging from the water that now streamed down him as if he were a mountain, no more harm. He swore a lot, which she expected.

He even got up, although he wobbled. His legs were like large logs.

"Brecht," Kaylin said softly. "Sorry about waking you, but we need to talk."

"Bar's closed." This wasn't evidence that he was actually awake; Brecht could say this in his sleep. She'd seen it.

"We don't want to talk when the bar's open," Kaylin replied. "Too many people. And some of them, we'd have to kill."

"Not in my bar."

She shrugged. "We'd try to take the fight outside."

He closed his eyes and rubbed water off his face. Didn't work. Dropping the bottle, or the half of it that he still held, he tried mopping his face with his apron. Given that that, too, was soaked, it didn't help much either. The swearing that followed, on the other hand, seemed to do him a world of good.

He shook himself, like a Leontine waking, and then his bloodshot eyes narrowed. "Is that Elianne? And Severn? Together?"

Before she could frame a reply, he muttered, "I've got to drink something better than swill." But he continued to stare at her, and after a minute, he snorted. Water flew out his nostrils. "Do that again," he added, "and you won't be."

"Together?"

"Alive." He frowned. "Who's the nob?"

"Tiamaris. He's a—a friend."

Suspicion, which was his natural expression, chased surprise off his face. "A friend of who?"

"Mine, sort of. Look, Brecht, we need to—"

"Yeah, I heard you. You need to talk. Tell you what. You go behind the counter and get me a bottle of—"

"No," Severn said.

Brecht cursed him for a three-mothered cur. All in all, it was almost affectionate. "What do you need to talk about?" he said after he'd finished.

She started to speak, stopped and waited.

He lost about four inches in height. "I should have known," he said softly. "Look, Elianne—"

"I'm called Kaylin, now," she said quietly.

"Shit, I barely remembered the old name." Which was probably true. "You got out," he added. "We heard about it. I thought it was a lie—I thought you were dead, like the others."

She closed her eyes. She could not look at Severn.

Severn said nothing.

"But it's started again," the old man continued. His hands were over his face when she opened her eyes. Old hands, now. Seven years had changed him. "Connie's lost her boy. I found him."

"What did you do?"

"I sent a runner. You don't know him," he added. "He came after your time. I sent a runner to the damn Lords of Law."

She nodded.

But Severn didn't. He stepped in, toward Brecht, and grabbed him by the shirt collar.

"Severn—" she began.

"He's lying," Severn said. Menace enfolded the scant syllables.

"Lying? Why?"

"I don't know. Why don't you tell us, Brecht?" Before she could say another word, Severn's long knife was in his hand. Brecht was no fool; he didn't even try to reach for a bottle.

"Severn, this is stupid. Look—the Lords of Law *have* the body," she snapped.

"They have it now. Brecht, who did you send the runner *to*?"

Brecht was absolutely stone still.

And Kaylin, caught by Severn, by the change in him, was still as well. But she was a Hawk. She'd spent seven years under the harsh tutelage of both Lord Grammayre and Marcus. The hair on the back of her neck began to rise, and her arms goose-bumped suddenly.

She looked at Tiamaris and saw that his eyes were a deep, unnatural red; that he had already turned away from the pathetic bartender and the not so pathetic Shadow Wolf.

Toward the door. The open door.

In it, the answer stood. And he smiled. "Why, to me, Severn," he said softly, in perfect Barrani. "Thank you, Brecht. You've done well, and you will be rewarded." His Elantran was also perfect, and she was surprised to hear it. Then again, Brecht probably didn't speak any Barrani worth listening to. Unless you liked inventive cursing.

Kaylin wasn't certain that that reward wouldn't be death; Severn's eyes were black. She knew what that meant. Hated it. Without thinking, she reached out and grabbed his knife hand, curling her fingers round his wrist.

He stared at her. Stared at the hand that she had willingly placed around his wrist. Understood what she was asking, understood that she would never ask in words.

Severn slowly released old Brecht and turned at last to face the outcaste Barrani lord known, in this fief, as Nightshade.

CHAPTER 4

He was tall.

Taller than either Teela or Tain; taller than Tiamaris. He had hair that was a shade darker than ebony, and it was long; it slid down his back like a cape.

Teela and Tain made her feel ungainly, clumsy and plodding. Nightshade—lord of this fief—made her feel worse: young again. Afraid. Just standing there, in the door, his hands idling against the wooden frame. They were ringed hands, and she hated that.

In fact, had she not been so unsettled, she would have hated him. But, like the rest of the Barrani, he seemed above any emotion she might offer. His eyes were cold, emerald-green; they did not blink once. She hoped it stung. She knew it wouldn't.

"So," he said quietly, sliding back into Barrani as he withdrew his hands from the door frame and stepped into the bar. He gestured without looking back, his fingers flicking air as if he were brushing away a speck of dust.

Behind him, two guards followed; they were, by their look, Barrani as well.

Three. Against a single Barrani, she and Severn had a good chance—on a very lucky day. But against three? None whatsoever.

Her hands fell to her daggers.

The fieflord raised a dark brow. "Do not," he said softly, "insult my hospitality. Had I wished you harm, you would never have reached this…place." He glanced around the innards of the bar.

She said nothing. She had heard his name whispered for years. In the fiefs, it was common. Outside of them, his name was also known, but the Hawks at least didn't feel any need to speak it with respect, on the rare occasions they used it at all. She'd gotten used to that. She'd forgotten too much.

Kaylin had never met the fieflord. Was certain that she would have remembered even a passing glimpse, had she had one. Because although the Barrani had all looked alike to her when she had joined the Hawks, and it had taken months to become used to the subtle ways in which they differentiated themselves when they could be bothered, she would have known that *this* one was different.

She almost called him Lord Nightshade, and that would have been too much. Too much fear. Too much reaction.

As if he could hear her thoughts, his gaze met hers. "So," he said softly. "You are the child."

Not even that word could make her bridle.

He moved toward her, and Severn moved, slowly, to block him. The Barrani at the fieflord's back moved less slowly, but with infinitely more grace. They were cold, deadly, beautiful—and utterly silent.

"Severn," the fieflord said quietly. "It has been many years since we last spoke."

Kaylin couldn't stop her brows from rising. "Severn?"

Severn said, quietly, "Not enough of them."

The fieflord moved before either she or Severn could; he backhanded Severn. And Severn managed to keep his footing. "I will, for the sake of hospitality, tolerate much from outsiders," the fieflord said. "But you were—and will always be—one of mine. Do not presume overmuch."

"He's not yours," Kaylin said sharply, surprise following words that she wouldn't have said she could utter until they'd tumbled out of her open mouth. She spoke forcefully in Elantran, her mother tongue. Barrani, if it came, would come later; to speak it now was too much of a concession. Or a presumption. Either way, she didn't like it.

A black brow rose; she had amused the fieflord. Then again, so did painful, hideous death by all accounts.

"And do you claim him, then, little one?"

"The Lord of Hawks does," she replied.

He reached out slowly, his hand empty, his palm exposed. Gold glittered at the base of his fingers, but he carried no obvious weapon. His fingers brushed her cheek.

As if she were a pet, something small and helpless.

"The Lord of Hawks has no authority here," he replied softly, "save that which I grant him."

"He has authority," Tiamaris said quietly, speaking for the first time.

The fieflord's hand stilled, but it did not leave her face as he turned. His eyes, however, widened slightly as he met the red of Dragon eyes. Unlidded eyes, they seemed to burn. "Is she yours?" He asked casually, and this time, he *did* let his hand fall away.

"She is as she says."

"She has not said who she serves," the fieflord replied. "And if I am not mistaken, she was born in the fiefs." He turned to look at her again.

"I—I serve—the Hawklord. Lord Grammayre. And so does Tiamaris."

"Really?"

"I have offered him my service," Tiamaris replied softly, "and it has been accepted. While I am here, I am his agent."

The fieflord surprised Kaylin, then. He laughed. It was a rich, lovely sound, and it conveyed both amusement and something she couldn't quite name. "Times have changed, Tiamaris, if you can serve another."

"I have always served another," was the cold reply.

Kaylin had never seen a Dragon fight. Had a bad feeling that she was about to. The Barrani guards had forgotten Severn, forgotten her; they were drawn to Tiamaris as if he were the only significant danger in the room. Which was fair. He was.

The fieflord, however, raised a hand, and the Barrani stiffened. She knew some of the silent language of thieves, and saw none of it in the gestures of the fieflord. They knew him well enough that that gesture was command.

"It is strange," the fieflord said softly. "I know both you, Tiamaris, and the young man called Severn by his kind. But the girl? She is at the apex of events, and I have never met her." He held out a hand, then.

She stared at it.

"Leave her be," Tiamaris said, and his voice, soft, was suddenly louder than Marcus's at its most fierce.

"I intend her no harm," the fieflord replied. He had once again turned the full emerald of his eyes upon her, and she could not help but believe his words. "And I intend to make clear to the people of my lands that I intend they offer her none. Will you gainsay me?"

"I will not have you mark her."

The fieflord said, quietly, "She is already marked, Tiamaris."

To that, the Dragon offered no reply.

Which was too bad; it might have helped her make sense of the fieflord's words. She stared at his hand; he did not move it. After a moment, it became clear to her that he intended her to actually *take* his hand.

"I am not patient," the fieflord said, when he realized that she wouldn't. "And I have little time to spare. You are here because of the sacrifices, of course. And it is in my interest to see an end brought to them as well."

Still she stared. Might have gone on staring, dumbfounded, had Severn not said, curtly, "Take his hand."

Her fingers touched the fieflord's palm, and he closed his hand around hers.

Magic coursed up her arm. Her right arm. She was rigid with the shock of it, and angry. She tried to pull free, and wasn't surprised when she failed.

"What are you—"

"Silence."

She could feel the magic as it rode up her shoulder, sharp light, and invisible. She *hated* magic. But she bit her lip and waited; she was already committed.

Severn swore.

Tiamaris's brows rose. "Lord Nightshade," he began, but he did not finish.

The magic broke through her skin, questing in air as if it were alive. She could see it. Judging by the expressions of her companions, everyone could. It twisted in the space just above her, and then it coalesced into a blue, sparkling shape, like a ward.

It touched her cheek, in the exact same place that the fieflord had. A lesson, for Kaylin, and one that she would not forget: he did nothing without cause.

"You bear my mark," he said quietly. "And in this fief, it will afford you some protection." He paused, and then added, "This *is* a fief. It will not protect you from everything. Mortal stupidity knows no bounds. But in the event that you are harmed by *any* save me, they will pay."

He let her hand go, then. "Now, come. It is late, and we have far to travel."

"Travel?" Her first word, and it wasn't terribly impressive. Then again, Severn said nothing at all.

"You are invited as guests to the Long Halls of Nightshade," he replied, with just the hint of a bow. "But sunset is coming, and in the fiefs—"

She nodded. In the fiefs, night meant something different.

Her skin was still tingling a half hour later. The fieflord walked before them, and the Barrani guards, behind. Sandwiched in an uncomfortable line between these two walked Severn, Kaylin and Tiamaris, the wings of their namesake momentarily clipped.

"Severn," she said, in a voice so soft he should have missed it.

Severn nodded, although he didn't look at her.

"My face—what happened?"

"You—you've got a blue flower on your cheek," he said quietly.

"A *flower?*"

"Sort of. It's nightshade."

"It's *what?*"

"Nightshade," Tiamaris said quietly. "The namesake of the fieflord. It's a...herb," he added.

"I have a tattoo of a *flower* on my face?"

Severn did look at her then, his brow arched. "You would have liked a skull and crossbones better?"

"Or a dagger. Or a sword. Or even a Hawk. A *flower?*"

"A deadly one," Tiamaris said, with just the hint of a smile. "But it is very pretty."

Had he not been a Dragon, she would have kicked him. Or had she not been shadowed by armed Barrani. As it was, she glowered.

Which broadened his smile. Dragon smile. "You should feel…honored. In a fashion. This is the first time that I have seen a human bear the mark of the fieflord."

She turned the words over, picking out the information they contained. "How often have you seen him mark anyone else?"

"Not often," Tiamaris replied, his eyes now lidded. "And no, before you ask, I am not going to tell you when."

She frowned. "Does the Hawklord—"

"Lord Grammayre knows much," he replied. "And if he feels it necessary to enlighten you, he will. Until then, I suggest you pay attention to the—"

Cobbled streets. Badly cobbled. She caught her boot under the edge of an upturned stone and tripped. Severn caught her arm before she made her way to the ground.

"Severn?"

"What?"

"When did you meet the fieflord?"

"Back when we were both in the fiefs," he said. But he didn't meet her eyes.

"Why didn't you tell me?"

"Because I didn't want you to know."

"All right, I guessed that. Why?"

He shook his head. "Don't ask, Kaylin."

She heard the change in his tone, and she suddenly didn't want to know. "You know where we're going?"

"No. When I spoke to him, he didn't invite me into his Hall."

"Should we be worried?"

The look he gave her almost made her laugh. It would have been a shaky laugh. She held it. "I mean, more worried?"

And he shook his head and cuffed hers gently. "You haven't changed at all," he said, with just a hint of bitterness.

The manor of the fieflord was *not* a manor. It was a small keep. Stone walls circled it, and beyond their height—and they were damn tall—the hint of a castle behind them could be seen, no more. The stone work of the walls was in perfect repair, and that made it suspect in the fiefs, where nothing was perfect.

The castle would have looked ridiculous had she not been in the presence of the man who ruled the fief from its heart. She'd lived most of her life in Nightshade, and she'd only once come near the keep. Rarely come down the streets that surrounded it. She'd spent a good deal of time honing her skills at theft, and no one survived stealing anything from the fieflord or his closest advisors. And in the end, they were happy enough not to survive; it was all the stuff in between that was terrifying.

She saw no one on the streets. It was not yet dark, but they were empty. She wondered if they'd been cleared by the Barrani guards, or if people were just unusually smart in this part of town. She didn't ask.

The tall, stone buildings around the keep were better kept than those at the edges of the fief, but they were still packed tightly together, and they still felt old. As old as anything in the outer city. Shadows moved in the windows, or perhaps they were drapes closing; the movements were quick, furtive and caught by the corner of a wary eye.

Between some of those windows, gargoyles, carved in weathered stone, kept watch like sentinels on high, smooth wings folded, claws extended about the edge of their stone bases. She had often wondered if the gargoyles came to life when the last of day waned. She was careful not to wonder it now. Because in the shadow of the fieflord, it seemed too plausible.

The road to the keep was wide; a carriage could easily make its way to the gate, pulled by four—or even six— horses. But the gates themselves were behind a portcullis that discouraged visitors.

They certainly discouraged Kaylin.

She turned to Tiamaris, but Tiamaris didn't blink. He nodded, however, to let her know that he was aware of her sudden movement.

"Welcome," the fieflord said softly, "to Castle Night-shade." He stepped forward as they approached the gates, and he placed a hand upon the portcullis.

It shivered in place, but it did not rise.

"Follow me," he said. "Do not stop. Do not hesitate, and do not show fear. While you are with me, you are safe. Remember it."

He spoke to Kaylin in his resonant Barrani, and although she'd spoken nothing but Elantran, she knew he knew that she understood him perfectly. Then again, she was a ground Hawk; all of the Hawks had to speak Barrani, or they weren't allowed on the beat. She wondered, now, why she had thought it was such a good idea.

It seemed, to Kaylin, that he spoke *only* to her.

Dry-mouthed, she nodded.

He stepped forward *through* the portcullis. As if it were shadow, and only shadow. Drawing breath, Kaylin looked to either side for support, and then did as he had done: She stepped into the gate.

It enfolded her.

She screamed.

When she woke, her head ached, her mouth was dry and she would have bet she'd had a *terrific* evening with Teela and Tain in the bar down the street—if she could remember any of it. That lasted for as long as it took her to realize that her bed was way too soft, her room was way too big, her door lacked bolts and had gained height and her windows were nonexistent.

That, and she had a companion.

She reached for her daggers. They weren't there. In fact neither were her leathers. Or her tunic, or the one pair of pants she had that hadn't been cut to pieces.

Lord Nightshade stood in the center of the almost empty room. If there were no windows, light was abundant, and it was both soft enough to soothe the eye, and harsh enough to see clearly by. The floor beneath his feet was marble and gold, and he seemed to be standing in the center of a large circle.

"You will forgive me," he said, making a command out

of what would, from anyone else, have been an apology. "I did not expect your passage here to be so…costly. Your former clothing was inappropriate for my halls. It will be returned to you when you leave."

The when sounded distinctly like an if.

She wasn't naked. Exactly.

But her arms were bare to the shoulder, and she *hated* that. She never, ever wore anything that didn't fall past her wrists, and for obvious reasons. The thick distinct lines of swirling black seemed to move up and down her forearms as she glanced at them. She didn't look long.

Dizzy, she rose. Her dress—and it was a dress of midnight-blue, long, fine and elegantly simple—rose with her, clinging to the skin. It was a pleasant sensation. And it was not.

Teela and Tain were the Barrani she knew best, and they never came to work dressed like *this*. It made her wonder what they did in their off hours. Which made her redden. She wondered who had changed her, and that didn't help.

But the fieflord simply waited, watching her as if uncertain what she would do. She lifted her right arm, and saw that the gold manacle still encased it, gems flashing in sequence. A warning.

"Yes," he said softly. "That was…unexpected. I have not seen its like in many, many years—and I suspect not even then. Where did you get it?"

"It was a gift."

"From the Lord Grammayre?"

She nodded.

"It did not come from him. Not directly." He stepped outside of the golden circle inlayed upon the ground and approached her. But he approached her slowly, as if she were wild. "My apologies," he said, less of a command in the words. "But I wished to see for myself if you bore the marks."

"And now?" she asked bitterly.

"I know. If you are hungry, you may eat. Food will be brought. These rooms have been little used for many years. They are not fit for guests."

"Where are my—where are Severn and Tiamaris?"

"I found it convenient to leave them behind," he replied gravely. "But they are unharmed, and they know that you are likewise unharmed. If they are wise, they will wait."

"And if they aren't?"

"These are *my* halls," he said coldly. "And not even a Dragon may enter them with impunity."

"But he's been here before."

The fieflord raised a brow. "How do you know that, little one?"

"I'm not called 'little,'" she replied. She wanted to snap the words; they came out sounding, to her ears, pathetic.

"And what *are* you called now?"

"Kaylin. Kaylin Neya."

His other brow rose. And fell. "Interesting. Yes, you are correct. Tiamaris has indeed visited the Long Halls. If any could find their way in, uninvited, it would be he. But I think, for the moment, he is content to wait. It will keep your Severn alive."

"He's not mine," she said. *And I don't want him alive.* But she couldn't bring herself to say the words to the fieflord. Didn't want to know why.

He held out a hand.

She tried to ignore it. But she found herself lifting hand in response. As if this were a dream. He took the hand; his skin was cool. Hers was damp.

"These are the Halls of Nightshade," he said quietly. "Come. There are things here I wish you to see." Without another word, he led her from the room.

She expected the doors to open into a hall.

So much for expectation. They opened instead into what must have been a forest. Not that she'd seen forests—not up close—but she'd seen them at a distance, when Clint had taken her flying to the Aeries of his kin. Here, the trees grew up, and up again, until they reached the rounded height of a ceiling that she could only barely glimpse through the greenery.

She walked slowly, her hand still captive to the fieflord's, but he seemed to be in no hurry. And why would he? If he didn't manage to get himself killed, he had forever. Time meant nothing to him.

At his side, in waking dream, it could almost mean nothing to her. She touched the rough surface of brown bark, and then moved on to the smooth surface of silver-white; she touched leaves that had fallen across the ground like a tapestry, a gentle riot of color. All of her words deserted her, which was just as well; she didn't have any fine enough to describe what she saw.

And had she, she wouldn't have exposed it. Beauty meant something to her, and she kept it to herself, as she kept most things that meant anything.

"There is no sunlight," he told her, as if that made sense. "But outcaste or no, I am still Barrani Lord—they grow at my whim."

"And if you don't want them?"

He gestured. The tree just beyond the tip of her fingers withered, twisting toward the ground almost as if it were begging. She stopped herself from crying out. It was just a plant.

She didn't ask again, however. And she kept her wonder contained; she looked; she touched nothing else. He had offered her a warning, in subtle Barrani fashion. She took it.

"Where are we going?"

"To the heart of this forest," he replied. "Be honored. Not even my own have seen it."

"Your children?"

His brows drew in. "Are you truly so ignorant, Kaylin?"

"Apparently."

His hand tightened. It was not comfortable. Another warning. But he chose to do no more than that, and after a pause, he surprised her. He answered. "I have no children. I am outcaste."

Outcaste was a word that had meaning for Kaylin, but in truth, not much. Although one human lord served as Caste-lord for her kind, the complicated laws of the caste did not apply to the rank and file. It certainly didn't apply to the paupers and the beggars who made a living—or didn't—in the fiefs. The Leontines, the Aerians and the humans—mortal races all—were not defined in the same way by caste; they were more numerous, and their lives reached from the lowest of gutters to the highest of towers. Not so, the Barrani.

"I spoke simply of my kin, those who chose to follow me. The forest speaks to them, but it speaks in a language that is…not pleasant to their ears. They will not hear it, and remain. And I am unwilling to release them.

"I release nothing that is mine."

She said nothing for a while. For long enough that she found the silence uncomfortable. Not awkward; awkward was too petty a word. "Did you build this?"

"The forest?"

"The…Long Halls."

"No."

"The castle?"

"No. I have altered it over the years, but in truth, very little. It was here, for the taking." His smile was thin. "I was not, however, the first to try. I was the first to succeed."

"It had other occupants?"

"It had defenses," he replied. "And I forget myself. You ask too many questions."

"Questions are encouraged, in the Hawks. When they're not stupid."

"Indeed. Here, they are not. The answers can be fatal." He stopped in front of a dense ring of trees; their branches seemed to interlock at all levels, as if they had deliberately grown together. She didn't like the look of them. But then again, at the moment she didn't like the look of herself, either. What she could see, that is; the dress, the funny shoes, the bold, black design on her arms. She drew her arms down.

His hand came with one. "You do not understand the marks you bear," he said, his voice a little too close to her ear.

"And you do?"

"No, not completely. But I understand some of their significance. In truth, I'm surprised that you still survive."

"Why?"

He smiled, but he didn't answer. Instead, he lifted his hand and touched the trees that barred their way. They shuddered. There was something terrible about that shudder, something that looked so wrong she had to turn away. It was as if the trees were silently screaming.

But they parted. Like curtains, like great rolling doors, their limbs untwining, their trunks shifting. Roots moved beneath her feet—or something did. She really wanted to pay less attention.

"Come," he said, when there was room enough for passage.

Her hand fell to her hips, and came up empty. Daggers, of course, were someplace else. But the desire for them, the reflex, was still a part of her. And it was growing stronger.

"Nothing will harm you here," he told her, the smile gone. "You bear my mark. You are in my domain."

I've lived in your fief for more than half my life, and it wasn't ever safe. But she said nothing. And it was hard.

The trees were not as thick as they appeared; the darkness of their branches curved above like a roof or a canopy, but it lasted a scant ten feet, and then it was gone.

They stood in a great, stone room, beneath the outer edge of a domed ceiling that gave off a bright, green light. And as they walked toward the center of the room, that light grew brighter, changing in hue. She looked up; she couldn't help it.

Above her, carved in runnels in the smooth, hard stone, were swirling patterns that were both familiar and foreign. She lifted a hand. An arm.

"Yes," the fieflord said quietly. "They are written in the same tongue as the mark you bear. It is known as the language of the Old Ones."

"I—I don't understand."

"No one does. There is not a creature alive that can read the whole of what is written there. But I have never seen the writing glow in such a fashion. I believe that the room is aware of your presence."

"But who—or what—are the Old Ones?"

His frown was momentary, but sharp. But he surprised her. "Once," he said softly, "you might have considered them gods."

"But the gods—"

The derision was there in the cold expression the word evoked. "Mortal gods?" He shrugged. "Mortal gods *are* mortal. They exist at the whim of your attention, and your attention passes quickly."

She didn't like the room. He continued to walk; she

stopped. But although he was slender, he pulled her along, her feet scudding stone. Dignity forced her to follow, given how little of it she had.

She forgot the ceiling, then.

The floor itself was alive. Where she stepped, light seemed to squelch like soft mud, and it flared in lines, in swirling circles, in patterns.

"Here," he said softly, and stopped. "Go no farther, Kaylin. And touch *nothing* if you value your life."

If she'd valued her life, she'd have stayed out of the fiefs. She nodded.

In the center of the room, laid against the floor in sapphire light, was a large circle. It didn't surprise her much to see writing across it. She couldn't read it, of course; it was almost the same as the writing that was carved high above her head. But it was different. It seemed to *move*.

"This is the seal of the Old Ones," he said quietly, "and from it emanates the power that defended the castle against intruders." Against, she thought, the fieflord.

She stared at the seal. The writing seemed to sharpen, somehow. Light flared, like blue fire, and it grew in height along the patterns that had birthed it. She watched as it reached for the ceiling. Watched, forgetting to breathe, as the light from the ceiling dripped down.

When they touched, she cried out in shock, and then in pain; her arms were on fire.

"Stay your ground," the fieflord said, but his voice seemed to come from a distance—a growing distance. She reached out almost in panic, and was instantly ashamed of her reaction.

She would have reached out for Severn that way, once. And she'd already paid for that. She made fists of her fingers.

"Kaylin, *stay your ground.*"

Her tongue was heavy; too heavy for speech. She wanted to tell him that she *was* staying her damned ground, but she couldn't, and probably just as well.

The light was a column now.

She felt it, an inch from her face, from her hand. Her hand was moving toward it, fingers twitching, as if pulled by gravity. She'd fallen once, from a great enough height that she'd had time to think about just how much of a pain gravity was.

She'd choose falling any time.

She heard the fieflord. She *felt* his presence. But her hand moved, continued to move. Her skin touched blue fire. Blue fire touched her.

For just a moment, she could see, in the pillar of light, something that looked like a…man. The way that the Barrani fieflord did. But worse. She could not make out his features, and she knew that she really, really didn't want to.

Her hand sank through the light.

She heard a single word.

Chosen.

And then a different light flared; the golden manacle slammed into the pillar and it refused to move farther. She pushed against it with half of her weight and none of her will. She was losing ground.

She cried out; she couldn't help it. Years of training fled

in the panic that followed. She could see only light, could hear only the indistinct murmur of a stranger's voice, could feel nothing at all beneath her feet. She had feared the night all her life; this was worse. Her feet were moving. Toward the light, toward the pillar, toward what it contained. She bit her lip, and she tasted blood.

And then, just before she entered the column, before she lost herself entirely, the shadows came, and they came in the shape of a dark, precise crest.

She didn't recognize it. It didn't matter.

She hit it and froze.

The light scraped against its edges, seeking passage the way sun does through stained glass. But this lattice offered nothing; it wasn't, as it had first appeared, a window. It was a wall.

It was a wall with something written across it. She stared at it as the light flared, brighter now, and she understood the word in the same way she understood hunger, pain or fear: instinctively.

She could still taste blood. She could not feel her lips. But they moved anyway. Barrani was one of the languages that the Hawklord had insisted she study, and if she hadn't been his most apt pupil, she'd learned. She'd always learned any real lesson he'd decided to teach her, even the ones that scarred.

Her lips moved over the syllables; she had to force them. She couldn't make a sound, but it didn't matter.

Calarnenne.

The light went out.

"My apologies," the fieflord said softly. His arms were around her waist, his face against her neck. Black hair trailed down her shoulder in loose, wild strands. Pretty hair.

She tried to speak.

He lifted a hand and pressed his fingers gently against her lips. "No more," he said softly. "You have done enough. I have done enough. Come. We must leave this place."

Her knees collapsed.

Teela would have laughed at her. Tain would have shaken his head. But the fieflord did neither; he caught her before she hit ground, lifting her as if her weight were insignificant. He cradled her against his chest, and because he did, she saw blood well against the soft fabric of his odd tunic.

It was hers. Her cheek was bleeding.

"I…can walk."

He smiled grimly. "You can barely speak," he said, "and if you touch the ground again, I am not certain that I will be able to stop you from touching the seal."

There were so many questions she wanted to ask him.

Only one surfaced, fighting its way to the top. "Calarnenne?"

"Yes," he replied grimly. "My name. Do not speak it, Kaylin." His eyes were as blue as the light had been, and just as cold.

"Your name."

"I should kill you," he replied.

"Why?"

"Because you are now a bigger threat than even the Dragon."

She shook her head. She knew that. "Why did you—why your name?"

He stopped walking, but he did not set her down. The trees were above them now, and she found their dark presence almost comforting. "The mark," he said, touching her wounded cheek, "was not enough. You know the Barrani," he added, his fingers brushing blood away gently. "How many of them have given you their names?"

She shook her head. "I don't know."

The frustration on his face was the most familiar expression she had yet seen. It reminded her of the Hawklord. "None," he said curtly. "Because if they had, you *would* know."

When this didn't seem to garner the right response, he shook her. But even this was gentle.

"If you called their names, they would hear you. They would know where you were. And if they were not strong, they would be drawn to you. Names have power, Kaylin." He paused. Frowned. "They have power, if you have the power to say them."

And then he spoke the whole of her given name, her new name. "Kaylin Neya."

She felt it reverberate through her body as if it were a caress.

He laughed, then.

CHAPTER 5

He took her back to the rooms she had woken in, and there, she found her daggers. Her clothing, however, was nowhere in sight. When her brows rose, he smiled. His smile was so close to her face it was almost blurred; she could pretend it was something else.

Her arms *ached*. Her head hurt. And her cheek? It continued to bleed.

The fieflord set her down upon the bed. He reached out to touch her cheek and she shied away—which overbalanced her. She really was pathetic. "Don't."

The word displeased him; his face fell into its more familiar, cold mask. "I have no intention of harming you," he replied. "And I seek to take no screaming mortal children to my bed. Those who are fortunate enough to come to the Long Halls come willingly."

"Willingly." She snorted.

"Kaylin, I have perhaps made an error in judgment, and you have paid for it. Do not presume overmuch."

Another warning. Too many warnings. She fell silent. But she did not let him touch her again, and he didn't try. They were quiet for some time.

"My clothing?" she asked at last.

"It will return to you when you leave the Long Halls. It is, as I said, unsuitable." He rose. "We will return you to your Hawks for the moment."

She waited until he had reached the door; when he did, she rose. "I want to cover my arms," she said.

He said nothing; he simply waited.

Her legs were wobbly, and she made her way, clumsy and entirely graceless, toward him. When he offered her an arm, she bit back all pride and took it; it was either that or fall flat on her face.

Teela had taken her drinking when she had been a year with the Hawks. It had been something like this, but with more nausea. Not a lot more, though.

When he opened the door, the forest was gone.

In its place? A long hall. Funny, that. She felt magic as she walked through the door, and she swore under her breath. It was a Leontine curse. It would have shocked Marcus, if anything could.

"You will be weak for two days," he told her quietly, "if only that. Eat what you can eat. Drink what you can drink. Do not," he added softly, "be alone."

"Why?"

"I do not understand all of what happened, Kaylin. But I understand this much…by presence alone, you activated the seal. In my life, I have never seen it burn. And believe that I, and the mages at my disposal, have tried.

"It is not, however, of the seal that I speak."

"Your name," she whispered.

"Indeed. The giving of a name is never an easy thing. It is, in essence, the most ancient and most dangerous of our rituals. It is a binding, a subtle chain. In some people, it destroys will and presence of mind."

"You mean—"

"I did not think it would have that effect upon you, but it was a risk."

Her brows rose. He smiled, but it was a sharp smile. "Barrani gifts," he said softly, "have thorns or edges. Remember that."

Like she could forget.

"I would take the name from you," he added softly, "but I think I would find it difficult. And if the taking of the name was costly to you, the giving was costly to *me*." Clear, from the tone of his voice, which one of the two mattered more.

"Do not let go of my arm," he told her quietly. "We will meet some of my kin before you are free of the Hall, and two who have not seen the outer world for much, much longer than you have been alive. They will be drawn to you." His lips lost the edge that was his smile. "They will not touch you, if they see the mark—but it bleeds, Kaylin, and you will not let me tend it."

"I couldn't stop you," she said quietly.

"No. But in this, I have chosen to grant you volition. It is another lesson."

The Hall was, as the name suggested, long. It was tall as well, but not so tall as the great hall that opened into the Halls of Law. No Aerian wings graced the heights; they were cold, serene and perfect. Funny, how lack of living things could make something seem so perfect.

They walked for minutes, for a quarter of an hour, passing closed doors and alcoves in which fountains trickled clear water into ancient stone. She didn't ask where the water came from. She didn't really want to know.

But when they came at last to the Hall's end, there were tall doors, and the doors were closed. An alcove sat to the left and right of either door, and in each, like living statues, stood a Barrani lord.

She could not tell, at first glance, if they were male or female. They were adorned by the same dark hair that marked all of their kind, and it, like their still faces, was perfect. Their skin was white, like alabaster, and their lids were closed in a sweep of lashes against that perfect skin.

She heeded the warning of the fieflord; she held his arm. He walked beside her until the Barrani flanked him, and then he said, softly, "The doors must be opened."

Eyelids rolled up. Nothing else about the Barrani moved. Kaylin found it disturbing.

The doors began to swing outward in a slow, slow arc. She stepped toward them, eager to be gone; the fieflord, however, did not move. She turned to look at him, and her glance strayed to the two Barrani on either side of her.

They were speaking. Their voices were unlike any Barrani voice she had ever heard, even the fieflord's: they were almost sibilant. They reminded her of ghosts. Death that whispered the name of Nightshade.

But when they reached out to touch her, she froze; the dead didn't move like *this*. Fluid, graceful, silent, they eyed her as if she were…food.

"Peace," the fieflord said coldly.

They didn't seem to hear him. Icy fingers touched her arms. Icy fingers burned. Unfortunately, so did Kaylin.

The hand drew back.

"She is yours?" one of the two said. His voice was stronger now, as if he were remembering how to use it. The words held more expression than any Barrani voice she had heard, which was strange, given that his face held less.

"She is mine," Nightshade said quietly.

"Give her to us. Give her to us as the price of passage."

"You forget yourselves," he replied. He lifted a hand, and thin shadows streamed from his fingers. They passed over her shoulder, around the curve of her arm, without touching her. She froze in place, because she was suddenly very certain that she didn't want them to touch her.

"They smell blood," he said quietly.

It made no sense.

"They are old," he added softly, "and they have chosen to reside here in Barrani sleep. They are also powerful. Do not wake them, Kaylin."

"You rule here."

"I rule," he said softly, "because I have not chosen to join them. They are outcaste, and they have been long from the world." He paused, and then added quietly, "They were within the castle grounds, even as you see them, when I at last took possession. They fought me. They are powerful, but they seldom speak."

"They're speaking now."

"Yes. I thought they might. You have touched the seal," he added.

"Will they leave?"

"No. They are bound here, but the binding is old and poorly understood. Blood wakes them. It is a call to life."

The lesson, then. She raised a hand to cover her cheek.

"She bears the mark," one of the two said. It confused Kaylin until she realized they weren't talking about the fieflord's strange flower; they were talking about the ones on her arms. "Leave her here. Do not meddle in the affairs of the ancients."

"She is mortal," the fieflord replied. "And not bound by the laws of the Old Ones."

"She bears the marks," the Barrani said again. "She contains the words."

"She cannot."

Silence then. Shadows.

"She is almost bound," a flat, cold voice at last replied. "As we are bound. We grant you passage, Lord of the Long Halls."

Kaylin passed between them in the shadow of the

fieflord, but she felt their eyes burning a hole between her shoulder blades, and she swore that she would never again walk through a shadow gate, not even if her life depended on it. She'd been hungry before, but never like they were, and she didn't want to be whatever it was that satisfied that hunger.

"You will not speak of them here," he told her.

"I—"

"I understand that you will speak with Lord Grammayre. I understand that, if you do not speak well, he will summon the Tha'alani."

She shuddered. "He won't," she snapped.

"You already bear the scent of their touch. It is... unpleasant."

"Only once," she whispered, but she paled.

"Do not trust Lord Grammayre overmuch," he said softly.

"Your name—"

And smiled. "Not even the Tha'alani can touch it. No mortal can, if it has not been gifted to them, and if they have not paid the price. The name, Kaylin Neya, is for you. If he questions you, answer him. I give you leave to do so."

"Why?"

"Because the Lord of Hawks and the Lord of Nightshade are bound by different laws. We have different information, and I am curious to see what he makes of you, now."

He stepped through the doors, and they began to close slowly behind them. When Kaylin turned back to look, she saw only blank, smooth walls. But at their edges, top and bottom, she saw the swirled runic writing with which she was becoming familiar.

"Not even I can free them," he said quietly. "I tried only once."

She started to say something, and to her great embarrassment, her stomach got there before she did; it growled.

His beautiful black brows rose in surprise, and then he laughed. She wanted to hate the sound. "You are very human," he said softly. "And I see so few."

Which reminded her of something. "Severn," she said.

"Yes. Perhaps the last of your kind that I have spoken to at length."

"Why?"

The laughter was gone, and the smile it left in its place was like ebony, hard and smooth. "Ask him."

"He won't answer."

"No. But ask him. It will amuse me."

When they left the next hall, she heard voices.

One was particularly loud. It was certainly familiar. She closed her eyes, released the fieflord's arm, and stumbled as she grabbed folds of shimmering silk, bunching them in her fists. She lifted the skirt of her fine dress, freeing her feet, and after a moment's hesitation, she kicked off the stupid shoes, the snap of her legs sending them flying in different directions. The floor was cold against her soles. Cold and hard.

Didn't matter.

She recognized both the voice and its tenor, and she

began to run. The lurching movement reminded her of how weak her legs were. But they were strong enough. She made it to the end of the hall, and turned a sharp corner.

There, in a room that was both gaudy and bright—as unlike the rest of the Halls as any room she had yet seen—were Severn, Tiamaris and the two Barrani guards that had accompanied the Lord of Nightshade.

The guards held drawn weapons.

Severn held links of thin chain. At the end of that chain was a flat blade. She had never seen him use a weapon of this kind before, and knew it for a gift of the Wolves.

And she *didn't* want to see him use it here.

"Severn!" she shouted.

His angry demand was broken in the middle by the sound of her voice. It should have stopped him.

But he stared at her, at the dress she was wearing, at the bare display of shoulders and arms, her bare feet, at the blood—curse the fieflord, curse him to whichever hell the Barrani occupied—on her cheek, before he changed direction, started the chain spinning.

And she knew the expression on his face. Had seen it before a handful of times in the fiefs. It had always ended in death.

This time, though, she thought it would be the wrong death. She moved before she could think—thought took too much damn *time,* and she came to stand before him—before him, and between Severn and the fieflord, who had silently come into the room as if he owned it.

Which, in fact, he did.

"Severn!" She shouted, raising her hands, both empty, one brown with the traces of her blood. "*Severn*, he didn't touch me!"

Severn met her eyes; the chain was now moving so fast it was a wall, a metal wall. He shortened his grip on it, but he did not let it rest.

"Severn, put it *down*."

"If he didn't touch you, why are you dressed like that?"

"Put it down, Severn. Put it away. You're here as a Hawk. And the Hawklord wants no fight with the fieflord. You don't have the luxury of dying. Not here."

If he did, she wasn't so sure that his would be the only death. "Don't start a fief war," she shouted. Had to shout. "He didn't touch me. I'm not hurt."

"You're *bleeding*," he said.

"The mark is bleeding," she snapped back. "And I don't need you to protect me, damn it—I'm a Hawk. I can protect myself!"

He slowed, then. She had him. "I don't need protection," she said again, and this time the words had multiple meanings to the two of them, and only the two of them.

His face showed the first emotion that wasn't anger. And she wasn't certain, after she'd seen it, that she didn't like the anger better.

"No," he said at last, heavily. The chain stopped. "It's been a long time since I could. Protect you."

Tiamaris, Dragon caste, said in a voice that would have carried the length of the Long Halls, "Well done, Kaylin.

Severn. I believe it is time to retreat." And she saw that his eyes were burning, red; that he, too, had been prepared to fight.

"Your companions lack a certain wisdom," the fieflord said, voice close to her ear.

"What did you do here, fieflord?" Tiamaris's voice was low. Dangerous.

"What you suspect, Tiamaris."

"That was...foolish."

"Indeed." He made the admission casually. "And I am not the only one who will pay the price for it. Take her home. She will need some time to recover."

Severn slowly wrapped the chain round his waist again. He stepped forward and caught Kaylin as her knees buckled. His grip, one hand on either of her upper arms, was *not* gentle. Kaylin did not resist him.

"The deaths, fieflord?" Tiamaris said quietly. Or as quietly as his voice would let him.

"Three days," the fieflord said, "between the first and second."

"And it has been?"

"One day since the last death. If there is a pattern, it will emerge when we find the next sacrifice."

"Why do you call them that?" Kaylin looked up, looked back at him.

"Because, Kaylin, it is what we believe they are. Sacrifices. Did the Hawklord not tell you that?"

No, of course not, she thought, bitter now. Bitter and bone-weary.

"You will return to the fiefs," he added softly. "And to the Long Halls."

"The hell she will," Severn said.

They stared at each other for a long moment, and then the fieflord turned and walked away.

It was, of course, night in the fiefs.

And they were walking in it. Or rather, Severn and Tiamaris were walking; Kaylin was stumbling. Severn held her up for as long as he could, but in the end, Tiamaris rumbled, and he lifted her. He was not as gentle as the fieflord, because he was not as dangerously personal.

She preferred it.

"Kaylin," Tiamaris said quietly. "Do you understand why the fiefs exist?"

She shrugged. Or tried. It was hard, while nesting in the arms of a Dragon.

"Have you never wondered?"

"A hundred times," she said bitterly. "A thousand. Sometimes in one day."

Tiamaris frowned stiffly. "I can see that Lord Grammayre had his hands full, if he chose to attempt to teach you."

"I don't need history lessons. They won't keep me alive." The words were a familiar refrain in her life; they certainly weren't original.

"Spoken like a ground Hawk," Tiamaris replied.

She shrugged again. Although he wore no armor, his chest was hard. "I believe," he said quietly, "that I will let Lord Grammayre deal with this."

"No," she said, tired now. "I think I know what you're asking."

"Oh?"

"You're asking me if I've ever wondered why the Lords of Law don't just close the fieflords down permanently."

"Indeed."

"Hell, we've *all* wondered that."

"There is a reason. I think you begin to see some of it. The fiefs are the oldest part of the city. They are, with the exception of ruins to the West and East of Elantra, the oldest part of the Empire; they have stood since the coming of the castes.

"I...spent time in the fiefs, studying the old writings, the old magics. I was not alone, but over half of the mages sent with me did not survive. The old magics are alive, if their architects are not. There are some places in the fiefs that could not easily be conquered without destroying half of the city, if they could be conquered at all. They almost all bear certain...markings."

Her head hurt, and she didn't want to think. But she made the effort. "The tattoo," she said faintly.

"Yes. It is the only living thing I—or any one of us—has seen that speaks of the Old Ones. It is why you have always been of interest."

"Have I?"

He said nothing, then.

In the dark of the fief's streets, shadows moved. They were pale white, a blur of motion that hunched three feet above the ground. Severn cursed.

Kaylin was still dressed in the finery of Nightshade, but

she wore her daggers again; she hadn't bothered to change, because there was no privacy, and she wasn't up to stripping in front of everyone. Severn had taken her clothing. "What?" she asked. Too sharply.

"It's the ferals," he said.

She really cursed. She had always been able to outcurse Severn.

In the moonlight—the bright moon—she could see that Severn was right: the ferals had come out to play. And if the Hawks weren't bloody careful, some poor child would come out in the morning—to play—and would discover what the ferals had left behind.

She'd done it herself, once or twice. Whole nightmares remained of those experiences.

"Severn?"

He was already unlooping the long chain. "There's only two," he said softly. Nothing in his voice hinted of fear. Nothing in his posture did either. She wondered if he had changed so much that he felt none.

She hadn't.

Tiamaris set her down. "Don't move," he told her grimly. Her hand had already clutched a throwing knife; it was out of her belt, and the moonlight glinted along one of its two edges. But her hand was weak, and she knew she didn't have the strength to throw true. Wondered if this was the fieflord's way of getting rid of her.

Her eyes were already acclimatized to the moonlight. She could see the four-legged lope of the creatures that dominated the fief streets at night. They were not numerous; they didn't have to be. If you were lucky, you could weather the stretch of a night and never see one.

Unlucky? Well, you only had to see them once.

She hadn't seen them as a child. But later?

Later, Severn by her side, she had. She was caught by the memory; she could see Severn now, and Severn as he was. The seven years made a difference. The weapon that he wielded made a bigger one.

Hand on dagger, she stood between Tiamaris and Severn, and she waited. The quiet growl of the hunting feral almost made her hair stand on end; it certainly made her skin a lot less smooth; goose bumps did that.

The ferals weren't as stupid as dogs. They weren't as lazy as cats. They weren't, as far as anyone could tell, really animals at all. But what they were wasn't clear. Besides deadly. She felt the tension shore her up. Found her footing on the uneven ground, and held it.

The last time she had faced ferals, she had stood in Tiamaris's position, and between her and Severn, a child had cowered. Lost child. Stupid child. But still living.

She didn't like the analogy that memory made of the situation.

Severn waited, his chain a moving wall. He wasn't even breathing heavily. He spoke her name once, and she responded with a short grunt. It was enough.

The ferals leaped.

They leaped in concert, their jaws wide and silent. The moonlight seemed to cast no shadow beneath their moving bodies, but then again, it was dark enough that shadows were everywhere. Severn's chain shortened suddenly as he drew it in, and then it lengthened as he let it go.

Feral growl became a howl of pain; a severed paw flew past Kaylin's ear.

Tiamaris had no like weapon; he waited.

The feral that had leaped at him landed feet away, and it bristled. Tiamaris opened his mouth and *roared*.

That, Kaylin thought, wincing, would wake the entire damn fief. But she watched as the feral froze, and then watched, in astonishment, as it yelped and turned tail. Like a dog. Had she really been afraid of these creatures?

The one facing Severn lost another paw, and then lost half its face. It toppled.

"Kaylin?"

She shook her head.

"Come on," he said quietly. "Where there are two, there are likely to be more."

But Tiamaris said, softly, "Not tonight." He picked Kaylin up again, and he began to *move*.

They crossed the bridge over the Ablayne in the moonlight. The Halls of Law loomed in the distance, like shadowlords. "Kaylin," Tiamaris said quietly, "the Hawklord will be waiting."

"All right," she said, into his chest. "But I'd better be getting overtime for this."

If Kaylin slept—and she did—the Halls of Law never did. The crew changed; the guards changed. The offices that were a conduit between one labyrinth of bureaucracy and another, however, were empty. She was grateful for that. Severn had cleaned the blade of his weapon, and he'd looped it round his waist again. But he didn't leave.

The guards at the interior door were Aerian. Clint wasn't one of them, but she recognized the older men. They were a bit stuffier than Clint, but she liked them anyway.

"Holder," she said.

He raised a brow. "You went on a raid dressed like *that*?"

"I wasn't on a raid."

"Oh, even better. Look at your cheek. It's—" he frowned.

"It's stopped bleeding," she offered, but she had grown quiet herself. In the fiefs, it had seemed disturbing to bear a mark—but it had also seemed natural in a fashion that now entirely escaped her. Holder's dark eyes narrowed. "Hawklord's waiting for you," he said at last, lowering his weapon. "And you'd better have one helluva good explanation for him."

She nodded and went through the doors. Or rather, Tiamaris did, carrying her. Severn trailed behind.

When they reached the main office, she was surprised to find Marcus still on duty. He was not, however, surprised to see her, which made Kaylin look up at Tiamaris with unguarded suspicion.

"I sent word," he said quietly. "I made use of one of the mirrors in the castle."

"But the mirrors in the castle can't possibly be keyed to—" She saw his look and shut up, fast.

"You got her out," Marcus said, his words a growl. He was tired. Tired Leontine was better than angry Leontine—but only by a whisker. His were bobbing.

"In a manner of speaking," Tiamaris replied coldly.

Whatever existed between the sergeant and the Dragon was always, Kaylin thought, going to be an issue. But this time, Marcus let him pass without comment.

Severn stopped, though. "I'm not going up," he said quietly. "I'll wait for you here."

"I'll be a while," she replied, without much hope. "Go home."

He met her gaze and held it. And she remembered that she'd never really been able to tell Severn what to do. Oh, she'd always given him orders—but he'd chosen which ones he wanted to follow, and ignored the rest. She would have said as much, but he was angry. Tense with it, waiting to spring.

"Kaylin," Marcus said.

She shored herself up so she could look over Tiamaris's shoulder.

The Sergeant snorted. "You shouldn't be in the fiefs. Tell the old bastard I said so."

"Yes, sir."

The tower passed beneath her. It was interesting to see it from this perspective; interesting and a tad humiliating. "I can walk," she muttered.

"You will have to, soon enough," Tiamaris replied. He climbed the stairs without pause until he reached the doors that were, as always, guarded. Here he paused and set Kaylin on her feet.

She recognized neither of the two Aerians, and this was unusual. But one, grim-faced, nodded to Tiamaris. "The Lord of Hawks is waiting," he said quietly. "He bids you enter."

Tiamaris nodded.

Kaylin stared at them both for a moment, and then she moved past the guards and placed her palm on the door's seal, grimacing. Great way to end a very long day.

But the Hawklord must have been waiting, because the door rolled open, untouched. Startled, she watched before she remembered that two strangers were staring at her. Then she squared her shoulders and entered the room. Lord Grammayre was indeed waiting, but not in the room's center; he stood, instead, in front of a long, oval mirror on the east side of the rounded wall. Their eyes met in reflection; his were cool.

Bad, then. There were days when she could actually make him smile. Days when she could make him laugh, although his laughter was brief and grudged. There were also days when she could make him raise his voice in frustration. All of these, she valued.

None of these would happen tonight.

"Lord Grammayre," she said, bending stiffly at the waist before she fell to one knee. She had to place a hand on the ground to keep her balance; in all, it was a pretty poor display.

Tiamaris, in theory a Hawk, did not bend or kneel. He

offered the Hawklord a nod that would pass as polite between equals. "Lord Grammayre," he said quietly.

"Tiamaris. You almost lost her."

Tiamaris said nothing.

"Kaylin. Rise."

She rose. She *hated* formality in this tower more than she hated almost anything—because formality meant distance, and distance was the thing he placed between them when something bad was about to happen. Usually to her.

"Kaylin, I wish to ask you what happened in Castle Nightshade."

She nodded.

"You will come to the center of the circle before you answer, and you will stand there until I have finished."

She grimaced, but that was all the resistance she offered.

Tiamaris surprised her. "Give her leave to sit," he said quietly. "If she is forced to stand, I don't think she'll make it through the interview."

"She is a Hawk," the Hawklord replied coldly. A warning.

"She is a human," the Dragon replied.

The Hawklord's pale brows rose slightly, and he glanced at Kaylin. After a moment, his wings flicked; it was the Aerian equivalent of a shrug.

She made her way to the brass circle embedded in stone; she knew what it was for. "Don't cast until I'm in it," she whispered.

If he heard her, he didn't show it. But he did wait.

He approached her, and stopped. His feet grazed the circle as he reached out to touch her cheek. "This is a Barrani mark," he said.

She said nothing.

"Nightshade." The word sounded a lot like swearing. But colder. "Why?"

"He thought it would protect me."

"I doubt that, Kaylin," the Hawklord replied. "I doubt that very much. Tiamaris, can it be removed?"

"Not easily," Tiamaris replied. "And not at all without the permission of the Lord who made the mark. Not from a human."

Kaylin heard the distinct *that you don't want dead* that he didn't say.

"The likelihood of that permission?"

"In my opinion? None whatsoever."

"As I thought."

"I can probably cover it up," she offered. She'd become good at that over the years; black eyes and red welts never made the office staff feel secure.

Tiamaris shook his head. "Grammayre, have you taught her so little?"

"I have taught her," the Hawklord replied, distinct edge in the words, "what she is willing to retain." To Kaylin, he added, "The mark can be hidden from mortal sight. The Aerians might not recognize it. Most of the humans won't. But the Leontines will smell it, and the Barrani? You could cut off your cheek and they would still know. Don't," he added, as if it were necessary, "try."

He lowered his hand, but did not leave her; instead he reached down and lifted the arm that was bound by the bracer. He looked at it, and then he touched it carefully, and in sequence, his fingers dancing over the gems as hers had done.

It didn't open; it was a different sequence. He frowned. Stepped out of the circle. She reached out without thinking and grabbed both his hands; she was *that* tired. His brows rose a fraction; she felt the rebuke in the expression, and she forced her hands to let go.

But as he stepped outside the circle, his expression softened slightly, allowing a trace of weariness to show. "I trust you to tell me the truth as you perceive it," he said quietly. "But I do not trust the Lord of Nightshade. The spell is not a punishment."

He lifted his hands, and his wings rose with them, until they were at their full span. Like this, she found the Hawklord beautiful in a way that she seldom found anything beautiful. And he knew it. Had always known it. This was as much mercy as he was willing to offer. It shouldn't have made a difference, but it did.

He began to question her, and staring at his wings, at the particular length of his flight feathers, she answered him.

She told him of the Long Halls. She told him of the forest. And then, haltingly, she told him of the room beyond the trees. The circle that surrounded her turned a distinct shade of gold each time she finished speaking.

But when she spoke of the pillar of blue flame, he lifted a hand.

"Kaylin," he said softly, "are you certain?"

She nodded.

"Tiamaris?"

"She has seen what none of the surviving Imperial mages has seen," the Dragon said quietly, his flawless Barrani tinged with caution. "I am intrigued by her words, but I do not doubt them."

"Why?"

"You know well why. She bears those marks."

The Hawklord nodded grimly. "But what do they signify? Why does she bear them?"

"That has always been the question, Grammayre. The answer is of concern to the Emperor."

"I know. Kaylin—show me your arms."

She lifted them; they shook.

Tiamaris walked over to the circle's edge, but he did not cross it. He did, however, frown. "I wish to see visual records," he said, distant, his eyes a pale gold.

The Hawklord frowned in turn; he gestured at the mirror and spoke three words in quick succession; the mirror began to glow. Kaylin really hated mirrors.

The surface of this one shimmered and shifted; when it cleared, she was looking at her arms writ large; the Hawklord wasn't short, and it was his mirror. Tiamaris looked at the mirror for some time, and then looked down at her arms. "They've changed," he said softly.

The Hawklord frowned. He came to stand by the side of the Dragon, and he, too, examined the symbols that covered Kaylin's inner arm from wrist to elbow. "It's subtle," he said at last, "but you are correct." He looked at Kaylin, his eyes clear, almost gray. Magic.

"Aside from the mark of the outcaste, I see no difference in her," he said at last.

"Remove the bracer, Grammayre, and look again."

The Hawklord hesitated. Then he shook his head. "Not yet," he said quietly. "Kaylin, you have done well. Go home." He paused, and then added, "Do not remove the containment until I give you orders."

CHAPTER

6

Severn was, as he had promised—or threatened, she wasn't sure which—waiting for her. So was Marcus. There wasn't a lot of idle chatter going on, either, but they both looked up as she turned the corner and caught the wall with her free hand. Tiamaris had not accompanied her; he was closeted in the domed tower with the Hawklord.

Talking, no doubt, about her.

"Kaylin," Marcus growled.

She nodded stiffly. "Thanks," she said.

"For what?"

"For the—the bracer. I think it saved my life."

"Bad sign."

She nodded again. "Always is."

"You…lost control?"

She shook her head, hating the question. "No.'

"What happened?"

She hesitated. "I'm not sure it's not keyed—"

"It's not in the gem. It's not keyed."

Severn, watching quietly, added nothing, but there was an intensity in his gaze that spoke of the need to know.

"There's...old magic...in the fiefs. At least in Nightshade."

The hair on the back of the Leontine's neck rose so suddenly, it looked like slender quills. "You were exposed to the ruins?"

She frowned. "No. In the fieflord's Halls."

Marcus said nothing, which was always a bad sign. But he reached out, and after an awkward moment, she surrendered her wrist to his palm; the manacle shone there in the fading light, a dream of gold.

"What does it do, Sergeant?" Severn asked.

Marcus hesitated, and met Kaylin's brief glance. *It's up to you*, he seemed to say. She shook her head.

"He's your partner."

He's not. A lie. Not even a good one. She said, bitterly, "It inhibits my magic. We don't know how it works. I don't know where it came from; it was given to me by the Hawklord. But it's old. Maybe as old as—" She broke off, thinking of the Long Halls, and not liking any of the thoughts that were about to follow.

Turning to Marcus, she said, "The Hawklord told me to go home."

"Good. Go."

"Promise you won't wake me up?"

He growled again, but it was bluster. He wasn't annoyed—at least not at her.

"Your pride-wives are going to be really pissed if you don't get home yourself."

"Too late," he muttered. She glanced at him, and then glanced at the oval mirror on the far wall. "You turned it *off*."

"Rank has its privileges."

Meaning, of course, that she couldn't. She grimaced. Marcus was not a face to wake up to in the morning. And she often did.

"If the fieflord harmed you—"

She shook her head, too tired—but only barely—to be alarmed. "He didn't."

"The...dress?"

"He doesn't like our standard issue."

Marcus said something in Leontine, and Kaylin laughed. "Been a while since I heard you say *that*."

"Be careful, Kaylin."

"Always." She headed toward the door, and Severn followed. "I'm going home," she told him firmly.

"I know."

"You're not coming with me."

She repeated this at ten-yard intervals until she got tired of the monotony. She was too numb to be angry. Either that or she didn't want to get into a real fight in a very stupid dress. That's what she told herself. Too bad she had always been such a lousy liar. But she was tired, and she almost appreciated the company—Severn was alert.

Not that it was, strictly speaking, necessary. Kaylin lived in a small place, but she lived in a part of town that was frequented by Hawks and Swords. If there was crime, it usually wasn't something that was done outdoors.

"Kaylin," Severn said quietly, when they reached the building that contained her small room. "Don't trust the fieflord."

"I'm a Hawk, not an idiot," she snapped. She paused, and then added, "Why did you go to talk to him?"

He shrugged. "It doesn't matter."

"If it doesn't matter, answer."

He didn't. She knew he wouldn't.

They stood in the dark of the twin moons in an uncomfortable silence. Kaylin had no way of breaking it. She turned, opened the door and headed up the stairs.

Severn followed.

"Severn, *go home.*"

"I will. When I see you safely to yours."

"This wasn't a date!"

He said nothing. She snarled and bounded up the stairs. The tripping didn't help her much.

Offering a hand didn't help him.

She said, distinctly, "I don't want your help. I want to—"

"Kill me?"

"Something like that."

He shrugged. "Go ahead. I won't stop you."

She hated him, then. She gained her feet, stormed up the stairs, was out of breath by the time she fumbled with two locks and threw open her door.

The only light in the room was cast by mirror; the windows were shuttered. Had she done that?

Severn came up behind her, and she gave in to the inevitable. She walked into her home, and left the door open behind her. Was surprised when he didn't come in.

He stood in the frame of the door, gazing at everything as if he'd always been a Hawk. At last he said, "You live alone."

She nodded. "Easier, that way."

"You never liked being alone in the fiefs."

"Meant something different, in the fiefs. But I don't live there anymore."

"You do," he said softly. "We both do."

"Actually," a familiar voice said, "She doesn't. Kaylin, is he a friend, or does he need help finding the door?"

Kaylin almost laughed out loud. Teela had taken up a very casual lounging position against the stair railing, and she had a dagger in her left hand. She spoke Elantran, as she usually did when she was with the Hawks.

It had been a while since Kaylin had heard her speak anything else.

"He's a Hawk," she said quietly.

Teela's frown was subtle and lazy. "I don't recognize him."

"He's new."

"Must be, if he's hanging around *your* door." She eased herself off the rail, gaining her full height. After it became obvious that Severn had a slight advantage, she shrugged and relaxed again. "A bit scarred," she said to Kaylin, in her Barrani purr, "but sort of pretty. You're sure he's not with you?"

"He's not with me."

"He's not fond of being talked about as if he weren't here," Severn added quietly. He turned stiffly to Kaylin and said, "I'll see myself out."

Teela whistled.

"What?"

"I'd avoid him, if I were you."

"You don't much look like you want to avoid him."

"I'm not you." It always amazed Kaylin that something so tall could radiate essence of cat. Teela smiled and sauntered into the room; the door had been left open, and she had a habit of making herself at home—at least in Kaylin's home.

"Why are you here?" Kaylin asked.

"You're late."

"Late?"

"We're supposed to go out drinking. You forget?"

"I—" she looked down at the dress she was still wearing. At the circular script across her arms. She was dead tired. "Yeah. I forgot."

Teela shrugged. "Tain thought so. But it's you—you could have just been late. What's with the dress? It's not like—" She stopped.

She could stop so suddenly, stillness seemed menacing.

Kaylin turned her back and started to pull the dress up over her head. She had to struggle; her arms were stiff, and the dress wasn't exactly baggy.

"You can see the fieflord's mark," she said, when silk

cleared her face. She tossed the dress into the pile beneath the windowsill, and then rooted around in the pile beside the bed until she came up with a bed robe; she slipped into it, and after a minute of fumbling, gave up on the belt. Resigned, she turned to face Teela; the Barrani Hawk hadn't moved an inch.

"I would have seen it earlier, but we started drinking without you." Her voice sounded normal. Kaylin had, however, seen Teela break the arms of a drug dealer on the banks of the Ablayne while talking about the fact that her desk was a pigsty. She wondered if she should reach for her daggers. It wasn't an idle thought.

But she was so damn tired, it wasn't a possibility either. She sat heavily on the bed, never taking her eyes off Teela's face.

"He sent you into Nightshade," the Barrani Hawk said. Unblinking. Unnerving.

Kaylin nodded. "Is it bad?"

"It's bad."

"How bad?"

"How many people have you seen with a mark like that?"

Kaylin shook her head. "None."

"In Nightshade?" Teela was aware of sparse details of Kaylin's past; all of the Hawks were.

"Never." She paused, and then added, "Do you know how to remove it?"

Teela shrugged. Kaylin felt herself relaxing.

"Sure. I could cut off your head."

"Thanks, but I'm sort of using it."

"Not for much, if you've got that. When did it happen?"

"Today."

"You allowed it?"

"I didn't exactly get a chance to offer permission," she snapped.

"Why did he…mark you?"

"How the hell should I know? He's Barrani. I'm not."

"No. Clearly."

"And if I were, what would I be doing?"

"Playing corpse. Or rounding up other Barrani and heading into the fiefs to kill the man who marked you."

"Was that an offer?"

"Maybe." The Barrani eyes were glittering; they'd shaded from perfect green into perfect blue. It was a *bad* sign. "Kaylin—those marks are forbidden to mortals."

"He's not exactly on the right side of the law. He's a fieflord."

"You don't understand what it means, do you? No, don't bother." Teela crossed the room and slung herself heavily over the bed. Great. It wasn't a large bed. "It's a symbol of ownership."

Kaylin shrugged. In as much as a Barrani could look outraged, Teela managed it. "He's the fieflord," Kaylin said, weary. "He owns all of Nightshade."

"What I said was true, Kaylin. You don't live there anymore."

"No." She wedged herself onto six inches of bed, and then added, "Tiamaris said it can't be removed by anyone but Nightshade."

"He's right."

She was quiet for a minute. "Teela?"

"What?"

"If I weren't a Hawk, would you have killed me?"

Teela shrugged. "Maybe. It's not safe to bear a mark like that. Not outside of his fief."

"Why?"

"Ask the castelord. No, on second thought, *don't* ask the castelord. In fact, don't see the castelord, ever."

"I'll add it to the list." She closed her eyes. "What's Tain going to say?"

"If you're lucky, a lot of Barrani that won't mean a damn thing to you."

Kaylin borrowed a Leontine phrase. She knew what her luck was like.

The mirror woke her in the morning.

When exactly in the morning, she couldn't say—but the phrase too damn early came to mind. She rolled off the bed.

There was no booming voice to accompany the unnatural sheen of the mirror's surface; no clear picture of Iron Jaw in full Leontine annoyance.

"Go away," she muttered. She pulled the bed robe tight and stood. Her legs were wobbling. Then again, had she gone out drinking with Teela and Tain, they would have been worse. If the inside of her mouth hadn't tasted like a hairball, the world would have been a better place.

The mirror continued to glow. She made her way to its surface and placed her palm against the lower right corner.

A face began to emerge from the too-bright light; a woman's face. She was Leontine, and she wasn't a Hawk. Shedding sleep, Kaylin straightened her shoulders. "Marrin," she said softly.

"Kaylin. I'm sorry to wake you—I mirrored the office, but Marcus said you weren't going to be in today." Her fur was a shade of pale gold; she was not young.

"I'm not—I've got today off. You need me?"

Marrin nodded.

"I'm not dressed, and I haven't eaten. How soon do you need me?"

The silence went on for just a stretch too long. Kaylin grunted. Breakfast could wait. Dressing, however, couldn't. She stared at her arm; the bracer reflected Marrin's image. After a moment, she clenched the bracer fist and ran her fingers over the gems in a quick sequence. It was the sequence that Lord Grammayre had taught her last: White, blue, white, blue, red, red, red.

The only sound in the small apartment was the quiet click of its hinges.

The river quarter was already crowded; the streets were full of either horse or people. Given the size of some of the people, it was just as safe to stay out of their way. Kaylin was grateful that it wasn't a parade day. Had it been, it would have taken her half the day to get to the foundling hall, and she would have been biting the heads off of more or less innocent bystanders about three minutes in.

She cursed under her breath at the various bakers' stalls;

she really didn't have to the time to stop, and had she, the money was a bit lacking. Her stomach, as usual, was ignorant of the basic facts of her life, and it growled every time she came close. Which, given the press of bodies, was about every ten feet.

Shadows moved across the bent heads of the crowd. She glanced up; Aerians were in the sky. It would be really useful to have wings about now. As usual, she made do.

The foundling halls backed out onto the Ablayne; they were gated, fenced and haphazardly guarded. Amos, the guard in question, was wandering around in front of the slender metal gate like a worried hen as Kaylin approached. As a guard, he was a great gardener. He didn't wear much armor, he had a sword that might have been sharp when he was four years old—whenever that might have been—and he wasn't, in his own words, as strong as he used to be. But he did like children.

He relaxed visibly. Bad sign.

"Marrin?"

"She's waiting for you in the front hall," he said. He had almost no hair, and what little he did have, he worried with shaking hands. "I'm—"

"Never mind. What's happened?"

"It's Catti." In spite of her name, Catti was a human orphan. All of the children in the foundling halls were. Leontines and Aerians were less numerous than humans, and much hardier; they seldom left children behind. And when they did? Someone kept them. Aunts, uncles, cousins, siblings—someone always wanted them.

The youngest of the foundlings often came to the hall with no name attached to them, and they were named by Marrin. Marrin had a Leontine's sense of humor.

"Catti? What's wrong with Catti?"

He shook his head and pointed to the closed doors of the foundling halls. They were modest doors, in a building of its size. She swallowed, nodded and ran.

When Kaylin had first come to visit the foundling halls, she had asked Marrin why the children in the halls were all human. Marrin had explained, quietly, that the halls were open to children of any race—but that only the human children seemed to make their way through its doors, or at least to its steps.

"The rest are wanted," Kaylin had said, bitter.

Marrin had shaken her head, growling softly. "Don't use that word," she had said, her *S*'s sibilant.

"Which one?"

"Wanted."

Kaylin had shrugged.

"Humans are all so fragile," Marrin had continued firmly, "and little things kill you. Plagues. Floods. Fires. Other humans. I don't want my children to think that they were deserted."

Your children, Kaylin had thought, with suspicion. But she had discovered, as she had been drawn, time and again, to the halls, that they *were* Marrin's children in every way that mattered. Marrin saw to it that they were housed, clothed and fed; Marrin bullied and cozened people into donating the things such a hall required. Where money was scarce, she was willing to settle for time—and the children were taught to read, write and perform skills that might make them useful to people who had the money to employ them.

Kaylin couldn't resent the orphans for their good fortune; she had thought to, but seeing them… they were just children.

And Kaylin had always had a weakness for children.

She swung the doors open and almost collided with Marrin. The Leontine was pacing.

"Marrin, what happened to Catti?"

"She fell," Marrin said quietly.

"From where?"

But the Leontine said only, "Follow me." Her tone of voice added, *quickly*. Kaylin did as the other children who lived in the foundling hall did: she obeyed.

Catti was in a low bed, covered by heavy blankets. She was not conscious, which was a bad sign. "You moved her?" Kaylin asked.

"She didn't walk here by herself," was the curt reply. Marrin really *was* worried.

And Kaylin could see why. Catti was breathing. But that was about all she was doing, and it was pretty shallow breath.

"Dock found her," Marrin added, in a more subdued tone.

"Is he still calling himself that?"

Marrin shrugged. "It's a phase," she said. Her paws were behind her back, but as she paced, Kaylin could see that the fighting claws were extended.

"Did he move her?"

Marrin nodded.

"Tell him not to, next time. Just...leave her, and call me."

"Is she—"

"I don't know. But I've seen injuries like this before." Not often, thank the gods. Whichever gods. Kaylin wasn't particular about religion. "Get some water," she added.

"You want me to bathe her down?"

Kaylin shook her head. "I'll need to drink it. I might not remember. Make me," she added, as she placed a palm against the girl's pale cheek. Catti had grown, in the last six years. At twelve, she still had a child's face, but the jaw was sharpening, the cheekbones becoming prominent; she wouldn't be a girl for much longer. She wanted to join the Hawks.

Kaylin grimaced. "I can't be disturbed," she continued quietly.

"I'll see to it."

"No, I mean—" But she shook her head. "It's different from the usual."

"How?"

Doctors were expensive, but because Marrin was so intimidating—when she had need—she could always find at least one who would call. It was after the doctors had come, and had left without a word, that she would summon Kaylin.

Because she knew as well as any of the Hawks did that Kaylin's gift was hidden, had to be hidden. By order of the Hawklord, and for much better reasons than that. Kaylin could heal. It was the rarest of the mage talents, and there were four known healers in the Empire—all of them seconded to the Emperor. They lived in a very rich and very pretty cage, and they healed at his command or whim; they stood by, waiting for assassination attempts to come and go so that they might flex their fingers.

But *their* talents? They were understood. Kaylin's had no real explanation. She had not trained for years in their use; they had come to her. Just as the marks on her arms had.

The Hawklord felt that the two were intertwined, and he did not trust the power. Kaylin was bright; she didn't, either. But given the choice between using it and not using it? She stared at Catti's pale face. It wasn't much of a choice.

It never was.

"Disease is easier."

"It's still life-threatening."

Kaylin nodded. "But it's easier." To kill something. "This is—I've never done this."

Marrin tensed, and her claws clicked together; it was the only sound in the room for some minutes, because Catti's breathing was almost inaudible. "I trust you," she said at last, speaking in the tongue of her people. It was a phrase that had multiple meanings, but it was only ever used in situations that involved life or death. Or both. Marcus had taught her the words just before she had taken the Hawks' Oath of Induction, but he had never been able to clearly explain what it meant to Kaylin's satisfaction. Her translation was off. But on some level, she *understood* it. She just couldn't put it into her own words. Funny, that things she couldn't explain could still bear so much weight.

She brought her free hand to Catti's face, and cupping pale skin between her palms, she closed her eyes.

Catti wasn't there.

Kaylin had expected as much, but it still hit hard—the sense of absence. The distance. She was frightened of failure, but she wasn't terrified—terrified would do her no good. Fear, as the Hawklord had taught her, had its place. But it was hard to keep it in its place. Years had given her a hope of doing so—but no certainty.

Catti.

She visualized. It helped. Better to think of Catti as she was—as she had been—at all ages. Kaylin's memory was like a kaleidoscope; fractured, but in a way that was arresting, even beautiful, if looked at the right way. As a child, Catti's hair had been bright red, but it had shaded toward auburn with the passage of time; it had grown, and been cut back, over and over again, as if it were unruly, something a gardener might curse at. Kaylin had seen it in braids, in pigtails and above the girl's wide ears; she had seen it in locks across the floor. It was too fine to sell, Marrin had told her.

Catti loved to talk. She loved to sing. She could do the former until the cows came home, but the latter? Not well, and mostly, not on key. It had never stopped her. She liked to sing at Festival, when the orphans were allowed to stage plays in the streets; she liked to sing during parade days, when they were given a holiday from their endless string of lessons and chores; she liked to sing at night, as if she were a mother, over the beds of the youngest of the foundlings. They didn't mind that she couldn't hold a tune.

As Catti had gotten older, she sang less; she had become more self-conscious about the fact that she couldn't sing *well*. Kaylin had blessed maturity, but in time, she had learned to regret it as well. Then again, Kaylin had a voice that only a frog would love. But she had always known it. And in the fiefs? Less to sing about.

Severn had a good voice.

Aie, and she wasn't going to think about Severn here. Not here.

Catti. Think about Catti.

Think about Catti walking. Catti running. Catti sliding down the banister—the last on a dare. Think about Catti chattering. Think about the first time they met: on Kaylin's first visit to the foundling halls.

Clint had pointed the building out to her when he had taken her on his ground patrol. She had had to make him repeat himself slowly, so that she could be certain the words she'd heard were actually the right ones. A whole huge building devoted to parentless children? She had asked Clint who paid for them. Had asked him what happened *after* they left the foundling hall.

He was patient, in a humoring-the-newbie sort of way; he answered her questions as if he didn't think them crazy.

He answered them over and over again, because for the rest of their patrol, she had asked about nothing else.

But at the end of the patrol? He'd taken her to the guarded gate. She had thought it odd, then, that this haven would need a guard, but Clint knew him, and Amos had greeted the Hawk with a gruff friendliness that didn't suit any jailer she had ever met.

Later, Clint explained that Amos was the *only* guard. But not then. He had taken her past the gate, and up the walk. Had pushed her up the stairs, as her feet seemed to become heavier with each step. And he had introduced her to Marrin, the Leontine on duty.

On duty being words that lost meaning and texture over time. Marrin was not the only adult who worked within the foundling halls, but she was the one in charge—and the only one who wasn't human. If the Hawks were graced with recruits from every possible race, the foundling halls, which could afford to pay so little, weren't equally blessed; they had Marrin. But Kaylin, even new to the Hawks, had met Marcus. She was polite and respectful when she spoke with Leontines.

Marrin had thought it funny, at the time.

"Sorry to disturb you, Marrin," Clint had said, "but Kaylin wouldn't talk about anything else for the *entire* shift, and you're better at handling children than—ouch!"

"Clearly," Marrin had said, in her dry, Leontine purr. She was amused.

"Ankle-biters," Clint had snorted.

"Kaylin is…a Hawk?"

"A new Hawk. Sort of."

"I'm a Hawk."

"Well," Marrin had said, taking Kaylin by the shoulder and ushering her gently into the halls proper. "I'm sure the children will be very pleased to meet you, Kaylin. At least three of them are determined to march up the steps of the Halls of Law the moment we set them loose. Poor city," she added, with the hint of a chuckle. "The fact that you *are* a Hawk, and at your age, will give them hope. Come and meet my children."

Suspicious, confused, Kaylin had done just that, while Clint waited.

Marrin might not have been foolish enough to call Kaylin a child in so many words, but she was mother enough that she wasn't willing to let Kaylin find her own way home. Clint had put up a fight, but not much of one. She could see him clearly as he was on that day: standing alone, his gray wings folding behind his back, his arms across his chest. He wore the surcoat of the Hawks—and the sword that she really couldn't lug around on her hip without destroying the scabbard—and light armor; he wore regulation boots that had clearly seen years of use. She would outgrow three pairs before hers would at last look like that—and the quartermaster had been *very* particular on that point. He seemed to resent that fact that she'd outgrown them before they'd developed holes; it was, in his opinion, a waste of good leather.

Clint was smiling, but it was a slight smile; it might have been a trick of the light.

Catti had been the last child to make it into the open space at the top of the banister where so many of Marrin's group speeches were given. She had tripped over Iain's outstretched foot, and had turned and smacked him in the head before she'd realized that everyone on the landing was watching her. Her muttered apology lacked any sincerity whatsoever, but Marrin let it pass with a huff of breath.

"And this is Catti. She's not very punctual, unfortunately."

And there she was: three feet nothing, a spindly armed, redheaded girl who exuded both delight and defiance in equal measure. Wearing the undyed linen that marked the foundlings, her hair pulled back in a braid that was already fraying, her cheeks pale and freckled. She had Barrani eyes, at least in color.

Punctuality is highly overrated, the older Kaylin wanted to say. The younger Kaylin had said nothing; she was busy trying to remember what the word punctual actually meant. They met for a moment—older self, younger self—as Kaylin in the present reached out to grab hold of *this* Catti before she disappeared.

Catti had always been part of the foundling hall, to Kaylin.

Catti was here. Faint, in memory, but *here*. Kaylin held fast, building on that memory; giving it roots. She couldn't have said why—and she wouldn't have to. No one would ask. Her hands were warm, now; her arms were tingling.

She called Catti quietly, and no one answered. Had this just been the damn plague, someone would have.

But this was the wrong thought; it drifted away from the necessary memories into others that belonged in the foundling hall. She let it go.

Catti. Catti, I'm here.

Beneath her palms, she was aware of dry skin, of delicate cheekbones. She let that awareness spread, thinking of Catti; holding the memories that not even Catti was aware of. She became aware—slowly—of limbs that were still bird-thin, of a body that puberty wasn't finished with yet. White skin. And beneath that, muscle—not much of it, though—and vessels, lungs, heart. Beyond these, spine.

Catti's hands on her hips, in mimicry of Kaylin. Catti's finger, flexing in air as if she could by dint of will force her fingers to extrude the claws of a Leontine. Catti singing, singing, singing, in her off-key voice.

The body and the memories were too far apart; one was firmly rooted in Kaylin, and the other was outside of her. She had to knit them together, and she didn't know how.

But before she did that, she had to make the body whole. Had to find what was broken, to find things that she still had no words for—although her visit to the examiner's office with Clint had done wonders for her vocabulary, and had only cost her her lunch.

There. Something wrong. Something broken. No; not just one thing; many things, small things, things that her fingers felt too clumsy, too ungainly to fix. She lost them— and more; she lost hold of her power for a moment.

Panic. This had happened before, and it had taken time to find her way back to it. She wasn't a mage—she had no fancy, theoretical words to describe what she knew. She only had certainty, and at the moment, it was the wrong kind.

Something cool touched her lips.

She swallowed, tasting nothing; she was barely aware of the motion of her own body, she was so caught up in the motionlessness of Catti's. As if it were more her own, more familiar, than the one she'd lived in all her life.

She could return to herself; she'd done that before. But if she did, she would lose the girl. And she could not face Marrin as a failure. Had promised herself, the day she first laid hands upon the brow of a fevered, bone-thin foundling, that she would *never* fail another child again.

And so she continued to struggle; to catch the slippery strands of unreliable power; to bind them, thread by thread, until she could grip them tightly again. They seemed to resist; it was harder this time than it had been when she had hovered over Sesti's near-disastrous birthing. Kaylin's eyes were already closed. Catti's face, the sound of her off-key voice precious, became all that she was willing to see or hear.

And holding power, she fastened it to herself, extended it and began to tie it in odd knots around Catti's injuries—the ones she could see, and the ones that she was almost afraid to touch. Delicate work. And vital.

More threads. More strands. She gathered these as well; felt the tingling spark that ran along them as a shock. She didn't let go; instead she built them into a weave that was strong enough to contain both her and Catti. It was, she thought, like a cocoon. She wondered what would emerge from it.

Hoped that it would be Catti, whole.

Quietly, she called Catti. She asked her to sing.

And this time, power flowing between them, Catti heard her. Her voice was broken and rasping, an awkward combination of sound; it was—as always—slightly off-key. Kaylin felt the sharp pang of joy, the anxiety of hope, as she joined her voice with Catti's; if Marrin was still there, and if Marrin could hear them, she was almost to be pitied. Kaylin hoped she was someplace else—one didn't pity a Leontine. Not more than once.

But she heard the soft huff of Marrin's breath, and she opened her eyes—at least she thought they were hers—slowly. Saw, for a moment, the ceiling of the room, from entirely the wrong angle. Catti's vision and hers mingled.

It was not a good way to see the world.

Kaylin toppled from the bedside, but the floor didn't hit her; Leontine arms did instead. They were warm, and very strong, even given Marrin's professed age.

"Catti—"

"She's awake," Marrin said, the purr deep-throated and loud, it was so close to Kaylin's ear. "But I have a feeling you shouldn't be."

"Sounds good to me," Kaylin muttered.

And then she wasn't.

CHAPTER 7

Kaylin slept off the worst of her numbing exhaustion in the foundling hall, if something so interrupted could be *called* sleep. In ones and twos, the foundlings came to visit her, and if Marrin wasn't present, they poked her or pulled her eyelids up just to see if she was awake.

Even Dock came, but Kaylin was tired enough that she called him by his given name, Iain, and that put him in enough of a mood that his sullenness was almost its own presence. Had she been a bit more awake, she'd've asked him why he called himself Dock—but she was thankful for small mercies.

Marrin came to chase him out of the room, and after the foundlings were in bed—or as much in bed as they ever were, given that they showed so little fear of Leontine outrage—Marrin called Amos from his position at the gate. It was dark, now, and the doors should have been locked, which meant in theory that he could go home.

Marrin sent him by way of Kaylin's place, and he helped Kaylin walk down the streets. They were emptier, she'd give them that. And given the way she was lurching at the almost unbearable weight of her own body, she was grateful.

He knew better than to ask her what she'd done. Instead, he saw her to the outer door of her building, and hugged her briefly, in silence, before he watched her walk up the stairs.

She remembered opening the door.

She remembered stumbling into the room; latching the door behind her was so much of a reflex that her fingers did the work while her mind started to blank. She made it to the bed.

Kaylin was going to break the damn mirror, never mind that the cost of replacing it would come out of her meager pay. As mirrors went, it was pathetic; it wasn't at all flattering, besides which she hardly ever saw her own face looking back at her on the days when she did use it. On the other hand, given how she was feeling, she was pretty sure that even Marcus's face would be an improvement over hers.

Improvement or no, she could hear his growl transmitted through the magical silvered glass. Had there been a time in her life when she'd been stupid enough to long for magic? Probably. She carefully failed to remember it as she rolled out of bed.

Someone had forgotten to pull the blinds over the window. The problem with living alone was that she always knew who the guilty party was. The mirror's glow threatened to out-bright the sun's light. She winced as she looked at the floor. She'd memorized the way shadows fell beyond the perpetual laundry heap: it was late. Very, very late.

"Kaylin Neya, I *know* you're there!"

"Coming," she said, putting on her best morning voice. "Haven't we already done this this week?"

Marcus said something unflattering in Leontine. She shrugged. She did this just before she snuck into the mirror's widest view; no point in adding to his annoyance. If that were possible; with Marcus, it was hard to tell.

"I'm getting a little tired of it myself," Marcus snarled. "But apparently Caitlin doesn't have enough of a voice to wake you up." Caitlin was the birdlike woman who served as his secretary—on the very rare occasions Marcus actually needed one. He wasn't a great believer in paperwork, and usually only saw to it when under threat of death. Or worse.

She took a good look; Marcus wasn't in dress uniform. It couldn't be that bad. Then again, she was in yesterday's clothing, and was certain, from the slight lift of his golden fur, that she looked it.

"Neya, do you have *any* idea what time it is?"

"Past midday?"

"Good guess. How much past midday?"

She winced. "I'm almost out the door," she said.

He snorted. He didn't, however, call her a liar. "Good. I

don't suppose it will come as a surprise to you that the Hawklord is waiting?"

She closed her eyes. "He'd have to be," she said, bending out of the mirror's range and reaching for her boots. Took her a minute to realize they were still on her feet. It was going to be a *long* day.

Clint, as it happened, was on duty at the front doors. It wasn't his favorite job; in fact, it was no one's favorite job, and the Hawks and Swords shared it in rotation, resenting the fact that the Wolves were given a bye. It did, however, have completely regular hours, something often denied people whose jobs took them out on investigations, and given Clint's family situation, this was a good thing.

"You look like crap," he said, frowning.

She lifted bleary eyes. "You look like Clint."

"Nothing wrong with your eyes." He laughed. She still liked the sound; it took more than a late morning to make her too grouchy to appreciate it. Unfortunately, more was coming. Clint's perfect face got very serious, and she didn't like it.

"What?"

"You're investigating in the fiefs," he said quietly. Word, it appeared, traveled. In how much detail, she didn't know—and she wasn't allowed to ask.

She nodded. She *really* didn't like it.

"Get your butt indoors," he said, lowering his pike. "Now."

"Clint—"

He shook his head. "You were at the foundling halls yesterday."

"Great. Does everybody know?"

"Marrin mirrored in here, first. Yeah, I'd say everyone knows. Well, everyone who wasn't sleeping at their desk."

She snorted. But she had no reason to worry about the foundling halls at the moment. She took the steps two at a time, and managed not to trip. Fear did that.

Marcus was, of course, waiting for her. The fact that the office was bustling—and gossiping—all around him eased Kaylin's mood somewhat, but she was cautious.

"Morning," she said, and then, looking out the window, added, "Afternoon."

"Yes," he said, deadpan, which was pretty much standard. "It is." He stared at her, his eyes unblinking. "You're all right?"

She nodded.

"Marrin called."

"I know."

"She managed to get you at home?"

She nodded again.

"I told you to take the day off."

"You told me to take two days off," she countered.

He shrugged. "Hawklord had other ideas." He motioned toward the doors at his back. "He's waiting in the tower."

She started to make her way past him, and he caught her shoulder in his clawed grip.

"Where's your armor?"

"Home."

"Quartermaster is going to have your ears."

She lost a few inches as she deflated. "We're going out?"

"Yeah. All three of you."

And she remembered Severn. Squared her shoulders. "Could you—"

"Yeah. But the other two are already equipped."

Sometimes whole weeks were like this.

The stairs were longer than usual. Or her legs were weaker. Given the magical protections placed upon every square inch of the huge building, she bet on the latter. And cursed it.

She passed guards at the levels between Tower and everything else, and nodded; they nodded back. They recognized her. She wondered privately if she were winning—or losing—them any bets. It hadn't escaped her notice that betting on the time of her arrival was an office pastime. Sadly, her attempts to end the betting always failed; punctuality was never going to be her strong suit.

"Kaylin," the Hawklord said, when the doors to the tower rolled open. "Good of you to join us."

She had the grace to flush, and she bowed a little lower than absolutely necessary. There wasn't much difference between that and what was in theory necessary, but she managed. She'd learned early that if she couldn't be on time to save her life, she'd better cultivate the unseemly art of groveling.

"Lord Grammayre," she added, as she rose.

"You were at the foundling halls yesterday?"

She cringed, but nodded. "Yes, sir."

"I see. I think you spend too much time there." He turned toward the tower's other occupants, and her heart did that heavy flip-flop that was often called sinking.

"Morning, Kaylin," Severn said, with a mock smile.

Tiamaris merely frowned.

"You been waiting long?" she asked the Dragon, without much hope.

"A mere two and a half hours" was the curt reply.

She said nothing to Severn, but even had they been friends, this would have been understandable; Dragon tempers were legendary, and Dragons were reputed to take offense at odd things. Like, say, being kept waiting in cold stone towers for hours on end.

"Sorry," she said, meaning it. She would have exposed her throat—she often did that when confronted with an angry Leontine—but she wasn't sure if it would have the same cultural meaning for a Dragon, besides which, she was attached to her throat.

"You have a mission," the Hawklord said, when it was clear Tiamaris had nothing further to add.

She straightened up. "Sir."

He met her level gaze, and held it for a moment, as if examining her expression. Which was a bad sign.

His words were worse. "There's been a third death," he said softly.

She didn't ask him what he meant; it wasn't necessary. "Where?"

"In Nightshade."

"I know that. Where in Nightshade?"

He looked up, and then away to the long mirror. "Recall," he told the hated silvered glass. "Pay attention, Kaylin. The image is aerial; the quality is poor. The report was sent hours ago, but it was sent to the Hawks." He paused, and then added quietly, "Nothing has been touched. Inasmuch as anything can remain untouched in the fiefs. The child was poor, and no family claims him; he had little to steal."

"Retrieval, sir?"

He nodded. "Bring the body back to the halls. The examiners are waiting."

Severn began to walk toward the doors. Kaylin was staring at the moving images that flickered across the mirror's sheen. She didn't look long, though—it was clear that Severn knew where they were going.

Tiamaris was quiet all the way down Old Nestor. The barkers and the merchants that habitually shouted out the value of their wares fell silent when they met his glare; she wondered if it was because he was a Dragon, or if it was because he looked one step away from murder. Either way, she was impressed; if she could cultivate a look like that, it would take a lot less time to get anywhere in Elantra. At least when she wasn't dressed as a Hawk, and of course, given their destination, she wasn't.

Severn matched her stride.

"Where were you?" He asked.

"None of your business."

He shrugged. "The Wolves frown on tardiness."

"The Wolves frown on *everything*."

His brief staccato laugh surprised her. But as it was true, he didn't demur. "I'm under the impression it's not looked on favorably in the Hawks, either."

She shrugged. "I'm still a Hawk."

"Yes. Apparently there are bets in the office about that."

She rolled her eyes. Severn was like her; born to the fiefs. He could probably find betting in the Imperial Castle without putting his mind to it. "You play?"

"Not yet. But having met the Hawklord, I think it unlikely that you get dismissed."

"Not while I'm still breathing." She banked sharply to avoid a wagon. "Where are we going?"

"Four corners," he replied, the trace of smile freezing. Without it, his scars made his face look dangerous. She wondered if it had always looked that way; if she had just been blind enough to miss seeing it. It wasn't a comfortable thought.

"You look like shit," he added.

"Thanks."

He shrugged. "What the hell were you doing yesterday?"

"I told you—"

"None of my business. I heard. But we're partners now," he said quietly, "and that makes it my business."

"It doesn't."

"It does if you're too damn tired to be useful."

They reached the foot bridge over the Ablayne. Men were talking in the shadows of the bridge on the far bank.

She wondered what they were doing, and if she should break it up.

But Tiamaris strode across the bridge without pause, and she let that be her answer. She knew why she hesitated; she didn't want to find that body. She'd found them before, but never as a Hawk. There were reasons why she had never returned to the fiefs, and freedom was not the only one. Not even the best one.

Severn knew. He was quiet, and he was present. She walked a while in his shadow, letting him lead. Or letting him follow Tiamaris's lead. Hard to say which; neither of the men looked like they were particularly good at following anyone else's orders.

Then again, neither was Kaylin.

She cursed when her boot got stuck in what could charitably be called mud. Severn smiled slightly; Tiamaris, heavy-footed lout, frowned. She pulled the short heel free, wiped what could be wiped off on the stone and wet dirt—not a lot of help—and kept walking.

The fief of Nightshade enveloped them all slowly. Without thinking, Kaylin lifted a hand to touch the mark on her cheek. Marrin hadn't even mentioned it, and she'd almost forgotten about it—gods knew the mirror didn't actually show her *her* face that morning. Well, afternoon.

Severn caught her worrying it, and pulled her hand away. "Leave it," he said quietly. "It may come in useful." The words were cool, and she saw that he offered them with some hesitance. But fief-born, he was practical—any weapon in a fight was not to be sneered at.

During the height of day, the streets of the fief weren't empty. They thinned markedly when the fieflord's patrols were nearby, but this time, when Kaylin and Severn chose to avoid them, Tiamaris didn't argue. He rolled his eyes, crossed his chest with taut arms and waited—as if they were children and these were games.

And they were, Kaylin thought. But they had seemed so serious when she had been young here. She adjusted her daggers a tad self-consciously, and when the fieflord's guards had passed, she followed Severn. He never spoke much, but his lack of words here wasn't an improvement. He was going to the Four Corners.

She was following.

There was a singular lack of imagination in the fiefs with regards to everything but betting; the Four Corners could have been the intersection of any two streets. But in this case, it was the intersection of the two widest streets. The hovelled remains of mansions girded either side, and weeds sprung up in every conceivable patch of open ground that existed between the street and the buildings themselves. There was no glass in the lower windows, and the windows that could be reached by an expert stone's throw were long gone as well; but the third and fourth stories of the worn, stately buildings still boasted yellowed glass that had thinned slowly at the heights. Bars crossed that glass, indicating panes; the people who lived here now were too poor to use the steel structures that might keep thieves at bay.

Didn't matter anyway; none of the doors had locks worth shit, and no one bothered to try. The rooms in these mansions were irregular in size, and they were all occupied, often by multiple families. The sounds of arguments drifted streetward at any time of day.

At any time of day but this one.

The Four Corners was almost tomblike in its silence.

Which meant one of two things. The first, and less likely, was that the body had been discovered by the children, and news had traveled down either street. News did, and that type of news? It made parents who could stay at home grab their children and hide them. Or start looking for other accommodation.

The second, and more likely, was that the fieflord's men were present. Kaylin glanced at Severn; saw he was thinking the same thing. His hand had fallen to his sword, although he still wore his chain. Hers were now on her daggers.

"Where?" she asked Severn.

He nodded to the northeast corner. "In the hall of the second floor. There."

"It was hours ago?"

He nodded again. "But the boy had no kin here. I doubt anyone's seen to the body. I'm surprised word reached the Lords of Law at all."

"Our people are here," she replied softly.

"So," Tiamaris said, speaking for the first time in a while, "are his."

"Nightshade's?"

"Yes. Barrani, all."

"How many is all?"

The Dragon frowned. "Four," he said at last. "And none of them are young."

As she had never been able to correctly guess the age of *any* of the Barrani, she shrugged. She knew what his answer would be if she asked him how he knew, and as she didn't much care for magic, she didn't bother. "We can't take four," she said to Severn.

He snorted. "On a good day, we *might* be able to take one."

Tiamaris said, quietly, "It won't be a problem."

The hair on Kaylin's neck rose. She hated that, and reached up to pat it down.

"Tell you what," she told Tiamaris. "You go in first."

He smiled, a lazy slow smile, and headed toward the building's door. "Try not to get in the way," he said, as he kicked it off its hinges.

"Hey!" Kaylin shouted, at his retreating back. "That wasn't necessary!" But he was already gone. She looked at the ruined hinges and shook her head. "Uptowners," she said, with a grimace.

Severn laughed. "I thought you were one?"

"Piss off."

Severn side-stepped her, and nudged his way into the wide foyer ahead of her. She took the rear through lack of choice, but she pulled a dagger from her belt and began to follow quietly. In a building of this age, it was damned hard. The floorboards were a type of alarm; they creaked with every step.

Anyone who lived behind the closed doors here would know that someone had entered, and they'd even know how many they were. But no one—no one smart—would open a door to see who they were—not after the way Tiamaris had let himself in.

They made their way up a rickety staircase that had at one time been grand; it circled the foyer beneath the cracked and water-damaged ceiling that towered above them. Once, she knew, men of power and wealth had chosen to call this place home. She couldn't imagine what had driven them across the river from this place—but clearly something had. They had abandoned their finery, and in the end, that finery had aged and withered, like hothouse flowers do. But what they had built still stood, and it was at least useful to those in the fiefs who had little way of earning a living.

She had lived in a building like this once.

Severn lifted a hand to his lip, motioning for silence; it annoyed her. As if she would suddenly start gabbling here.

But Tiamaris had cleared the landing, and headed down the main hall toward what had once been either bedrooms or guest rooms; in the mansions, it was hard to tell, and she had little enough experience in the homes of the powerful and moneyed on the right side of the Ablayne to be able to tell the two apart.

She didn't need to. She wouldn't be entering any of them. At the far end of the long hall, she could see the four Barrani guards that Tiamaris had detected. They were armed, and they wore what was, for the fiefs, fancy dress: surcoats with an emblem that was owned by Nightshade.

They had already drawn swords, and they waited the approach of the Dragon in perfect silence.

Kaylin had the strong urge to be somewhere else. Then again, Barrani spoiling for a fight always had that effect on her, even when she knew them and they were theoretically on her side. She managed to ignore the urge; she walked a bit more quickly, to catch up to Severn.

Tiamaris stopped twenty feet from the closest of the Barrani. He tendered the man an unexpected bow. It was brief, even curt, but it said much. "We have been sent by the Lord of the Hawks, from the Halls of Law, to retrieve the body you guard."

Body? Kaylin glanced at the floor. She couldn't see a thing. But as she stared, she felt it; a flicker of elusive magic. They'd cloaked the boy. And that took skill. She wondered if it was this magic that Tiamaris had sensed at a distance, but she doubted it.

"The Lords of Law do not rule here," one of the Barrani replied. The words were cold, but they were surprisingly polite. "And we have been sent by *our* lord to secure the same body."

"That would be unfortunate," Tiamaris replied, stepping forward. "The fieflord of Nightshade has allowed us entry into his domain for the purpose of investigation."

"For that purpose, yes," the Barrani replied again. "But for no other. Look, if you must, but the body will remain in the keeping of the fieflord." Cold, stilted language. The Barrani at their best.

The stranger lifted a hand, and dropped it like a blade; the curtain that had hidden the body fell to one side.

Kaylin closed her eyes. It was as much instinct as drawing daggers had been. But it was a weakness she couldn't afford; she forced herself to open them, to look, to live up to her namesake. Hawk.

In the silence, Kaylin heard the tinkling links of moving chain. The Barrani heard it, too, and they shifted their stance. They were going to fight.

Tiamaris shifted as well, but before he could move, she reached out and touched his sleeve. It didn't startle him; he might have expected it. But he did not spare her a glance.

Severn did.

"Kaylin, don't—"

She shook her head. "We can't fight," she told him quietly. "Not here. Not yet." She pushed her way past him, and edged her way past Tiamaris. It shouldn't have been difficult; the hall was wide. But it was.

She walked past the Dragon, and approached the Barrani. She moved deliberately, and slowly, and as she came within ten feet of the body, she sheathed her weapon, her hand shaking slightly.

The Barrani looked at her; all of them were suddenly riveted by her presence. She knew why. They did not speak, but they made no attempt to stop her as she finally approached them and knelt before the corpse of the young boy.

His face was frozen in a rictus of agony. It shouldn't have

been; the body was long past rigor mortis. His eyes were wide, open, frozen upon whatever they had last seen. It made her stomach knot suddenly in revulsion, in anger.

Reaching out, she closed his eyes; felt the stiff curl of thick lashes against the inner flat of her palms. The boy's arms were bare, and across them, in dark swirls, were symbols that she recognized.

"His thighs?" she asked.

"Also marked," one of the Barrani said.

She pulled aside the rough blanket that covered the dead boy's torso, and almost instantly regretted it. The stench was overpowering. Familiar. "It's the same," she said, speaking to Severn. Only to Severn.

He started to approach, and one of the Barrani *moved*. He moved so quietly Kaylin was aware of his absence only when he was standing in front of Severn, barring his way.

She covered her mouth with her hand for a moment, and then, bracing herself, she rose. "We need the body," she said quietly.

The Barrani said nothing.

But the mark on her cheek was warm, and she understood what it meant. For now, right here, she understood. She didn't care to look farther, and that was a gift from her years in the fiefs.

"I claim the body in the name of the man whose mark I bear," she told them calmly.

They exchanged a glance. In humans? It would have been an uneasy glance. But these Barrani gave nothing away. She waited, tense, while they made a decision in silence. The Barrani who had done *all* of the speaking tendered her a bow. It was brief, but it was deep.

"You take responsibility," he said gravely, "for your lord's displeasure."

"I do." She would have quibbled with the use of "your," but she knew it would gain her nothing. Had to bite her tongue not to do it anyway.

"Then take the body. We bear witness."

"Tiamaris," she said quietly.

The Dragon stepped forward. This time, no one tried to stop him. He came to stand by Kaylin's side; she felt his shadow as if it were warm. "I can carry him," he told her.

She didn't want to touch the boy. Rising, she nodded. Severn was at her side in an instant, and he, too, looked away as Tiamaris wrapped the slender corpse in the blanket that hid the injuries that had killed him.

She felt an arm around her shoulder, and she didn't even shrug it off when she realized it was Severn's. She was that numb.

They made an awkward procession through the streets of Nightshade. The Barrani guards fell in before and behind them, and they cleared the streets by presence alone. She was almost grateful, and she hated that. She would have been one of the children in hiding, in a different time. Now? She was entwined with the cause of their terror, and she didn't like the change.

The Barrani followed them only to the edge of the borders; the bridge across the Ablayne. They seldom traveled this far during the hours of daylight; she wondered what orders they'd been given.

But they allowed the Hawks to pass out of Nightshade in silence, and Tiamaris carried the body down Old Nestor, retracing the path that had brought them here from the Halls of Law.

How long had it been? Hours, she thought. But hours spent in the fiefs felt different than the hours spent outside of it. They marked her, shadowed her, haunted her. She hated the fiefs. But even as she left them, she glanced back. Her history was there.

And here, in the arms of a Dragon.

Clint was still on duty, and Tanner was beside him. The smile that usually crossed Clint's face when he caught sight of Kaylin vanished in the face of a Dragon; Kaylin couldn't see Tiamaris's eyes, but she could guess at their color by the sudden change in Clint's demeanor.

Tiamaris went in, unhindered, and he was shadowed by a grim and silent Severn. Only when they had passed did Clint lower his polearm slightly, more to get Kaylin's attention than to block her way, although it had the advantage of doing both; she wasn't moving quickly.

"Kaylin?"

She met his eyes in silence.

He shook his head. "Remember what Marcus told you," he said, and reaching out, he brushed hair from the sides of her cheeks. His fingers were callused and rough, but his touch was gentle; it was a dichotomy that she had always liked.

"What was that?" she asked, standing still a moment, a step below him.

"You can't save everyone."

She grimaced. "We have to try," she said.

"Trying is fine. Failing is inevitable. Don't let it devour you."

"It's not me that's devoured," she said bitterly.

"Yes it is." He lowered the polearm. "It's just not *only* you." He touched her shoulder with his free hand. "We'll get the sick bastard."

"Won't bring the boy back."

"No. But it'll stop other boys from coming in like this. That's what you think about. Remember it."

"Clint—"

"I think the Hawklord's waiting. I know Iron Jaw is." He stepped aside.

She walked past him, and then turning, touched his feathers. They jerked under her palms, but just this once, he let it be. She wanted to fly. And in a fashion, she did; she turned and ran through the Aerie hall toward the Tower of the Lord of Hawks.

CHAPTER 8

Instead of hitting the stairs to the Hawklord's Tower, Kaylin banked left when she reached the office that was at the center of the Hawk's nest, as the Hawk's wing of the Halls of Law was often called by anyone who wasn't a Hawk. She hoped to avoid Marcus, Teela, Tain—in short, everyone who wasn't part of their mission.

She was half-successful. The office was still crowded, but it was crowded in the way offices are when most of the people working in them have already sent their brains home and are packing up to follow: noisy, chaotic and not really all that productive. During a normal day, she half liked this, because it was possibly the best time for day's end gossip, and gossip had a life of its own. She could find out who was engaged, who was no longer engaged, who had gained—or lost—weight; she could find out who had

stomach troubles, who was pretending to be sick, and who
had developed gout. Hanging around those lively desks,
she knew which Hawks were working on which cases,
who had scored tickets to any of the various balls, dances,
concerts or plays that were the bane of a Leontine, who was
pregnant, who was trying or who had birthed a child.

But it seemed obscene, at times like this, that life *could*
be normal. She knew this wasn't fair, and she knew that she
wouldn't feel the same way when she managed to get a
grip—but she also knew that she was, at best, a wet blanket. At worst?

A spoiled brat.

And it had been years since she'd lived up to that; it was
no time to start a second childhood now. Not when she'd
finally proved, after so much effort, that she'd managed to
grow out of her first one.

Behind the office lay the Tower; to the left down a long
stretch of hall and through a set of fancy, heavy double
doors, lay the rooms that the examiners occupied. The examiners were not, strictly speaking, Hawks; they served *all*
of the Lords of Law. But when they chose to enter one of the
three towers, they served discreetly at the behest of the particular Lord who ruled the tower they were called to. For
this reason they were trusted by the Lords, and mistrusted
by the Hawks, the Wolves and the Swords. Your own, you
could count on. But someone who claimed no ties or loyal-
ties?

Still, if Kaylin were being truthful, there were always one
or two who bore the crest of the Hawks and mimed the loy-

alty without ever letting it sink roots. At least the examiners were honest about it.

She crossed her fingers—well, eight of them—and prayed that she'd find Red beside the body. Or that she'd find the *right* body. Murder wasn't exactly uncommon in Elantra. But a lot of the murder victims never made their way here; this was a place of—as the Hawklord liked to call it—last resort.

Here was where the special cases were delivered. And the boy? Special case was literally written all over a third of his body. It was written over a third of hers. She was dizzy, and stopped as she passed through the doors. Wondered if it was magic—because magic was the only guardian the doors required—or lack of sleep. Or food. But her arms ached; her thighs ached. Bad sign, all of it. She almost turned back.

But she couldn't. She owed the boy that much, whoever he was.

She knocked on the first closed door, and made her first mistake. Her second knock netted two for two, and not in her favor. Third time was lucky—in some circles. But not hers. She'd almost given up, but some innate stubbornness made her venture to the fourth, and she didn't have to knock—the door swung open when she touched it.

Magic, of course, played no small part in its inward swing; her hand was tingling painfully as she withdrew it. She was always half-surprised that those magical whatsits didn't actually leave scars or blisters.

On the other hand, Red was there.

She had no idea why he was called Red, because he wasn't. His hair was black, except for the gray bits, and his beard, likewise colored. His eyes were brown, his skin a sun-dark shade, his hands laborer's hands. Which, given his work, was a tad strange. He didn't even *wear* red. It would have looked gaudy on him.

But it was the name he answered to, when he bothered to answer, and she'd gotten used to using it, same as everyone else in the Hawks.

"Red," she said. "Thank god."

"Which one?"

"Take your pick. I'm liberal."

He laughed. No one else in the room did. And as she looked, she realized that Red was to be the one mercy the room afforded. The Hawklord was there. Marcus—curse it—was there. Tiamaris. Severn. These, she could live with, even Severn.

But the Imperial mages were there, and she hated the mages. They were pompous, arrogant, self-important and, above all, powerful. She never trusted powerful mages. The brief amount of history she'd been forced to endure before she'd been inducted into the Hawks had made it clear that *all* of the worst crimes facing the Lords of Law were instigated by mages—in the best of cases. In the worst? Caused by them. They were like walking death.

Oh, she had nothing against a little magic; that could be found on every third street corner. It was the hoarding, the cold gathering, the expensive use that bothered her. It certainly bothered her now.

"Private Neya," the Hawklord said coolly, well aware of her distaste, "I trust you remember Callantine?"

And they all had pretentious pseudo-Barranian names. Which was fine, if they were Barranian—but this one wasn't. "Yes, sir."

"Good. Callantine?"

"I don't remember all of the Hawks," the man replied. "She seems young for one."

The Hawklord's expression was as clear a command as she ever got, but just in case she missed it, Marcus stepped in and surrounded her left shoulder with claws. He didn't close them. Much.

"I admit I'm surprised at the speed with which the fieflord surrendered this particular body," the mage continued. "He's newly dead."

She really, really disliked mages.

"Kaylin," the Hawklord said, ignoring the comment, "I want you present at the examination."

She nodded, but she tensed. The one thorough examination she'd witnessed had left her nauseous for days, and she had no desire to repeat the experience.

"Red?"

The examiner had already donned his gloves and picked up his scalpels. He handed one to Tiamaris, and the Dragon took it without comment. As if, Kaylin thought, he was used to presiding over such vivisections.

"There's not much to cut," she said, without thinking. "He's already been opened up pretty thoroughly." She couldn't keep the bitter anger out of her voice, and didn't bother to try.

Red glanced at her, and offered her a weary grimace. "I'm

not going to cut much," he said quietly. "But I want to examine the skin beneath the tattoos, and I want to take a look at the edges of those cuts, as you call them. You don't have to—"

"Yes," the Hawklord interrupted, voice grim. "She does."

Red frowned. "Lord Grammayre," he began, but Marcus chose that moment to growl. As Leontine went, it was pretty monosyllabic, but it shut Red up.

Kaylin looked at the wall on the far side of the door. It was one long mirror that started at waist height—her waist—and went up to the ceiling. She could see herself clearly in it, and wished she couldn't; she looked like crap. Which was about how she felt.

But the mark on her face? It was an intricate design of thin, dark lines now. Prominent. She lifted a hand to cover it, and caught Callantine staring at her cheek.

"Lord Grammayre," he said, "I would like to examine the girl after this is over." He spoke in Barrani.

"She's a Hawk. She understands Barrani," the Hawklord replied. "And I believe that the examination in question will be at her discretion."

Kissing the Hawklord was out of the question. And given his sense of humor, Kaylin didn't—but it was a near thing. She tried hard not to look at Callantine as if he was something she'd managed to scrape off the bottom of her boots, and turned her attention to Red.

Severn was standing beside him. Not so close that he got in the way, but close enough that Red was twitching.

"Severn," Kaylin said quietly.

He looked up as if surprised to see her, he was that focused. Something about his expression made her move. Toward him. Her brain caught up with her slowly.

"Don't disturb Red," she told him. "He needs a lot of space when he works."

Red said, "He knows. He's only new to the Hawks…he's been with the Wolves for a while now." He glanced at Severn, and then back at the boy.

Her eyes were drawn there as well.

"He's between ten and twelve," Red said quietly. "I would say ten, but in the fiefs, food is scarce enough it's hard to judge." His voice was dry, almost uninflected. The first time Kaylin had seen him work, she had thought he was a monster. She'd been younger than, and the corpse on the slab had been older.

In time, she understood—barely—that he *had* to be this dry, this distant, in order to do his job.

It's just a body, he told her, after that first time. *It's dead. It feels nothing. No pain. No fear. That's what I think of, Kaylin. You think of what it must have been like to die. You wonder what they were thinking. How they were feeling. If they were terrified. I don't. Because right now, there's not a damn thing I can do to make it worse. And if anything I can do can help the Hawks find the killer, I think the dead will forgive me.*

She tried to remember that now.

He cut very little to begin with. He examined the boy's frozen mouth; pulled his eyelids up to look at his eyes. He spoke very little as his examination turned to the gaping, terrible wound that had once been an abdomen. It wasn't bleeding.

That was the other thing Kaylin had learned to appreciate, with time: bleeding meant life. It meant there was still a *chance*. And this boy? He'd had none.

"Arms are bruised," he told them quietly. A nebulous them; he didn't bother to look up to see if anyone was listening. He might have been talking to the mirror. In fact, given Records, he probably was. "Wrists are cut—he was bound. No rope detritus in the scrapes…they probably used leather straps."

"Manacles?"

Red shook his head. "Unlikely. If magic was involved. His ankles are likewise marked."

He continued to speak, and Kaylin lost track of his words. It took effort. She closed her eyes. Opened them. Took deep breaths.

Marcus touched her shoulder; she barely felt him.

"Hawklord," the Leontine said curtly. He was the *only* Hawk who called him that in the line of duty.

The Hawklord said, "She stays." Just that.

There would probably be an argument, but it would happen later. Marcus didn't care for mages either, and he wasn't about to show departmental divisions in front of them. He'd wait. But his fur was starting to stand on end. Normally, this would bother her. But nothing was normal, now.

Oh, it was bad. It was worse than the first time she'd watched such work, Clint by her side like a comfortable rock.

Because this was personal.

"Records," Red said. He laid his scalpel down beside the boy's face.

The Hawklord nodded and gestured. The mirror's sheen began to move in an iridescent ripple, as if it were a serpent. A large one. She stared at the image that coalesced, hating it, mesmerized by it. It was another body.

"Which one?" she asked quietly.

"The previous body," Red replied. "As you can see, Lord Grammayre, the cause of death, the method of death, is the same. Inch for inch, the cuts are identical."

The Hawklord nodded.

"Arms," Red told the mirror, and it obliged; the image shifted and changed. He had covered the boy's abdomen, and now lifted his exposed lower arms. "I believe the marks are the same," he told the Lord of the Hawks.

"I concur," Tiamaris added.

"And the first of the three deaths?" the Hawklord asked.

Red nodded; the mirror shifted. No faces were shown, and Kaylin was grateful for the lack. But only barely.

Another set of arms—hard to tell that they weren't the same, but the Records seldom botched a command—appeared, with the same intricate swirls running from inner elbow to inner wrist. "The same," Tiamaris announced.

Red began to tuck the arms under the heavy sheet. He pulled it up to expose the thighs, and they went through the same comparisons.

Only when they had finished did Kaylin speak. And she spoke to the mirror. "Records," she told it, voice shaking. It did nothing.

With an angry snort she ducked between Marcus and Red, and made her way to the flat, huge silvered glass. She placed a sweaty, and not entirely spotless, palm against its surface and said, "Records, damn you."

"The mirror is not keyed to you," Callantine began, in his arrogant, condescending ice-block of a voice.

She had the satisfaction of seeing the mirror react. Too bad all of the reflective surfaces were inactive—she would have liked to see the mage's face.

"Time, seven and a half years ago. Victims from the fief of Nightshade. Tina," she added quietly. She thought it would kill her to say the name.

But only the good died young.

"Inner arm, from elbow to wrist. Right and left."

The mirror struggled for a moment. Kaylin had no idea how the magic actually worked, and she didn't much care. The natural curiosity of a mage had never been a part of her life. She did her job. She did it well. And she never asked too many irrelevant questions. Well, okay, she tried really hard not to.

The tattoos came up in sharp, bright colors: black and white. She hated the pallor of dead skin.

"Tina?" The mage said quietly. He was obviously not a frequent visitor, at least not for these files.

"It was the name of one of the victims," Kaylin replied, in the tone of voice she reserved for people who belabored the obvious.

Callantine's frown made it clear how much he appreciated being on the other end of condescension. "Her family name?"

Severn answered before Kaylin could, which was probably a good thing. "She was born in the fiefs," he said quietly, no apology and no contempt in the cool words. His scars spoke a different story, and in color; they were whiter than usual.

"Ah, of course, of course. Continue," Callantine said.

But Red ignored him for the moment. "Tiamaris?" he said, speaking the name with just a trace of hesitation. Kaylin filed it away for later.

"The same marks," the Dragon said. His voice was flat. Kaylin wondered if that was what passed for exhaustion among the Dragons. They were a mystery to her. She wanted them to stay that way. After all, the Emperor was a Dragon, and nothing she had ever heard about him in office parlance suited the words "gentle" or "merciful."

"Reginald," Lord Grammayre said quietly, "that will be all. Callantine and his assistants will examine the body now."

Had it been any other day, Kaylin would have snickered. *Reginald.* Red, however, ignored the name; he picked up his scalpels and his gloves, and vacated the slab. If standing ten feet away from the corpse could be said to be vacating.

Callantine, whatever else she could say about him, was clearly an expert at his craft. He didn't gesture, and he didn't mumble—and Kaylin knew, from her short lessons about how to recognize magery before it killed you, that the lack of focal constraints denoted either great power, or certainty. Usually both.

He *touched* the boy's arms. She wanted to pry his hands

off, and held her own in fists by her sides. Because it wasn't reasonable, it made no sense, and it would get her in trouble for sure.

"They are like the other marks," the mage said, after silent moments had passed. "They are not…tattoos in any traditional sense of the word. They are not composed of ink or dyes."

"What are they composed of?" Kaylin asked.

Callantine raised a brow and looked to the Hawklord for permission to answer her question. The Hawklord nodded grimly.

"Flesh," he replied. "To our spells, the symbols and the skin are no different. If it were not for the obvious visible artifacts, magic would not detect them at all."

"But they were laid there by magic."

His brows lowered. Kaylin had only barely managed to keep the accusation out of the words. "Yes," he said curtly. "By magic."

"Whose?"

"If we had an answer to that," the mage replied, his careful composure fraying slightly, "there would be no more deaths."

And it came to Kaylin that this arrogant, smug, pretentious bastard was actually one of the good guys. He wasn't a Hawk, but he wanted what the Hawks wanted. Hell, she thought, he wanted what *all* of the officers of the Lords of Law wanted. She would never go drinking with the son of a bitch, but she could work with him. Petulance was not an option. It was a strong desire, but it was not an option.

She hesitated for just a moment. No, honest now, for much longer than that. And then she reached for the buttons of her cuffed sleeves.

Claws caught her left hand; hands caught her right. Marcus's claws. Severn's hands.

"Thank you Kaylin," the Hawklord said quietly. "That will be all."

They didn't drag her from the examination room. Exactly.

The office cleared when Marcus reached his desk. It wasn't subtle, but then again, it was almost past shutdown anyway. One or two of the desk-for-life Hawks gave her a sympathetic wince behind Marcus's back, but they were smart enough not to actually put any of it into words.

"What," Marcus said, shaking her arm, "did you think you were *doing?*"

"I was going to show him—"

"I *know* what you were going to do, you idiot."

Usually when you know the answer to a question, Kaylin thought sourly, you don't waste time asking it. But she was smart enough not to say so.

"The mages—"

"Kaylin, there are one or two who *do* know some of the particulars of your past and the marks you bear. They don't know *who* you are. They just know that we know how to find you. They know that Lord Grammayre has chosen to take personal responsibility for you or your subsequent actions, and that he has been granted—gods know why—Imperial dispensation for his claim. They *don't* know you're a Hawk."

She snorted. "It's the Hawklord. Could I *be* anything else?"

"Dead," he said quietly.

Severn sat heavily on Marcus's desk. He had nothing to offer, and he kept his hands to himself after that initial contact. But he was stone silent, and although he had never been much for chatter, his silence was all wrong.

She was drawn to it. Then again, she'd tried to kill him the first time she'd seen him in the tower, so that probably didn't say much.

"Tiamaris knows," she said quietly. "And if he's not an Imperial mage—"

"He's not."

"He's not a Hawk."

"He is, according to the Hawklord, *exactly* that. He is honor-bound to leave all information he gathers within our ranks *in* our ranks."

She started to speak and Marcus growled. "It's clear you don't understand the Dragon caste," he said, as his claws extended.

"You understand them," she countered, "and it's not making you any more comfortable."

He hissed. It was the Leontine form of an angry sigh. "I understand Dragons well enough to know that their presence is trouble. They don't like to follow. They lead. It's in their blood."

"Is that why there are so few of them?" she asked, flippantly.

His silence turned that flippancy on its ear.

"Yes," Severn told her, when it became clear that the answer was beneath Marcus. "That's exactly why."

"Something happens to the rest," she said slowly. It wasn't exactly a question.

"Something happens to the rest," he agreed.

"I'm not happy about his placement," Marcus added.

"I'd guessed."

"But it seems that he has become fond of you."

Given Tiamaris's perpetually dour expression and his utter lack of patience with her, this came as a bit of a surprise. "How does he treat people he doesn't like?"

"He probably eats them." Marcus shrugged.

"That would break at least three laws."

"Not really. Suicide isn't illegal."

"And being disliked by a Dragon is on record as a form of legal suicide?"

Marcus snorted.

"Got it."

"Callantine is an ass," Marcus added, shifting the conversation. "He's serious about his work, and he's good at it—but he's a mage, and he cares a lot about reputation and prestige. Mostly his. Don't trust him."

She nodded.

He rolled golden eyes. "Kaylin—"

Severn stood up. "I'll take her," he said.

"Where?"

"Anywhere. Not here."

"Good. Her stomach is growling."

Kaylin flushed. "I didn't have time to eat—"

"You could try waking up in the morning like the rest of us."

"Yes, Marcus."

"Get out of my sight," the Leontine added. His claws had found purchase in his desk, and by the looks of them, they were about to add a new furrow or four to its surface.

"Yes, Marcus." She started to walk away, turned, and added, "can I be given access to the old records?"

He didn't even ask which ones. "Yes. But study them in Grammayre's tower. Don't study them anywhere else."

"But the Hawklord—"

"Will say yes."

She *really* didn't want to see that discussion. She beat a retreat as quickly as possible, and only when she was out of Marcus's sight did she realize that she'd tacitly agreed to be led somewhere by Severn.

They stopped outside of a tavern that Kaylin dimly recognized from her walking rounds. It was far enough from home—hers—that she'd only been in it on the one or two occasions when the tavern's owner had seen fit to call in the Hawks. Given that it was only once or twice, she figured it was a fairly quiet place.

"I eat here a lot," Severn told her, as they stood beneath the faded sign that listed on uneven chains above their heads. The sign might once have been decent; years of sun, rain and the occasional rowdy teenager had done their damage. The name, however, could still be read—by those who could read. The Spotted Pig.

"A lot?"

"A lot."

"Which is your way of telling me not to do anything embarrassing, right?"

"Pretty much."

"I'll do my best."

"Which means?"

"I won't start a fight if you don't."

He shrugged. But the shrug was stiff, and his smile was a jerk of lips, more reflex than expression. She told herself she didn't care. Sadly, she'd been telling herself that a lot in the past couple of days, and it was beginning to grate on her nerves.

Everything was.

Severn entered the tavern, and she entered behind him, like a shadow. Like, in fact, the shadow she had once been, when he had been safety—and more—in the fief of Nightshade. She stopped walking, but he didn't notice.

The Tavernkeep came out from behind his bar. "Severn," he said, with a broad smile. The smile lasted until the man was close enough to see Severn's face. Kaylin couldn't, but she didn't need to.

"Bad day?" The man asked, turning back to the bar. He didn't wait for an answer. Proof, if she needed it, that Severn *did* eat here a lot; the man certainly understood his mood well enough, and he wasn't offended by it.

"It was," Kaylin told him quietly.

The man stopped at the only obvious entrance to the liquor cache behind the bar and stared at her. After a minute, he frowned. "I've seen you before, haven't I?"

She pointed at the small white and gold Hawk embroidered on her tunic; she hadn't bothered with full surcoat because the walking beat wasn't hers today.

"Never forget a face," he said, with no modesty whatsoever. "Are you with Severn?"

"Sort of."

"Take your regular table," the man told Severn's back. As Severn was clearly moving with a purpose, Kaylin figured this was just formality; she wasn't wrong. But the man walked over to her, extended a large, callused hand, and smiled. Broad smile. All teeth present. "If you're a friend of Severn's, you're welcome here." His voice matched his smile; it was a little too loud, a little too friendly, and somehow completely genuine.

But he lowered it a little as he leaned closer. "But given that I've never seen the two of you together, let me give you a bit of advice, girl. What's your name?"

"Kaylin," she told him. "Kaylin Neya. Private. Hawks."

"Right. I'm Burlan. Burlan Oaks."

It sounded like a street sign. Or an intersection. "You made that up, right?"

"Smart girl. But not too smart. Look, I know a bit about Severn—as much as anyone here does—and I'm telling you that today is *not* the day to spend time in his company. You turn around and go home. He won't hold it against you; he doesn't have that kind of temper. But I think he needs to sit at that corner table on his lonesome for a while."

"Probably," she said wryly. "But if I walk out that door, he won't. Sit there," she added. "I'm a Hawk. I can take care of myself. But thanks for the warning."

Severn was absolutely silent. The silence was just... unnerving. She stared at the side of his face; at the pale white line that traveled from his ear to the underside of his chin. Ferals had given him that.

She remembered it clearly; it was the first time she had ever used the power to heal, and it had been entirely by accident. Now? If it happened today, and she could touch him before the bleeding stopped, he wouldn't even bear the scar.

But she wouldn't heal him.

She stared at her hands, forcing her eyes away from his face. "This would have been a luxury," she said, without thinking.

"You haven't eaten his cooking yet. Don't be so quick to judge."

She looked up; a smile had creased his eyes without touching his lips. It was there and gone. "Severn—"

He said, "You haven't changed."

"And you have?"

"Not much."

There was a lot of awkward silence.

Burlan—she really wanted to know the name he'd been born with, because she couldn't imagine it could be worse—dropped two large bowls in the center of the table, and followed them with spoons and large rags that were so uneven it took Kaylin a minute to recognize them as napkins. If that's what they were. She eyed them dubiously.

Her stomach was less picky and more embarrassing. She ate just to shut it up.

But as she was chewing—and the meat in the very heavy stew was surprisingly free of fat, gristle or bone—something occurred to her. "Severn, when exactly did you request your transfer?"

He watched her eat for a while before he picked up his spoon. Which meant, of course, that he wasn't going to answer.

"It was after the first new death, wasn't it?"

He chewed slowly. As if he were counting.

"How did you know about it?"

"It's not a secret."

"It's an open secret. It's not talked about much, not even in the Hawks. The Wolves were sent out hunting—we'd know, if they were sent into the fiefs. Hell, the Swords would know. How?"

"Just eat, Elianne."

"Kaylin."

"Kaylin, then."

"You were waiting." It was an accusation. She couldn't help it. All of the anger that she had kept in check in the examination room had turned inward, and her anger had a bad habit of hanging around.

"This is not the place," he told her quietly.

"This is as good a place as any." Not true. Not true at all. She bit her lip. But his silence, his lack of expression, were more than she could comfortably handle. And she thought she'd passed through the examination with flying colors. "You knew. You knew it would start again."

"No," he told her, continuing to eat with deliberate, slow movements. "I didn't."

"You suspected."

"And you didn't?" Scorn. The first display of real emotion he'd shown yet. Wasn't exactly what she wanted, but it was better than nothing.

"No."

"You were hiding," he said. "You've always been good at that."

"It was after the first death," she repeated, ignoring his comment.

He gritted his teeth and nodded.

"How long have you known that I've been with the Hawks?"

"Long enough."

"How *long*?"

"Six years."

She put her spoon down. Soup splashed over the flat rim of the bowl. "Six *years*?"

"About that."

"And you never said anything?"

This time, his smile was all edge.

She hesitated, and then said, "All right, I deserve that. You knew I'd try to—"

"Yes. I knew."

"I didn't know you were a Wolf."

"You weren't looking for me."

"No. I thought I'd left you behind."

"You did," he said quietly. "But you came to the Hawks looking for something. You found it," he added bitterly. "And I had no place there."

Something about the way he said the words killed the anger. And she needed it. "Who's doing this?" she whispered.

"I don't know. But I'm a Hawk now…you're a Hawk. We've both learned enough to earn that rank. This time, things will be different." He spoke the words as if they were a promise.

But this time was built on last time. She closed her eyes. "I'm not ready for this," she said quietly.

"I know."

"I was happy here."

"I know. It's why I stayed with the Wolves."

It wasn't the answer she was expecting. But she was no longer certain what to expect. She picked up the spoon and played with it. "Were you?"

"Was I what?"

"Happy with the Wolves."

He shrugged. "I'm not a happy person," he said after a moment had passed.

"Why did you join them?"

"Why did you join the Hawks?"

She shook her head.

"Don't ask me to share what you won't."

She nodded. Fair enough. "You're right about the food," she added with a grimace.

He continued to eat. She tried not to backslide into the examiner's room. Memory was treacherous.

But not, apparently, just hers. Severn put his spoon down. "Come on," he said quietly.

"You're not going to finish?"

"I'm finished." He shoved his hands into his pockets and waited.

She followed him; the tavern wasn't empty, and the streets weren't empty either. But no one went near Severn, and by extension, Kaylin was likewise avoided.

They didn't walk far. They came to a squat, two-storey building, and Severn stopped at the door. He took out a key, slid it into the lock, and twisted it. Looked back at her as she realized that she was standing just outside of his door.

"This is yours?"

He shrugged. "Not all of it."

"It's…bigger. Than my place."

"You wanted to talk," he said quietly, pushing the door open. He waited. Something about his expression was off; she'd never seen it there before.

"Severn?"

"No," he said, waiting. "I won't talk about anything you don't want to talk about."

She nodded, then, and walked past him into the open hall. Stairs led up at angles, and a wide arch separated the front room from the hall. Her brows rose. "They're paying you a helluvalot more than they're paying me."

"I was old enough to *be* a Wolf when I joined them."

She didn't ask him about the shadows. Because she wasn't certain she wanted to know. Being a Shadow Wolf— a Shadow *anything*—was a tricky business. It meant that you could do anything at all at a simple command. And that you were trusted to do it *only* then.

Not all of the men and women who lived in the Shadows lived up to that trust. She'd seen it, as a Hawk.

And she knew what Severn was capable of.

"If this is neater than my place, I'm leaving."

"You know where the door is."

She rolled her eyes. "Boots?"

"Leave 'em on if you want. I don't care."

"Tell me someone else does your cleaning."

"Someone else does my cleaning."

"Liar."

"You didn't say it had to be true." He led her into what would have been a sitting room in a large home; she'd seen them before. It was, sort of. There was a fireplace here, and grates. There was a long couch, and a functional wooden one; there was a table just one side of the window. The window, even though it fronted out onto the street, had no bars.

The colors were subdued, and Kaylin noticed that this room lacked a mirror of *any* size. She hesitated until she noticed the carpet beneath her boots, and then she cursed and took them off.

"Why did the Wolves let you go?"

"I asked."

"That's it?"

He shook his head. "The Wolflord and the Hawklord are

not the same. The Wolflord knew why I asked, and he granted the request. He was not at all certain the Hawklord would comply. Kaylin, *what* are you doing?"

She frowned. "What do you mean?"

He had taken care, she realized, to put distance between them; when she had perched in the corner of the couch, he had taken the wooden chair. He left it now, crossing the carpet to kneel by her side. Well, to kneel on the carpet to one side of her feet. He was a lot taller than she was.

He caught her hands in his, and only when he did did she realize that she'd been fussing with the cuffs of her shirt. "My arms are itchy," she said, half-apologetically.

But he didn't immediately let go, and his expression didn't sink into the familiarity of exasperation. He met her eyes, his gaze intent; Hawk's gaze. Moreso than hers would ever be.

"Let me see," he said.

"See what?"

"Your arms."

She nodded, and he carefully undid the buttons that held the cuffs together. He pushed the right sleeve up to the bend of her elbow, turning her wrist gently so that the marks were exposed to the light in the room; it was mage-light, not fire, and it was steady and bright. Or as bright as he wanted it to be. He really *was* making more than she was.

But she forgot to resent it when she heard the single word he spoke. He set her arm down gently, but she felt the sudden tension in his hand; he rose, walked over to the chair, grabbing its broad back in either hand, as if to steady himself.

She almost cried out when the wood cracked.

Almost. But she looked at her arms instead, at whatever it was he had read there, and she froze.

The marks were different; the writing was slightly thicker, the swirls almost smudged. "It's—it's changed."

"Yes," he said, without looking at her. "It's changed."

And she knew that he'd both expected it, and feared it. "Severn—"

"It was all for *nothing*," he said bitterly, and he turned, then, shoving the chair to one side, his gaze intent, almost wild.

"All for—" She stood. "I don't—I have to go."

He said nothing at all as she grabbed her boots and fled; she was three houses down the street before she stopped to put them on.

CHAPTER 9

"Kaylin?"

"Morning, Marcus."

"Yes. It is. Morning," he added, his eyes narrowing. "Are you certain you're Kaylin Neya?"

"Ha ha."

"Well, you've got the right sense of humor."

Meaning, of course, none. She glared at him balefully.

"You *did* sleep last night, right?"

She said nothing, choosing to let the dark circles under her eyes speak for themselves. They were a perpetual adornment, and this morning, she'd actually owned the mirror for long enough to see them clearly. Made her miss the wake-up calls, and almost nothing did that.

Caitlin, looking interminably cheerful, breezed by with a quick stop for a good-morning hug. She seldom hugged anyone, but she never missed hugging Kaylin. Caitlin might be a paper-pusher, but she somehow managed to keep Marcus in line—or what passed for it—in most situations; she didn't much like his temper, but then again, no one in the office did. She was older than she looked, and she'd been on duty, as Marcus's aide, the day Kaylin had been introduced to the Hawks. Kaylin thought of her as birdlike, and it was true; she'd taken Kaylin under her wing, adopting her. She'd showed Kaylin how to navigate the mass of paperwork that often landed on Marcus's desk—because Marcus wasn't going to get to it anytime soon—and made her feel at home.

Or rather, made her feel as if she had one.

Caitlin had found her her apartment. Caitlin had argued the rent down to something that was "only outrageous." But Caitlin didn't hover during any of Kaylin's conversations with Marcus. She was smart.

And she was gone, with just a momentary cluck to indicate that she, too, noticed a substantial lack of sleep. One day if she was lucky, Marcus was going to hire someone thick. The mirror began its sonorous whine.

"Don't answer that," Marcus said.

"I wasn't going to."

"Severn booked off."

"Good."

"Kaylin—"

"It's none of your business, Marcus."

Leontine fur rose.

Kaylin shrunk. Exposed her throat in a perfunctory way. Marcus growled.

"I have to see the Hawklord," she told him, as his claws brushed her skin. They stopped.

"What happened?" His voice dropped. Not an octave; Leontine voices weren't that musical. But it did deepen, which was never a good sign.

"The marks," she said quietly. "They've changed."

He cursed in Leontine, but he kept it short. "Tiamaris is already in the Tower," he told her, as he shoved her in the direction of the doors.

"Figures."

Lord Grammayre was also in the Tower, which was less of a surprise. Kaylin entered, and the doors swung shut behind her. She bowed, rose and offered the Hawklord a passable salute—which is to say, passable because there was no one to be offended by its lack of precision—and took a deep breath.

Tiamaris frowned. "Kaylin," he said, nodding almost formally. "I wasn't expecting to see you this early—"

"—in the morning. Join the queue."

"Kaylin," the Hawklord said, his frown more severe.

She nodded and muttered a brief apology, which Tiamaris failed to notice. Maybe the Dragon wasn't so bad after all.

"Are you here for the Records?" the Hawklord asked. The frown hadn't shifted; it deepened. Luckily this one wasn't entirely her fault.

"Marcus spoke to you?"

"At length. For Marcus," he added.

"I'm here for the Records. Sort of." She turned to the mirror. "Records," she said firmly. And then, after a pause,

"Subject—Kaylin Neya." The mirror here was, of necessity, smaller than the mirror in the examination room had been; the images that began to coalesce were bounded by a long oval. She had to reorient her vision; it was either that or turn the mirror sideways, and she had a good idea of how popular that would make her.

The Hawklord came to stand by her side. "Kaylin?"

She shook her head and undid her buttoned cuffs, pushing them up to her elbows. Exposed, the marks looked less threatening than they had the previous evening, but not by much. She held them out before the mirror's image, and waited.

"They've changed," Tiamaris said quietly. If he was surprised, she didn't hear it in his voice. "Is this the first time they've changed since your arrival?"

"In the Halls of Law?"

He nodded.

So did she.

"And we have no earlier records of them?"

"We have some," she said, trying to keep the resentment out of her voice.

"The Tha'alani," the Hawklord said, by way of explanation.

"May I?" Tiamaris asked her. He did not look at the Hawklord, and she had the feeling that if she said no, he would leave the Records alone. She was surprised at how grateful she felt, and she gave him willingly what she would have resented otherwise: her permission.

He was better at mirrors than she was, no question; he didn't even *speak*. Instead, he touched the silvered surface—something the Hawklord had promised to break her fingers for if she ever did the first time he'd let her practice mirror skills here.

Images rushed past—solid, clear images, not the hazy things that Kaylin often invoked. She watched in fascination as he dredged them up from Record bowels, slotting them into the meagre space until he had five different sequences, all of her arms.

"This would be the first time you noticed the marks?" He asked her, pointing to one of them.

Spider-thin, like webs, ash-gray. "Yes," she said, although she herself could no longer remember what they had looked like.

"And this would be seven years ago?"

"Give or take six months."

He nodded again. But instead of fear or resentment, she felt curiosity, and she let it guide her. The marks, the earliest ones, had changed over the course of—

She swallowed. Too much to think about, here.

"They did change," he said softly. "With the earlier killings." He didn't sound surprised. In fact, she suspected that he had already studied them. She didn't ask when; she owed him. He stared at the surface of the mirror, and the writing became larger in each of the images he had chosen. He'd picked one set of marks to focus on. She could see that they had darkened—that took no study.

But she could also see that some part of the swirling pattern *had* shifted.

"I...guess so."

"When did you first use your powers?"

She looked at the Hawklord for the first time.

"He is aware of them," the Hawklord replied evenly. "The mages were not. What were you—"

"Thinking?"

"I hesitate to use the word."

She was silent for a full minute, and then she said, "I was thinking that the mages might be more useful if they had more information."

The Dragon and the Aerian exchanged a glance.

"I want it stopped," she added bitterly. Her hands started to shake, and she let the sleeves fall. "I don't want to go back to that room again. I don't want anyone to be brought there. Not for this. Not because of *these*."

"And exposing yourself would accomplish this how?"

She shrugged. "I don't know. You've always said I don't appreciate mages—it's true, I don't—but I don't always know how the little bits and pieces of information I gather on a case are going to fit together, either."

"Admirable," the Hawklord said, as if it were anything but. "But in this case, misguided. Yes, it may give them insight—but the cost for that insight would be too high. You will not take that risk again."

"Yes, sir." She hesitated; Tiamaris was still studying the different marks, as if he hoped to force meaning out of them. She let him. "Did the mages do *anything* useful?"

"That's the Kaylin I know," the Hawklord replied dryly. "Callantine took some of the skin with him. He retreated with his coterie."

She rolled her eyes.

"I believe it is his intent to visit the oracles."

"Oracles?"

"Before you indulge in pointless contempt, may I repeat your own words? Information comes from unexpected sources."

"I certainly wouldn't expect anything useful out of oracles," she said, not bothering to hide her scorn.

The Hawklord chose to ignore it. "There have been three deaths in the fiefs, and in shorter span than any previous deaths of this nature. If the mages are ignorant of the reasons, they are well aware that three is not the desired number; they know that more will fall. The mages are not certain of anything in this investigation, except for the presence of magic. They are aware that the markings are linguistic. They are *not* aware of what those marks mean."

Tiamaris looked up. "Grammayre," he said. Kaylin thought he was unaware of the dropping of the honorific, and the Hawklord didn't seem to notice its absence either. Not something Kaylin could get away with. Not, in fact, something *any* of the Hawks could. What was Tiamaris, to the Hawklord?

"Tiamaris?"

"Look." The mirror had shifted. When, Kaylin wasn't certain. "These are the marks on the boy's arms. And this, this and this—the marks on different victims. They are, as you know, the same."

The Hawklord nodded.

"These are Kaylin's arms, as they first appeared. These are her arms now. Can you see the pattern emerging?"

The Hawklord didn't frown; his face didn't change at all.

Kaylin looked at Tiamaris. And then she looked at her arms. "They're changing," she said softly. "Into what was written on them. On the dead."

"Yes," Tiamaris said quietly. "That is my guess."

It was more than a guess; given the visual cues, she could see it clearly herself. She had been afraid of dying, once. It was a better fear. "You don't think when they change, if they do change completely, that it's going to kill me."

"No, Kaylin," he said softly. "Not you."

"What do you think it will do?"

His utter silence was not a comfort.

"Tiamaris?"

"I don't know," he said at last. And he wasn't telling the truth.

She called him on it. "You're lying."

And took a mental note as his eyes went straight from a flat gold to a bitter, bright red: Don't ever call a Dragon a liar.

The Hawklord stepped between them. He did not touch Kaylin, and he certainly didn't raise a hand against Tiamaris, but his presence had a calming effect. Sort of. "She was raised in the fiefs. She has little understanding of the Courts, and as you've chosen to study here, you must expect this."

Tiamaris nodded grimly. "I was not lying," he told her, in a voice that would have frozen the entire Ablayne in an instant. "I do *not* know what will happen."

"You have suspicions."

"If you have half a thought to spare," he replied, "so do you. You've seen the seal in the Long Halls of Nightshade—you've seen the writings of the Old Ones. You know that this is an old magic." The red left his eyes; they were now a burnt orange, and receding into their usual gold. "But it is true, Grammayre, I forget myself. Kaylin, I told you—mages died in the study of marks like these. They were on stone walls, stone tablets, golden spheres. Not a single such mark has been found upon anything living save you.

"But the writing on your arms when it first appeared is substantially different from the writing that was placed upon the sacrificial victims. And given the nature of their deaths, and the significance of the writing, there is only one conclusion that *can* be drawn."

"I'm a danger."

"Yes." Before she could speak, he raised a hand. "The gift that you have shown—the healing—is not a dark art. It *is* a rare one, and the fact that you evince it at all, given your deplorable lack of education, makes you unique. It also," he added softly, "must make the task the killers have undertaken somewhat more difficult. If I had to guess, from my scant knowledge, I would say that the early writing speaks, in some way, to your impulse to heal. The writings upon the sacrifices speak to death, and only death. Here," he said, images shifting, "is the earliest image we have of the symbols on your arms. Do you see this sigil?" It was a circle, a small circle, simple and adorned with something that might have been stylized leaves. "I believe this is a token. It means not death, but a natural end, a natural beginning.

"This," he said, quietly, as he shifted his focus to the arm of a faceless dead corpse, "is death. It is a circle that is divided, and it loses the sense of nature. To change these in writing is simple. But there is more than writing here. I believe they attempt to change some essential part of the nature of the magic. Were you a different person—"

"She would never have left the Tower alive," the Hawklord said quietly.

"Would that have been better?" Kaylin asked softly.

"It is a question you must answer," the Hawklord replied. He was grim now. Cold. "But it is not just for yourself that the answer will be offered. My judgment hangs in the balance as well."

She swallowed. "Tiamaris," she said softly, "will you stay?"

He raised a brow.

"While I...study the Records. Of the previous deaths."

"Ah. Yes, Kaylin. I will stay. I have much desired the opportunity to question you, and it has long been denied me."

"When did you ask?"

"It is not relevant," the Hawklord replied, lifting a hand. "Tiamaris."

"Lord Grammayre."

Hours passed in the tower room. The shadows lessened as the sun reached the center of the domed ceiling; Kaylin hardly marked the passage of time. Her neck was stiff; she had to pace to keep her legs steady. Tiamaris worked the mirror; he had offered it to her, and she had done nothing—her way of declining.

The first hour had gone by in silence. Silence had never been her strength. She might have hated people who felt the need to cram a lot of words into a silence just to fill it, but she was honest enough to know that she hovered on the edge of being one of them. Silences were barbed in unexpected ways; with words, you generally knew where the traps were.

But there were some times when words were so inadequate it was almost obscene to use them. She hovered between the two impulses, and spoke only partway through the second hour. "How many?"

He could have pretended not to understand her, but he had some pity; although he was crisp and intent, her color had faded to something between gray and green.

"Thirty-eight."

"Right. I knew that." But she *hadn't*. She'd known the number. She'd understood it, the way she understood most numbers. She'd never wanted to get closer to it than that. And this? Even though her hands weren't actually *on* the bodies, they might as well have been. The Records had far less sympathy than the Dragon did; they were clear, crisp, concise; they captured everything.

And what they didn't, she could fill in: the smell. The temperature of the skin.

"All of the deaths took place in Nightshade."

Tiamaris nodded.

"Can you—can the Records map them for me?"

"There is no obvious pattern—"

"Can you just get me a map?"

He nodded. But as he lifted a hand, as he turned to face the mirror fully, he asked the first intrusive question. "Kaylin, do you know *all* of their names for a reason?"

She hadn't spoken the names out loud. And she didn't much mind being called a liar; she almost said no. But it wouldn't help. The truth might lead to answers she didn't already have. But it was too much, for the moment; she changed the subject instead. "When I was younger—when they were happening—I thought it was happening *everywhere*. We didn't read much. We couldn't. We didn't have a sense of what was going on outside of our fief. We thought there were hundreds of deaths.

"We thought the outer city didn't care."

"And now?"

"Didn't matter how much you cared, did it?" She said bitterly. Then she stopped. "It does. Matter. It just didn't make a difference."

"And if it didn't make a difference then," Tiamaris said, his back still toward her, "you can't see how it's going to make a difference now."

She nodded.

"You're here."

"I meant a good difference." The mirror shifted suddenly, as if it had taken time to gather and sort the information she'd requested, and then spit it out all at once.

Tiamaris said something about small mirrors under his breath; she would have laughed at any other time. But in this one, she watched Nightshade unfold. It wasn't a map in the traditional sense of the word, it was an aerial capture of the actual buildings and streets. There were no obvious signs, but the mirror provided small words that ran along the street lengths in a bright, glowing gold. "That one's wrong," she said, without thinking.

"Which one?"

"That street name. That's not what it's called."

"That's what it's *officially* called."

She rolled her eyes.

"Keep in mind," Tiamaris said, as small red points began to flash across those "official" streets, "that these lights indicate where the bodies were discovered. They don't indicate where they were killed."

She nodded. "Are they coming up in the…right order?"

"They should appear in the sequence in which they were discovered," he said. Each word chosen carefully to provide distance. She had always hated that; today she felt the hypocrite for her appreciation of the attempt.

She watched. The mirror offered each new light slowly, and she had to assume that was because of Tiamaris's silent command.

"Do you want the names?" He asked quietly.

She looked up; was surprised to see that he was now watching her, and not the mirror. But she shook her head, watching a disaster that she was powerless to prevent as it unfolded. Time was always her enemy; the past was just another part of time. When she was feeling particularly low, she daydreamed about being able to travel through it, as if it were the Ablayne; that she could somehow go back, armed with knowledge, and prevent each and every death from occurring. That she could find them *before* they died. That she could heal them all.

It was her most visceral desire.

"Kaylin?"

"Can you tell me if anyone else has…done this?"

"Done what?"

"Mapped the deaths. Like this. Accessed this information."

"Records are kept for each access," Tiamaris replied thoughtfully. "But that information is classified—"

"I don't give a damn about classification. Can you get me that information?"

"Why?"

She ground her teeth. "Because I need it," she said.

"No."

"Can you tell me if a particular person has done this?"

"Which person?"

"Severn."

He hesitated. "Kaylin," he began.

"Please."

"The question will be noted," he told her. His way of encouraging caution. As if. When she didn't reply, he said, "Yes. Severn accessed this information."

"When?"

"Six years ago."

"Six years—he was barely a Wolf! I didn't get access to Records until—no, sorry. Never mind. Was that being recorded, too?"

"Probably."

She added a lot of colorful, multilingual swearing. Let some scholar chew on that.

"I can see why Lord Grammayre considers you a challenge," the Dragon said. But he smiled, and if it was weary, it was genuine.

She watched as the map at last played itself out. She stood beside the mirror, counting red, blinking lights; counting deaths. Naming them silently, because she could. She had met them all, some more than once, some a lot more.

"The only thing they have in common," she said quietly.

"Is their end in Nightshade."

She shook her head. "I knew them all. At least to name." She lifted a hand, but didn't actually touch the mirror; old lessons had taken a very firm hold. "You're right. There's no clear pattern." But she was lying.

"Where are you going?"

"To get something to eat. I'm hungry." Another lie.

Tiamaris wasn't a hypocrite; his expression made clear that he knew she was lying, but he didn't accuse her of doing so.

After the nonevent that was lunch, she returned to the Tower. Tiamaris was still there, and the mirror—what she could see of it on either side of his broad back—was no longer graced by images of the dead; it was littered instead by swirling sigils. Some were on stone; some were on parchment; some on cloth. She tried to peer round his shoulder and he lifted a hand; the mirror went dead.

"Sorry," she muttered.

He looked up, as if only just aware of her presence. "No apologies are necessary," he told her quietly. "But I believe Sergeant Kassan expects you to go on patrol."

"With who?"

"I am not entirely certain."

"Which means not you."

He shrugged. "I am not often sent on patrol."

"You're not really a Hawk."

His raised brow was the whole of his answer. "Kaylin," he said, as she was turning for the door, "I have studied this case for almost seven years, and for reasons of my own. I have a question that I wish you to answer, but I will accept silence." The tone of his voice was odd. She was enough of a Hawk to understand it, but enough Kaylin to question.

"You don't normally have to accept silence, do you?"

"Not normally, no. But nothing about this case is normal."

She hesitated, and then nodded.

"Where did you live, in the fiefs?"

He missed *nothing*. "Why?"

"You are free not to answer the question," he said, his frown deepening. "But you are not free to waste my time with idle games."

She closed her eyes. "Map," she said softly. When she

opened them, it was already there. So were the lights, the trail of the dead. She walked to the mirror, and lifting a finger, pointed to the center of the random pattern. "There," she said quietly. "Near the Four Corners."

He passed a hand over the mirror; she thought the map might disappear. Instead, three more lights joined the original thirty-eight.

"Yes," she said softly. "Close to there."

"They don't know you left."

"I don't know. I'm not sure what proximity has to do with anything. The deaths occurred in the fiefs, but my arms are still changing."

"Thank you." He lifted a hand again, and the map vanished. "You are free to go."

She almost made it out, but had to turn again. "Did you tell him to kill me?"

He said nothing.

"Tiamaris, did you tell the Hawklord to kill me?"

"What do you think?"

She had no answer to offer.

Teela was waiting for her by Marcus's desk. Marcus was absent; Leontines did eat. They didn't cook much, though.

"You took your time," the Barrani Hawk said. She eased her backside off the newest set of claw marks and shrugged. "They're keeping you busy."

Kaylin nodded. "Tain's not coming?"

"I thought I'd give Tain the afternoon off." As she spoke, she eyed the mark on Kaylin's face. Kaylin cringed. She'd forgotten it was there. Then again, she seldom saw her own face.

"I haven't changed," she muttered.

"You got here on time," Teela pointed out with a grin. Everyone was a comedian.

"I heard there was some trouble at the foundling hall."

Kaylin shrugged. "Did *everyone* hear about it?"

"Pretty much, if they were within a mile of the office." Teela's frown was all surface; her eyes were narrowed. This was her worried expression. Funny how much like a threat it looked.

"Why?"

"Marrin's loud when her kits are threatened."

"She *is* a Leontine."

"Yes. And she couldn't reach you. Marcus was in a bit of a mood—it's probably a good thing she didn't come down to the Halls in person."

"Why?"

"Oh, the usual—two angry Leontines, a lot of hissing, a lot of claw, fang and fur." Teela shrugged. "He did eventually tell her you were at home."

"How eventually?"

"She had to tell him what happened."

Kaylin shut her eyes. "She'd hate that," she said at last.

"She did."

"Marcus?"

"He didn't add much. He's male. He knows when to step aside." She twisted the club in her hands—it was regulation. For a Barrani. Which meant it was almost four feet long, and it was made of something that looked like wood until it hit you. Teela wore her full street uniform, but she didn't bother with armor. For the Barrani, armor was optional. Kaylin wore leather, although it was hidden by the drape of surcoat across which the emblem of the Hawks was embroidered in something that looked like gold. Given the office budget, it was probably something else. She never asked.

"Where are we going?"

"Barker's."

"Why?" Barker was a short, stout, weasel of merchant. He made oil seem clean.

"You haven't been paying attention, have you? We've got four and a half weeks until full High Festival in Elantra."

Kaylin rolled her eyes. "And Barker's selling counterfeit licenses again?"

"He's human," Teela said, with a shrug.

"Hey, I resent that!"

The Barrani woman laughed. "You would. No, we have no proof that he's attempting to sell counterfeit licenses. Yes, he probably is. He tries some variation on this stupid scheme every year."

"He must have gotten lucky once."

"Probably. Either that or he's *incredibly* optimistic."

"He's Barker," Kaylin said, shrugging. She paused, and slowed down.

"What?" Teela asked, turning and striding back.

"Why have you been assigned Festival duty?"

Teela shrugged. "On report for hangover?"

"Hah. If that was a problem, Iron Jaw would have arranged for a permanent state of Festival in the city. You're senior. You've managed to avoid this for what—the past five years? You *hate* Festival duty."

"It's not Festival yet," the Barrani replied. And then she reached out and smacked the back of Kaylin's head. "Don't be so observant."

"You asked to be assigned."

"Do I look like a masochist?"

"Only when you're drinking with Tain." Kaylin found her stride again. "Are you worried about me?"

"I have no idea how humans manage to survive in the Empire. It must be the fact that they breed like rabbits," Teela replied. "You are *all* so direct, you're like walking targets."

"It's part of our charm."

"It is. Which means I've probably spent too much time in human company. I'm hardly fit for Court."

"Good thing you're not part of it, then."

Teela laughed. "You've never been to Barrani High Festival haunts, have you?"

"No."

"Good."

"Teela—the mark doesn't change me."

"Not yet," Teela said quietly. "But it *can*. It gives him power over you. It's—it's as close as a human can come to giving their true name. Names have power."

Kaylin almost told Teela, then. That she had the fieflord's

name. She wanted to know if that evened the scales any—but she couldn't bring herself to ask. Wasn't certain why.

"If you're not strong enough—and very, very few humans are—the Barrani Lord who marked you can use you in a number of ways. He can see through your eyes, he can hear through your ears. But it's…more than that."

"Thanks. That's enough." But it wasn't. "Could you do this?"

"Mark you?"

"Mark anyone."

"You really are too observant. And you have a big mouth." Teela shrugged. "I've never tried." Which was as close to admitting a lack of power as a Barrani of any stripe could get; they had their arrogance to tend to, after all. "Ownership, among the Barrani, means something different. Don't forget it."

With the mark on her face, Kaylin thought that unlikely.

Teela came to a full stop outside of a very large, very functional three-storey building. It was ornate to the point of being ugly, in Kaylin's opinion, given that gargoyles and carvings seemed to populate any stone surface that threatened to be smooth. Gold, magically protected against mythical thieves who might spend hours trying to pick it off—as if—was also used in abundance, in particular across the surface of the huge plaques that proudly proclaimed the establishment's name, and the conditions under which the lowly might petition for membership.

Kaylin disliked the Merchant Consortium on principle. Merchants lived the daylight hours on the other side of the heavily guarded doors, and just in case incoming visitors were a threat, they put magical glass wickets between themselves and the mundane world. They also layered paperwork in piles so thick it was a miracle there was any floor at all in sight.

But the floors, as they always did, gleamed.

The Merchant Consortium had its own guards, and they fancied themselves a shade worthier than the guards of any save the high nobles. Which the Hawks demonstrably weren't. They therefore sneered as they stepped—slightly—out of the way to let the Hawks through. If they were superior, they weren't stupid.

Kaylin doubted the superiority, though. When she was younger, she'd hated the guards for their smugness; now they were just another part of the Consortium, and at that, temperamentally suited to the job. They were paid a lot—but then again, if you were guarding something that didn't deserve or command loyalty, you probably had to be.

The merchant wickets took up the largest part of the first floor, but there were doors—guarded as well—that led to offices and the upper gallery. The merchants had their own dining hall, of course, and their own cooks; they hired their own mages. They were like a little fiefdom of their own.

But in a fashion, they answered to the Lords of Law; they answered to the Emperor. And they paid—as they often bemoaned, and at length, their *taxes*. Which in theory paid *her* salary. She tried to remember this as she headed across the floor.

Teela caught her shoulder, and Kaylin stopped walking.

Stopped moving pretty much instantly. The Barrani seldom shouted a warning; the lack of subtlety was often beneath them. But when they touched you, when they gave you any signal at all, you paid attention.

"What?" Kaylin whispered. Only a Barrani would have picked the sound out of the din in the hall.

"I think we'll come back later," Teela replied. Her lips were inches away from Kaylin's left ear.

"What's wrong?"

"Nothing. Just turn around—now—and head back out the door. Beside me."

Kaylin frowned. But she'd known Teela for all of her life with the Hawks, and she obeyed instinctively.

They made it halfway across the floor when she heard the voice that she *knew* Teela had been trying to avoid. It was a lovely, deep voice, something far too perfect to be human, and it spoke in perfect Barrani. High Barrani.

"Oh, come, Anteela. Will you not even stop a moment to offer or accept the greetings of your kin?"

Teela swore. In Elantran. Her hand tightened on her club, but her face slid into that remote perfection that Kaylin always found so disturbing. The Barrani Hawk straightened her shoulders, pulling herself up to her full height before she turned. The fact that she interposed herself between Kaylin and this newcomer was not lost on Kaylin; Kaylin was absolutely still.

Or as still as one could be, in comparison with a watchful Barrani.

"Lord Evarrim," Teela said, in carefully modulated High

Barrani. Kaylin could see her back, and only her back—but her posture was *perfect*. "I tender my services at this time to the Lords of Law, and my time is not my own."

"The Lords of Law are mortal," Lord Evarrim replied, his voice drawing closer. He must be important, Kaylin thought, because all around her, the din of idle chatter and heated barter had begun to die out. "But even mortals are not without an understanding of our graces. It has been many years, cousin. I did not think to see you here when I set out this morn."

"Nor I," Teela replied. "And had I, I would have been certain to garner permission to remain. But you understand the weight of a freely given pledge, Lord Evarrim."

"Indeed I do, and I have always marveled at your ability to offer it so carelessly to those who cannot possibly prize it fully." Kaylin could hear his steps now. "But come...there has been no battle within the Consortium walls, and no idle theft. Surely your business here cannot be so vital that you would offer offense to kin?"

Teela was silent, assessing his words.

At least that's what Kaylin thought she was doing, until the club moved. It moved swiftly; Teela offered no warning at all. But it moved to bar his way.

He came into view then, moving carefully, his face as neutral as Teela's certainly was. Kaylin saw him, and she almost lost her voice: he looked like Nightshade.

No, she thought, don't be an idiot. They *all* look the same to a human. But they didn't, anymore. Tain, Teela, the other Barrani, had slowly become familiar enough that she could tell them apart. In the Hawks, they made an effort—an effort she truly appreciated at times like this—to help their comrades differentiate them.

But this Barrani—he was high caste. Kaylin was certain of it. Not the castelord; that would have caused groveling bows and utter obedience in even Teela. But he was important enough. His hair was long, dark and fine; it fell past his shoulders. His forehead was adorned by a slender, platinum tiara, and in its center, a ruby was caught, as if in sunlight. He wore red robes, with emerald edges, and boots of a similar color; his skin was pale and completely without blemish.

And his eyes were blue, bright, perfect, when she met them.

But his brows rose as he stared at her, and his expression shifted slightly—he was surprised. Shocked, even.

"What is this, Anteela?" He asked, sparing no glance to Teela. His eyes were upon Kaylin, and she felt trapped by them.

"She is a Hawk," Teela replied quietly, the club not wavering an inch, "in the service of Lord Grammayre." She might have spared herself the words, for all the attention he paid them.

"You," he said, his voice cold and distant, his words dropping from the most formal of Barrani to the more common variant. She doubted he would ever lower himself to speak a merely *mortal* tongue. And didn't doubt for an instant that he knew them all. "What do you bear?"

And Kaylin understood, then. She said nothing.

"Lord Evarrim," Teela began.

But the Lord was not interested in Teela. He stepped forward, and stopped when his robes touched the side of the club. "Do not," he told Teela, "threaten me."

"I have offered no threat," she replied evenly.

"Stand aside."

"I have my duty."

"And I, mine." He reached out, then, his hand moving as quickly as Teela's club had, and touched Kaylin's cheek. Or tried to.

Light flashed, like magefire, beneath the tall ceilings of the Merchant Consortium.

CHAPTER 10

Lord Evarrim did not so much as cry out, but Kaylin could see the blisters that marred his perfect, slender hand. He withdrew that hand slowly, as if fire and its consequence meant nothing to him. Thus it was with the Barrani; weakness was something to be abjured. Death was easier.

She shook herself; she was *thinking* in High Barrani, and that usually gave her a headache that was only equalled by too much time in bars with Tain and Teela. Who thankfully almost never spoke Barrani, never mind its Court variant. She wondered why. No, amend that. She'd wonder why when it was safer.

She had thought she'd had the whole of Lord Evarrim's attention before; she'd been wrong. Just how wrong was evident when he drew as close as Teela would allow, his eyes now bright, sharp, hard as the edge of cut sapphire. Sometimes beauty could be prized and appreciated; sometimes it could be coveted. And sometimes it could only be feared.

But Kaylin Neya was a *Hawk*. She held her ground.

Her cheek didn't even feel warm.

"Who are you?" he asked, the cadence of the Court dropping from the words as if they were a mask. What was left was simple death.

"Private Kaylin Neya, of the Hawks, under the command of Lord Grammayre, Lord of Hawks." She chose formality behind which to hide, but hedged her bets; she answered in Barrani. That the words had the advantage of being true was just a bonus.

"I am pleased to make your acquaintance," he said softly. It was Barrani-speak. She wondered if he was armed. "And is that all you are called?"

"It is."

"I...see. The mark you bear, child, is of interest to me."

So much for polite and Barrani. She slid into Elantran, and held that position. "One of the things I'm *not* called is a child."

"By your reckoning, no." His smile was slight. Sort of like the edge of a razor was slight. "Forgive my choice of words."

Oh, she'd stepped into dangerous territory. Barker would be a welcome sight, about now—but the man was a stone coward, and there was no way he'd chance the floor this close to a Barrani Lord. Not when magic had just made an explosive statement.

Teela gave her a warning glance, and with a lot of effort, she swallowed her pride and forced herself to speak Barrani again. "There is nothing to forgive, Lord Evarrim."

"I am pleased to hear you say so. Has your companion seen fit to discuss the significance of the mark you bear with you?"

Her companion?

"He means me," Teela said, speaking the first Elantran she'd uttered since Lord Evarrim had approached.

If Lord Evarrim understood her, it didn't show.

Kaylin stopped herself from shrugging, but it was a near thing. "It's a mark," she said, trying to keep her voice as flat as a Barrani's, and failing utterly. "It was given to me to...aid in our investigations in the fief of Nightshade. Anyone who serves him there won't hinder me. And no one who serves him will harm me."

"Is that what she told you?"

She loathed high caste Barrani, and briefly toyed with the idea of telling him to ask Teela if he wanted to know what Teela had said. "No. That's what Nightshade told me."

"I see." He seemed to draw closer, but it was a trick of the light; the hard, solid line of Teela's favored beat weapon hadn't moved an inch. "The last, at least, is truth—no one who serves the outcaste will harm you. But it is not proof against those who do *not* serve him."

She did shrug, then. "I am capable of taking care of myself."

"We shall see if that statement is true. It is almost certain to be tested." He turned to Teela. "What was his purpose in marking her?"

"I was not there, Lord Evarrim. I did not see the mark given."

"Ah, that was careless of me. Of course not. Has he formally acknowledged her?"

Teela said, quietly, "He is outcaste." As if that was an answer.

"He is, but he has always been…what he is. And he has chosen to publicly claim an *Erenne*. Not even the castelord has done so in centuries."

"It's against the law," Kaylin said, half-hopefully. It was what she'd been told, after all.

Lord Evarrim's eyes darkened; they were almost a midnight blue. She'd never seen that before.

"Is she a fool?"

"She *is* mortal."

"She is. But I sense that she is more. Must be more. Were she so limited, the mark would have consumed her when I touched it." His gaze returned to Kaylin. "Have you consummated your relationship?"

Her brows rose. "Our *what?*"

"Human, indeed." His smile was cool. "The caste do not speak with the outcaste. It is our law. You, however, are not beholden to our laws or customs. Tell Nightshade that Lord Evarrim reminds him that what he has not fully claimed, he cannot hope to hold long, if the interest of the castelord is involved."

On a cold day in Hell, Kaylin thought. She'd gone past the not-liking-where-this-was-going part of the discussion and into the force-herself-not-to-speak-and-make-it-worse part.

"The castelord will be most interested in your observations, Anteela. We will speak again, you and I. The High Festival comes, and it is time, at last, that you took your place at Court."

Kaylin glanced at Teela, surprised. Teela had always disavowed the Barrani High Courts, and Kaylin had just assumed it was because she wasn't part of them. Seven years, she'd known the Hawk. Barrani really *were* good at keeping secrets.

"And you, Private Kaylin Neya. Perhaps we will see you there as well. It has been many years since a mortal attended our High Festival celebrations, and perhaps it would be…amusing." He stepped back, then, and lifted his arm, exposing his palm. Across its flawless mound was a tattoo. A black tower.

He was an Arcanist.

"Marcus is going to have a fit," Kaylin said, when the Merchant Consortium was a hundred yards behind their quickly retreating backs. "He sent us to talk to Barker. We didn't."

Teela, silent up until that point, and utterly graceful in the stiff, regal way of her kind, stopped walking. She closed her eyes, took a deep—and obvious—breath, and then shook her head. Hair cascaded down her shoulders as Kaylin watched.

"Do you have any idea who he was?" the Barrani Hawk demanded of Kaylin, when her shoulders had receded into their more familiar height, and her language, into Elantran.

"Lord Evarrim?"

"Very funny, Kaylin."

"If it is, you're not laughing much."

"Short of walking into the audience hall of the Barrani castelord, we couldn't have announced your presence in a worse way."

"We didn't exactly announce—"

She turned and pointed at Kaylin's cheek—but she was careful not to touch it.

"Oh. Right. Sorry."

"What in the hells was Evarrim doing at the Consortium?"

"Trading. I hear that even the Barrani high caste will lower themselves to do that from time to time. First time I've seen it, though."

"I've told you before, you're entirely too trusting."

"Uh, Teela—there *isn't* anything else to do at the Merchant Consortium, unless you're a merchant. And I can't think of a high caste Barrani who wouldn't have both his legs chopped off first."

"Can you think of any high caste Barrani at all?"

Kaylin shrugged. "There was Lord Navalos. You know, the Barrani who was involved in that magical—"

"Thank you."

"Oh. Rhetorical, right?"

"Good guess."

"Does the fact that he's an Arcanist make it worse?"

"Oddly enough, no. It doesn't make it any better, but it doesn't make it worse." Teela's eyes narrowed. "What exactly have you been told about the Arcanists?"

"They're mages. Sort of. But more arrogant, more secretive and a lot less friendly." Kaylin's knowledge of magic stretched as far as the Hawks. And the Hawks and the Arcanists didn't have what could be called a working relationship. Or any relationship, which was good, given that the only other alternative was an investigation involving the Arcanum.

"Spoken like Kaylin," Teela said. "They're an order of mages that is *not* beholden to the Dragon Emperor. They're about as powerful as the Merchant's Spice Guild."

Kaylin whistled. "I don't remember Arcanists trying to destroy the city or assassinate the Emperor, though."

"You're not old enough." She straightened her shoulders. "Marcus will forgive us the lack of Barker. We'll just tell him that we're waiting until close enough to the festival that we can pick up his forgeries and charge him. We made a lot of money off him one year in fines, if I recall correctly."

"Yeah. And we didn't get to keep any of it, either."

"Marcus bought us drinks."

Kaylin snorted. "And I was sick as a dog the next day, and put on report because of it. I lost two days pay. Some reward."

Teela laughed. Kaylin felt her shoulders relax at the sound. Not that Barrani laughter was without its barbs, but at least it was normal.

"Teela?"

"What?"

"What's an *Erenne*?"

"Never mind."

* * *

Teela didn't go directly back to the offices the Hawks occupied, however. Or rather, she didn't go straight to Marcus. Instead, she strode over to a closed door, placed her palm on the plaque in its center and said, "Open the damn door. We need to talk."

It was Tain's door.

"Why's he in the office?"

"He lost at gambling, and he has to fill out our reports."

Great. He hated reports as much as the next Hawk. "Where were you gambling?"

Teela shook her head. "Let me do the talking," she said, as the door swung open.

"You want me to wait outside?"

"No. He's going to know sooner or later." She stuck her head into the office, and reappeared. "On second thought, good idea." She stepped inside and closed the door behind her.

The offices were supposed to be soundproof. So it wasn't a good sign when Kaylin heard a muffled exclamation. She couldn't make out the word, but she didn't really need to; the tone of voice, given that it was a Barrani speaking, said enough.

She tried to stop her shoulders from curving inward as she waited what seemed an hour.

The door opened, slammed into the wall it was theoretically part of, and swung almost shut again. Almost, because Tain was in the frame. He stared at her face, and only at her face. Then he uttered a string of Leontine curses. Leontine was the favored language for office cursing. But coming from the throat of a Barrani, it lost its growl; it sounded too smooth. Too kittenish. Not something she was about to tell Tain.

He turned to look back into the office. "And when exactly were you planning on telling me this?"

"You've got eyes," she heard Teela say, in her lazy drawl. "I figured you'd notice sooner or later."

"Don't just stand there," Tain added, glaring at Kaylin. "Come in. This isn't something we want bandied about the office as gossip."

Good luck, she thought. But given his demeanor, she slid into the office and let him slam the door shut. Which he did.

"Kaylin, when did this happen?"

She shrugged. "A couple of days ago."

He exchanged a glance with Teela; Teela raised a brow.

"The Hawklord sent me into the fiefs. I can't talk about—"

"It's the sacrifices, right?"

"I *can't* talk about it," she continued, through clenched teeth. "Not to anyone, unless the Hawklord is present. I'm bound."

Tain cursed the Hawklord's flight feathers. Kaylin was actually shocked.

"And you *met* Nightshade."

She nodded.

"Why did you—"

"She didn't," Teela said quietly.

"He couldn't mark her without—"

"She's a human, Tain."

He stopped talking for about a minute.

"Has a human borne a mark like this before? I thought you said—" Kaylin looked at Teela, who was notably silent. She hadn't been telling the truth. What a surprise.

"Humans have been marked by Lords before, before the Emperor forbid it," Tain told her coldly. "But not with *that* kind of a mark." He looked at her as if she'd lost half her mind. "It's *his* mark. It's not just an ownership sigil, it's not just a binding mark, it's clearly," he added, with a slight trace of disgust, "not an enslavement. Exactly. Teela—"

"I thought it was safer if she knew less. She has a human temper." She paused, and then added, "And she's never been called to the Barrani High Courts. What were the odds?"

He opened his mouth, and closed it again slowly. "You're probably right." Given that this was as much expression as he ever showed, Kaylin was unsettled. And annoyed.

"If I know more, I can—"

"Can what?" The words were very, very cold. She had a suspicion they would drop below freezing if she mentioned Nightshade, and shut up.

She didn't have a chance to vent, and probably just as well; Teela and Tain were almost as good as human in most ways, but they could hold a long damn grudge, and over the smallest things.

"You met Lord Evarrim?"

"In the Merchant Consortium."

"What the hell was he doing there?"

Kaylin threw Teela a look, and Teela shrugged. "I've had this conversation already," she added. "I don't know why he was there."

"Did he already know about the mark?" Tain had calmed down. Not in the way that normal people did; his calm descended without warning, sort of like a summer storm.

"I would say it wasn't possible," Teela said, choosing her words with care.

"Tiamaris—"

"Tiamaris wouldn't tell him anything." Kaylin was surprised to hear herself saying the words. But she believed them. "Dragon honor," she added. "He's not allowed to discuss things that happen in our Tower outside of our Tower, and Marcus believes he won't."

"And you didn't talk to anyone else about it?"

She shook her head.

"Didn't see any of the Barrani besides Teela?"

"No." She frowned. "Imperial mages were in the examination room yesterday."

Tain's eyes narrowed. "*Which* mages, Kaylin? Think carefully before you answer."

"Callantine."

"And?"

"Three of his cronies. And no, before you ask, I don't know their names."

"Can we dredge it out of Records?"

"Not without setting off eighteen different mage alarms," Teela told him.

"Can we get *permission* to dredge it out of Records?"

"Not on this case," his partner replied quietly. "If Grammayre bound her, he's serious."

"He couldn't bind the mages."

"The mages probably have their own reasons for keeping things quiet," Teela told him. But she didn't disagree.

"Then he *could* have known."

Teela's frown was thoughtful. "He could have known that she was marked, yes. But he wouldn't have known that we were going to the Merchant Consortium. The duty roster's not exactly public knowledge."

"He's an Arcanist."

That term again. "Are they like oracles, but real?" Kaylin asked.

They both looked at her as if she were an idiot. Given that, she decided asking questions couldn't make things any worse. "Tain, what does this mark mean? Why did he ask Teela if I'd been acknowledged?"

"That's not quite what he asked," Teela said quietly.

Kaylin colored slightly. "Yes, but I understood the *other* question."

"What would that be?"

"The one," Teela said, knowing Kaylin wouldn't repeat it, "about consummation."

She had thought Tain couldn't look more annoyed; she was wrong. His expression didn't change, but his color did; he lost most of it. Given how the Barrani tended toward the pale, it was noticeable.

"Don't look at me," Teela told Tain. "I made it clear to

the Hawklord that sending her off with two fledglings was a damn bad idea. Even if one's a former Shadow Wolf, and one's a Dragon."

"It should have been safe enough," Tain replied. "She's *human*. It's not as if she's…" He raised a hand to his brow. "Kaylin, does Lord Nightshade know about your powers?"

She started to say no.

"Kaylin?"

"I—I don't know."

"What do you mean, you don't know? Did you tell him?"

"No!"

"Did you use any of them in his presence?"

"No."

"Then—"

"He saw the marks," she said at last. She hated to mention them; it made her arms itch.

"Don't scratch," Teela told her, batting her hand away.

"But—but I didn't *use* power. It's just…" She couldn't bring herself to mention the seal. "Someone else may have told him. Years ago. He wouldn't have known it was me."

"But he did." Damn Barrani observation, anyway. "This is…"

"Bad?"

"Worse than bad," he said quietly. "But at the moment, Lady willing, it's not *quite* your problem. He's outcaste. It may not mean as much—" He paused, and his eyes narrowed. She hated the color blue. "His name?"

Teela's brows rose when Kaylin failed to answer. And fell

again, dark, thin lines. "His name," she whispered, shaking her head. "No wonder."

"What? What's no wonder?"

Tain looked at her for a moment. "It's the mark," he said at last, "of a consort. And he would not have made *that* mark if he thought he could control you with a lesser one."

While she was gaping, they continued to speak.

Teela turned to Tain. "Lord Evarrim tried to touch the mark. It made quite a light show in the Consortium. I should have guessed, then. But I was trying to make sure our mascot got out alive."

Kaylin bristled slightly. She hadn't been called the company mascot since her fifteenth birthday—at least not since she'd upended the pitcher of beer over Tanner's head.

"You didn't see Evarrim," Teela added, dropping the honorific as if it were garbage. "What Nightshade wants has to be of interest."

"Why is Nightshade outcaste, anyway?"

They both fell utterly silent.

"Go deal with Marcus, Kaylin. Tain and I have a lot to discuss."

"Is this going to happen with *every* Barrani Hawk?"

"Pretty much."

Kaylin borrowed the Leontine phrase that Tain had finished with. But she opened the door and went to find Marcus.

She found Severn instead.

He was standing by one of the open desks—the paperwork pool, as it was affectionately called by anyone who didn't have to spend time doing any—chatting with Caitlin. Kaylin was surprised at how annoying she found this. It made her forget to feel uneasy. Possessiveness did that; it wasn't her best character trait, but she hadn't quite found a way to ditch it.

Caitlin saw her first—but she was certain that Severn was aware of her before Caitlin looked up. "I hope things went well with Marcus the other day, dear. He's been in a bear of a mood."

Kaylin had always found that phrase funny, given it was Marcus. She found it less funny just by its proximity to Severn.

"It was all right," she said.

"Did I tell you that I love your tattoo, by the way? It's not one I would have guessed you'd wear—it's too delicate, for one—but it sort of suits you."

Could the day get any more surreal? "Thanks," she managed. "I thought you'd booked off?" she added, acknowledging Severn indirectly.

He stared at her, as if words were too raw to use.

She'd gotten good at it, over the years.

"I came to speak with Lord Grammayre," he said at last. "But he's in a meeting."

"He wants to see you, though," Caitlin reassured Severn, patting his arm. As if he needed it. "He should be done in half an hour."

Severn thanked her politely.

Kaylin wanted to tell him to can it, but she didn't want

to hurt Caitlin's feelings, or worse yet, worry her. She said nothing.

A lot of nothing.

"You hanging around for a reason?"

It's my damn office? These are my friends? She shrugged instead of speaking. "Don't know. Does this meeting have anything to do with me?"

Severn shrugged. "Maybe."

"Then yes."

His smile was thin, but it was there.

She wanted to talk to him, then. It was a sudden, stupid impulse. She wanted to ask him all of the whys she hadn't stayed to ask him in the fiefs. She wanted to get his word that she would never have any need to ask them again. She was frozen with the sudden need.

And he knew it. He had always known her best.

But he walked away from her, toward the Tower doors. He didn't look back. She didn't have the courage to call him.

The Hawklord did. Or rather, the Hawklord had the authority to call *her*. She was sitting on top of Marcus's desk, chatting with Caitlin about Caitlin's youngest daughter, when the small mirror went off.

"I hate those," she said.

Caitlin grimaced. "Not half as much as I do." Which was probably true. "Lord Grammayre wants to see you," she added.

"Figures. Did he say about what?"

"It wasn't verbal, dear. But at least he's not at the top of the Tower, and that's something. He's in his office," she added.

Kaylin shoved herself off Iron Jaw's desk and went upstairs.

The Hawklord's office, such as it was, was half the size of the open room that Marcus ruled; it was also about a tenth as crowded, and at the moment, aside from the man at the desk just one side of the entrance, it was empty. The outer door, unlike the doors of the heights, was unguarded by even the most perfunctory of magics. It was wide, and it made a lot of noise when it was pushed open—and unlike most of the magically greased monstrosities the Halls of Law boasted, it *did* need to be pushed.

Kaylin didn't bother to knock first.

"Hi, Hanson."

Hanson, a man closer to fifty than forty, looked up from his desk, as if the creaking hadn't actually alerted him to her presence. He smiled, leaning to the right to get a clear view of her; his desk looked like the wreckage of a library. Then again, it usually did. "He's just inside," he told her, placing the flat of one hand on the top of a teetering pile, most of whose spines she couldn't even read. "But he's not alone."

"Is he in a mood?"

"Hard to say. He's just come back from a meeting with the other Lords of Law, if that's any help."

"It is," she said, shoulders sagging, "and it isn't. Thanks anyway."

* * *

"Kaylin," the Hawklord said, when she entered his office. "The last time I summoned you while Severn was in my presence, your behavior was less than appropriate. I trust you won't make the same mistake this time?" He was seated on an Aerian stool; Aerians weren't overly fond of chairbacks, and with good reason. It was one of the subtle ways in which the high caste Barrani could offer offense—they simply used the finest of thrones in which to entertain their winged guests.

Not that she'd ever been present when this had happened, but Clint's years of guard duty on the Hawklord's behalf had left him with hundreds of stories, and he liked to share.

"Private Neya?"

"No, sir."

"Good. Please come in." He had the Hawks' love of paperwork written all over his severe expression, but unlike Marcus, he actually did his. He also attended all meetings that had his name attached to them, and he never swore in front of his superiors. Not, at this point, that he had many.

She entered the room slowly, as if every slat that composed the floor was trapped.

"I have a question to ask you, Kaylin."

Whenever he used her name this often, it was bad. Then again, conversations with the Hawklord recently hadn't exactly been good. She found herself inexplicably missing the good ones; he was not always so severe, and not always so distant, as this case had made him become.

But he knew the value of distance, much as she hated it, and he wasn't above using it.

"Yes, sir?"

"Where is your bracer?"

She froze. Looked guiltily down at her unshackled wrist, and back up at the Hawklord.

"I believe I gave you an *explicit* order. Contrary to popular belief among the rank and file, an order is not a request." He lifted his hand to his brow and closed his eyes, giving every impression of being in possession of an extreme headache. "I am, however, aware that Marrin called, and with some urgency, and for the moment I am content—barely—not to put you on report for insubordination. Where did you leave it?"

She took a deep breath. "At home."

"Whose home?"

And frowned. "Mine, last time I looked. Well, mine and the roaches. And the mice."

The Hawklord turned to Severn, who had been utterly silent the entire time. Silent enough that she could almost forget he was there, given the Hawklord's grim demeanor. "Severn, if you please."

And Severn reached into his satchel and pulled out the bracer. She stared at it. "Where did you—were you in my—"

"No, Kaylin, he was not," the Hawklord replied. "He *claims* you left it with him."

He'd covered for her. Or he'd tried; clearly he wasn't used to the Hawklord yet if he could be that stupid. It would have meant more, but she was stuck on the question of how he'd gotten his hands on the manacle in the first place.

"Severn," the Hawklord said quietly, although he didn't look away from Kaylin, "I do not know how the Lord of the Wolves responds to prevarication. I, however, find it unacceptable in any man who professes to serve *me*. Do I make myself clear?"

Severn said nothing.

"Give Kaylin the bracer," he added.

Severn handed it to her. He was closer than he seemed.

"How did you get it?" she asked him quietly.

"It was at my place."

"But I didn't *wear* it to your place."

"No," the Hawklord said, "you didn't."

They both looked at the man to whom they owed their allegiance.

"I've told you before, Kaylin, that it is an old artifact, and its nature is not *fully* understood."

She hesitated. "How old?" she asked.

"Old," he replied softly. "It was taken in Elantra by the Dragon Emperor at its founding. It is not marked, as so many artifacts of the Old Ones were—but we believe it to be their work. This is *not* to be discussed with *anyone*. Is that clear?"

She nodded.

"There is a reason that it—unlike anything else the quartermaster has seen fit to give you—has never been damaged or lost, in spite of your best attempts to do either."

And waited.

"But in the past, it has always returned to *me*." He looked long at Severn. "It appears, Severn, that you have been chosen its new keeper."

Kaylin touched the gems in sequence as Severn watched. She would have turned her back toward him, but she felt that she owed him this: he had lied, in an attempt to cover for her.

Oh, it was dangerous, to have him here. To have him as one of the Hawks. The past was sharp, and bitter—but the present had an imperative that made all memory shaky.

"It's not just armor." It was Severn's way of asking a question.

She shook her head. "No," she said. "It's not." It snapped open as she finished the sequence.

His brows rose slightly. "It's not hinged."

"Not that we could see, no. But yes, it does open. Don't ask me how." She unbuttoned her sleeve, lifted her arm, and let the folds of cloth fall slowly toward her elbow. As the Hawklord watched, she snapped the bracer shut. The lights did their customary little dance, and then went dark.

"It's supposed to dampen your power," Severn said quietly.

She nodded.

"Why?"

"I don't know. I don't know how it—"

"Why does your power need dampening?"

She hesitated.

"Kaylin—when we were in the fiefs, the *only* thing you could do was heal. And it wasn't exactly life-threatening. What's changed?"

"Everything," she said flatly, the words heavy with meaning. With accusation that she couldn't quite keep out of them.

"It's not necessary that you have that information, Severn," the Hawklord added quietly.

She saw Severn's expression snap shut. His face was almost Barranian as he turned slightly to look at the Hawklord. "What are the criteria for being keeper of this... manacle?"

Kaylin winced. "That's what *I* call it," she said. "It's not what it's generally called."

"It is not," the Hawklord told them both, "generally called anything."

Severn nodded.

"As for your question, you might find a more satisfactory answer if you ask Tiamaris. I myself am now...uncertain." And not pleased about it either, if she was any judge. "Tiamaris is still within the Tower," he added, looking down at the paper on his desk.

"Come on," she said to Severn. "That was a 'get out.'"

"It was a dismissal, Kaylin."

"Yes, sir."

The Dragon was waiting. She'd read that, in one story or another, during the months and years she'd been forced to learn how to read in the two and a half languages she knew.

This one, on the other hand, wasn't forty feet long, and didn't have scales worth killing for. Or, as so often happened, dying for. "The Hawklord sent me," she said, by way of apology for the interruption.

"And Severn?"

"Funny you should ask that. Umm, it sort of involves Severn."

Tiamaris turned away from the mirror, blanking it. Not that he had need to; his body blocked most of its surface from view. "How exactly?"

"Well, it's the—" She lifted her arm. Gold shone there in the light that poured in through the glass dome.

"I see. What of it?"

"Severn found it."

Tiamaris frowned. "Found it?"

"I put it down. He picked it up."

"And?"

"I put it down in my apartment. He picked it up in his. They're not the same," she added.

The frown grew more pronounced. Tiamaris crossed the circle in the center of the tower's floor and held out his hand. "Let me see," he said evenly.

Her hand was already out before the words had died into stillness. Something about his voice demanded obedience—and she'd obeyed. She didn't much like it.

And Tiamaris? She didn't think he'd even noticed. The whole of his attention was focused on the gems that studded the bracer's surface in a straight line. He touched them, pressing them carefully and quickly, his fingers moving fast enough that Kaylin couldn't hope to memorize the pattern.

"Tiamaris, why did the Hawklord send me to ask you about the—the manacle?" Severn spoke in a low voice, his gaze intent; Kaylin realized that he hadn't even blinked as Tiamaris had touched the bracer's gems. She'd bet money—her own—that he could repeat the sequence. He also spoke, damn him, in Barrani.

Then again, it was the only language she'd heard Tiamaris use.

"It's not a manacle," the Dragon replied, his fingers still dancing across the hard surface of gems. They glowed at his touch. He looked up at Severn. "You've known Kaylin for how long?"

"Fifteen years."

"And your relation to her?"

"We were friends."

The dragon's golden eyes were unblinking; the opaque inner lid hadn't closed. He stared at Severn.

Severn stared back.

Tiamaris said, "Records." It was a challenge; Kaylin knew it because she'd seen him manipulate the records without once lifting his voice. Severn either didn't know or didn't care; she couldn't decide which way to bet.

But when Tiamaris stepped to one side to reveal the mirror's surface, it wasn't reflective; it was full of motion. And her first thought, watching it, was *Do I really look that insane?*

The answer, of course, was *only when I'm trying to kill someone.*

She watched herself try to kill Severn. But this time, removed from the anger, she watched Severn *not* try to kill her. She turned to look at his face, but it had shuttered completely back in the Hawklord's office, and it hadn't opened a crack.

"Your point?" he said softly, when the mirror once again clouded, and the Records fell silent.

"You have an odd notion of friendship, even for a human."

Severn shrugged. "The bracer?"

"It's…keyed to Kaylin."

"It dampens her magic."

The dragon raised a brow. It fell after a moment. "It does that, yes," he said slowly. "But that is not all it does."

"What else does it do?"

"It records," he replied. "Not in a way that we can access by mirror; not in a way that can be accessed by any who don't actually touch it, or know the sequences to activate it."

"And the rest?"

"You *are* a Hawk." His inner lids dimmed the gold of his eyes. "It protects her," Tiamaris said at last. "From what, we cannot fully say. It is an old magic. Unique, in Elantra. And it was given to Kaylin because of her—"

"The marks."

"Yes. Although she feels ambivalent about it, she should feel honored. None of us were certain that it would accept her." He didn't say who "us" referred to, and no one wasted breath asking.

"And if it didn't, as you say, accept her?"

Tiamaris did not reply, which, as far as one of the two observers was concerned, was answer enough.

"Why did it go to Severn?" Kaylin asked, wanting to shift the conversation in any other direction.

"That would be the question." Tiamaris offered her an odd smile. "But if I had to guess, I would say that it chose Severn on the basis of its imperative—it protects you, and it feels that that protection is best served, at this time, by Severn."

"Do I get any say in this?"

"None whatsoever. But if it helps at all, Kaylin, neither does the Hawklord."

It didn't.

She looked at Severn.

Severn looked at Tiamaris. "If this…artifact is old, how did you know what it would do?"

The dragon's inner lids rose, opacity in motion. "There are scholars," he said at last.

"There are no markings on it. Nothing that would hint at—"

"I cannot say more, as it concerns the Emperor and his mages," Tiamaris said coolly. "But by the time it was given to Kaylin, there was some strong suspicion about its nature. It was not, I think, intended as a kindness when it was first created. It was meant as a cage."

Severn looked at Kaylin. "But you trusted her enough to give her the keys."

"That much is not known in all circles," the dragon said, warning in the words.

Severn, ignoring the words, met Kaylin's gaze and held it, just as he had held the Dragon's. In the end, it was Kaylin who looked away.

CHAPTER 11

Marcus was less than thrilled by the verbal report Teela gave him when Kaylin's back was turned. No, she thought sourly, be fair; Teela would have given him the same report had Kaylin been standing beside Marcus, frantically gesticulating while *his* back was turned.

"I'll send someone else to talk to Barker," he growled. "In fact," he added, glaring at Kaylin, "I'll send someone else to cover *your* beat until things settle down."

"And that would be when?"

He shrugged. "Ask the Barrani."

Which told her nothing at all. Nothing is what the Barrani would probably say.

Severn, by her side, shrugged. "Go home," he advised her, "or file your own report. Most Wolves don't mind a break from active duty."

"I'm not a Wolf."

"Obviously."

She stared at the bracer on her wrist, and then shrugged. "I don't want your protection," she told him quietly.

He shrugged. "Doesn't seem to matter what you want."

"Never did, did it?"

Utter silence. She turned and walked away, remembering too much. Her dead. The past.

Severn didn't follow this time.

But Teela met her as she left the Halls, and Teela escorted her home. She felt as if she was thirteen again, and she didn't like it.

"What is it with you and Severn anyway?" Teela asked quietly, when she'd reached the door that led to Kaylin's apartment.

"History," Kaylin said.

"No shit."

Kaylin had always privately believed the only reason Teela and Tain—and the rest of the Barrani Hawks—chose to use Elantran was because mortal languages were more colorful. As in, she could swear a lot using them.

"He's from a place I never want to go back to," Kaylin said, relenting a little. "Because I never had a choice about being there at all." She shoved her key into the first lock and twisted it a little too viciously.

"Suit yourself," Teela replied. "But I'd say, if you asked me—"

"I'm *not* asking, Teela. Maybe tomorrow." Maybe never.

Teela shrugged her long, elegant Barrani shrug.

"I got taken off the beat," Kaylin added, as she unlocked the second lock.

"I know. It's better that way. First, you can't stand Barker, and you don't have to talk to him. Second, you *may* get out of Festival squawking. Third, Lord Evarrim is high caste, and if he's not above the law, he's not exactly conversant with its finer details." She was quiet for a minute, almost reflective. "You know that the laws governing the different races are sometimes based on…unusual context."

"I'm not a lawyer."

Teela didn't even chuckle.

"Teela—"

"You really don't want to be involved with Evarrim."

"He can't be worse than Nightshade."

"Worse? No. Better? Hardly."

"He's not outcaste."

"Kaylin, the word outcaste, when applied to humans, means something like 'going to jail if you get caught.' It doesn't mean the same thing for the Barrani. Or the Dragons. No, don't bother. I'm not going to explain the difference. I like my tongue in my mouth. Or in—"

"Spare me."

Teela smiled, but it never reached her eyes. "Get some sleep."

Kaylin tried.

Her stomach started a long conversation halfway through the first hour, and she ate some stale bread and dry cheese just to shut it up. But as she lay beneath the sill of the unshuttered window, she gazed up at the falling night sky, and she counted stars. The bracer on her wrist was heavy and cool, a companion of sorts. It kept her safe, or so the Hawklord said. Still…

It had gone to Severn.

Tiamaris had spoken of protection.

And Kaylin had said *nothing*. It was a betrayal of the dead. The dead she hadn't buried. The dead she hadn't saved. She turned over, grabbing the pillow that had flattened with years of use. It was too late for laundry; too late for shopping.

Just too damn late.

Go away, Severn. Go back to the Wolves. Go back to the Wolf Lord. Stay away from *my* life.

Spoken, silently, over and over again, as if it were a prayer.

She was on time the next morning, but given that Teela was her companion, Clint only snickered when he saw her.

"You look like crap," he said cheerfully.

"Thanks."

"It's the dark circles under your eyes. That and the fact they're barely open. Teela, you should show a little pity."

"I did. I didn't let her see a mirror on the way out."

"You barely let her dress, by the looks of it. Kaylin, you do know your tunic's inside out, right?"

Kaylin hated morning people, especially *in* the morning. She said something rude, and Tanner laughed. "Get it out of your system," he said, as she pushed past them. "Iron Jaw only likes swearing when he does it."

* * *

Marcus, on the other hand, was being harried by Caitlin to finish filing the monthly report that the Lords of Law demanded, so most of the swearing in the office that morning was his by default. You couldn't outswear a pissed off Leontine—for one, the volume made it difficult to do with dignity.

Kaylin slid across the floor to the desk that was, in theory, hers. It wasn't cordoned off by four walls and a door; it hovered at the edge of the paper-pushers, which suited her junior status. She had no idea what she was supposed to be doing, but given Marcus's mood, she didn't ask.

And Marcus didn't provide the answer.

The whole of the day turned around the sudden flare of the inbound mirror. She looked up when it went off—but then again, so did the rest of the office.

"Caitlin, who is it?"

Caitlin frowned. The mirror was on the wall nearest her desk, because she was in theory its custodian. The frown deepened slightly as she glanced around the office. "It's…Marrin."

Kaylin sighed and got up from her desk. "What is it this time?" She asked, fingering her bracer's studs without really thinking about what she was doing.

Marrin flared into view.

Her fur was on end, her eyes were wide, even wild, and her claws were at *full* extension. She said something in Leontine, and she spoke so quickly, Kaylin missed half of it. The unimportant half.

"*What?*" she shouted, as she ran toward the mirror.

Marrin spoke again, and again her angry hiss of a Leontine cry rang out in the office; it was louder.

Marcus looked up. He reached the mirror before Kaylin did, no mean feat given their respective starting distances. But his fur was also on end, and his claws—his claws were also at their full extension.

She'd seen this before, but seldom; he was responding to a female Leontine in distress. She *didn't* want to be the dead person that had caused the distress. Because that's what he was going to be, given Marcus's demeanor, and unpleasantly dead, at that.

She would have let him handle the situation, but she had recognized the only thing in Marrin's Leontine that was urgent: Catti.

"Marcus," she said, just as urgent, her voice as low as she could pitch it, her demeanor submissive. She barely noticed that the various office workers were slowly shoving paperwork into the safest receptacles and edging away from their desks.

He turned, spinning so suddenly, Kaylin was afraid she was about to be disembowelled. But she didn't flee, and she didn't show obvious fear. Not of Marcus. He'd taught her that, and she'd learned quickly.

His fur slowly flattened, and if his claws didn't retract, he spoke to her in Elantran. "Catti is missing," he said.

She swallowed. "Missing?" She turned to the mirror. Marrin was still at the full height of her distress, and her eyes literally glittered with suppressed rage. Given that this *was* suppressed, Kaylin never wanted to see the foundling hall's mother unleash.

"Marrin, I *need* you to speak to me in Elantran. I need you to speak quickly. *What happened?*"

And although Marrin looked no different, her vocal chords struggled with the unnatural sound of human vowels, human consonants. "Dock came, five minutes ago."

"He reported?"

She nodded.

"Catti didn't run." It wasn't a question.

"If she did, she blew out her window—on the second floor—and blasted half her room to cinders first."

"She's not—"

"She wasn't in the room when it happened, no."

"Is there—"

"There's blood," Marrin said, the growl overtaking the syllables. She had to struggle to hold it back. "Not a lot of it. It's hers."

"I'll be right there."

She felt a hand on her shoulder, and she *snarled*. Marcus, however, flexed his claws. She spun to face him, and the claws pressed fabric into her skin.

"Not alone," he told her.

"I have to go now."

"Take someone with you."

"No."

"Kaylin—"

"*No.* This is *mine,* Marcus. It's mine. I need to—" She said something in Leontine. "They *trust me.*" It was the phrase slightly changed, that he had taught her in his attempt to impress upon her the importance of the Hawk's Oath.

And he accepted the whole of its meaning. "Go, then," he said. "But Kaylin, *if* mages are involved, you *call* the Hawks. Understood?"

She nodded.

"Fail," he said, as she bolted for the doors, "and you'll be on report for so long, you'll feel like you're on the other side of the Law."

Amos was waiting for her. He didn't bother to speak; he sent her running up the steps, and he followed her, leaving the gates untended. His hair, white to start with, looked like half of what age had left him had been torn out. His eyes were red; had he been a Leontine, he'd be out in the streets questioning people. Which would essentially be the same as killing them.

"I kept her here," he said, as Kaylin struggled with the front doors. She knew he meant Marrin.

"Good job," she managed to get out, as the doors gave. "I don't envy it." And then she was running.

Marrin wasn't waiting for her in the hall, which was the worst sign possible. Kaylin hesitated for a moment, and then she tore up the stairs, taking them two and three at a time. She was out of breath before she started, and her thighs felt the stretch, but she ignored them.

She had to see the room for herself. Because she knew that's where Marrin was, trying to pick up the scent.

But when she hit the open doors to Catti's room, they

were circled by the foundling hall orphans, and she had to skid to a stop not to crash into them, or through them.

Dock was wild-eyed. "Kaylin!" he cried, as if she were a minor deity.

She caught him by the shoulders. "Tell me what happened," she said. It took both time and effort, and she paid that price.

"I was in my room." She didn't ask him why. He was at an age where he saw a whole lot of his room. "I heard a noise," he told her. "It sounded like—like something breaking. And then I heard Catti scream." He had a candle-stick in his hands, and Kaylin realized that it was meant to be a weapon, his only one. She would have given him a lecture, but there wasn't any point. She couldn't do anything to make him feel worse, and she hadn't the heart to bawl him out for his attempt to go to Catti's rescue.

In the fiefs, they'd used small clubs, when they could find them—and a candlestick was as good a club as any, if markedly more expensive.

"What happened?"

"I ran to her room. The noise was coming from the room—and—and there was fire. Beneath the door. I couldn't open the door—it was stuck." There were no locks on the doors in the foundling hall rooms. Not that Kaylin was aware of.

"I ran to get Marrin," he said. "I ran—"

"You did the right thing," she told him.

"Marrin *broke* the door." He flinched. "But Catti—"

"I'll see the room now, if you'll let me pass."

He looked up at her in surprise, and then he nodded. He shoved another boy to one side and they made room to let her pass. "Marrin's mad," he added softly.

Kaylin could see that for herself, but it took a moment.

She saw the room first. The windows had been shattered; the glass was across the floor. The room was indeed blackened, as if fire had been released in a sudden white-hot burst. The bedding was still smouldering. But it wasn't any of these things that was significant.

On the floor, in a circle that stretched from window to door—it was, after all, a foundling room, and not a large one—were symbols that she half-recognized. Swirling, circular symbols. She blanched.

Marrin stood in the center of the circle.

"Here," she growled, as Kaylin entered the room. "The scent ends here." She spoke in Leontine, and Kaylin didn't ask for anything else.

But she shook her head. If Marrin was raging, Kaylin was something else entirely. She wandered into the room, bending to examine the circle, as she'd been taught. She didn't touch it. But she should have ordered Marrin out of the room; should have ordered her not to touch anything either. Should, in fact, have done as ordered and called the Hawks.

She couldn't. She could barely think. "Not here," she whispered, over and over again. "Not here, too. Not *here*."

Marrin's anger lost its edge as she approached Kaylin.

"Where is Catti?" she said, no accusation in the words. "Kaylin?"

Kaylin shook her head. No; she just shook. Her hands were opening and closing in bunched fists of their own accord; the bracer was warm and tight.

"Not here, too."

The fiefs came back, in force. This small room? It could have been hers. But it wouldn't have been only hers. It would have been a room she shared with Steffi and Jade and Severn.

Oh, the names—she hadn't thought them, couldn't bear to think them—for years. She struggled through it, working as hard as she had *ever* worked. The Tha'alani might as well have been attached, like lamprey, to the thoughts, sucking them out while she struggled against the invasion. They *wouldn't* leave her.

Her dead.

Her failure.

"Kaylin—what—"

And *that* voice. She spun, in a crouch, as Severn entered the doorway.

Severn, here.

Not *here*. Not *here*.

He saw it coming a moment too late, and he went flying out of the door as she launched herself at him, daggers suddenly welded to her palms. She was screaming something, but the words were so raw they might not have existed had she not known what they were, what they *had* to be.

She had never, ever faced him.

She had never made him pay.

And she *would not* let him touch these children, this

retreat, this small protectorate that had given some meaning to her life.

She roared, Leontine in her fury, and the children must have fled, because they were nowhere in sight. She didn't want them to be; she didn't want Severn to see them. To learn their names.

She would kill him first. She *had* to kill him first.

She knew what would follow if she failed.

He was ready for her the second time, although she gave him no opportunity to draw his chain, to arm it; he had his club instead, and it was a poor weapon. She had seen him fight. She had watched him on purpose.

And he had seen her fight, or so he thought. She was about to show him how wrong he was.

She charged, daggers out, and shifted at the last moment, launching herself into the air, her feet coming down against his chest. Clint had taught her that; it was an Aerian maneuver. And if she lacked the plummet that gave it most of its strength, it had its effect; Severn staggered back, down the wide stairs, fighting for balance.

He didn't speak. He didn't try to talk to her. He defended himself.

"Fight!" She roared, years of anger in her voice.

He backed away, and she followed.

Drew blood when they closed.

Drew blood again, as he stumbled back, out the doors.

She saw Amos; she flew past him, as if she had wings. He was pale, his mouth open.

She had to kill Severn. She *had* to. Because it would start again, here, and that would kill her. But it would kill more than her, and she had taken oaths, profound and private, that it would *never* happen again.

The stairs to the foundling hall evaporated beneath her feet; the gates passed her by; she was in motion, and Severn was in motion as well. Wouldn't be, had she had time to remove the bracer.

He'd be dead.

But she didn't have time. She tried only once, and he almost broke her wrist with a quick snap-kick that numbed her hand, causing her to drop one of her two daggers.

She didn't even notice the pain; she spun on a foot, roundhouse feinting before she caught him full in the shoulder; the dagger left her hand as he jerked back.

She had to stop him. She was screaming now, incoherent with the need. But he understood it, and he was the only one who had to.

He had to go on the offensive now, and she felt a vicious satisfaction as he swung the club. He feinted low, and missed her jaw as she vaulted back. It was an acrobat's jump. Teela had taught her that because Teela always thought it important to know how to get out of the way at the right time.

She heard shouting, saw people fleeing as Severn tossed the club aside and pulled his sword. The dagger was still embedded in his shoulder, and blood was seeping from beneath its pommel. He was slower than he should have been, but it was a flesh wound, and he'd probably taken worse.

She leaped up, then. The sword passed beneath her as

she kicked. He fell to the ground, and she passed just above him, and outside of the awkward arc of his sword. He cut her tunic. She laughed.

"You're slow!" she shouted.

"And you talk too much," he said. He was beside her, bleeding, his sword swinging at the level of her shoulders. She bent back; it flew above her, inches from her bent torso. She could see it catch light and shadow, and she continued her backward bend, catching the cobbled stone in her hands and flipping away from him, end over end. She stopped at a safe distance, and then she reversed the motion; she'd left a dagger behind in the street, but she had others. She started to run, tensed and leaped up, twisting in the air, her feet already pointed and aimed.

But the leap carried her high.

High indeed, too high. She felt hands under her armpits, and heard a familiar voice in her ear. "Don't try it," Clint said, all affection and all amusement stripped from the depths of his voice. "Or I'll be forced to drop you."

He carried her skyward, making more of the threat with each passing second.

And she saw, as her eyes cleared, as the cold wind gave her face the most gentle of bracing slaps, that the sky was full of Aerians, and the ground, littered with their shadows.

There were no other people beneath her; no one save Severn.

"You don't understand!" she shouted at Clint. "You don't understand."

"No," he said, his grip tightening. "I don't. None of us

do. But if you can't make the Hawklord understand, he'll give what's left of you to the Tha'alani. What the hell were you *thinking*?"

She couldn't tell him.

She couldn't tell any of the Aerian Hawks who had come in force to the foundling halls. She could see one of them fly through the wreckage of Catti's window, and she knew, then, who had called them in on her. Marrin.

But if Marrin understood, she would have been helping.

Shaking, Kaylin fell silent, the whole of the fight deserting her.

"Consider yourself on report," Clint said, his voice shifting slowly into the voice she knew. He let her go, and she fell a dozen feet before he caught her again, this time in a more familiar position.

"Deal with your history, Hawk," he said, in as severely parental a voice as she'd ever heard him use. "Don't let it destroy you."

"I thought the Hawklord was going to do that," she said, turning her face into his chest.

"Probably." He would have shaken her; she could tell by the tone of his familiar voice. But it was hard to do while in flight. "Kaylin—"

"He'll kill them all," she said bitterly.

"Tell it to the Hawklord." And he took her to the Halls of Law, skipping the entrance that he no longer guarded, passing beyond the maze of halls, the inner sanctums, the offices with their gaping occupants. He flew instead to the dome of the Hawklord's Tower, and she saw that it was open, like a giant Dragon eye whose inner membrane has finally fallen.

But he didn't set her down until he landed, and he landed in the circle at the heart of the Tower's center.

The man known formally as the Lord of the Hawks was waiting, and his eyes were as dark a blue as any Aerian eyes she had ever seen.

"Kaylin Neya," he said coldly, "I am very disappointed in you."

Clint put her down in the circle, and then leaped up, taking to air. They exchanged words in Aerian, but the wind took them; Kaylin's Aerian wasn't quite good enough—it had too much of the streets in it. She couldn't understand what passed between them.

But she heard the word "magic" and "mage," and that was enough. The Hawks would be all over the foundling halls in a matter of minutes. And Severn? He'd probably be first among them.

She couldn't step out of the circle. She didn't even try; the wards on the floor had come, sizzling, to life, and she knew what they meant. The very first time she had entered this Tower, they had done the same. She'd been stupider then. She'd tried. Her forearms bore the diffuse scar of that single attempt.

But the circle was not a dome; she could stand.

And she couldn't. Her arms and legs were shaking too much. She bowed her head. It was almost a gesture of respect; it was arguably a gesture of penitence.

"Not enough," a familiar, cold voice said. She might have been thirteen again. She certainly felt it. "Kaylin Neya, you have publicly embarrassed the Hawks. You tried to kill an officer of the Lords of Law in full view of half the city."

That was an exaggeration. She didn't point it out.

"Worse, you started that attempt in the *foundling halls*. While the foundling halls and their funding has always been a source of resentment for you, they are not universally ignored by the high castes—killing people in front of orphaned children crosses several lines, all of them in the wrong direction. And you did both of these while wearing the uniform of the Hawks."

"Not the beat uniform."

Clearly, he wasn't making the distinction. "I have been patient," he told her, in a tone that clearly indicated his patience was at an end. "You will explain yourself, now. If the explanation is somehow satisfactory, you *might* be given the privilege of continuing to wear the mark of the Hawk. I will certainly be called upon to explain your actions to the Lords of Law, and Kaylin—it is *not* a comfortable position to be in. It will weaken the Hawks."

She nodded. It was all she could do. Honesty—*I didn't even think of the Hawks*—was so far from the best policy she tried to put as much distance between herself and it as she could. Found it wasn't as hard as she wanted to believe it had become.

"I have been tolerant. Your first attempt to greet Severn was recorded, but it was not…acted upon. It was, I admit, a weakness, and I regret it now.

"You have been given leeway. You've been allowed the privacy of your past. What the Tha'alani took from you on the occasion of our first meeting was *only* what was relevant *to* that meeting. You've lost the right to that past now. It will be either public knowledge, or *my* knowledge, or you will never leave this Tower."

He didn't add "alive," but he had never been one to state the obvious, unless pressed. Which she didn't.

"You have served the Hawks well in your years here. I am therefore reluctant to call in the Tha'alani."

She blanched.

"You have earned that much. But not more. What were you doing?"

She glanced at the mirror, and then away; she knew that he knew exactly what she had been doing. "I was trying to save them," she said bitterly.

It was not the answer he had been expecting; she saw that by the slight rise of his wings. They were already half-extended; it was as threatening a posture as an Aerian of his rank adopted. And his wings? They were pale and beautiful. He was pale. Beautiful in a way that was entirely different from the earthy ebony, the friendly affection, that was Clint.

"You were trying to save *who*, Kaylin?"

"The children," she said bitterly. "My children. The foundlings."

"By killing Severn in front of the population of Old Nestor?"

"By killing Severn," she agreed.

"Tell me."

"I don't know where to start."

"At the beginning," he said, his wings flexing.

"I don't know where it began."

"When did you first meet Severn?"

"I don't know." She closed her eyes. It was easier, that way. Because nothing else about this conversation was going to be easy. If conversation was the right word; she suspected interrogation was more appropriate. "When I was five."

"Five?"

"Five and something. I don't remember the exact day." But she remembered what had happened. Maybe opening her eyes was wiser; it gave her the anchor of the present, even if the present held the promise of very little future. "He was ten years old," she added. "At least we thought he was. I *know* when I was born. He doesn't. Know when he was."

"I understood that. Continue."

"I was five, and something."

"So your memories, without extraction, will not be reliable."

She swallowed. "These ones are."

"Oh?"

"I almost tripped over a feral."

His wings folded slowly; his arms crossed his chest. But his expression was marred by no new lines.

"I was out on my own. My mother was sick. She was dying. I didn't know it then, but she knew. She...had asked me to go outside. To play. Told me when to come home." She hesitated.

"You weren't punctual as a child, either?"

"Not really." As a child, she hadn't known what the word meant. Not that her mother had used it. "I knew it was getting dark, though. And I—" She shook her head. "I was playing with sticks and rings."

"In the streets of the fief?"

She nodded quietly.

"The feral?"

"Only one," she whispered. "And I would have died, there. I froze. But Severn was there, somehow, at the lip of the alley that led to our place. And he had food. He threw it—really threw it—and it must have hurt like hell; it was meat. What passes for meat, in the fiefs. The feral hesitated, and this strange, tall boy grabbed my hand and dragged me all the way down the alley." She could feel his hand in hers; could feel how large it was, how warm, and how steady. She had thought, then, that he hadn't been afraid. "He knew my name. I asked him his. He told me. He wanted to speak to my mother, and that was the only time his hand tightened, the only time I was uncomfortable. But I wasn't afraid of him.

"I don't know what they talked about, Severn and my mother. He made me wait in the kitchen. But when he came to get me, his anger was gone. I think—now—she must have told him she was dying.

"Severn lived close to us. He liked my mother. I don't remember why. But he started to run errands for her, and he would take me with him. He would go shopping for her when she wasn't well enough to shop. Happened a lot, but

I still didn't understand. I was selfish," she told him. "He was older, he knew so much, he was willing to talk to me, and I was just a kid," Kaylin added, remembering. These memories weren't so harsh. They would—without the rest—be almost happy. She couldn't afford that. "But when she got…paler, he stopped taking me with him so much. I was afraid I'd annoyed him, but he was always happy to see me. I didn't understand why I couldn't go with him, not then. I do now. He probably stole more than he bought. He usually came by with too much. She hated that," she added softly, seeing her mother with adult eyes, instead of the un-questioning allegiance of a child's. Seeing, as well, other truths. "But because of me, she didn't question him too harshly.

"I adored him," she added, bitterly. "I looked up to him. He was *ten*. And he understood death. He knew that my mother wasn't going to last the winter. He never told me. He just helped us, and waited."

"What happened, then?"

"When she died, I had no place to go. I couldn't afford the room she had rented. I couldn't afford to bury her—not like you bury people in the outer city. The dead don't care—that's what we say in the fiefs. The living can still starve. My mother told me that a lot in her last few weeks.

"She just didn't wake up one morning. I didn't know a doctor. But I knew—I knew she wouldn't wake up. I tried," she added, remembering the slack, cold skin of her mother's face. "I tried really hard to wake her."

"Did you find anyone to help you?"

"You really don't understand the fiefs," she told him, but without heat. She had become resigned to this over the years; it was something that was so natural it was like the weather. "I just…stayed there. With her. Until Severn came. He always came," she added, "in the winter. Every day. I don't know why. I didn't know what to do, and Severn did; he told me to walk, with him, and I went. We never came back. I was still five. He was still ten.

"He taught me how to live like he lived. He taught me how to look harmless and pathetic, and he took me to the edge of the fief. I used to beg along Old Nestor, just across the Ablayne. I used to look at the Outer city people, with their warm coats, and their new boots, and their money. I used to hate them," she added, dispassionately. "But I'd take their money anyway. He taught me how to take it when they weren't in the mood to give, too. We worked as a team.

"He didn't like it," she added. "No more than my mother had. But it was the fiefs…stealing was better than starving." She brought her hands together, as if she were praying. It was the only way she could stop them from shaking. "I'm not proud of it," she told him, staring at her fingers. "But I'm not ashamed of it either. It made me who I am."

The hard part was coming now. She almost couldn't say it. And the Hawklord knew. His silence was cool, but when she finally glanced up at his face, it was different. He was waiting, now. Would wait.

"When I was eight," she said, her throat tightening, "I still adored Severn. He was thirteen by then. I thought he was a man. I thought he could do anything. It was winter—everything desperate happened in the winter."

"Winter in the fiefs is harsh," the Hawklord said quietly. Not, of course, to tell her anything she didn't know. But the reminder that he understood was steadying.

"We were looking for food," she continued, staring at the subtle gleam of the circle's edge. "Or money. I had outgrown my clothing, mostly. We had a room to live in, but not much else. But on that day, we found Steffi instead."

"Steffi?"

The walls of her throat closed. She bowed her head, trying to force her eyes to stay open. To stay dry. Her hands were moving in an open and close rhythm that spoke of heartbeat. "She was a year younger than I was." Every word was surrendered slowly; each was anchored in emotion, and if she wasn't careful, emotion would come with them until it was all that was left.

And what emotion?

She hit the floor hard with the flat of her palm. "She was really pretty. Not like me. Her hair was very pale, and it was long; her eyes were blue. Her skin was blue, too—but that was the cold. When she warmed up she was like a little, perfect doll. I thought of her that way," she added, dispassionate, as if bitterness could be buried, or amputated. "As if she were mine. Because I found her in the snow.

"Severn didn't want to keep her. But I did. I begged him. I pleaded with him. I even threatened him," she added, a thin wail that sounded like laughter adorning the words. "I told him I wouldn't go home without her.

"And in the end, he was angry with me. But he let me keep her. He brought her back to our place."

She bowed her head.

"Kaylin. *Kaylin.*"

She looked up to meet his eyes, and saw instead that his wings were extended. Had the circle not been shining, she would have leaped from its confines to run straight into his arms. She had done that before. More than once. But she'd been younger, then. "You wanted to know," she whispered.

He said nothing.

"He was good with her, in the end. He treated her almost the same way he treated me. Steffi was…a bit high-strung. She was afraid of Severn for weeks. But she trusted *me*. And in the end, because I trusted Severn, she let her guard down. He would go foraging for us. She wasn't well," she added, as if it mattered. "For three weeks, she coughed all the time, and she was hot. I thought she would die.

"I wish she had, now."

CHAPTER 12

Lord Grammayre gestured, and the circle guttered inches from Kaylin's splayed fingertips. "Kaylin," he said quietly, offering her, wordless, the freedom he had threatened to take from her.

But she was there, now, in a place she had promised herself she would never revisit. There was no way out. There never had been. "No," she told him. "I chose this."

Lord Grammayre was not, had never been, friendly. Not jolly, not affectionate. Had he, she would never have learned to trust him. He was not, however, without kindness—had he been, she would also have been unable to trust. "I think I understand," he told her quietly. "It is not an excuse for your behavior, but I—"

"No," she said, more firmly.

His wings didn't shift. But his arms fell to his side.

"Are you recording this?"

"The mirror records."

"Good." She took a harsh breath. "Because I *never* want to have to say it again. Steffi was the third member of our family. Of what I thought of as our family. I told you she was cute—and she knew it—and that she was only a year younger than I was, something Severn *always* felt the need to remind me. But I thought of her as a baby sister, as the sister I had always wanted, and had never been lucky enough to have. She called me big sister, too. She wore my clothing when my back was turned. She ate my favorite foods. Sometimes I wanted to strangle her. But I never wanted her to leave. I loved her," she added softly, as if the words had never been said before.

"She was with us for almost a year before we found Jade."

"Jade?"

"I didn't name her."

"She was another girl?"

"Another girl," Kaylin nodded. "As different from Steffi as a girl could be. Jade was two years younger than I was, maybe two and a half. And she was scarred, from forehead to cheek. She was darker than Steffi, and her hair was a mess of curls, no matter *what* we tried to do with it. She didn't talk much."

"You found her in the winter?"

"In the winter," Kaylin nodded. "And at night."

His brow rose.

"The ferals were out, then. We were watching them from

the window in the room; the table was against the wall, and we could stand on it, press our faces against the glass. There was glass there—I think Severn stole it. I never asked.

"But I saw her, wandering in the streets below our window. She was furtive, like she was afraid of something—I know the walk. And there was reason; there was a man on her tail. With a knife. I called Severn—Steffi and I liked to look out, but it wasn't something he did often—and he joined us, just watching. Then he sighed and looked at me, and I must have—I must have looked at him in the way I did when I thought he could do *anything*.

"So he rolled his eyes and told Steffi to stay indoors. He told her not to answer the door, if anyone came, and told her to hide, and then sneak out, if anyone got in. Me, he handed a large club. We went out after that strange, small girl. We should have died. It was night, and we knew better. But..." She shrugged, almost helpless. "The ferals were out."

"And this...Jade?"

"She was their meal. Or would have been, if Severn hadn't found her in time. I remember it. He was standing in the moonlight, in the open street. He had a long knife, and a club. He was—I think—afraid, but none of it showed. I didn't think he was afraid, at the time—my impression is all hindsight. He shouted at Jade, and Jade almost ran, but I was there too, and I was quieter. I told her to stay between Severn and me; I told her not to scream, not near the ferals. I can still smell their breath."

"But?"

"He cut the leader. He kicked. The leader drew back, and had no one else been out, it would have gone badly. But someone else *was* out—the man who had been hunting Jade. They ate that someone else instead.

"Jade wouldn't talk about it. We didn't press her. We caught her by the arms and we ran. The man was stupid. Maybe he was drunk. He screamed a lot, and it drew the rest of the feral pack. We made it back home to Steffi. She was just waiting for us, all white. She'd been watching from the window. She'd ignored every word Severn had told her. I would have, too.

"This time, when I asked Severn if we could keep this child until we found someplace else for her, he didn't argue. He said, 'only until we can find her a place.' But he knew what that meant. Steffi knew it, too. She took Jade by the hand, and asked her name. Jade answered." She shuddered. "I was nine," she told the Hawklord. "I had a stick. I called it a club. Severn had two, and a dagger. He'd been trying to teach me how to use them, and I'd been trying real hard not to learn.

"But after that night, I learned. Jade was bleeding from the shoulder to the wrist, but she was…she wasn't screaming. She was almost smiling. Steffi asked her who the man was—Steffi wasn't even with us, but she'd seen it all from the small window—and Severn told Steffi to shut up. He never asked Jade. And because he didn't, I didn't.

"But Jade never hated the ferals the way the rest of us did."

"Jade was seven?"

"Seven and a bit. Her mother was dead, she said. Severn didn't believe her."

"He said as much?"

"No. But I knew Severn. He let her lie. Steffi was sort of happy to have Jade at home, because it meant that Steffi wasn't the baby anymore." In spite of herself, Kaylin smiled at that memory. "Jade was furious being called a baby, but hers was a sullen fury, and it was hard to hate Steffi for long.

"We made it through that winter. Steffi and Jade slept together. I slept with them sometimes, and sometimes with Severn. It wasn't—" she reddened. "We were kids," she said at last. "He never touched me. Not like that. But it was crowded, we couldn't take a step without hitting each other. Severn talked about finding us a bigger place. Things were going well, sort of. Steffi was a better thief than I was. Everyone liked her instantly. It's easy to steal things from people when you've already charmed their socks off.

"But we didn't find a bigger place. None of us could read. None of us could write. Severn was fit for work, but not the type of work we wanted. It would have kept him away for too long, and it would have meant working for the fieflord. That's not a job with a long life expectancy in the wrong areas of the fief. Too many people with too much to prove, and the fieflord isn't without his challengers."

The Hawklord nodded quietly.

Kaylin continued to talk; she couldn't have stopped had he ordered it—not without magical bindings to enforce the order. And she spoke nonsense, because now that she'd finally started, she wanted to tell him something that would make her children as real to him as they had been to her.

"Jade could sing. She used to sing for us, sometimes. We'd join in, but really, it was her voice that was special. She knew a lot of songs. I don't know from where. She was never as friendly with strangers as Steffi was—she was always too self-conscious about her scars. But she trusted us, in the end, and her song was one of the few things she thought she could offer us, because I certainly couldn't. I loved the sound of her voice." Kaylin's stopped for a moment. "I can't do this."

Lord Grammayre waited. He had always known when to wait.

"You don't want me as a Hawk," she told him quietly.

"It's not the first time you've said that."

"It's as true now as it was then."

"What did I tell you, then?"

"That you made your own decisions," she replied, wooden.

"That hasn't changed."

"Don't you regret it?" she asked him softly, staring at her hands.

He didn't answer.

"When I was ten," she said, when she couldn't stand the silence for another second, "everything changed." She lifted her arms. Beneath the buttoned shirt, the tattoos were alive; she could almost feel them crawling across her skin. "It was winter again. Sometimes I think the whole of my life in the fiefs was lived in winter.

"The marks appeared. We were listening to Jade sing. I was waiting to tell a story. I told them stories, and they were patient enough to pretend they were interested. Severn was leaning against the wall by the door. We didn't have bolts," she added, "and in the winter, people could get pretty desperate."

"But Steffi suddenly pointed at my arms. I think she may have shrieked. Steffi wasn't a screamer. Didn't matter— Severn was off the wall as if it were suddenly on fire. He was across the room by the time I figured out what Steffi was pointing at.

"He held my wrist as the marks began to write themselves across my skin. He watched them. We all did. It was scary," she added softly, remembering. The way they had huddled together in a room that was warm because it was small and it held so many of them. The way Jade had come to her side, had put a skeletal arm around her, as if the marks were scars. As if it made them more alike.

"But it stopped at the elbow. I didn't notice the marks on my legs for another day, and I didn't tell the kids. I told Severn. I was old enough by then to be a little self-conscious, but not much. He was Severn.

"We waited. We waited for three days for something else to happen. Steffi thought it was the plague. Severn told her she was an idiot. Oh, there were a lot of tears, then.

"But it was two weeks before we got what seemed like an answer, and it was a grim, terrible answer."

"The first of the victims," the Hawklord said.

She nodded. "A boy," she added quietly. "My age. Benito. I knew him. He was the son of one of the two grocers that would actually let us near his stall. The grocer had seven children, and he knew what hunger did to the young. He knew that we would steal anything we could when his back was turned—and he did. Turn his back, I mean. He turned it just often enough. We paid him whenever we could," she added. "And it was from his brother that we heard the news.

"His brother was really shaken. He talked about the marks. He talked about the death. He told us to be careful. He didn't know about the marks on my arms," she added, "because Severn made me cover them up. Even then.

"Jade was terrified for me. Severn said nothing. But after that day, he never let me out of sight. We waited, just waited. And a month later—another death. That was Tina," she added bitterly. "She lived at the farthest reach of the fief. Before my mother died, we would sometimes play together.

"The deaths happened once a month. And every time one happened, we were frightened and relieved. Frightened, because a madmn was running free in the fief—not even the fieflord was able to catch him, and by that time, the fieflord had been informed. I hadn't met him, then. I never wanted to. But we were relieved because it wasn't me.

"Your power?"

"I was getting to that." But she wasn't; she was cataloguing every death. Giving it a name. And she would have done so until the hours had dwindled into night, and from night, into morning. He stopped her. "It was maybe six months after the marks appeared. A small boy had been thrown off the back of a cart, and he was lying in the road. He was bleeding. I thought he would die. I made it to him first, and I picked him up—Severn told me not to but I couldn't help myself.

"He was shaking, and he was cold—he was barely awake. But I felt the cold, in him, and I felt other things, broken things, things that were somehow *wrong*. I couldn't tell you what they were—not then. But I could mend them. I knew it.

"And I did. I helped the boy to his feet as his father got control of the cart and came running back. I didn't tell his father what I'd done. Severn was holding my arm, and he shook his head. I always listened to Severn," she added bitterly. "The man took his son, thanked his god, and thanked us for trying to help. He tossed us a couple of coins. We didn't have a lot of pride. We took 'em and thanked him.

"But when we got home, Severn questioned me, and I answered him. He told me—he made me promise—that I would never tell anyone else. I asked him why—I was so naive then—and he told me that if I did, someone would come to take me away, and he'd never see me again. I hated that thought, and when he explained that if I could heal a stranger, I could heal someone powerful, I understood why he had made me promise, and I never spoke of it. But I did use the gift, and he let me.

"I used to think that I could find the children. The ones who were killed. I used to daydream that I could find them *in time*, and I could heal them all. I thought they were all like me, somehow—that they were healers, and that someone wanted to kill them all, rather than leave their gift in the fiefs."

"You were wrong."

She nodded quietly. "But the marks changed. I didn't notice it, then. Severn must have. I can see this now, but then? It was just Severn, and he had always been my protector. He didn't tell us when a new death had occurred, if we weren't together when he found out about it. He didn't tell us where. Sometimes we didn't find out at all. I had no idea that the deaths were happening only in Nightshade. I think Severn must have." She shook her head. "I got better at clubs and daggers. I got better at defending myself. Severn was larger, and faster, than any of us, but he pushed me, and I improved. I didn't want to teach Steffi and Jade. I wanted to protect them. I guess I wanted them to *be* children for as long as they could. It's not long, in the fiefs. They were mine," she added, "and I was Severn's.

"But when almost three years had passed, and the deaths hadn't stopped, Severn left us alone one night. He made me stand in his spot by the door, and he promised he'd be back—but he wouldn't tell me where he was going."

She closed her eyes.

"He came back almost a day later. The waiting was bad," she added. "We knew the fiefs. We knew it was night. We knew he might never come back at all. But I wasn't five anymore, and I had Steffi and Jade to think about. We could steal enough between the three of us to keep the room if we had to, and we could scrounge enough food so we wouldn't starve. We'd never done it without Severn, and if I hadn't had the two girls, I'm not sure I wouldn't have panicked. But I *did* have them.

"When he came back, I was happy—for about five minutes. But everything about him was wrong. He was—he was hurt, somehow. He was frightened. I'd never seen him frightened before, not like that." She closed her eyes. "I was thirteen," she said softly. "I trusted him."

"He watched me like a—like a Hawk. He asked questions, about the marks on my arms. They were just a part of me, by that point. No one had killed me yet. I answered him. That was all."

"But three days before the long night, he sent me out foraging for food. He gave me money, so I wouldn't have to steal single—he never trusted that. I went shopping. I suspected nothing. *Nothing*.

"And when I came home to the room..." She was shaking now, eyes closed. She couldn't find words. And she couldn't leave them alone. Struggling, she said, "The blood." It was soft, a whisper of sound. "The room was covered in blood. It was everywhere. And Severn was there, part of it, covered in it. His hands were still wet."

Her eyes were dry. "Steffi and Jade were dead. I don't know if they fought him. I don't know if he slit their throats in their sleep, or if—" her throat closed.

"I saw him. I *saw* him, and I knew. I screamed. I screamed at him. I—"

"You ran."

"I had to run," she said quietly, the intensity of the words a quality more than a sound. "I knew I couldn't kill him. I knew I had to."

"Where did you go?"

"It doesn't matter. I went. I never looked back. I didn't even bury them—" her arms were locked, rigid, beneath her breasts; her body was weighted toward ground. She could taste blood in her mouth; could feel it in her cheeks. Her eyes were dry. She wanted them to be dry.

"He killed them," she said softly. "I saw it. He didn't even try to deny it."

"Why, Kaylin? Why did he kill them?"

"I don't know!"

The Hawklord said nothing for a long moment, and then he crossed the stone floor and knelt in front of her. He didn't touch her. He didn't try.

"I came here, in the end," she continued.

"Six months after you left."

She nodded. "Please don't ask me where I was."

"I won't. I can guess, and it's not relevant. Records, end," he added, as if it were an afterthought.

"Do you understand?" she cried. She looked up, forcing her eyes to open. "Do you understand why I had to try? He came to the *foundling halls*. He came to *my children*. I can't let him—ever—" Her fist slammed stone, slammed gold inlay. "They were *my children*," she shouted. "They were mine. And they trusted us both. I failed them. He killed them."

His arms enfolded her, then; she might have shoved them away, but his wings followed, covering her and hiding her from the sight of the sky.

* * *

He did not let her leave the Tower for another hour, and it was spent in silence, in the peculiar warmth of the harbor his wings granted the wingless.

"I'm on report?" she asked him, when he at last withdrew.

He met her eyes, his the pale gray of Aerian thought. She didn't know what color hers were; human eyes didn't change to reflect what was captured beneath the closed lines of composed expression. Not that hers was composed. But he gave her the time to do it.

"I cannot judge you," he said quietly. "And if I were given only your words as guide, I could do little else but judge Severn. I make no excuse for him, Kaylin."

"There *isn't* one!"

"No," the Hawklord agreed gravely. "None. But at times, from the remove of age, if there is nothing that excuses, there is often something that explains."

"You won't see him killed."

"Not by you." The Hawklord's face was shuttered. "You've killed before," he added, before she could take offense at his protectiveness, his desire to shelter her. And she would have—but only as a blind. A screen.

"I—"

"But except for that one time, it was always in self-defense. It was always in a clean fight."

She flinched, thinking that he would speak of the time she had lost control of her power—and had discovered what that loss could mean.

But instead, he said, "You've always been fond of children." He knew. He dismissed it. "This is different. The fight is internal, and it is not a fight that anyone but you can finish."

She grimaced. "And not by killing Severn."

"Do you honestly think that would bring you peace or closure?"

She nodded sharply.

"Then you are still young."

"Can he just get away with this?"

"The fiefs are not the demesnes of the Lords of Law," the Hawklord replied.

"That's only practice. In theory—"

"In practice," he continued quietly, "the fiefdoms have been ceded to their fieflords. Even if I desired his death, in this, I would have to defer to the Wolf Lord."

"Then talk to him—"

"And I will remind you that Severn was a Shadow Wolf. The Wolf Lord knows what he is capable of, or he would never have inducted Severn into the ranks of the Shadows. Not all crimes are forgiven when one chooses to serve the Lords of Law—but those crimes committed in foreign territories are not considered crimes for the purpose of our evaluations." He took a breath, held it and then settled his wings. "Severn will be here within the quarter hour, Kaylin."

"Here? Why?"

"You are not the only person to face suspension. Although the truth in this case is somewhat stretched, it does take two to fight."

"Then ask him why," she said bitterly. "Ask him. I hope you get an answer."

"And you will not ask him?"

She shook her head. "Not in this lifetime."

"Why?"

"Because I don't care."

His eyes narrowed. He didn't argue, however. "You are on report," he told her quietly. "See Marcus. If you can convince the Sergeant that your actions in no way materially harmed the Hawks, he may even agree to partial pay while your case is reviewed."

Marcus was waiting for her. Severn was not. She had no idea how he intended to climb the Tower stairs, but he intended to do it unseen. As her hands were already gripping the pommels of her dagger in a movement as old as her memory, this was a decidedly Good Thing.

But Marcus growled when he saw her, and she noticed that not even Caitlin had remained in the office. She wondered idly if every department that served the other Lords emptied this way, but doubted it; no one else had a Leontine at its center.

His claws were extended. "Private," he said curtly, the growl extending the *r* in the first syllable.

"Sergeant."

"The Hawklord took his time. I see he was considerate enough to leave something for me."

She shrunk. She was tired; bone weary. She'd been cut, although she didn't remember when; when the fury was on her, pain didn't make much of an impression unless it was damaging enough to slow her down.

She expected questions; he had the right to ask them. She expected anger, and had already lifted her throat in reply. But his eyes were small and warm.

Without preamble, he said, "You're on report."

She nodded.

"You might never make it *off* report."

And nodded again. She'd already lived through the loss of one family, and if she desperately wanted to avoid losing the second, she knew that she'd made her choice in the foundling halls.

"If you weren't already skeletal, I'd suspend you without pay."

Which meant he wasn't going to. She should have been grateful—but she saw that he didn't expect it. He turned his golden shoulders away, and she saw that the fur on his back, the fur that peaked as it followed his spine to the base of his skull, was on end. It wasn't just his claws.

"Marcus—"

"Private?"

She'd earned that. It stung anyway.

"What am I supposed to do?"

"Keep out of sight of the Barrani high caste," he replied evenly. "Severn is also on report, and you are forbidden any contact." He paused, and she saw that the extended claws were held in a state of tension; it was warning enough that she braced for his next words.

"We don't have time for this. We don't have the luxury

to endure and ignore your little tantrums. Catti is still missing. Marrin is…enraged. And terrified. We *needed* you on this case," he added, spitting as the last word drew to a hiss of a close. "And we don't have you.

"If we find her body, I'll mirror you."

She closed her eyes, then. Begging never worked, with Leon-tines. She came close anyway.

"I've put Teela and Tain on the case," he added. "And I believe that Severn will also join them."

"But—but you said he's on report—"

"My initial information suggests that he wasn't trying to kill you. If he acted in his own defense, he will likely be on duty by the time his interview is over." He watched her, daring her to argue.

And she had enough of a grip that she didn't.

"The Dragon is doing research now. There is one question that he asked of me, and I will pass it on. If you choose to answer, your answer will be funnelled through me."

"I'll answer," she said quietly.

"He wants to know if you healed this child recently."

"Didn't he ask Marrin?"

"He asked," Marcus replied, with a mirthless smile. "But she was reluctant to reply, even given the seriousness of her situation." He hesitated, and then added, "You understand what this means?"

She was dumb.

"She considers you her kitling, Kaylin. You are as much her kin as Catti, and she will not surrender the one for the other. No *Pridelea* would. She did however tell him he could ask you. If she considers you kin, she also considers you adult. Which, given the ferocity of your attack, is a high compliment."

"But she—she called the Hawks—"

"No," he said quietly. "The Hawklord sent them, and at speed. She would have let you rampage."

"Yes," Kaylin replied, lifting her chin without hesitation. And then, to be clear, she added, "I healed Catti."

"Was there anything unusual about this healing?"

Kaylin swallowed. The bracer on her wrist was heavy and cold. She nodded after a moment.

"How?"

"She was dying," Kaylin whispered. "Not—not of illness, not of the plague, not of infection. She was—she had—fallen. She…hurt her back."

"It was broken?"

Kaylin nodded.

Marcus clicked his massive jaws. "And you healed her?"

"I healed her. I *had* to heal her," she added. "And it was… hard. It was harder than any healing I've ever done."

"Was it different?"

"Yes. I had to—" She stopped speaking.

"Yes?"

Intuition informed her next question. "Tiamaris thinks they took her *because* of the healing."

"He is not inclined to share anything he hoards. He's a Dragon. And in this case, his hoard is information. Had I asked, he wouldn't have answered, and he didn't volunteer the reply." His smile shifted; it was still all teeth, and there was an edge to it that made Kaylin think about taking a few steps back. Like, say, thirty of them, as fast as she possibly could. "But he is not as clever as he thinks he is."

"That would probably be impossible."

"Either that, or knowing you're on report, he wishes you to have the information, and he expects that you'll be able to wheedle it out of me, as he is forbidden to offer it in any other way."

"Can I?"

The Leontine's growl grew louder. "You press your luck," he said. "I lied. He didn't ask a single question, he asked a number of questions. They all lead to the one that you asked me, and Dragon scent is strong. If I had to bet—and that is a phrase I'll thank you never to attribute to *me*—then yes, I would say he believes that it is entirely because of the healing that Catti was taken."

"How would they know?"

"I don't know. And at the moment, your source of information is limited."

She nodded and began to walk to the doors, but he stopped her, claws on her left shoulder. "Had you not been wearing the bracer, you may well have destroyed half the foundling hall. Don't remove it."

"I won't."

"Where are you going, Kaylin?"

"To do civvy things," she replied, keeping the sweet sarcasm out of the words.

"Remember that you are forbidden Severn's company, if you need the reminder."

She almost swore. Almost. Instead she said, "Severn won't have the answers I want."

"You can't find the girl on your own. Don't try."

"Marcus, don't ask that."

"It wasn't a request. I want you as a Hawk, Kaylin—but if you remain here, it *is* as a Hawk." He paused. "Lord Grammayre must have been satisfied with whatever it was you offered him. He's my superior, and I'll accept that."

Which would be a change. A huge change. It was getting harder not to talk.

"And because he is satisfied, he will face down the Lords of Law, and short of Imperial writ ordering otherwise, he will see you returned to your place in my pride. When you do," he added, and this time, he took care to keep the depth of his growl out of his carefully modulated words, "you need to resolve your past with Severn."

"I could have done that this afternoon."

His growl returned in force. "In front of Marrin's kits?"

"No," she said, and she hung her head. "I'll never do that again."

She held the posture for as long as she could. It took effort, because she already had a destination in mind, and she'd spent a lot of daylight hours in the company of the Hawklord; she couldn't afford to lose more of them.

But she stripped her surcoat off before she left the office, and handed it to Marcus. He bunched it into a ball and threw it over his shoulder. Since this was what she usually did with it at home, there wasn't a lot to complain about.

* * *

She went home, and found a mirror message waiting for her. The color of its triband pulse was neutral; she couldn't tell who'd sent it, and she almost failed to look. But she didn't.

"Kaylin Neya," a familiar voice said. She scanned the mirror's surface, but there was no accompanying image. *I guess Tiamaris didn't trust Marcus to be as perceptive as he is,* she thought wryly.

"Marcus will not tell you this because he doesn't fully apprehend your danger. But you *are* in danger, if you did what I think you did. I cannot remain here. The mirror I use is not a mirror that can be used—or recorded—by the Lords of Law.

"The child, Catti, is a gift to our enemy. If we do not find her, you will be in more danger than you have been in with any other death. Do *not* remove the bracer. Whatever else you choose to do on your leave, do not do that."

"Okay," she told him, although she knew he wouldn't hear it; the mirror wasn't open to conversation at this point. She sat on her bed, pulled off her boots, wrinkled her nose. And then she reached for the dress she had taken from the castle of Nightshade, and with a shudder that had nothing to do with sweat, she peeled off the rest of her Hawk uniform, and she pulled the dress over her head. The softness of cool silk was its own shock.

Daggers didn't exactly accessorize the dress well, but she put them on anyway. Then she cleared the mirror and looked at her face. Flinched. There was a livid bruise beneath her right eye, and her lip was swollen. She couldn't help but notice these, even though she was searching for something else.

The mark of Nightshade lay against her cheek, and if her face had been bruised in the fight, nothing had disturbed the intricate scar.

She pulled her hair back, shoved it unceremoniously out of her face, and went hunting through the sediment of laundry for something that looked like a cloak. She found one—well, it had a hood—and donned it. The two, dress and cape, looked incongruous.

It pained her to acknowledge that Marcus and the Hawk-lord were right, but she did—there were no witnesses. She needed to somehow lay her past to rest, and killing Severn was out of the question.

But she wasn't thirteen anymore. She knew where Severn had gone when he had disappeared that night. She knew where he *must* have gone. And she knew that something he had learned from the fieflord had sent him back to murder their family—their children.

Nightshade was of the Barrani high caste, outcaste or no. Teela had implied as much, although she'd've cut out her tongue before she said it. And Kaylin knew—from years spent tagging along after the twins—that the Barrani were famous liars. The more powerful and significant they were, the more deadly the lies.

He had lied to Severn.

He *must* have lied to Severn. And Severn had been eighteen.

If Kaylin couldn't vent her fury on Severn, she could always find another target. A deadly target. She straightened her shoulders and looked in the mirror again, this time seeing past the mask of bruises that time would dismiss.

No thirteen-year-old, here. No child.

But her fists clenched.

No Catti, either.

She gathered some small amount of coin, her daggers, and no sign at all that she had ever been a Hawk.

The mirror flashed.

She answered it, because she had to walk past it anyway, on her way to the door.

Marrin's face filled her view. "Kaylin," she said. The growl was gone. Not even Marrin could sustain the killing frenzy for more than hours at a time, although Kaylin was certain that when her strength returned, the rage would return as well. How could it not? Catti was still missing.

"Marrin," Kaylin said quietly.

"Have the Hawks—"

Kaylin didn't bother to tell the Leontine she had been suspended. "No."

The breath that escaped cut Kaylin in a way that rage couldn't.

"I'm going to look for her," Kaylin continued softly. "And I swear to you, Marrin, that *this* time, I'll find her before—before—"

"Good."

The mirror's light guttered. Kaylin leaned her head against the silvered glass, knowing it would have to be cleaned. And then she made her way to the door. She took care to lock both locks behind her; she wasn't certain when she was going to be back, and if this wasn't exactly the fiefs, she still knew how to be cautious.

When it suited her.

CHAPTER 13

The keep of Castle Nightshade stood apart from the fief it dominated in the distance, like a justifiably arrogant aristocrat—the ones Kaylin was never sent to interview when the Lords of Law were reluctantly summoned. Before its walls, cages dangled from their respective chains; they were empty. If someone had offended the fieflord recently, he—or she—was already dead, and their bodies no longer on display.

People met her gaze, and one or two, made bold by numbers, even held it. But the mark that was almost an embarrassment in the Outer city afforded her legitimacy in the fief; no one dared to raise a hand against her. It would have been useful, when she'd been younger.

But she had the idea it would have been expensive as well. How expensive had yet to be determined, and she was here to do just that. Inasmuch as any Barrani could be, Teela was her friend—but the fact that Teela wasn't telling her everything was a certainty. Then again, if she wasn't actively lying, it meant a lot—the Barrani probably lied more easily than they breathed.

The gates that had swallowed her whole on her first visit were waiting; they were lowered. Kaylin wondered if they had ever been raised, but she didn't ask; instead, she approached them.

As she did, Barrani slid out of the shadows; there seemed to be small guardhouses built to either side of the gate, although she hadn't seen them on her first visit. Then, she had been almost panicked, and she had let confusion be her guide.

She was done with confusion, for now.

One of the two Barrani guards met her gaze and held it. He was perfect, his face unscarred, his weapons—two swords, which only the Barrani in the fiefs seemed to favor—silent in their sheaths.

She didn't bow as she approached them. Nor did she hold out her hands, palms up, to show she was unarmed—which wouldn't have meant much if they were at all competent. She simply walked.

To her surprise, the guards bowed. If there was reluctance or stiffness in the motion, she thought it was due to lack of familiarity with the gesture. As guards of a fieflord, that high caste social nicety couldn't be called on often.

Certainly not by a motherless foundling or the orphans she'd built into a brief, necessary family.

"Kaylin Neya," one of the two men said. They were both men. The Barrani women seemed to stay on the right side of the law, at least as far as the fiefs were concerned. They probably had the choice.

She said, without preamble, and in possibly the best Barrani she'd ever forced herself to use, "I've come to see Lord Nightshade."

"He has been waiting for you," the guard replied, standing to one side. Like a mirror image, the other guard did the same.

She had the strong feeling she could have spoken in the *worst* Barrani she'd tried in years, and his answer would have been the same. Which was sort of a pity, because it left nothing standing between her and the lowered portcullis.

"It never goes up, does it?" she asked, without much hope.

Neither guard deigned to answer, and she squared her shoulders, lowered her chin, and walked forward.

This time, she didn't pass out.

The room that she entered was the room that she'd last seen, but this time she had a chance to notice it; it didn't contain an angry Hawk and an equally angry Dragon. In fact, to her surprise, it also contained no Barrani guards. If the fieflord could feel threatened in his keep, it wasn't by someone like her. She wasn't sure whether or not to feel insulted. Settled on an emphatic not.

The ceilings were lower than the ceilings of the almost mythic Long Halls—at a paltry twelve feet—and there were gilded candelabras on gleaming, tall tables that rested against the stone walls to either side of the entrance. The floor was a pale shade of smoky green, and her boots sounded a lot louder as the heels slapped against it.

All in all, the room resembled the front hall of many a fine manor—or at least, of the few she'd been given permission to enter in her duties as a Hawk. Her background in the fiefs left her an unsuitable candidate for the "delicate negotiations" demanded of the Hawks when dealing with personages of importance and influence—mostly money. Money didn't frighten her, and it didn't impress her; unfortunately, on the wrong days, it started resentment simmering. And her face was rather expressive.

In fact the only intimidating thing in this room was the fieflord himself. Unfortunately, he was the only thing that needed to be intimidating. He wore a lot of black. And a smile.

"Kaylin," he said, lifting a hand and inclining his head in a perfect nod.

"Lord Nightshade."

"I offered you the hospitality of my home when last you visited, but you were not in a position to truly appreciate it. Let me offer it again."

"I'm still not in a position to appreciate it," she replied. She lifted her hands, pulling the hood of her heavy cape back from her face.

He was at her side before she could see him *move*. At her side, and towering over her, although his expression was smooth and cool, flavored with the condescension that all of the Barrani showed the lesser races. Which, of course, meant every race that wasn't either Barrani or Dragon. At the moment, she wasn't entirely certain about the Dragon part, either.

He removed the cloak from her shoulders, and she deliberately avoided noticing the flicker of disgust it evoked. The cloak's fabric was a rough weave, which suited her, and it wasn't a particularly attractive color—because those cost money, and she didn't spend all that much time looking at herself anyway.

He took the cloak carefully and set it to one side. Which side, she wasn't certain, because he didn't leave it hanging on the wall.

"I want that back when I leave," she told him, in as firm a voice as she could muster.

"Are you so certain?"

"Completely certain. It's useful when—"

"Ah, I was unclear. I meant, that you will be leaving."

Her hand fell to a dagger. She had to struggle not to say something offensive, because she wanted information. That, and her life.

"If you must draw weapon, draw it here. It is the only room in the castle in which it is unquestionably safe to do so." He spoke without apparent concern, but she had enough experience with Barrani not to trust his nonchalance. She let her hand drop away.

"I didn't come here to fight," she told him.

His smile was a thin edge of perfect lip. "No?"

"No. I came here to talk."

"Human speech is often colorful, and often augmented by pathetic attempts at violence."

"I also didn't come here to be insulted."

To her surprise, he laughed, and she had to admit that even Clint's voice didn't have the depth of velvet Nightshade's did. "No indeed, and you remind me of what I seldom offer in the fief—my hospitality. It is deplorably lacking. Come, Kaylin Neya." He offered her an arm.

She stared at it. Hoped that she didn't *look* like she was staring at a dead snake. A minute passed, and then another; it redefined the word awkward for Kaylin. She realized, as she continued to stare, that he *had* forever, and he was going to hold his arm out in front of her like a challenge for about that long. So she took it, sliding her fingers across the crook of his elbow; it was a reach.

He led her past the...vestibule, or whatever it was called when it was this damn big, and toward a familiar wall. She flinched, and he stopped walking. "Do you not wish to enter the Long Halls?" he asked her softly.

"Does it matter?" was her bitter answer.

"For today, Kaylin, as you are my guest, I will tender you an answer seldom heard in my keep. Yes, your will in this matters, as you so quaintly put it." Before she could speak, he lifted a hand, and brought it an inch away from her slightly open mouth. "Before you make that choice, however, you must understand that beyond that wall, beyond the sentinels who wait, there is a certainty of safety. Not in those halls, nor beyond them, can anything attack me within the keep without first paying a price."

Something about his wording was odd. "The same price," she asked, with just a shade less bitterness, "that you usually extract from people you're pissed—" she switched abruptly into Barrani; it had fewer colloquial phrases she could spit herself on "—from people who've displeased you?"

His brow rose, dark and perfect arch. "No. It is not I who extracts the price, but the keep itself. It can be circumvented. I have done it. But it is not without cost, and few are those who live who could survive the paying."

She met his gaze, held it, wondered at the way his eyes shaded from the deep green of emerald to something that added blue to its brilliance—like a hint of depth or danger. "Yes," she said, remembering that breathing was important. "It matters. I don't want to go back through those doors." And her eyes traced the symbols above it.

"Very well. You are not yet known. It is unlikely that we will be interrupted. Let me lead you instead to those rooms in which I entertain those who wish to offer favor, or to receive it."

Although his legs were longer than hers, and his step just a shade lighter, his stride was cut by a third to match her hesitant steps. She *really* wanted to feel less clumsy, less graceless, and less… fat. Something about the Barrani just made her self-conscious. Well, except for the drunk ones.

They certainly made her lose focus. She drew breath, shifted the weight of her shoulders down her back, and lifted her chin, hoarding words. Well, truthfully, biting them back. Not yet, not yet—and timing was often everything.

He led her not to the room in which she'd first awakened; her memory wasn't much to write home about, but she was never going to forget that marbled floor, that high ceiling and that particular sense of exposure. Instead, they entered through a wide set of double doors—ones that were gilded wood, and adorned by what seemed to be growing vines. It was better, she told herself, than walking through runed stone. But not by much.

Her arms felt naked, and her skin was rumpling itself into that rough state known quaintly as goose bumps. Why, she didn't know; she'd seen her share of geese in her life, and they didn't seem to have them. Not, at least, while they were alive and feathered.

"I entertain infrequently," he told her, as the doors rolled wide. "Please forgive the state of this chamber. It has seen little use since I first took up residence within the castle."

She said nothing, arms stiff by her sides, as if by keeping them still she could avoid drawing attention to them. It took a bit of will; she often fidgeted, and rarely sat—or stood—at attention, even when Marcus was in the worst of his moods.

This was her excuse for missing her first glimpse of the two thrones that stood at the far end of the long chamber, up three steps and on a flat that seemed a little too reflective. Neither would have suited an Aerian—they were both high-backed, with long, confining arms to either side. Never mind that the backs looked like cushioned velvet, and the chairs themselves were adorned with inlay and gilt; they weren't the chairs she was accustomed to seeing in the Halls of Law.

And in the fiefs, they hadn't owned chairs of any type; certainly not these ones. It was *so* hard to remember why she'd thought it was a good idea to come here.

The chairs weren't exactly close to the doors. In between them and the aforementioned doors were tall pillars, each carved in the likeness of a man, or one of the mortal races, in various states of dress. Or undress. Barrani craftsmen—artists, she amended—must have labored here a long time, to capture so exactly the fey and wild expressions of the various people; the snap and flow of moving hair, the exposed chins of heads thrown back in laughter or song, the folds of stone that hinted at a fabric that was much lighter, and much softer.

They made her uncomfortable, although everything about the castle did.

His laughter was low and quiet. She didn't much like it, and didn't join in—which, given he was Barrani, wasn't as socially awkward as it might have been. Her fingers stayed on his arm until he reached the first of the chairs; there he lowered the arm, and she at last—thankfully—let go.

"I have taken the liberty," he told her quietly, "of preparing a…chair?…for your use. You may sit in it safely. No one else can." He stood at her side—a little too close—and waited, the command in the posture like a loud order shouted in her ear.

"Why?" she asked him, stalling.

He said nothing, but his lips folded in frown. She *really*

hated Barrani frowns. Feeling as if she were thirteen again, and new to the Hawks, she forced herself down into the seat, her arms folded tightly across her chest.

It was enough of a surrender; he took the chair to her left, with a great deal more grace than she had. "This is, as I said, a room seldom used. Even had I come here with a consort, it is unlikely that we would have entertained many guests. The outcaste may not be convenient and they are not easily killed—but shunned? We are indeed that, by our kin."

He spoke without evident bitterness, as if he were discussing the weather. And Kaylin was familiar enough with the Barrani that she had to stop herself from either flinching or asking him, again, why he was outcaste.

"However, the halls need not be empty while you are resident here." He lifted arms from the rests, and as he did, light sprang up against the walls to either side; left or right. She couldn't fix the hall's orientation; here, with no windows to grace its interior, east, west, north or south had no meaning. Things were either before the thrones, behind them, or to either side.

And to either side, to her great astonishment, the pillars seemed to capture the light he'd summoned, swallowing it until they glowed with it.

She was about to say something, but speech deserted her when the statues stepped off of their bases and began to move, roving freely along the length of the halls. They were not all human, although she did not recognize this immediately by sight; she realized it by the sounds of their voices.

They were musical voices, full of the promise of youth, and not yet the blight of it; their sunny ignorance was so infectious she almost wanted to call it innocence. There, a man with dark, long hair, had pulled a closely clasped lute from his chest, and his fingers stretched sideways along its taut strings, evoking a music that his speech—which was lovely and utterly foreign—did not convey.

Beyond his back, a woman with hair of fine gold—much finer than that which adorned Kaylin's chair—came to his side, her fingers trailing the curve of his shoulder. He wore nothing from the waist up, which wasn't a distraction; she wore nothing from the waist up, which was. Kaylin had been in her share of fights in the line of duty, but even had she avoided them by hunching behind a much-hated desk, her skin would never have been so fine and so perfect as this girl's.

Beyond them both, she caught the orange-gold glint of Leontine fur; a solitary Leontine, but one who did not seem on the prowl. He wore nothing at all. But he moved to speak with someone who made her skin crawl: Tha'alani. The only thing that was missing was an Aerian.

As if he could hear the thought, Nightshade said, "They fly high, and are difficult to call to hand. None of the Barrani hunt birds."

Music filled the hall, and the dance of these bodies as they began to intermingle also filled it in a different fashion. Light flared, multihued and almost impossible to trace to its destination, from the ceiling above. It was beautiful.

And it wasn't.

Mouth dry, Kaylin brought her arms to the throne and clutched the rests for all she was worth.

"Any of them would gladly bear the mark you bear so reluctantly," he told her.

"Are they captives?"

"Do they look confined?"

"They were *stone!*"

"Indeed."

She was silent for a full minute. "Are you an Arcanist?"

"I? No, Kaylin. I have never much liked organizations, and the sense of belonging, the need for it, is often human."

"But you—"

"They sought immortality," the fieflord continued, as if she hadn't interrupted him. "And in a fashion, they have it here. They are not aware of the passage of time, in this place—they are aware only when they wake." He paused, and then added, "I have much interest in things mortal—things that both fade and change. Even in death, you are not like the Barrani."

Her arms were tingling. "You used the castle's magic."

"I dared it, yes. And this is one of many results. Not all are so fortunate. Not all," he added quietly, "are so unfettered in their beauty."

"This is beauty?" she asked him softly, the question denying the statement. She started to rise. His hand caught hers, although the thrones were not side by side.

"If they displease you," he said coldly, the threat evident in his voice, if not his words, "I can dispense with them entirely."

The music stopped playing the moment the words left his mouth, and the light in the hall changed. The revelers looked up, their silence sudden; it was clear that they had heard him, although he'd spoken softly. She was certain they would have heard him had he not bothered with words at all.

"Well?" he said softly. Death in the voice. Theirs. Maybe hers. She couldn't separate it easily.

"Leave them," she told him, hating herself. "Unless you want to free them and send them back to their—" she paused. "They have families?"

"Not among the living, no. And the world, I fear, is much changed in their long absence from it."

She'd seen what he'd done to the trees, and she knew firsthand what the price of flippancy was. She shook her head. "Let them be. If this was their choice—"

"You may ask them, if you doubt me."

She shook her head again. "Just...let them be." Because they *were* beautiful, each and every one of them, and some part of her didn't want to see that beauty come to an abrupt end.

"If you desire their company," he said quietly, "I will give them to you."

Watching their silent, drawn faces, she winced. He could have hit her and gotten less of a reaction, and she hated her face for expressing so much.

"I don't want them," she said, without force, but not without conviction. "And I don't want you to be able to use them against me."

He smiled as the words left her mouth. She almost gaped. It had been a thought, a ferocious one, but she hadn't meant it for sharing. He touched the side of her face, his fingers brushing the flat surface of his mark.

Her head snapped back at his touch, as if he'd struck her. And he had. The whole of his name, in long, drawn-out syllables, resonated throughout her entire body.

"You do not understand the gift," he told her, and his voice was almost gentle. Beneath it, she heard something darker.

"No," she said, her own voice thick and hesitant. "I don't." She reached up and pushed his hand away, breaking the contact and drowning out the sound of his name. A name that might have been, for a moment, her own. Her cheeks were flushed, her face red; she knew it, although she couldn't see herself. Fingers lingered over his hand, and this, too, was a shock, because they were hers. They left damn fast.

She pushed herself up from the chair.

"You have already accepted my mark," he told her, rising in her wake.

"I haven't," she snapped back. And realized, slowly, that it was almost true.

His eyes narrowed. "Speak." It was not a request.

"You don't own me."

"No."

"And the mark doesn't mean what it—what it could mean." She recalled Lord Evarrim's question clearly.

His eyes turned a shade of remarkable blue. The statues

were statues again, although they were no longer in the neat, even rows that pillars occupied. "I had hoped," he said softly, "that this would not be such a difficulty. These others you see," he added, lifting a careless arm and gesturing across the width of the hall, "came to me. They came willingly."

"Good for them."

"And you, Kaylin?"

"I came to ask you a question." She hesitated as he drew closer, and closer still; her breath was a little too shallow. She opened suddenly dry lips and spoke a single word. His name.

And he stopped, his fingers an inch—less—from the underside of her exposed chin.

"Very good, little one." The words were at odds with his expression. "But I have time."

"All the time in the world," she said sweetly. "But I don't. I'll age," she added, staring at faces caught in stone and marble. "I'll die."

"Will you?"

Something in the words brought her up short, and she stared at the marks on her arm, her stomach beginning to fold in on itself—the first sign of incipient nausea. "It's your name, isn't it? It's not the mark that gives you the power to—that makes me talk."

He could have pretended to misunderstand her. He didn't. Nor did he move away; he was a shadow that seemed to grow to surround her. He filled the whole of her vision. "Yes," he said, voice still gentle. "My name gives you much."

"It doesn't—doesn't seem to. I'm not reading your thoughts."

"I am not, as you so quaintly and superstitiously put it, reading yours. I doubt they would have much information or amusement for me. But you have not yet learned to school your expression." He paused, and then added bitterly, "nor have you had the need. The Barrani High Courts were not your home."

His fingers made contact with her skin as he spoke the last word, and she felt, again, a shock of recognition. The peal of his name. She wanted to speak it; felt her lips moving over the syllables, awkwardly and in silence, as if they were a desperate, private prayer. And as she did, memory intruded, and with it, the dour, scarred face of a man she hated more than she hated anything.

The outcaste Barrani eyes were still a clear, deep blue, but he withdrew the hand. "Hatred," he said softly, "comes, at root, from another source. If he is to be the great hatred of your life, it is because your life was founded on its opposite.

"But it appears that you are not yet finished with Severn. I would kill him, if I thought that would ease the bindings."

"If anyone's going to kill him, it's going to be me!"

"Indeed. I believe you have already tried twice, and you have failed twice. This is not an accident, Kaylin Neya. There is some part of you, some weakness, that desires *answers,* as if answers are paltry excuses. You cannot even admit this to yourself. You hide from it, but you are not perhaps as skilled at hiding as you hope. Those answers will find you, because in the end, you will not be able to turn away from them."

He caught her face suddenly in both hands, and she saw just how deep a color blue could be. But she didn't struggle; didn't pull away. His lips brushed her forehead, and she closed her eyes. Three men—three men had kissed her in that fashion in her entire life.

She trusted only one of them, and not with her life.

"What did you come to ask of me?" he said, as he withdrew, his eyes shading now to an emerald darkness, as if she had somehow satisfied the anger beneath their surface.

"I want to know what you told Severn when he came to you."

"In the fiefs?"

"When we both lived here."

"Ah."

As if you didn't already know that, you son of a—but even in thought, it wasn't a safe word. It was a lot harder to control her thoughts than it was her mouth. And she had never been a champion at the latter.

"Then come. Let us retire from this chamber. You will drink with me," he added quietly, "as I reflect."

He led her to another room, and although it was finely appointed, it was small. She was grateful for it; she looked at the walls, noted with relief the absence of any statues— or mirrors—and almost failed to notice the delicate paintings on the walls to her right and left. They had no frames, and their colors were washed out, the remnant of something bright seen through a haze of fog or smoke, but she saw that they were of Barrani. But not Barrani she recognized; they had long, pale hair and golden eyes. That much she could see without approaching them—and his demeanor didn't grant permission for closer inspection.

Instead, he gestured to a low divan, and she walked toward it hesitantly. His smile was brittle as she sat at its farthest end. "You must learn not to let fear govern your actions," he told her casually, as he also sat.

"I'm here."

"Indeed you are." His gesture brought movement from the far wall; the doors opened, and what must have been Barrani servants walked in. They were attired entirely in white; it made their dark hair gleam in astonishing contrast. They brought tall pitchers with long necks, and they also brought silver cups; these they filled in perfect silence.

Only when she had taken one of the two did the servants depart. And only when she brought the cup—hesitantly—to her lips, did Lord Nightshade begin to speak.

"Severn did not speak to me within the walls of the keep. He sent word to me, through my guards, and I chose to meet with him in the fief." He toyed with the edge of his cup before drinking, and she thought this was just done to unsettle her.

"He was…an odd child. I see few human children," he added quietly, "few mortal children. But in Severn, there was almost something worth using. I would have taken his service, had he offered it. Has he ever mentioned that?"

"You know damn well he never—" *careful*, she thought, and bit the rest of the sentence back, holding it as if it were on a very thin leash.

"Oh, indeed, he could not have offered it freely then. His loyalty was elsewhere. He was afraid," he added, staring at her obliquely over the cup's glimmering edge, "of me. But the fear was balanced by a greater one. It is seldom that this is the case, and I admit I was curious.

"I knew of the deaths, of course," he added, his eyes brushing past her face, as if his gaze were physical. "I had my own mages seeking those who committed the crimes within *my* fief."

She felt his anger viscerally, as if it were her own. For a moment, it was; they were one person, in the quiet of a small, elegant room. Hard to disentangle herself, then. But she did.

"He had come to me, he said, with information about those deaths. We did not…treat him kindly. But we did not injure him overmuch. I knew at first glance that his was not the hand behind those deaths."

"Because he wasn't—"

"A mage. No. He was, in his fashion, wise. And he was—as are all of my people—desperate. He would not have sought me otherwise. He told me of you."

She was utterly still.

"Not by name," he added softly, "and not willingly. We bartered for information, in a fashion. To receive what he needed, he had to give up what he hoarded."

"What did he—"

"He asked me if the deaths had occurred in any other fief."

She closed her eyes. Could still see his, burned on the inside of her lids, like sunlight on the unwary eye.

"He suspected the answer, and it was not costly. I told him no. He then asked what the marks on the corpses of the dead children signified. And I, Kaylin Neya, asked him when and where he had seen them."

"We'd all heard about them—"

"Oh, indeed. But his knowledge was more than that of hearsay. He could describe their color, their form, the place where they began and ended, almost as intimately as if they adorned him. He was…reluctant to part with that information, and I'm certain you understand why.

"But in the end, he answered, because I would not answer his questions otherwise. He told me that he had seen them…on you. I would have forced him to take me to you, then—but he would have died first. And my power, my presence *is* known. If someone of like power was watching my movements, I would have led them to you. I was not, however, pleased. I considered the killing," he added quietly. "And decided against it."

"I wish you had," she said bitterly.

"Do you? Do you really?"

"I tried to—"

"Kaylin, my name binds us. You cannot lie to *me*, even if you can lie to yourself. You have never truly tried to kill Severn. You have raged against him, you have injured him. You have even let others believe that you meant his death.

But I know you now. Had you intended his death, he would *be* dead."

There was nothing she could say. It was still damn hard to say it.

"I…was interested in you. I confess it. It is an interest that has grown with time, and I confess that I am old enough that very little holds my attention. Had I realized how close you were—" He shook his head and his smile was thin. "But I asked him if the names of the dead had meaning to him.

"I knew them all," he added softly. "I listed them. All. He was a quiet boy. Almost a man—on the edge of the act that would define him. He didn't have to answer. Words are often merely a barrier, a set of curtains pulled to one side or the other that cannot change the face of the window.

"He knew them. Which meant, of course, that you did."

"And you—you thought someone with your power—" Thought caught up with words. "You thought you knew who might be doing this."

She wanted to run. It was a terrible impulse and she was on her feet before she could fully name it for herself.

But so was he, the cup in his hands crashing to the floor, its contents a spray of dark liquid beneath, and upon, their feet. "Perhaps. But I may have been in error, and if I was not, I was not yet ready to face him." His hand was on her wrist—her bound wrist—and he cursed for the first time as light flared between them.

From the scent of singed flesh, it wasn't just for show.

But when she looked at his face, it was smooth and

expressionless, and the angry Barrani word—a word she actually *didn't* know—might never have left his lips. "Do not run in the Long Halls," he told her gently. "They change, and often suddenly. More than one visitor has been lost within its walls, and I will not have you be one of them."

Her legs were shaking. She told herself this was due to lack of sleep, of food. But she sat stiffly only because she knew he wouldn't continue until she did.

"I do not understand the marks you bear in their entirety. I would examine them, but it discomforts you, and I will bide my time. You bear my mark now, and you bear my name. Even if you do not accept the truth—and you are very good at refusing to accept truth—you *are* part of me."

"You understood something," she said, mouth dry. She wanted to change the subject. Unfortunately, there wasn't anything safe to change it *to*. Small talk had no place in these halls, no place in front of this Lord.

"Yes, Kaylin Neya. After speaking to your Severn, I understood that the sacrifices were chosen *because* the names were known to you. They were chosen because of their ages. There was not a child older than twelve or younger than ten among the victims. I guessed that whoever was making those sacrifices in *my* domain was drawing closer and closer to where you resided. That something about those sacrifices was meant to speak to you, and through you, to the marks you bear, and not to your benefit.

"I asked him only one further question in return for the answer I offered him."

"You asked him," she said dully, "if the marks had changed."

His black brow rose slightly; his eyes were a shade of deep, calm green. "Very good, Kaylin. That is exactly what I asked him. He did not choose to answer, which was of course answer enough.

"I do not know who is behind this. I can guess, but I will hold that guess a while. It is not the act of a sane man, but neither is it the act of a mad one. I would guess that it is not the act of a man at all."

She thought of the seal, then, and the man of blue flame. Thought of the Long Hall, with a door of stone that looked like it was part of the wall—probably because most times it was.

"I could number the deaths. I could count them. And numbers, in the ancient world, had power."

She didn't ask him how he knew because she didn't want to know. Hawks were hunters; Hawks were scouts; Hawks were gatherers of information. She was suddenly glad that she hadn't worn anything that bore her insignia. "What did you—tell him?"

"I told him the truth, and only that—that if the numbers were as I suspected, the time was coming when the last sacrifice would be offered, and the power of the sacrifices made manifest." He was silent for some time, and then added, "This particular type of sacrifice was once simply called death magic. There is a strength in it that living magic cannot rival."

"Sacrifices are made *to something*," she said bitterly. She knew it for fact. There were a lot of gods in the Empire; more than she could name were worshipped every day in the City of Elantra alone. She'd gone in with Tain, Teela and most of the Aerians when they'd destroyed the makeshift temple to one of them; there were *some* gods that the Dragon Emperor frowned on. Or, Kaylin thought, with chagrin, ate. She hadn't been present when the Emperor had arrived at the building; Clint had grabbed her by the armpits and had flown her up to the Hawklord's Tower just ahead of the small Royal army.

"If they were sacrifices—dammit, if they *are* sacrifices—who the hell is the power of the death magic *feeding?*"

"Do you really not understand?"

His gaze was level; intent.

But if he had accused her of lying about Severn, he didn't repeat the accusation; he merely frowned.

"They are made, Kaylin Neya, to *you.*"

She was glad she was sitting. Falling flat out on her butt would have been more indignity than she could have handled with grace.

But she shook her head, over and over again, as if the simple act could erase the words. No, not the damn words—the utter, implacable certainty that they were *truth.*

"Severn was old, too old to become a sacrifice. He asked nothing. But I knew from his expression that he clearly understood the risk."

"What risk?"

"Kaylin, you bear power. You *are* power. Perhaps you *are* human. Perhaps you were merely mortal until those marks and sigils began to write themselves across your skin. He understood the significance of the numbers, the timing of the sacrifices, the phases of moon. And he was bright enough.

"He asked me why the sacrifices had to be connected to you.

"I told him, truthfully, that I did not know. But I also told him that the greater the bond, the greater the power that would be channelled from the death to its recipient."

"How could you know that?"

"I couldn't."

"Then it was you—"

"But Kaylin, I was not wrong. I told him to think of you—whoever you were, girl, boy, child—as a chrysalis. I did have to define the word for him," he added, "but I assume your education in the Hawks makes such explanation unnecessary."

She swallowed. "It's the stage between caterpillar and whatever crawls out of the damn cocoon."

"Indeed. The sigils are your cocoon. The sacrifices? They are meant to make certain that what, as you so quaintly put it, crawls out of the cocoon is wed to the death magic and the dying itself."

She swallowed. "What would—what would happen to me?"

"I am not entirely certain."

"You're lying."

His eyes changed shade again, swiftly, as if at passing cloud. But although they did, he spoke as calmly, and as clearly, as before. "I told you, Kaylin, my name gives you much. Yes, I am not being entirely truthful. It is my belief that you would rise from the ashes of your mortality as a goddess—an ancient force, and a very dark one.

"And I told your young protector that it would take one more death for the tally, and one for the wakening. Two. I thought it likely that those two would have to be close to you in ways the others hadn't—if not the thirty-ninth, then certainly the fortieth." He hesitated; she knew this not because she could see it, but because she could almost feel it.

"I asked him, Kaylin Neya, if he had any idea of who those two might be. I told him to send them to me, and he asked me if I could protect them. I didn't have to answer, but I am not kind, not even by Barrani standards. I merely told him that their deaths would be less hideous, and far less costly to Elantra—and the whole of the Empire—than the deaths they would otherwise face."

The world shattered. She held the shards together, and they cut her and cut her and cut her. She sat, her hands dangling loosely over her lap, her sightless eyes staring at the bright reflection of lights on a hard floor.

"You have what you came for," he told her quietly.

She could not be certain how much time had passed. Didn't want to be.

"Why is it happening so quickly now?"

His arm was around her shoulders, and for just a moment, she took comfort from his presence. Dangerous moment, and short one; she pulled away.

Was aware that he let her.

"If I stay here—"

"I would keep you here. It was my intent. Had I not been forced to surrender my name to you, Kaylin Neya, it *would be* your intent as well." His smile was lazy and compelling; it was also unpleasant. But he rose. "There would be safety, I think, for a small time were you to remain within these walls.

"But only a small time. Someone is hunting you, and it is someone who knows what those marks mean. I am hunting him," he added softly, "and not without success. But you are not as malleable as you were, and I...think...the sacrifices are happening quickly because your enemies have little time. You are no longer standing on the brink of adulthood—you have crossed the threshold, but the transition is incomplete. You cling, still, to the memories of your childhood. If I am not mistaken you have already used the power granted you in ways that would not suit their interests, and in the using, you have anchored some measure of it.

"If they wait, Kaylin Neya, you will become something entirely beyond their control. Their ability to rewrite what is written is slipping from their grasp.

"And now, I fear you must return," he added quietly, "to your Hawks. I will see you escorted to the bridge."

"I don't need an escort."

"It is meant as a mark of my regard, no more."

"I don't need one."

He bowed, then. It surprised her. "I have never been

interested in the weak or the infirm, although many of my kind are. You have become a fledgling Hawk—fly, then, Kaylin, but do not look away from what you *must* see." He offered her an arm, and she found that she needed it. Touching it drove Severn's image away, and she needed the distance.

They walked in silence, the warmth of his arm both comfort and accusation.

"Kaylin, one other thing."

"Lord Nightshade?" She turned just at the edge of the coruscating light that was the portcullis.

"Tell Lord Evarrim—tell any of the high caste Barrani—that if they so much as touch you without my leave, they will be at war."

CHAPTER 14

"Gods damn it, Kaylin, you are *on report*. What do you think that means?" Marcus's growl filled the room, and pretty much silenced the office. People, however, could be bloody suicidal when it came to satisfying curiosity, and they didn't drop their work and flee instantly at the tone of his voice.

"That I wear civvies when I visit?"

"That if Clint let you in, he's out of a job."

She gave him her best I'm-harmless-and-really-sorry smile which was, unfortunately, a different variety of sorry.

"I should have you thrown out of the office. By the window," he added, glancing in its direction. There was only one, and it wasn't much of one; windows and security didn't exactly speak the same architectural language. Kaylin doubted she'd fit without causing structural damage. Then again, Marcus habitually caused structural damage to things like his desk. But even as he turned back, his fur flattened; his outrage was strictly for show. She was part of his office pride, as close to family as she could be, while being furless.

"I'm sorry." She hoped it didn't sound as lame to his ears as it did to hers; the Leontines had an acute sense of hearing. And smell. And touch. Oh, hell, and temper, while she was making mental lists. "But I need to know—"

"On report," he replied firmly, "means that you're out of the loop. You're suspended. Which means," he added, spreading his glare across the office in an even cloud, "that no one talks about internal matters or investigations with you." He stretched his claws across his desk, but didn't embed them. "The Hawklord's not happy." He might have been talking about the weather, except he never did. "The Swordlord is underimpressed as well."

"The Wolflord?"

"What do you think? Severn was seconded to the Hawks, but the Wolflord is proprietary. He wants reasons. And the Hawklord isn't inclined to give 'em."

She put her hands flat against the scored surface of his desk and bowed her head. Her arms were stiff. "Marcus—"

"I'm going to lunch," he announced to the office at large. "Don't follow me," he added.

She waited until he'd made his exit—his overly obvious exit—and then turned to Caitlin.

Caitlin didn't manage to dredge up a smile. "You haven't slept at all, have you?"

"Some," Kaylin managed. "Caitlin—"

"They haven't found her." She looked up to see Marcus's back vanishing between two doors. "And not for want of trying, Kaylin. Marcus spent the whole of last night closeted with Imperial mages."

At any other time, Kaylin would have winced. Marcus's love of the Imperial Order of mages was just one rung up from his love of paperwork. But today? She loved him for it.

"And," Caitlin added, before she could find words to express her gratitude, "he spent early this morning closeted with Arcanists." She looked down at her desk—at the papers and missives that girded it—and picked out one. Kaylin didn't really notice what was on it; she was having trouble assimilating the word "Arcanist."

"They don't work with—"

"The Lords of Law. No. Apparently the Emperor added his voice to the Hawklord's request." Her tone implied "and high time," but she was wise enough not to say it. "This, in case you're too dumbfounded to read it, is a request sent out to the titular head of the Oracular order."

"*Oracles?*"

"Them too. If you insist on hanging around the office, you'll probably see her in about, oh, half an hour." She paused, and then added, "This is the first meal that Marcus has taken a break for since Catti disappeared." She didn't have to add what they both knew: He wasn't eating. He was giving Caitlin strictly forbidden time with Kaylin.

"Has Marrin called?"

Caitlin nodded quietly. Although she could be sharp-tongued, none of that edge was applied to the pride-mother of the foundling hall. "Three times. Her fur's on end, and she can't keep her claws sheathed."

"I'm surprised she can even speak."

"She couldn't. Not our tongue. But Marcus took those calls."

Kaylin sagged against the desk. "Caitlin—when am I going to be off report?"

"I don't know, love. Trying to kill a member of the Hawks while *in* the orphanage requires a bit more than the usual bureaucratic muttering. I've done every bit of paperwork I can—but the favors you need called in, I can't call."

"Teela—"

"She's out with Tain." Caitlin hesitated a moment, and then added, "And Severn."

"But—but—"

"He was put on provisional report, but he voluntarily submitted himself to the Tha'alani. It was made clear, and instantly, that all the aggression was yours. I'm sorry," she added, and meant it. It was one of the things Kaylin loved about her. "Clint and Tanner are on the doors, but the Hawklord has every other Aerian in the skies; he's pulled in reserves we haven't used for years. If the—the kidnappers can be seen, they'll be found."

"We don't have *time*."

"Kaylin, you're special, I'll grant that. But you're one Hawk. Every other Hawk knows what the timing is like, and every single one of them has taken a personal interest in this." She reached out and caught Kaylin's shaking hand between hers; hard to tell which were shaking more.

Kaylin pulled away and shoved hair out of her eyes. "Where's Tiamaris?"

"The Dragon?"

"The same."

"He's at the foundling hall. Kaylin—"

"Tell Marcus where I'm headed. If he needs me."

"He's not going to be happy."

"Probably not. But he won't be surprised, either."

Amos wasn't guarding the gates. He was probably somewhere on temple row, or worse. He'd never been a guard capable of dealing with this kind of situation; the worst he'd seen usually involved a defiant child's attempt to run away in a snit.

The gates were therefore open, and the path between the street and the foundling hall was utterly unoccupied. It was midday, give or take an hour; this was unusual. And it wasn't. Kaylin let herself in, shut the gates at her back—or tried; as gates went, they lacked a little in the latch department—before she walked briskly down the path and up the steps. The front doors were shut, but she tried the handles; they creaked as she turned them.

She wasn't stupid enough to enter the hall quickly. Had the situation not been urgent, she wouldn't have been stupid enough to enter at all without mirroring Marrin first.

But Marrin's sense of smell was at least as acute as Marcus's; probably more so, given her state of anxiety. Although she was in the vestibule before Kaylin managed to enter, she wasn't—yet—in full aggression mode. Which is to say, she didn't leap forward and try to tear out Kaylin's throat.

But her claws were bright and fully extended, and her eyes were all the wrong shape and color. Kaylin's Leontine was pathetic—most of the mortal races couldn't manage good Leontine because they lacked the right vocal chords for it—but she used it anyway, because Marrin didn't look like she was going to *hear* anything else.

"Marrin," she said, holding both of her hands up, palms out and empty, while also elongating and exposing the line of her throat, "I've come about your kit."

Marrin growled.

Words were embedded in the sound, but Kaylin had to work for them.

"I know." She kept her Leontine as level and simple as possible. The first was hard, the second was a necessity. "The birds are in the air. The mages are on the ground. The Wolves are hunting." She paused, and then added, "Where is the rest of your pride?"

The question seemed to calm Marrin—if calm was a word that could be applied in a situation like this. "Upstairs," she told Kaylin. "The Dragon is watching them."

"And their teeth?" It was the Leontine equivalent of asking about their health. Or the closest one Kaylin could think of.

"Cutting," Marrin snarled back. But she drew herself in, and if her fur didn't settle, her hands came down to her sides. "Kaylin, *where is Catti?*"

Anger, Kaylin could cope with. Had spent a life coping with. But this was worse. Without thinking, she tapped the bracer that bound her wrist. "I don't know," she whispered, reverting for a moment to her native tongue before she thrashed once again with the curled growl of Leontine. "But we're about to find out."

Marrin's eyes widened.

Kaylin hated to give her hope. Hated to, and had to— because if she couldn't, there wasn't any, and that was worse. "I need to speak with the Dragon," she added quietly.

Marrin turned and leaped up the stairs, taking them four at a time, her gait a great lion's gait, and not the two-legged walk that civility demanded. Kaylin followed as quickly as she could, but Marrin was at the flat of the landing before Kaylin was halfway up.

Her roar must have been audible from the street; it stopped Kaylin dead in her tracks for a moment. But it was answered by a deeper, resonant roar, and Kaylin, frozen, knew that she had, for the first time in her life, truly heard a dragon's voice.

She wondered if the children were crying, or if they, too, were frozen by something so primal it was almost beyond fear.

Tiamaris met her when she managed to get her legs under her to start moving and had reached the top of the stairs. He was dressed in the same robes he always wore, the crest of the Hawk—denied her—glittering across his chest. But his eyes were red, and their lids were all that prevented them from erupting in flame. Or so it seemed to Kaylin Neya.

Without preamble, she said, "I went to speak with Lord Nightshade."

Dragon eyes shifted. Whatever burned in them seemed to lose fire and heat as he stared at her face and the mark that adorned it. Minutes passed, and she waited, her hands deliberately by her sides, her throat still slightly exposed.

But when he answered, he spoke in his normal voice. It was the only thing about him that was normal, and she guessed it was costly. Everything was, these days.

"What did you tell him?"

It wasn't the question she expected. "I told him *nothing* about the foundling halls," she snapped. Had she the eyes of any other race, they would have shifted color in an instant.

He held out a hand, his expression smoothing into its frustrating lines of neutrality. Frustrating and familiar. "I make no accusation, Kaylin. The fieflord is *not* the hand behind this."

She swallowed, and had the grace to mutter an apology. "Why did you ask?"

"Because he gives little away without exacting a price, and it has been his way, in past endeavors, to offer an exchange of information—if he has information that you seek." He frowned, and then added, "I have been in need of information in his possession in the past, and speak from experience. I have not, however, had the questionable fortune to bear his mark."

There was a question in that, and she chose to ignore it. "He told me what he thinks they're after."

"They?"

"Whoever's doing this," she whispered. Her throat was still raw from her short attempts to speak Leontine. "But if I had to bet, I'd put money on you already having the same suspicion."

His lower lids rose, then, and his eyes were a bright orange, a mix of gold and Dragon red. She met them, unblinking, because there was a challenge in it, and the color could go either way. She was hoping for gold.

"It's about me," she told him quietly, lifting her arms, the sigils they both knew hidden by her customary long sleeves, the edge of the bracer gleaming. "I don't know why, or how, but these marks were written there by something old. And something else—probably also old—is trying to rewrite them in the only way they can."

He nodded; gold ringed orange.

"When they finish rewriting them, I won't be me anymore."

He nodded again.

"This is why you counseled the Hawklord to kill me."

He didn't deny the words; they were spoken with quiet certainty and no anger at all. Because she hadn't any. Had she died the day she'd first encountered the Hawklord in his Aerie, Catti would be *here*.

"I don't understand why he didn't listen to you," she added, her shoulders slumping.

"But seeing you, here, as you are now, I do, Kaylin Neya. Come. It is not…wise…to speak of this near Marrin."

She nodded, and let him lead her down the hall. Only

when she saw the gutted room that had once been Catti's did she hesitate; he had chosen the scene of the crime for privacy, and it was not a private she wanted to be part of. "Step carefully," he said, without looking back to see whether or not she was following. "The Imperial Order of Mages have been at work here, and they have marked much."

"And the Arcanists?"

"Theirs is a more subtle work." And those words, less subtle, were a closed door. "Kaylin?"

The not-quite-Hawk swallowed, ditched hesitation and crossed the threshold.

"He told you much," Tiamaris said, and she felt as if she had somehow stepped full into a child's story, although the door at her back still opened into a hall that was, to the eye, normal. Another world. Her world, she thought numbly. The one that was worth protecting. She had once promised herself she would never believe that anything was worth protecting in that way again—because she had believed she would never find another family.

Fear of failure did that.

"He pretty much said it had to be…death magic."

Tiamaris's brow rose. "He told you that?"

"He told me that this type of sacrifice used to be called death magic. And I take it that goats don't count."

Her attempt at humor caused a raised brow, which was about all it deserved; it was dismal.

"He is correct. It is a forbidden art," he added. "Forbidden to study. Forbidden to practice. These are obvious. It is also not an encouraged topic of conversation."

She nodded; she could understand why.

"What else, Kaylin?"

"That I'm the—the thing they're making these sacrifices to."

He nodded. "He can't protect you." It was a flat statement. Because it was, she didn't bother to tell him what he already knew. "Kaylin, a different question. Marrin was not forthcoming—her wards were more so, until she told them to be silent."

She nodded again.

"Marrin called you a few days ago. Before Catti disappeared. It was about Catti?"

"Yes."

"What did you do here?"

Tiamaris was a Hawk. Even if Kaylin was certain he already knew the answer to the question—and his early mirror message made clear that he *did*—she answered it. "I healed her."

He granted her something. "I spoke with Sergeant Kassan. He was forthcoming, but he doesn't understand your power; his answers were vague, and they were not enough. How did you heal the child?"

"What do you mean, how?"

"She wasn't ill."

"No."

"She was injured?"

"She was dying," Kaylin said, the words uninflected.

"Of her injuries?"

"She'd fallen." Kaylin closed her eyes. It was easier, that way. "She'd fallen and she'd broken something. Her back. More than her back. I've seen it before."

Tiamaris's single word made her open her eyes again. He was staring at her with a kind of…surprise. It wasn't awe; he *was* a Dragon. "Was she even conscious?"

"She was barely breathing. No, she didn't wake up. Not until—not until after."

"Kaylin, I *know* you almost failed magical history."

She winced.

"I know you almost failed practical magical knowledge as well."

"And math," she added, for good measure.

"Numbers are not a concern here. But magic *is*. You must know that healing magic is extremely rare in the Empire."

"I know. It's why the—my power can't be used openly. Not if I want to be a Hawk."

"You use it openly."

"I use it among people who won't talk about it later."

His smile had teeth. Real ones; the figurative ones, she was used to. "Children talk," he told her quietly.

She felt a flash of anger, like a summer storm. "You came here to weasel information out of *orphans?*"

"I came here," he replied, dignity intact, "to stop Marrin from entering her berserk phase."

"You—" She stopped. She couldn't think of another Hawk—with the possible exception of Marcus, and that wasn't a certainty—who could say that and mean it.

"If Catti is found dead—and in private, we must both admit that this is becoming a likelihood given the fact that she obviously left by magic, and she is in the same age range as the rest of the victims—the foundling hall still needs Marrin. And her orphans are not likely to recover from a berserk Leontine—if they do, Marrin is not likely to survive it. The Lords of Law will have to attempt to contain her."

There was only one way to contain a berserk Leontine. Kaylin swallowed.

"There isn't a healer alive who could accomplish what you accomplished, if I understand what you are saying correctly. How did you do it?" His eyes were gold now, but they were unblinking in their intensity.

"I—I don't know."

"You have to, Kaylin."

"But I *don't*."

He waited patiently, and she realized that he intended to wait for whatever incoherent babble she offered as an answer. "I—I couldn't hear her," she said, after a pause. "When I touched her. When I called her. There was *no* answer. It was as if—as if she was already dead. I couldn't *feel* her."

"And you normally can?"

"Normally, the children I'm called for are fevered, but they're *there*. Catti wasn't. She was—she wasn't there. I had to find her first."

"How did you find her?"

"I—I remembered her."

"How?"

"I just—I remembered her. As a small child. As a girl, the first time we met. I remembered her singing—she has a voice that's almost worse than mine. I remembered her hair. I remembered her smile. I just—I remembered *her*. And I held on to that while I built—" She stopped.

Tiamaris drew closer, his steps light for a man of his size and weight. When he touched her shoulder, she almost cried out, but his hand was gentle. "Kaylin, if we are to have any hope of finding Catti alive, you *must* answer this." His breath smelled faintly of smoke. Before she could speak, he smiled. It was the first smile he had offered her, and it was weary beyond belief—but there was a very real hope in it.

And hope was its own kind of terror.

But *gods* she wanted it. Grabbed onto it, babbling. "I couldn't hold her, even with those memories. I…I could feel the power. The magic, I guess—I don't know if that's what you'd call it, because I failed magic preliminaries, too. But I could almost see it. I grabbed at it—it was all thin strands, almost like hair. Or webbing. Or—something.

"I built it into a…net. No. A bridge between us. Something that could bind us together. I didn't know—at the end—who was Catti and who was Kaylin, and I didn't care. I only knew that she had to survive. Because I promised Marrin. Because she's one of—" She stopped. Her eyes rounded, her head rose in a snap of motion.

She saw the understanding in his eyes.

"They *knew*," she said softly. "Somehow, they knew. Someone must have told them—someone—"

His grip tightened. She struggled against it for just long enough to know she wasn't going to find freedom without another fight in the foundling halls.

"They know," he said softly, agreeing. "And no, Kaylin, no word was necessary. If you must find traitors, you will be *no help at all* in saving Catti's life."

He could have slapped her with less effect. She almost wished he had. "And you must have understood some part of the importance of that bridge yourself," he added softly. "Because you attacked Severn when he came to you here. Some part of you must have expected him to understand what you didn't consciously understand.

"I know what Severn did in the fiefs," he added. "And you were not wrong. Had he known—" But he stopped speaking of Severn.

"You used a magic that is inimical to death magic in a fashion—its very antithesis. You gave power, you *gave* life. They are attempting to refashion the power that you bear. The words that you don't understand, they understand. To use the power, Kaylin, I think you must, in some fashion, invoke the symbols. The fact that the use was inimical to their nature, their intent, would be a beacon."

"But Catti—"

"She is marked, by you," he told her softly. "Invisible to the eye, you have left the signature of your power in places that no one else could begin to touch. Her life was in your hands…it is still in your hands."

His face had lost some of its stonelike stiffness. He caught her bound wrist in his hand, and unbuttoned the cuff that concealed almost all of the gold. His large fingers pressed the glittering gems in a quick sequence: white, blue, white, blue, red, red, red.

"You are still bound to her, and she to you."

"You *knew*."

"No, Kaylin. I suspected. But had I known—" His eyes did not change color; the membranes did not rise. He was the Tiamaris she had walked the streets of the fief with. "It would be safest—in ways you cannot imagine—to kill you now."

He was considering it, and worse, she was letting him.

"Because they have in their hands not a single sacrifice, not like the thirty-eight seven years ago. They have something that contains your essence. They have a window into your…soul." The last word pained him.

"My soul?"

"It sounds overly dramatic for my taste."

Great. A literary snob.

"But killing you would not save the child." The bracer snapped open in his hands. He let it drop to the floor.

She watched it. "But the Hawklord ordered me to—"

"Leave it, Kaylin. It will find its way."

"Why are you—"

"Because while you wear it, you cannot trace the bindings you made to heal that child. Your magic is hidden and contained—even from you. Perhaps especially from you. And your enemies—no, Kaylin, *our* enemies—can do what the bracer prevents you from doing. They already have, or they would never have taken Catti, because they would not have been able to *find* her. You have two choices. Possibly. You can find the threads of that binding within yourself, and you can cut it entirely."

"And what would that do?"

"Two things. The first—and perhaps the most important to Elantra—is that it would close the door. It would make of her sacrifice something only as significant as the others have been, no more. They would lose their purchase into the heart of your power. The second, I believe it would kill her, but you would at least grant her a painless death."

"No."

He showed no surprise at all at her answer. But he'd expected it; she knew enough of him by now to know that much. "Or you can find the bindings, and strengthen them."

"I'll—"

"And *if* we cannot find the child in time, you will surrender everything human about you, and the child's death—all of the childrens' deaths—will seem paltry and merciful in comparison to what you will *then* be capable of doing.

"Yes, I counseled Lord Grammayre to kill you. I will not lie. He chose not to heed my advice—and it was costly to the Lords of Law to receive it—not because he was certain he could protect you, and not, in the end, because he was certain that the threat you presented was over. He refused because he thought, even then, that you were a fledgling, that you had come to him in his Tower, wings broken, and that he might somehow make you whole."

"But that's not—that can't be—" She was shaking. "Do you *know* why I first climbed up to the Hawklord's Tower? What I tried to do?"

If he did, he was kind enough not to answer. And he was Tiamaris enough to ignore the interruption. "I thought him reckless, then. But the gift that you used to heal that child—there is not another like it. Not in anything save legend, and history old enough to *be* legend to the mortal races. Even now, I can still think of his action as reckless—but I better understand it, and what he did not do, I will not do until it is clear that there is no other choice."

"And what if it's too late?"

"I will die." He brought his hands up to her face; they were both hard and warm. He could crush the whole of her head between them. "And now I too will take the greater risk, Kaylin Neya. Think of your Catti. Find the bridge that you built—and crossed—in order to save her life. Find only that."

"And then?"

"We will cross it." He paused, and the hesitation was profound. "I must call Severn," he said at last.

"No!"

"I will call Severn, Kaylin, because the child is almost certainly in the fiefs, and your history together lies there as well."

"Our *history*—"

"He has a part to play," the Dragon said softly. "It is not yet finished. He knows you better than anyone, save perhaps Lord Grammayre. He knows what made you. He understands you."

She didn't want to answer that. Or to face it.

"But they took Catti from the upper city—they could be *anywhere!*"

"And the bracer," Tiamaris continued, without pause, "went to Severn—he is its keeper. I believe that when we leave the foundling halls, it will return to his hand, and he will know."

She swallowed.

"Our enemies are in the fiefs," he told her, "because that is where the source of their power is. All of the ancient magics in Elantra, half-remembered and slumbering, are there. You are beginning to understand Severn, and I would pity you for it, but we do not have the time.

"Choose—Severn or Catti."

She swallowed. "If he tries to hurt her—"

"I will kill him myself."

The words should have been a comfort, because there was no lie in them, and not the least bit of doubt that he could.

"Severn," she said thickly. Because she was almost close to tears, and she couldn't speak any other way.

She wasn't certain of what to expect when Severn met them in the vestibule of the foundling hall, Marrin barring his way, her fur on end.

Tiamaris had a grip on her arm that would leave bruises, but it wasn't necessary, all breath—and all motion—went out of her when she met Severn's eyes. They were dark, and lined with shadow, and his chin was lined with stubble that would get him hauled across the carpet had he been on dress duty. He wore chain mail beneath the surcoat of the Hawks; he was dressed for ground duty, girded by sword, and belted, as was his custom, by long loops of chain.

He met her eyes and flinched. It wasn't what she expected. Couldn't say what she *had* expected. But when she opened her mouth, he lifted a hand, staying his distance.

"I brought your gear," he told her quietly, and she saw that he carried a satchel over his left shoulder.

"I'm not allowed to wear it."

He met Tiamaris's glance. "Your call."

"Wear it."

"You weren't the Lord of Hawks, last I looked."

"Nonetheless I will take responsibility for your disobedience." He raised a Dragon brow in Severn's direction. "You bribed the quartermaster?"

"I didn't bother to speak with the quartermaster," Severn replied, his broad shrug causing a cascade of sound that was only barely muffled by the satchel. "He had business to attend to—the reserves are taking up most of his time. And frankly, there aren't many Hawks her size. It wasn't hard to find her kit. We're going to Nightshade?" he added, eyes on Tiamaris.

"That depends," Tiamaris replied evenly. He turned to Kaylin.

"I don't know," she whispered.

Marrin, still standing between Severn and Kaylin, looked back. Her lips were pulled up over exposed, yellowed fangs. Give Severn this much, Kaylin thought; he wasn't even tense.

"I can find Catti," Kaylin told her, in the harsh, resonant tones of the Leontine. She reached up and brushed Tiamaris's hand away; he let her go. "I can bring her back. Marrin, she's part of my pride as well."

"I'll go with you."

"You can't," Kaylin continued, with far more certainty than she felt, given Marrin's state. "Because I can't stay, and no one else will protect the children the way you can. They need you here, until this is over. They've only got you." It was a low blow. But she'd learned, in the ranks of the Hawks, to use the weapon at hand as quickly and efficiently as possible once the need for a weapon had been established.

Marrin didn't hesitate. She stepped out of the way and let Severn pass. But as he did, she added—with the first sign of humor she'd managed to show—"Please, no more fighting in the foundling hall."

Kaylin laughed. Hysteria did that.

Severn didn't. He handed Kaylin the satchel. "Put the armor on," he added, before she could say a word. "All of it."

She was aware of Severn's presence as they left the foundling halls; couldn't help but be aware of him. He walked to her left, and Tiamaris, to her right. The sun's light had slanted; they'd wasted time in talk, and the shadows had begun to lengthen against the ground. What there was of it, that is, that wasn't occupied.

Severn and Tiamaris wore full Hawk uniforms. She wondered if they'd bother to take the time to ditch them when they reached the fork point of Old Nester at the bridge across the Ablayne. So far, they hadn't gone into the fiefs as Hawks—as servants of *any* of the Lords of Law. But she looked up as the thought crossed her mind, and she saw that Aerians were in the skies.

Caitlin, never prone to exaggeration, had given in to understatement. It was as if the Southern Welt had been emptied in its entirety, and sunlight glinted off the armor that some of the Aerians were strong enough to bear in full flight. They certainly didn't fly without their colors, and they were circling the fiefs in wide arcs that brought them just above the peaks of buildings.

"The Wolves are out," Severn told her quietly.

"The Wolflord called a hunt?"

"He hasn't emptied the hall," was the calm reply, "and he hasn't called in his reserves. But yes, he's called a hunt."

"On *what?*"

"The Imperial mages were able to pick up something in the mess left in the foundling hall. They've set up a trace, of sorts. They worked the night to do it, but they've enchanted small crystals that are attracted to—" he paused and frowned. "You didn't do well in basic magic, did you?"

"Does *everyone* read my transcripts?"

A smile tugged at the corner of his lips, changing the shape of the scars she was familiar with. She was numb; told herself she was numb. But it wasn't true; she was comforted to see even this hint of levity.

She didn't understand herself, and she didn't have time to try—praise whatever gods for small mercies.

"But if they could do that, then I don't need—"

"They won't find her," Tiamaris said quietly.

Severn actually bristled. "You've barely served as Hawk," he said curtly. "You've *never* served as Wolf. When the Wolves hunt—"

"They have to know what they're hunting. And the magic—" he said this with more disdain than two syllables of fact should have been able to contain "—that the Imperial Order can concoct on such short notice is seldom considered…efficient."

The crowds, thinning with every step they took, parted at last by the banks of the Ablayne, and they made their way to the bridge. Hawks' crests glinted as if light were pride, and she knew that Tiamaris and Severn had both made the decision to wear their uniform. She knew it was foolish; they were going into the fiefs, and they wanted as little interference as possible.

No time, she thought. She couldn't *feel* Catti. She couldn't feel whatever it was that bound them. Her breath was shallow now, as if she'd just run a four-minute mile.

"Severn," she said, without looking at him, aware even then that she had the whole of his attention. "I went to talk to the fieflord."

He didn't ask when. Didn't need to.

"He told me what he told you."

She wanted him to talk, then. Almost needed to hear his voice. Because if she did, she'd know.

"Kaylin," Tiamaris said softly, warning in the word.

But she turned to Severn anyway, to look at the face she had seen, even miles away in Castle Nightshade. "Catti is important to me," she said, her voice low. She was more vulnerable now than she had been in over seven years in his presence. "She's more important to me than I am."

He said nothing.

"I need to be able to trust you."

When he continued to offer her silence, her hand rose; she held it stiffly in the air, as if it were a signal and not the first half of a slap.

"I trusted you," she continued, and her voice almost broke. "And I needed to. Then, in the fiefs. But I didn't know… after…that I'd need to trust you ever again." Bleeding would have been easier, and less painful. She scraped herself raw, hating it. "And I do. Need to. But it *doesn't* mean the same thing, here."

"Kaylin—" His voice. Breaking, just as hers was breaking, more in her name than she'd managed to put into all of her words combined.

"There have to be things that are more important than my life. That's what it means to me—being a Hawk. Being… being Kaylin Neya. When I took the oaths, I was ready to die. I *wanted* to die."

His hand rose as well, but the gesture was so different from hers, so shorn of violence, it was painful too.

"I can find Catti because I healed her. Because I had to use some sort of power I'd never used before. It's why she was taken."

His whole expression turned to stone. Not ice; ice was colder and thinner. "Don't—"

"I have to. I have to ask this. If you ever cared for me—"

His fingers touched her unmarked cheek.

"It almost killed me," she whispered, acknowledging at last what she had only acknowledged before with blade and fury. "What you did. What happened that night. It *did* kill me. Maybe you had to do it—maybe you saved the City. Tiamaris thinks so, even if he's never said it to me. And I—don't care.

"Save her. Think of Catti. Please."

She might have said more, but her arms suddenly started to *burn*. She couldn't stop herself from crying out, and she only stayed on her feet because Severn was there, in front of her, his face her whole field of vision.

"They're starting," she whispered, as every one of the swirls and sigils upon her arm began to crawl with secret fire.

Biting her lip, pulling herself up, she began to run.

She couldn't have said where, but the why—the why was clear. Somewhere in the fief of Nightshade, the killers had started to make their marks upon Catti.

CHAPTER 15

She outpaced Severn. Whole years of her life had been narrowly defined by the fact that she couldn't even *keep up*. She heard him curse, but he didn't call out, didn't ask her to slow.

Movement cooled her arms. Fire, hidden beneath a layer of cloth and leather, banked as she ran, but it brought her no comfort at all—she knew, when it started again, it would start up her legs, and she couldn't afford to stumble, or to slow. Catti didn't have the time.

Hold on, she thought. No desperation in the words; just command. Or prayer. Or some mixture of the two. Kaylin, like most of the fieflings, had no professed religion. The gods were like the weather; sometimes good, sometimes bad, and either way, always beyond her.

People dived out of her way. They dived out of Severn's—or maybe Tiamaris's. The Dragon kept up, hardly breathing. She was certain, however, that she heard stone crack at least twice; these roads had been solid stone in a different age, and he was eroding some of the skeletal structure that survived. It was as if he was so focused on running, and only running, that he couldn't be bothered to expend the concentration necessary to keep his step light.

Another time, and this would have surprised her. Or terrified her. But she had just enough of basic Hawk training—the one thing she'd been damn good at—to keep her aware of what was happening around her; she had nothing left to react with. Catti, she thought. *Catti.*

And something in her heard an answer.

It wasn't a word. And it wasn't a scream—it wasn't strong enough for that. She had never heard Catti whimper; the little redhead with the defiant shove and the off-key voice had always been too strong a child.

But she *was* a child. And the fiefs weren't her home.

We're coming for you, Catti. We're coming to bring you home. Hold on. Wait for me.

It went out of her in words, but the words weren't spoken; they were like filaments, bright and airy, things seen like the palest of stars only out of the corner of the eye. She couldn't look at where they went, but it didn't matter; she *knew.*

She turned a corner. Hated the building that stood in her way, forcing her to alter her path. Felt something rise in the folds of that momentary hatred. Power. If she'd had the time, and the bracer, she would have donned it—

but that would kill Catti. Instead, she tried to forget the reasons she'd been given the damn thing in the first place. She ran through the surge, ignoring it. Praying, although it was pointless.

Here, the pain that was sudden in ferocity, surprising even though she'd expected it, helped her. It was a full body *slap*, a vicious reminder of what she needed to do. It took everything she had not to stumble or fall, and she willingly gave her all, shortening her stride for a few lousy steps while her inner thighs burned.

It gave Severn time to catch up; time to touch her shoulder, but not time to speak. He wouldn't, though; she turned to look at him, and he read everything he needed to read in the expression that contorted her face.

"Four Corners," he said, and it made no sense. But he spoke to Tiamaris; the Dragon rumbled in reply, his voice a shadow of his roar, but something stronger and fuller than his normal speaking tones. How much did a Dragon hide, when he walked the streets of the city?

How much did she?

She kept running, she kept breathing. The breathing was harder. Even Severn was glistening with sweat, and he was a wolf—he was used to running the city streets. Used to running these ones, probably the *only* Wolf who was.

But the streets shortened; the stones gave way to holes, grooves that were dried mud or flattened straw. This was one of the older streets in the fief. She couldn't remember its name, and didn't try. Because she looked up and finally saw the building that she *knew* she had to enter.

It was surrounded by black gates. Rust showed through the patches of oddly glistening paint, and it took her a moment to realize that it wasn't rust. She cursed.

"Watchtower," Severn said, which was more of a curse in its way than hers. "The gates are around the other side," he told Tiamaris.

"We don't have time!" Kaylin shouted.

Tiamaris looked first at Severn, and then at Kaylin. His eyes glinted red now, a deep, crimson color, shorn of inner lid. She had never seen it before.

"Get out of the way," he told her.

She obeyed him without thought, and half-wondered if he'd used some sort of voice-of-command magic. Whatever it was called. She *really* wished, for just that minute, that she had been a better student.

The Dragon Hawk reached out, gripped two of the thick iron bars in his hands, and tensed. Kaylin waited, because she thought he was going to bend them wide enough to allow passage.

She was wrong.

He *tore* them from their moorings, and with them, the whole fence face. Running here hadn't winded him; this barely made him grunt. But he did; she saw the muscles in his hands stand out in relief, as if chiselled there. His expression was stone. Red stone.

She was grateful that the streets had already emptied in a terrified rush, because had anyone been standing near them, they would have been crushed by the fence as it slammed into the street just inches to their back, probably shattering the few stones that remained of an ancient road.

Not that it would have mattered much, in the end: this was the fiefs, and the rule of law wasn't worth a rat's ass.

She ran across the newly uprooted earth, and nearly tripped as she noticed the mooring points planted in the ground; they were ebony. Ebony meant magic. If she'd had a minute, she would have been beyond impressed with Tiamaris.

But the pain had reached its height, and although it was sustained, she knew what would happen when it finally peaked. Knew it wouldn't take long at all, either.

She felt Catti's terror, and for a moment, she was back in the foundling hall, in the healing trance—bound so thoroughly to the young girl's life she couldn't separate her feelings from the child's: the terror was identical.

And there was a wall between her and it.

Old stone, smooth, cracked—maybe—by years of ivy growth. There were no windows here. There never had been. She'd always wondered why it had been called a watchtower.

From a painful remove she heard Severn speak of death, although he wasn't aware of it. "The gatehouse is on the other side."

No. No time. The gatehouse would be guarded. And even if it weren't, if it were barred, it would be too late.

Too late for Catti.

She could feel the power twist in her like the muscles of a very traumatized abdominal wall. Funny, how all those stupid technical magical words never left an impression no matter how many damn classes she'd been forced to sit through. She had watched a full autopsy only once and still remembered every clinical word Red had used.

Nausea overwhelmed her, but it wasn't the nausea of memory. She could taste blood.

She screamed. It came out in a *roar* that only a handful of Hawks would have recognized. They weren't there. Severn was. Tiamaris was.

And the wall was. She threw her hands at it, balled fists striking stone. Again. A third time. Skin left the sides of her fists, followed by a dark smear of blood.

"Catti!" Kaylin screamed.

And the wall shattered.

Stone shards flew in every direction; dust rose in an ominous cloud, an airy shroud. She lunged through them all, and came out looking like a crazed sculptor's interpretation of a spiny leaf-eater. She ran headlong into the pain, and because it was everything she could feel and see, she almost died.

But because it *was* everything, because she had once again totally lost it, she didn't. She caught the sharp point of an edged spear with the flat of her crooked arm and snapped it off; it sheared a gash in leather, dislodging stubborn bits of what had once been the external wall.

The head snapped off in her hand, the gleam of metal dulled by dust. She reversed its unbalanced, awkward weight and threw it back along the jagged wood of the shaft it had left.

Heard it strike something, heard the grunt that accompanied the strike.

Heard, blessed by it, terrified by it, the thin wail of a child's scream.

Catti. Catti. *Catti.*

And holding her down, surrounding her like priests out of a story that was too grim even for children, four robed men, all of a height, slender and perfect in build. The hoods hid their upper faces.

But the tapered edge of their perfect jaws were unmistakable: Barrani jaws.

They were *Barrani.*

But they weren't. She'd seen Barrani for seven years. She'd lived with them—briefly—investigated them, patroled with them, and eaten their food; she'd listened to their language, learned to speak it, envied their beauty, their musicality, their utter certainty of grace, and their endless, immortal life. They had made her feel awkward, ugly and just a little stupid simply by existing, because their lives made them everything that she would *never* have the time to be.

But until today, she'd never met a dead Barrani.

And she yearned for the whole range of awkward that the living Barrani engendered, because corpses didn't move without a lot of very, very illegal magical help.

Didn't think.

And yet these corpses did. And one of them, eyes the gray of night storm, did worse: he smiled.

* * *

She leaped up, toward the four, toward Catti who was *still alive*. It was all that mattered, that she was still alive. Had Marcus been there, he would have been beyond furious with Kaylin. Anger, she had learned quickly, was no good in a fight—it was more of an enemy than your armed opponent, because it meant you were fighting on two fronts.

Fear had its uses, she'd been taught that too. But you had to be able to parcel it out, to *use* it. Not to be used by it.

Old lessons. Old, hard-learned, and utterly useless. She cried out in terror, in rage, in something so raw that there wasn't a single emotional word that could describe it. Against one Barrani, she had no chance.

She knew it. And even if she had failed math, betting had been her only leisure pastime in the fiefs; she knew the odds against four.

And she'd take those odds.

But the *other* nine that closed in in a silent circle were more of a wall than the wall had been. She couldn't get past them; the power that she'd used to draw down the walls didn't leave her enough to destroy the Barrani. And she would have, and slowly, had she had the power.

They'd buy the time the others needed to kill Catti. The four already had blades out, curved blades, with flashing symbols, things that were also part of dark story, old legend. The pain in Kaylin's thighs, so insignificant compared to the rest of her pain, was fading; the runes had been written.

All that was left was punctuation.

Her life is still in your hands. You can let her go, Tiamaris had said. *It would be a more merciful death.*

This close, words like ash in her mouth, she felt the bonds between her and Catti, held them tight. Daggers were in her hands, and she was already in motion; whatever held the magic didn't need limbs.

But these Barrani were unlike the ones she'd trained with, drilled with, and patrolled with; they *let* the blades hit. One embedded itself in the center of Barrani chest; the other in an eye.

And neither of them made a damn difference.

The power that had destroyed the wall ebbed; she'd pay for it. She always had. But not now, she thought, willing it to be the truth, even if her body didn't really believe it.

"Let her go!" she shouted, in Barrani.

No one answered but Catti.

No; that wasn't true. The Hawks did.

She didn't know how much time had passed, but she knew she was no longer alone; she wasn't facing nine robed Barrani on her own. Tiamaris was by her side. "Kaylin." She didn't recognize his voice.

He turned, lifted Severn, and said something that she also didn't recognize.

But Severn did. He nodded, tensed and was catapulted through the air above these silent Barrani as if he were an iron ball. His knees and his chin were tucked into his chest, his sword drawn and held tight to his body as well, as he traveled end over end like an acrobat.

The watchtower ceilings went up forever. Tiamaris had noticed it; Kaylin, who loved heights, had noticed nothing. Severn and the Dragon had just over a week of bearing the name and crest of her beloved Hawks between them; she had seven years. But they lived up to the crest.

Her mouth went dry as Severn landed, legs astride Catti's slender, struggling body. His sword edge glistened with a lavender light; lavender and gold.

Terror had so many names, so many faces. She would have given in to all of them, but Tiamaris growled a warning and she had just enough time to get out of his way—because he suddenly needed a lot more room.

She discovered, then, that the word Dragon wasn't just an honorific.

He should have been red.

It was a stupid thought.

But she could *see* herself in the sudden shift of what had looked like human skin as it broke, and broke again, like earth in the hands of the gods. Small mountains with jagged ridges erupted from Tiamaris's skin, and there *should* have been blood, muscle, sinew—something more than this: the burnished, bright, shining scales of bronze; things that caught light, reflecting it, and with it, a distorted image of her own self.

She couldn't see beyond him, he grew that fast.

She couldn't see his head until his jaws opened and snapped to her left, leaving roughly a third of a Barrani on either side of his mouth. He had wings; she saw them flex, snapping in air. She'd heard big birds were dangerous, and she *knew* that Aerians could use their wings to bone-breaking effect in combat—but it wasn't like this.

Before she could gain her bearings, four of the nine had fallen. But the other five were in motion, and they were wary. Slow—slower than any other Barrani she'd ever faced, they circled. On the other hand, any other Barrani she'd sparred with would have been gone as far as their long, perfect legs would carry them. Even living forever, life was precious. Maybe more so, because there was so much more of it to lose.

She had single claws, one in each hand. She skirted the Dragon—she couldn't think of him by name—and he let her pass; the smell of smoke wafted on the breeze of his anger, his roar.

Barrani spears caught his flank, and the roar shifted, but it didn't still; it went on and on, as if it were an ancient, primal incantation. She would remember it forever.

But more, she would remember this: Severn.

Fighting.

What she almost couldn't remember: to breathe. Severn was bleeding from several wounds; his armor was rent, and his forehead was glistening the red that the Dragon was missing; he wore no head-band; the blood was dripping down, toward lashes and eyes. His bladed-chain still hung in loops around his waist; he hadn't space or time to unwind it, to set it spinning, to make it deadly. Instead, he relied on his sword. And the Wolves, she thought, as she ran, leaping up the stairs that led to the four robed men, should be *damn* proud of him. Against four Barrani, he was still standing.

And Catti—Catti was still alive.

Severn had their attention. Kaylin reached out, grabbed the back of a hood's cowl, the flesh that lay beneath it, and pulled. Her dagger cut air, and more: skin, flesh, windpipe.

It shouldn't have worked. They *should* have been faster. She knew this on some level, even as she shoved herself over and past the man she had in theory just killed.

And she saw that two of the fighting Barrani were missing hands. They bled. That was good. But they didn't seem to notice, and that was decidedly bad. Severn shouted something, but she couldn't make out the words; the Dragon's voice drowned them out, made them insignificant.

No. Not insignificant, never that.

She had thought Severn would kill Catti. She had thought—Severn gestured, then, and staggered as one of the Barrani daggers hit him. What his words hadn't done, this did. She had time to duck, to hit the ground, to roll, and the shadow of robed arms passed over her. The arms of the Barrani without a throat.

Learning to roll *to* her feet had taken about three weeks of constant bruising, and Tain had enjoyed every damn minute of it, because none of the bruises were on him. If she survived, she'd thank him. Maybe even buy him a drink.

He always called her flat-footed, and "clumsy Kaylin" had been his nickname of choice until she'd hidden a mouldering sandwich in his desk for three weeks. Flat feet, on the other hand, were right beneath her as she bent at the knees and side-snapped, clipping the underside of that jaw, her boots squelching in blood. She kept her knee up, pivoted and kicked back, knocking the knife arm of one of the Barrani before Severn lost an eye. Motion was important. Balance, more so. Her daggers were working, and her hands were red, but they didn't seem to have as much effect as the momentum of her weight behind the edge of her soles.

Catti was *alive.*

She could have done a little dance, and in fact, that was precisely what she *was* doing—but it was a Barrani dance, and they often ended in death. She kicked Barrani head when one of the priests—yes, that was the damn word for them—bent over Catti; he staggered back. His dagger had left a signature mark just above Catti's navel, and it was one of three. It wasn't deep, though.

They *had* been trying to kill Catti.

Severn, Severn, Severn.

She dropped her leading foot to one side of Catti, and felt Severn's foot brush hers as he took up the position she'd left open at her back. From this vantage, Kaylin could see that the marks on exposed thighs and arms were glowing; they would forever be her definition of black, but they were *still* glowing.

Gods, she thought, not particular about which, if they survived, she'd pay attention in magic class. She'd even *volunteer.*

Her roundhouse was her slowest kick, but it was her highest; she brought her leg up, hit a forearm. It didn't break, but it spun, causing the Barrani it was still attached to to spin with it. Severn was using his sword, and bits and pieces of Barrani bodies were piling up around them, but the parts they weren't attached to anymore just kept on coming.

And then she saw bronze light, the great, triangular head of a dragon, and she smiled. Not even the fetid scent of death that clung to the smoky breath was enough to dim its vicious edge.

The Dragon snapped up two of the four, and as he tossed them aside, he spoke. Caught in the roar a throat that large would have to make, she heard command.

"Get the child out of here. *Now.*"

Severn still faced two; she was free to move. Free to do what, until this moment, had been her only desire. She hesitated, and Severn said, "Damn you, *do it,*" and this time, his lips close enough to her ear that the words blended and carried with the Dragon voice, she obeyed.

She bent, scooped Catti up in her arms and ran toward the Dragon. Catti should have been beyond terrified, but she wasn't. Her arms were bound at the wrists, but she tried to reach up and throw them around Kaylin's neck anyway.

Kaylin shook her head. Catti wasn't the child she'd remembered first in the trance that had been their healing; she was heavy. She was twelve, the right age. The wrong age.

"Sorry," she muttered, as she twisted the girl around and threw her over her shoulder like a sack. The weight unbalanced her; there was no way she could both fight and carry the girl.

But she didn't have to. She brushed past the hard scales of the Dragon's girth, and stopped only for a second because she could see where they had been torn up, cracked, or riven.

But he was a Hawk. Kaylin was a Hawk.

And Catti was one of the people the Hawks had been created to protect. No choices to be made there; she left through the door her power had made and stepped into the full, blinding light of the quarter-day sun.

Severn was two steps behind her; he almost shoved her out of the way. "Get to the gate-line!" He shouted, and she nodded, still carrying Catti. When she stumbled, he swore at her. In fief-tongue, the dialect that made every upper city dweller sneer.

He took Catti from her shoulder, and she let him, stopping only long enough to give the girl a look that was meant to comfort.

It melted, though.

The rock melted as well.

Behind them, in the watchtower, Tiamaris of the Dragon caste had at last unleashed the most feared of Dragon weapons: his fire.

Severn shed his shirt and passed it to Kaylin. It was, as far as shirts went, a bloody, horrible mess; it made her laundry piles look pristine by comparison. But she knew what it was for, and she quickly cut the thick ropes that bound Catti's arms, massaging blood back into the girl's wrists.

"Wear this," she said softly, and pulled it over Catti's head. It caught in her red thatch of hair, and it fell down her shoulders like an ungainly dress.

She cut the ankle ropes as well, and helped Catti to her feet. "We're in the fiefs," she told the foundling. "The fief of Nightshade."

Catti's dark eyes were both bruised and wide. "Was that a Dragon?" she whispered.

Kaylin nodded.

"Cool! You have a Dragon!"

"Catti, he's *not* mine. He's a—"

"Hawk," Severn said quietly. "And while you're wearing my shirt, so are you."

She frowned at this stranger, and Kaylin was suddenly fiercely glad that Catti hadn't seen them fight in the foundling hall. "What do you mean?"

"Look at your chest," he said. And then, with a wry frown, added, "your waist."

Across it, injured in the same way that the Dragon had been injured, its gold broken and red with drying blood, was the emblem of the hunting Hawk, on a field of gray-blue. Broken, it still had power; perhaps, to Kaylin's eye, it had more power, because its flight had been tested, and it hadn't faltered.

"It's a Hawk," Catti said, her words and tone subdued.

Severn had to bend to bring his gaze level with Catti's, and his expression was utterly serious. "Yes," he said softly. "And most people—like Kaylin—have to earn the right to wear it. You were brave, Catti. You've earned the right to wear it for today. That makes you a Hawk, right now, and the Hawks don't speak about things like this."

She nodded.

Kaylin smiled, because she knew what the next question would be.

"Not even to Marrin?"

"Marrin is a special case," Severn replied, relenting. He rose. "Lord Tiamaris," he said, in a tone that Kaylin had never heard him use. Would have bet he couldn't, even to the Wolflord himself.

She turned. Framed by jagged, listing rock, Tiamaris stood. Gone were wings, great jaw, long tail; gone bronze, glittering scale. He had hands again, and feet—bare feet, blackened by soot. He wasn't wearing much. And not even Severn's kit would have covered him, anyway.

"Catti," she said softly, "stay with Severn." She looked at Severn, and something in his expression made her look away. But he said nothing as she made her way back to Tiamaris.

He was... singed. Bleeding. His face was bruised, and his jaw looked like it had been slammed against the floor by, oh, a hundred of the fieflord's best thugs. But his eyes were red, a brilliant red that had nothing at all to do with rubies.

"Tiamaris," she said, reaching out with the flat of her palms.

"Don't," was his curt reply. He stepped back, and she would have followed him, but something in his voice still contained the resonant power of a different form.

"Lord Tiamaris," Severn repeated, his voice clear and crisp beyond Kaylin's turned back.

The Dragon's inner membranes rose, lidding his eyes, muting their color. His outer membranes fell next, and his face twisted—literally—in something that might have been pain. Kaylin, realizing that she knew very, *very* little about Dragons, couldn't tell—and she was smart enough not to ask. But she watched as bronze scales—large as small shields, worked their way out of his skin, flattening across a large but human-sized chest, and working their way down.

When he opened his eyes, he caught her staring, and he offered her something that felt like the memory of a smile, as it couldn't be caught by simple gaze. "Kaylin Neya." He spoke the name as if she was no part of it.

But she nodded anyway.

"I apologize to you, and to your charge, but before we return Catti to the foundling hall, we must repair to the Halls of Law." She nodded again, started toward the broken wall, and realized that there was a reason he hadn't moved.

"By the power invested in me," he told her, almost gently, "I must refuse you entrance."

"But the Hawks will need to see—"

"No," he said quietly. "They won't." He waited there until he was certain that she would obey his command. And because he was injured, because she *knew* he should be carted off to the medical division—any of the three—as quickly as he could be made to walk there, she acquiesced.

Only when they were back on the fief's roads—themselves something like the memory of a real road—did she realize that he hadn't actually said *whose* authority was invested in him.

Before they had managed to make their way to the bridge that signaled safety—if you called home something other than the fief of Nightshade—shadows cut the ground. Not building shadow; they had a habit of moving about as slowly as the sun did on her way up or down.

But these shadows made Kaylin look up in wordless delight—because they were cast by Aerians, the closest embodiment to the name of the Lord of Law she served. She would have known them anywhere, because that dance of momentary darkness cast against the earth had always been a yearning and a delight.

Here, in the fief of Nightshade, they meant that much more.

Only one of the Aerians landed, and he was old by Hawk standards: one of the reserves.

"Private Neya?" He said, sparing more than a glance to either of her injured compatriots.

She saluted him briskly—because of the three, she was the one who could, without pain. And then, as she saw the wind-born creases around his eyes turn down in the wrong expression, she added, "I'm not on duty."

"You are on report," was the reproachful reply. "But in this case, there is some small chance that Lord Grammayre will overlook your interference." He turned to Severn, and his wings folded in a stiff arch above his head. They shook slightly; he'd been in the air longer than was wise.

"That is the missing child?"

"Yes. Catti of the foundling halls."

"The god of flight grant you warm winds," the older Aerian replied softly. It was a stiff, conservative phrase, but it was said with so much meaning, Kaylin didn't mind. "Corporal Handred?"

Severn nodded.

"Handred?" Kaylin said, brows rising.

"It was my father's name."

"But you told me you didn't know who—" She stopped speaking as the other word caught up with her. *"Corporal?"*

He shrugged.

"You didn't feel the need to mention it."

"The Hawks seem pretty informal."

"I want to talk to Marcus."

"Wait until you're off report. I hear, with the Leontine that there *is* actually a rank below private."

"Yeah. Corpse."

He laughed. The old Aerian rose to the sound of it, shaking his graying head. But his wings were white, and they were strong enough; stronger, perhaps, than they had been when all search had been in vain.

Clint flew when he saw them coming. Straight up, Aerian style, the equivalent of a victory salute. It caught the eyes of half the city—full, polished armor in this kind of sun usually did—but as Aerians had more or less been small, fleet clouds for the past day and a half, it wasn't as remarkable as it should have been.

When she reached the stairs, Catti was cradled—and sleeping—in Severn's arms. He, too, was bleeding, but he had insisted he was strong enough to bear her weight, and something about the bitter way he spoke those words made Kaylin let him, as if the burden was a gift.

And it was.

Clint was groundside, and he didn't even bother with the formality of the pole-arm. "Severn," he said, "you look like shit."

"You don't," Severn answered. His tone was all shrug, but he didn't otherwise lift shoulder, because he didn't want to disturb Catti.

"Aristo brought word," Tanner added. "Hawklord's waiting, and Iron Jaw's his new shadow."

"Is he happy?" Kaylin asked hopefully.

"Is he ever?"

"Um, I'm *not* wearing my crest. Both of you—you'll remember that, right?"

Tanner laughed.

"Marcus might be all right," Clint added. "I mean, at least you're not late." More in the words than humor; he reached out and gently touched the top of Catti's head. Not enough to wake her, just enough to make her presence *real*. Clint had always been tactile. His smile was weary, genuine and gone in an instant. "I should tell you something else."

Because she *wasn't* late, she waited.

"The Arcanum has paid a visit."

She rolled her eyes. "Clint—"

"And the representative hasn't left. Yet."

There was more. But it wasn't, apparently, for her. "Tiamaris." If he was surprised at how Tiamaris was dressed—and the scales could pass muster as very antiquated armor if you hadn't actually watched it grow—it didn't show.

The Dragon nodded briefly. "As expected," he said.

"What?"

He lifted half a singed brow in Kaylin's direction. "You really were a poor student, weren't you?"

"This is about magic?"

He snorted. The smell of something she wanted to call brimstone—and couldn't, because she had no idea what brimstone actually smelled like—tickled her nose hairs. "I read some of your transcripts," he said. "But even *I* have my limits."

"Go on in," Clint told them all. "But Kaylin?"

She had already made her way close to his beloved flight feathers. "Yes?"

"Mirror Marrin."

"She'll be here before I've finished the first sentence, Clint."

"She should know."

"Before I've finished the first *word*. She wasn't looking so…calm. And Tiamaris says that Catti needs to be examined before she can go home."

He cringed, the parent in him warring with the Hawk. The right one won; he said nothing else.

CHAPTER 16

The vaulted ceilings that were the commons for the Aerie were empty. If the Aerian reserves had been recalled, they had chosen other heights to grace with their weary presence. It was the first time that the central hall had seemed so empty.

"Kaylin," Severn said quietly. It was a question, and she shook herself, looking away from the empty heights. Catti was heavy, and blessed burden or no, she was still a burden.

Kaylin led the way to the doors that bordered the Hall of the Hawks. They were guarded, but not by Teela or Tain; not in fact by Hawks she recognized. These must also be reserves, although they weren't Aerian. They were, by the look of it, underslept humans—something she identified with heartily.

She answered their tired questions, assured them that the crisis—most of it—was over, and waited while they stepped aside to let them all pass. It seemed to take forever, but now that Catti was safe, she wasn't in a great hurry to actually face the Hawklord.

"Tiamaris?"

The Dragon looked down at her. He walked stiffly, and his stride was shorter than usual; she half expected to see a trail of blood in his wake. But she didn't touch him; didn't try. Her arms were too shaky, and besides, he'd made pretty clear that it was a strict no-go.

"Kaylin?"

"Why are you even here?"

He grimaced. "I cannot understand," he replied, "why you made such a poor student. You have an inexhaustible ability to ask questions."

She thought this was going to be the whole of his answer, but after a pause, in which three closed doors went slowly by, he said, "I was the only suitable candidate. I deal well with the mortal races."

At any other time she would have snickered. "The—your—"

"Transformation?"

"That."

"Yes?"

She hesitated. She understood what the word outcaste meant as it applied to her own race: it meant you were either in jail, were about to be or were incredibly unlucky with lawyers. It meant pretty much the same—

as far as she could tell, social niceties aside—for the
Leontines and the Aerians as well. If you managed to
somehow pay whatever you owed the courts, you weren't
really considered outcaste anymore.

But for the Barrani, it obviously meant something different. Kaylin had always had a sneaking suspicion that this
was because Barrani, at heart, were all sons of bitches, and
those who were officially outcaste were outcaste merely
because they had enough personal power to actually survive being *openly* rebellious. Nothing she had experienced
in Nightshade had done much to change that opinion, although for obvious reasons, she'd never voiced it.

But Dragons? Her mouth, as it so often did, ran ahead
of her brain. "Are you outcaste?"

He actually stopped dead, and swivelled his neck to
look—to *really* look—down on her.

"Kaylin," Severn said quietly, when Tiamaris failed to answer, "you *really* need to learn how to pay attention to
things that don't have wings."

"Dragons have wings," she said, half-defensive.

"Not in company that's supposed to survive them, they
don't. Look, Kaylin, even a Wolf cub knows that there are
no outcaste Dragons."

"And I was taught this *when*?"

"Obviously," he replied, with just a little heat, "you
weren't. I'm not sure whether this is a failing of the Hawks
or your own particular ability to not pay attention, but if I
was betting my own money on it, I know which way I'd go."

"Straight to some particularly hot corner of—"

"Children." Tiamaris raised a hand, his voice dry and inflected with something that might have been humor. "You did well today. Better, I think, than any of us would have guessed. Severn, however, *is* correct. There are no outcaste Dragons."

"But the Dragons *have* a castelord…they obviously have a caste system—"

"And the laws for dealing with the outcaste are determined in part by the ruling castelord of each race. Very good, Kaylin…you did manage to absorb that much in class. In the case of Dragons, that is the Emperor himself, and his decision has always been quite clear—there *are no* outcaste Dragons. I trust that my meaning is clear?"

She nodded.

"You've seen a Dragon, unleashed. Would you gainsay him?"

"No. And I wouldn't disagree with him, either."

Gold eyes rolled in mock disdain.

She winced. "I have to get it out of my system now. Because Arcanists? From anything I've heard—or seen, and I admit that's maybe two—they don't know what humor is. And if they've been around the Hawklord and Marcus for a while, neither will they."

"It isn't the Arcanum you have to be cautious around," he told her softly, as they approached the final doors. "Do *not* speak unless you are spoken to."

From the tone of Clint's voice, Kaylin had expected the office to be empty in the particular way it was when Marcus was in a mood. She almost tripped over her feet when she saw the exact opposite, and Severn almost tripped over *her* when she came up unexpectedly short. He offered her a friendly curse, and she actually apologized; she'd carried children before, and she privately thought of them as great, big blinders. He still held Catti, and his arms were probably locked and numb.

She looked up at him, and down at Catti, and seeing the two of them together, she couldn't think of a single thing to say that wouldn't break something. But she wanted to go on looking, and he knew it; he nudged her with his knee, wordlessly telling her to pay attention to what was in front of them.

What at first had seemed like a party—replete with foreign dignitaries in fine clothing, and a multitude of the races that made life in Elantra so exciting for an officer of the Lord of Laws—resolved itself into something a little more funereal. There was a whole lot of silence going around, like a quickly transmitted disease.

It wasn't made any better when Caitlin, looking harried but otherwise prim and proper at her desk, met Kaylin's eyes and winced. The wince disappeared as she saw who Severn carried, but the stiffness didn't. She got up, pushed her chair in, and made her way through the Hawks and the outsiders that had taken over the floor.

She didn't hug Kaylin, which was a distinct signal: things were formal. And Kaylin was so underdressed for formal she wished she *had* been late. It didn't help that there was actually someone in the room who looked worse for a change, because they were clearly with her.

"Kaylin," Caitlin said brightly. "Severn. Please come in. Lord Evarrim from the Arcanum chose to pay a visit in your absence, and as you *were* absent, he decided to…wait."

"I'm on report," Kaylin said, automatically. "He could have been waiting a long damn time."

"I believe Sargent Kassan made that *quite* clear. And in words that were vaguely less civil the tenth time. But as the Arcanum received a personal request to cooperate with the Lords of Law, from the Emperor Himself, Lord Evarrim resisted all attempts to be dislodged. He is not unattended," she added, lowering her voice.

No, Kaylin could see that. Teela and Tain, in spotless Hawk uniform, were almost under his armpits. They didn't exactly brandish their staves, but they didn't have to. She hadn't seen them look this Barrani-like in years. Three years. Well, if you didn't count the aborted attempt to visit the merchant.

"She wasn't talking about the Hawks," Severn whispered, as if he could read her mind.

No. She was talking about his four guards. "Maybe we could do this later?"

But Marcus had already seen them, and if Marcus had, every other person in the room, all quietly minding their own business, had as well. Kaylin squared her shoulders. "Don't let the Barrani touch Catti," she told Severn, out of the corner of her mouth.

"Way ahead of you."

She did turn to look at him then. As if seven years had never happened. It was almost too much. He met her gaze, and held it, and after a moment, he offered her a lopsided grin, something that never touched his eyes. It wasn't an apology; they both knew it. There wasn't one he could offer.

But he hadn't killed Catti.

And he could have.

All the whys she had refused to ask him, had refused to let him answer, gathered behind her lips; she closed her teeth on them, tried to swallow and blinked a few times.

"Later," he said. Not softly. But quietly.

For the first time since she had set eyes on him in the Hawklord's tower, she almost wanted that *later.* She touched Catti's face, in much the same way Clint had touched her hair, but for different reasons. And then she turned to face Marcus Kassan.

"Not in uniform, I see," he said curtly.

"No, sir."

"Don't 'sir' me," he snapped. He *was* in a mood.

"Yes—uh. Yes."

"Corporal."

Severn couldn't snap a salute without dropping Catti. But he did straighten out. "Yes, sir."

"You were given *strict* orders with regards to the off-duty Hawk in your company."

"Yes, sir."

"Did any of them include her presence?"

"No, sir."

"Against my advice, you were taken off report."

"Yes, sir."

Marcus snarled. Severn, new to the Hawks, didn't perform the requisite obeisance of exposing his throat. But Kaylin knew him well enough; even if he'd been a Hawk for years, he probably wouldn't. The fiefs were in him, and he'd lived them in a way that she could now admit she hadn't.

Because of him. He had been a lot weaker when he'd last carried her the way he was now holding Catti.

"Sergeant," Tiamaris said, in almost exactly the same tone he reserved for the word "children." "I required the Corporal's cooperation for work in the fief of Nightshade on behalf of the Lord Grammayre. Severn is subordinate to me, and I accept full responsibility for his presence here."

"And hers?"

"She was a civilian in need of protection," he replied, with such a perfect, deadpan expression Kaylin herself wasn't certain that she didn't believe it. And she *knew* better.

"The child, then, is Catti of the foundling halls?"

"Kaylin Neya identified her," Tiamaris replied. "I had no reason to doubt her word."

"And she was found?"

"In the fief of Nightshade."

"The fieflord—"

"Was not present. He had nothing to do with her disappearance," Tiamaris added.

Kaylin hated these conversations. She didn't see the point of people talking when everything they said was already obvious to everyone involved. At least paperwork had some vague point. Either that, or it was full of phrases and words that she hadn't bothered to master, so it seemed to be more important.

"Corporal," Marcus growled. "Report."

Tiamaris lifted a hand. "I think that...unwise, Sergeant Kassan. It is, of course, your call."

Kaylin was certain that Marcus would repeat his demand, and almost fell over when his jaws clamped shut.

"Lord Tiamaris."

Kaylin almost stepped behind the Dragon's broad back as Lord Evarrim of the Arcanum sauntered over. His four shadows sought to follow, but they were headed off by Tain; Teela joined him instead, and it was clear even to Kaylin that she would not have been his chosen escort.

It was also clear that, had she carried a dagger, he would have been its preferred sheath.

"Kaylin," she said quietly. It was a warning.

"Lord Evarrim," Tiamaris said, before Kaylin could speak. Not that she would have. "I had not expected to see you here."

"No, I imagine you didn't. There are, however, Imperial aides who are also recently arrived, and they will speak with no one. Not even Lord Grammayre, who is taxed by their presence." His smile was tinged with malice. "The mortal races are obvious and little patient. The subtle nature of immortal politics are obviously beyond their ken."

"At least we have the good sense to stay dead when we *are* dead," Kaylin snapped back.

Teela froze.

That was bad. Lord Evarrim froze as well, which was

worse. The moment went on forever, like one of those dreams in which you realize you suddenly have no clothing on in a roomful of vain, malicious nobles.

Tiamaris came to her rescue, such as it was. "Kaylin, Severn," he said quietly, "Much as I desire the ability to accommodate Lord Evarrim, I require your presence *now*. My apologies to the Arcanum," he added, tendering a bow to Lord Evarrim that was so far beyond what was necessary it had to be sarcastic, "but the Emperor's aides will not wait forever, and any attempt to keep them from me, now that they are alerted to my presence, would not be in your interests."

He put a bronzed arm around Kaylin's shoulder, and although the hand that fell across her shoulder looked gentle, it wasn't. Kaylin had the impression that his hand could have been cut off at the wrist, and his finger positions wouldn't change at all.

"Be cautious, Lord Tiamaris," Lord Evarrim said with a cold smile. "It cannot have escaped your notice that this one already bears a mark."

"In no way has it escaped my notice, Lord Evarrim. It has not escaped even yours."

Kaylin would have been shocked, but Marcus actually sniggered, and she couldn't add to that without earning Lord Evarrim's enmity. If she hadn't already done that merely by existing. She silently swore she would be eternally grateful to Tiamaris for his rescue as she crossed the floor, bumping into office-mates who, she realized, were at least as nervous as she was. Severn took a little longer to follow, as he didn't have the advantage of a Dragon's grip to ease his passage.

Everyone in the office was a Hawk, and all of them had seen active duty at some point in their tenure. They wanted to see Catti up close, because she *had* survived, and they had all been almost certain she wouldn't.

Proud day to be a Hawk.

But it was a bad day to be a Dragon, and Kaylin wondered how it was that eternity could actually wind up being so short. Because the aides that had been so obliquely referred to weren't human. They weren't Aerian, they weren't Leontine, and they weren't Barrani.

Which left three races, one of which she'd never actually encountered, given their racial agoraphobia, and the other two?

Dragon. And Tha'alani. Three of the former, and one of the latter, but one was enough if it wasn't dead.

Tiamaris's grip actually gentled, although his arm did not leave her shoulders. Which was a good thing. Sight of Tha'alani usually had two effects on Kaylin. The first involved a great deal of running, in the opposite direction, as quickly as humanly possible—and with her conditioning, that was pretty quick—and the second, when the first was denied her, throwing up.

But Tiamaris's body language, as the four aides approached, made her feel safe. That and unworthy of their attention, since they clearly had eyes for no one but Tiamaris.

"Lord Tiamaris," one of the Dragons said. His voice was not austere; it was ice. His eyes were that whirl of red-centered orange that was an instant sign of danger.

"Lord Diarmat." Tiamaris gave Kaylin's shoulder a squeeze—which she interpreted as a warning—before he released her and tendered the Dragon a bow.

Lord Diarmat was taller than Tiamaris, but he was more slender across the shoulders and chest. His hair was both shorter and darker, but his skin was a darker shade as well. He did not wear jewelery, which Kaylin considered a good sign, but he did wear the royal red, edged with platinum that was probably real, and cut across with the Emperor's emblem: a Dragon, in gold. He moved as if he wore no armor, and given her experience with Tiamaris, she knew he probably didn't.

"Lord Emmerian," Tiamaris continued, bowing to the second Dragon. "Lord Sanabalis." The third seemed older than the first two—graying hair did that—and returned the bow more readily. When he rose, there was an odd expression across his face, and it exposed lines that neutrality didn't. It wasn't—quite—a smile, but Kaylin felt herself drawn to Lord Sanabalis in a way that she wasn't to the other Dragons. Even Tiamaris, at least not when they'd first met.

He noticed her reaction, and he met her gaze with an open appraisal of his own. "Tiamaris," he said, his eyes not leaving Kaylin's face, "this is the girl?"

"Forgive my lack of...manners. Yes, this is Kaylin Neya. Kaylin, this is the Dragon who had the responsibility of tutoring me when I was considered young enough to be in need of lessons."

"He was a very focused student," Lord Sanabalis said, his golden eyes bright in a way that suggest liquid, not metal. "But unfortunately, he tended to choose his focus, and it was oft not the focus of his many teachers."

"This is hardly pertinent, Sanabalis," Tiamaris said, dispensing with the formality of the title.

"I see." The oldest of the Dragon aides turned. "Let me also introduce the fourth member of our entourage. This is Ybelline, of the Tha'alani."

Ybelline of the Tha'alani turned to look at Kaylin. So did her tentacles. Well, to be fair, they were more like long, dancing stalks that just happened to jut out of her forehead, and at a distance, they weren't as ugly, as, say, exposed Leontine teeth—probably because of the lack of blood— but Kaylin hated them with a passion. A meagre and stupid phrase which she intended to give real meaning.

The stalks didn't actually contain eyes—eyes were things that didn't pierce the surface, after all. But as far as menace went? Kaylin had made an inhouse motion that by law Tha'alani should be forced to bind the damn things to their heads with thick cloth—because no one *else* was allowed to run around the streets brandishing the most deadly of their weapons.

She had, of course, been denied the request, and also forbidden to make it through the usual bureaucratic channels, as it would reflect badly upon the multiracial makeup of the Hawks, and their leader. Especially their leader. She'd pointed out—loudly—that the Tha'alani didn't *join* anything; there certainly wasn't a single member of that race within the Hawks, so it shouldn't matter.

And Marcus had pointed out that there were worse things to be than a private.

So Kaylin smiled—in as much as that movement of lips could be identified as one—and bowed.

Ybelline's smile, however, was infinitely more gracious, and had it been on anyone else's face, it would have lit up a room. Or ten. In fact, if it weren't for those hated stalks, she would have been lovely; her hair was a pale, pale gold, her eyes were the color of brown honey and her skin—what little there was of it that wasn't covered by Imperial red—was unscarred and unbruised. She could almost give a Barrani a run for her money, and that could be said about very, very few mortals.

The smile faded, though, when Kaylin just couldn't match it. The bow became brisk and formal, and the Tha'alani turned back to Tiamaris, called Lord by three Dragons.

"The humans are necessary?" Lord Diarmat's voice was about as friendly as Kaylin's smile had been.

"They are my witnesses," Tiamaris replied, in measured tones. "But this is not the place for this conversation."

"Indeed. It appears that something that occurred within the fiefs has caught the interest of the Arcanum."

"The Lords of Law saw fit to ask the Arcanum for advice," Tiamaris replied, in his depths now. "And, as the Emperor's request was the one acceded to, I feel it is not my place to judge their presence."

"As you say. And what room in this building would do?"

"The West room" Kaylin heard herself say.

Tiamaris spared her a look.

"But we have a child who's been injured, and we'd *really* like to take her back to her—to her pride-mother."

"The child is not a matter that concerns us—"

"Lord Diarmat," Ybelline said, her voice soft, her expression…feminine. Wrong, to Kaylin's eye. "I believe that it is best that the child be examined. If her guardians will give consent—"

"Marrin of the foundling halls is her guardian."

"—I will ascertain that she is whole and unharmed, and that she is substantially the same child that she was before her abduction."

"I won't—"

"Kaylin." Severn stepped on her foot. "This is exactly what's going to occur. If you fight them, you'll just scare the girl, and you won't change anything else. There are worse Tha'alani than this one. Come. The West room."

They were joined by Marcus and Lord Grammayre. The former, the Dragons attempted to throw out—with words, of course—and the latter, they accepted without apparent qualm. It was a good deal less frosty in the West room than it was in the outer office, although given the amount of chatter—none—Kaylin couldn't say why.

"Kaylin." The Hawklord's wings were folded in a way that was just shy of tense.

She bowed, and made sure it was perfect.

"It appears you've been busy while on leave. I will not fault you for it. The child?"

"She's been injured."

"Marked?"

Kaylin swallowed and nodded.

He turned to the Tha'alani. "The child sleeps. I believe it would be best if she continue to do so. Can that be arranged?"

"Yes, Lord Grammayre."

"Tiamaris?"

"The child does not appear to be under the influence of magic," the Dragon replied, as if tendering a report. "Nor does there appear to be any enchantment that is active."

"Good. Ybelline?"

The Tha'alani nodded gracefully to the Hawklord. She failed to notice the way Kaylin tensed as she approached Catti, and even failed to notice the restraining hand that caught her upper arm.

Marcus, however, growled a warning. It wasn't pretty.

Kaylin could fail to notice many things, but not as gracefully as the Tha'alani did. She answered with a short Leontine phrase, and let go.

The stalks moved, elongating as Ybelline bent. The bend was, strictly speaking, unnecessary; she must have done it to make Kaylin feel less queasy. It didn't work, but Kaylin tried hard to appreciate the gesture.

She knew she was holding her breath because she exhaled—loudly—as those stalks touched Catti's forehead. Severn pushed strands of red hair out of the way, moving Catti gently so that she might be closer to the Tha'alani.

The woman's eyes closed. Minutes passed; Catti's expression shifted into a small smile. "She likes you," Ybelline said, and Kaylin started.

"Yes, she means you," Severn said.

"She trusts you," the Tha'alani continued.

"Is that pertinent?"

Severn, still burdened, stepped on Kaylin's foot. Kaylin tried to shut up; she knew the rules. One wasn't supposed to interrupt a Tha'alani investigation with speech. It apparently distracted them.

"Records," Lord Grammayre said. "Ybelline, we need to see what happened to the child. She is the only victim to survive, and this examination will be invaluable in our attempts to find her would-be killers."

Ybelline nodded.

And Kaylin, unhappy, nodded as well. She had known this would happen. Of course she'd known it. She just hadn't allowed herself to *think* about it.

"Catti would tell them," Severn said to Kaylin, and only to Kaylin. "She *wants* to be Hawk. She wants to be you."

"Catti's a child—"

"Not for much longer. If she is, now. She's asleep, Kaylin. She won't have to relive the experience. Wake her to get her permission, and she will."

Kaylin said nothing more. But it didn't last. "Severn—if I were her, I would still want that choice."

"You're not a child. You're *not* Catti. Let it go."

"They're *her* memories."

"Not all memories are a kindness."

"I wouldn't want to—" She stopped when Marcus growled. Sanabalis chuckled. "Tiamaris," he said, against convention, "I see that you have indeed grown in patience since I was last capable of being your teacher."

He was rewarded with two human glares and one Leontine chuckle.

Ybelline continued to stand above Catti, her hands by her sides. It was Ybelline's face that twisted, first in confusion and then in fear; it was Ybelline's face that froze in agony. Catti, peaceful, slept. And Kaylin, watching, felt the first twinge of something other than manic hatred for the Tha'alani. She had seen them work only rarely, and one of those experiences had been her own. But she had never truly watched their faces.

The last expression was a mingling of pain and something akin to joy. "You've arrived," Ybelline whispered, her voice carrying the texture of both of those sensations. She did not break contact, and she did not speak again.

They waited in silence, Severn, Kaylin and Tiamaris, remembering what they could of the quick, dark fight in the old watchtower.

But when Ybelline finally staggered back a step, it was Kaylin who moved to catch her; it was Kaylin who steadied her— and Kaylin had never willingly touched a Tha'alani in her life.

She knew, of course; the Tha'alani were sensitive to simple thoughts when they had even this level of contact. Stalks swivelled in the air, but they stopped just short of contact as honey-brown eyes opened.

"Kaylin," she said, with just a faint hint of question in the two syllables.

"You—you looked like you were going to fall," was the lame reply.

"The memories of the young are stark," Ybelline replied. "And bitter, in this case."

"In all cases." Sanabalis's voice was serene, his eyes gold. "It is seldom for reasons of peace or joy that the Tha'alani are summoned." He bowed to Ybelline. "You are afraid," he told Kaylin, "of what the Tha'alani see in you when they touch you. Did it never occur to you to think that they are not less afraid? It darkens them, always. And it wounds them. Very few of the Tha'alani can serve among the deaf for long."

"Deaf?"

He sighed. It was a gust of wind.

"Sanabalis," Ybelline said, her voice slightly cool, "that was unkind."

He shrugged. Kaylin realized she had never seen Tiamaris shrug that way. "So is she."

Ybelline began to speak, and Kaylin—who still held her by the arms—tightened her grip. "Don't defend me," she said. "I'll accept it. It's true."

"Fear does not make a kind person," Ybelline replied.

"Neither does envy. Could you *please* try to be a little less gracious?"

The Tha'alani woman laughed, and if her smile could light up, oh, the Imperial Palace, her laugh was better. Or worse, depending on how guilty one felt. Kaylin was caught between the two. She loosened her grip slowly, met Ybelline's eyes, managed not to flinch at the stalks, and

said, "If I ever have to face the Tha'alani again, could I call
you?"

"I am seconded to the Emperor," was the quiet reply, "but
in so much as I am able to choose my assignments, yes."

"You do her too much honor," Sanabalis said.

"She saved the child" was the serene reply.

"Not alone." Sanabalis's voice changed at the tail end of
those two words, and he turned away from Kaylin, from
Ybelline and from pretty much anyone else in the room who
wasn't Tiamaris.

"Kaylin," Marcus said in perfectly enunciated Leontine.
"Take Catti. Take Severn. Get out."

As he spoke, Lord Diarmat and Lord Emmerian stepped
toward Tiamaris; Tiamaris did not move. And Kaylin had
one of those sudden bad feelings that was a lot like losing
lunch, but without the mess.

"This room isn't big enough," she said, to no one in
particular.

"For what, Kaylin?" Sanabalis asked.

"One Dragon, never mind four."

Lord Diarmat frowned. "Tiamaris."

Tiamaris raised a brow at Kaylin.

"We have to stay. No," she added, after a pause, "I have
to stay. Severn, take Catti home."

"I'm not leaving without you. *We* can take Catti home."

"We're his witnesses. That's what he called us. And he
never says anything without a reason."

"Very good," Sanabalis replied. "She is not completely
hopeless, Tiamaris."

"I did not say *completely.*"

Kaylin shot him a dark look, but it was without heart. "When you—when it happened," she said, skirting what had suddenly become a dangerous word, "they felt it?"

"The entire Imperial palace felt it," Lord Diarmat replied.

"Meaning the Dragons."

"Meaning, as you quaintly put it, the Dragons."

"How?"

"That does not concern you."

"But it does. I was *there.*"

"Kaylin," Sanabalis said. He reached out slowly, but she wasn't fooled; when he touched her arm, his grip was like steel. "How often have you seen the change?"

"Never."

"Never?"

"I think even I'd remember that. Without help," she added, glancing at Ybelline. "It's not a big secret, is it?"

"Did you expect it?"

She started to say something cutting, and managed to shut herself up before it escaped. "Not that."

"Why?"

"Because I failed racial interaction classes."

"As *well as* magical classes?"

She gave up on the idea of pretending she was smart. Or pretending that the Dragons didn't know she wasn't. "Pretty much."

"Kaylin," Severn asked, both brows slightly raised. "Did you pass *anything* that wasn't practical?"

"Barrani."

He rolled his eyes. But his scar was whiter than it had been, and had he not been carrying Catti—still—she was certain his hands would be near some sort of weapon. It was damn hard to keep hers away.

"This particular part of Dragon culture is not studied in those classes," Lord Grammayre said. His wings flexed and settled. It was disquieting.

"I take it it's not exactly legal?"

"It does not have the approval of the castelord, no." Lord Diarmat frowned. "As Tiamaris well knows."

"And you're here to—to—"

"They are here to evaluate me," Tiamaris replied. "That is all."

"And if you fail?"

"I will be judged outcaste."

"You said there were no—oh." She turned to Ybelline. "You were sent to read *him*?"

"If it becomes necessary." Her reply was cool, now. "I do not, however, believe that it will be."

"That is not for you to decide," Lord Diarmat snapped. Kaylin could hear the echo of great jaws in the sound. She wondered what color he was.

"Blue," Ybelline replied. But it was a very quiet word.

"Tiamaris—tell them!"

"If," Sanabalis said, "you can contain your interruptions, he will do just that."

"And if you can't," Marcus added, "you'll be on the other side of the door. You decide in how many pieces."

"We entered the watchtower in the fiefs. It is an old watchtower," Tiamaris added, "and it is engraved in the style of the Old Ones."

Kaylin hadn't seen any symbols. She bit her lip. She also hadn't seen the entrance, if it came to that.

"The child was already marked, as Ybelline has seen. There were thirteen in the chamber."

"They were priests?"

"They were robed," Tiamaris replied. "And they carried daggers that were also marked in the old fashion. I believe the daggers were active at the time of their attempted use."

"The markings were," Kaylin added.

Marcus growled. A lot. But Sanabalis lifted a hand, granting Kaylin permission to keep her throat, at least until there were no Dragons present.

"What do you mean, Kaylin?"

"The marks on Catti's arms and legs. They were glowing."

"Tiamaris?"

The Dragon Hawk looked at Kaylin, and she knew she'd said the wrong thing, whatever that was.

"She was marked," he replied. "But I did not get close to her during the time the priests attempted to finish their ritual."

"Death magic."

"Of a certainty."

"How did you find the girl, Tiamaris?"

The Dragon's inner membranes rose. His eyes had shaded to orange. "I did not find her. Kaylin Neya did."

Six Dragon eyes, of a similar color, were not a comfort when they were suddenly all focused on *her*. Kaylin didn't squirm, but it took effort.

"How?"

Kaylin looked at the Hawklord, and the Hawklord nodded.

"I—a few days before she was taken—I was called to the foundling halls. She'd fallen. She'd fallen badly. I had to heal her."

Sanabalis stared at her, and the orange eyes in his friendly face were somewhat worse than the same color in the granite faces of the other Dragons. "How badly injured was she?"

"She was dying."

"Was she conscious?"

"No. She was barely there at all."

"Continue."

"I found her," she said, trying not to sound defensive. "And I brought her back. I healed the injuries."

"So. Tiamaris, this was not mentioned in your report."

"I was not aware of it until today, Lord Sanabalis."

"Very well. There was a connection between the child and Kaylin Neya. You used it?"

"Kaylin Neya did. She found the child." He paused, and then he, too, stared at Kaylin.

"We reached the watchtower," she said faintly, "and we made it in through the wall."

The Hawklord closed his eyes.

"And there were Barrani there. They were *all* Barrani."

The Dragons exchanged a single glance as if it were a hot coal. "Thirteen is a large number," Lord Emmerian said at last. "But in and of itself, it does not justify the extreme measures taken."

Kaylin hadn't finished. "But they weren't—" she took a deep breath. "I've seen dead Barrani before," she told them quietly, again looking to the Hawklord for permission. His wings flexed; his face, impassive, had turned an unusual shade of gray. "And they were usually missing things like, you know, their heads. Or their hearts. But these were different."

"Think carefully, Kaylin," Lord Sanabalis said. His voice was gentle. Gentle, in this case, was not good.

"They were dead," she told him. "They were all—I'd bet on it, with my own money—dead."

"Tiamaris?"

"There is nothing left of either their work or their bodies," the Dragon replied.

"You are certain of this?"

"I am certain."

"Thirteen," Diarmat said, in a voice as soft as Sanabalis's. "Are you *certain* the girl is not mistaken?"

"I ate one," Tiamaris replied. Had he been any other Hawk, Kaylin would have sworn he was joking.

But the reaction of the other three Dragons made it clear they took it literally, and if they were grim, they were satisfied. She wondered, then, what he'd be able to tell her about herself if he'd eaten her. Which was more stupid than her usual idle thoughts.

Lord Diarmat bowed. "Lord Tiamaris," he said quietly. "We will expect you in the Emperor's presence before sunset. You have been injured. See that the injuries are tended."

Good of you to finally notice, Kaylin thought sourly.

The only person in the room who could hear it gave a faint smile, and for the first time in her life, Kaylin didn't resent the idea that someone could pluck her thoughts, defenseless, from behind her closed lips. She met Ybelline's brief glance and actually smiled.

"Kaylin Neya, you are forbidden to speak of this to anyone," Lord Diarmat added.

"Ummm."

Marcus actually closed his eyes. "Kaylin…"

"Does Lord Evarrim count?"

CHAPTER 17

Apparently, Lord Evarrim *did* count.

Marcus, however, was not about to let the Dragons take it out on her—at least not right away. He looked at Severn, and said, "Corporal, go see the medics. Now."

Severn's hesitation was not marked in any way by nervous motion; he just stood there, waiting.

Waiting, Kaylin realized, for her. "I'll see that he gets there right away," she said, putting her hand on the small of his back and attempting to give it a subtle shove. "And we'll take Catti back to Marrin."

"No," Lord Sanabalis said, "you will not."

The hair on the back of Kaylin's neck rose. It might have been a bit more obvious, had Marcus's fur not got there first. The white-gold undersides of his close-skin fur were easily visible. So were his teeth; the black of his lips had pulled right off them.

"Were the current Emperor not so secure in his rule, there is every likelihood that he would demand the child's death."

"*Kaylin,*" the Hawklord said. "*Sergeant Kassan.*" He turned to Lord Diarmat. "My apologies, Lord Diarmat, Lord Sanabalis. The full context of your intent is not clear, and they *are* Hawks."

"Imperial Order does not require explanation." Lord Diarmat had drawn himself up to his full height while he spit the words out.

"No," Lord Grammayre said, "it does not. Nor does acceptance of Imperial Order require grace."

But Sanabalis relented. A little. "You care for the child, Kaylin Neya. That much is clear, from both your reaction and Ybelline's. That she cares for you is also clear, and we will trust your discretion in how she is told that she is not—yet—ready to return to her home.

"She is not safe there," he added. "Unless we leave Dragons in full force in the halls, she *cannot* be made safe there, and if the Dragons are forced to act—as Tiamaris did—the rest of the children will, in all likelihood, not survive."

"But what will you—what do you intend—"

"I give you my word," he said gravely, and she *knew* what that was worth to a Dragon, "that she will not be harmed. The guard that she cannot be given in safety in the foundling halls, she *will* be given in the Imperial Palace."

"She won't be turned over to the Imperial mages?"

"No. They may examine her, but I will be present for those examinations, and as we have already had the

Tha'alani's testimony, there is limited information that they can glean. They will not be allowed to enspell her."

"We need to explain this to Marrin," she said quietly.

"Marrin?"

"Her pride-mother. The Leontine who runs the foundling hall."

"Ah. I don't envy you the task. But I trust that you will survive it."

The medic on duty was Moran, an Aerian who would probably have been happier had she been born a Leontine. She had a great eye for detail—like, say, the ones you were failing to mention during her checkups—and absolute intolerance for stoicism. It made her oddly appropriate for the Hawks, but rather temperamental.

She was waiting, the duty table ready, when Kaylin managed to push Severn through the door. She clucked three times, which emphasized the birdlike build that most Aerians *didn't* have, flexed her wings in the universal gesture of disapproval and took Catti from his arms.

"Kaylin," she said, as she laid Catti on the table. "You look well." Bruises, unless they were the wrong color—and Kaylin seldom asked for a more precise definition than that—weren't a cause for Moran's concern.

"You found her," Moran added softly. "Has she regained consciousness?"

"She was awake when we found her," Kaylin answered. "But she had to be examined by the Tha'alani."

"Before she came here?"

Kaylin cringed. "The Tha'alani kept her asleep for the duration of the examination. You could probably wake her up if you wanted."

But Moran shook her head. "She's exhausted. Look at her eyes."

Her eyes are closed, Kaylin thought. But she obediently looked anyway.

"And her lips are cracked. She probably hasn't had much to drink for the last two days." She pulled the tunic up, frowned at the shallow abdominal cuts, and turned toward the cupboards in which she hid her healing unguents. Kaylin privately referred to them as poisons. "They'll heal fine," Moran continued, her voice soft. "And I don't think they'll infect."

"And the—the other marks?"

"They're not bleeding," Moran said. "And they're not wounds. I don't think they're tattoos—and if they are, getting rid of them is probably going to be more painful than putting them on was in the first place." She paused for just a moment, staring at Catti's face, a Hawk's pride in her gaze. "Good work," she told them, although she didn't look away.

"You," she added, to Severn.

"Severn," Kaylin supplied.

"Severn, on the other table." This was more like Moran's regular bedside manner. Probably the reason she didn't have a private practice. Her wings bent.

"She means it," Kaylin said, under her breath.

Severn sat down heavily.

Moran made him strip, and then let him have the sharp edge of her tongue. "You were walking around like *this*?"

"Clearly."

"He used to be a Wolf," Kaylin said, by way of distraction. "He's been a Hawk for a short time, so he's not used to the—"

"Spare me. I've done field work with the Wolves before. And the Swords. You Law people are *all* the same." She went back to the cupboards, grabbed bandages and something that looked suspiciously like needles, and came back to the table. "This will probably hurt some," she said. It didn't sound like an apology. "You've lost blood, but I imagine you know that by now. You've got enough scars."

Severn, flat out on his back, managed a shrug. "They didn't kill me."

"These ones won't either."

Because Kaylin knew Moran, she knew that this was a good thing, although Moran's tone of voice certainly didn't manage to convey it. "Can I watch?"

Moran shrugged, which was a clear yes. Kaylin grabbed a stool—Moran's wings made regular chairs a tad unwieldy—and dragged it over to Severn's side. She hesitated for a minute, and then caught his right hand.

His grip wasn't strong.

So much to say. Kaylin, often accused of loving the sound of her own voice, couldn't figure out where to start, and didn't bother. She just held his hand while Moran set about stitching him back together. He tensed several times, but true to form, didn't utter a word.

But he didn't close his eyes much either, and his gaze stayed locked on Kaylin's face.

When Moran was finished, and only barely, Kaylin excused herself. Severn started to sit up, but Moran started to stutter, and Moran won, as she so often did in the area she ruled.

"I'm just going to Marrin," Kaylin told him quietly. "I won't do anything else."

"You can mirror her," he said, through gritted teeth. Moran had actually *hit* him.

"I can. But I'd rather talk to her in person."

Which was more or less true. More true while she was in the Halls of Law, and less—and less—as she drew closer to the foundling halls. Leaving Catti with Dragons had taken on a whole new meaning, and she wasn't much liking it. She wondered if Marcus had *seen* Tiamaris go berserk before. Decided against, although it would explain a lot.

Amos was on duty, even though it was later. He was on his knees in front of the front gates, and it looked like he was trying to fix the latch. When he saw Kaylin, which was pretty much after she almost tripped over him, he stiffened and rose.

She smiled. "Catti's safe," she told him quietly.

All the stiffness went out of him, then. "I'm too old for this," he muttered. He often said it, but it had a different meaning today. She put a hand on his shoulder.

"It wasn't your fault," she told him quietly. "And you're

actually fond of children. This isn't supposed to be a prison, it's supposed to be a home."

"Kaylin—"

"I would have been happy, here. I am happy here," she added. "And I wouldn't choose a different guard for these gates. Is Marrin all right?"

"What do you think?"

"I think I'll go in and talk with her right now."

Marrin was already at the doors when Kaylin entered.

Kaylin held out her hands, and Marrin was across the foyer in a leap and a bound. Not really a good sign. Leontines could keep up a fight-ready response for a damn long while, but it took its toll.

Leontine nostrils flared.

"I would have mirrored," Kaylin said quietly. "But there are some things mirrors don't capture."

"You found her." She could pick up Catti's scent.

"She's alive."

"*Where?*"

"In the Halls of Law. Marrin—"

Marrin had already started for the door, and Kaylin managed—by dint of years of training—to beat her there. It was close.

"She's my kit too," the Hawk said. "But she's been marked. Like the other victims were marked."

"She wasn't harmed?"

"Not through lack of trying."

"Who?"

"If it wasn't worth my life, I'd tell you."

Leontine growls of this particular nature made the more distant threat less effective. But not by much. Kaylin was a Hawk, and if she hated Imperial bureaucracy as much as the next Hawk, she also played—mostly—by the rules.

"Marrin, it was because of *me* that Catti was taken."

Marrin stiffened. Her teeth were just a little too prominent. "What do you mean by that?"

"The healing," she said softly. "They took her because I healed her. Because the healing made a connection between us that *had* to be there if Catti was to survive.

"It's still there," she added, voice low. "If we bring her back, they'll just take her again."

"You didn't kill them?"

"We killed them."

"Good." It wasn't; Marrin wanted to eviscerate them herself. But she was old enough to be practical. Just. "But you don't think you killed them all."

"I'd like to think so," Kaylin replied. "But the Imperial aides don't."

"I want to see her."

"I know. But she'll be surrounded by Dragons. Can you handle that?"

The hiss was loud and long. Higher than Marcus's, but more menacing. Leontine women were always the greater danger.

"They want her at the palace. Catti would like it, I think. And she'll have so much to tell the others when she comes back."

"When or if?"

"When," Kaylin said firmly. "Definitely when. I know it's not over," she added. "But it's going to be."

"Kaylin. Kitling."

"Yes?"

"Don't do anything foolish." Marrin's fur was falling. Her lips were slowly lowering over those impressive canines.

"I won't do anything illegal, if that's what you mean."

"That's *not* what I mean, and you know it." She reached out, and her palm-pads were dry. Kaylin caught Marrin's hand and turned it over. The pads were a shade of pale gray, and cracked.

"Marrin!"

Marrin's dry chuckle almost made Kaylin cry.

"You're a Hawk," the mother of the foundling hall said, pulling her hand back and raising it to brush Kaylin's hair from her forehead. "But you're still one of my kits. Don't forget it. Don't let anyone tell you differently."

"Except Marcus?"

Marrin said something rude in Leontine. The equivalent of *men*, and in that tone of voice.

"I have to go back to the fiefs. We found her there," she added. It was hard, with Marrin, to be less than open. "And the answers are there as well."

"Answers? To what questions?"

"The ones about me."

"Kaylin—does this have anything to do with that mark?"

Kaylin self-consciously raised a hand to cover her cheek. "You noticed."

Marrin snorted. "Flowers are not your style."

"Yes. No. Maybe. I don't know. But—I'm going back to the fiefs. Catti's marked. And until this is over, she's not safe."

Marrin's eyes narrowed. "This has something to do with your marks?" She had never asked before.

"A lot," Kaylin replied.

"Will you take that young man with you?"

"Young man? You mean Severn?"

"The one you were having the…argument with."

Kaylin laughed. Only Marrin. "Yes," she said quietly. "Without him, Catti would have died."

"Is there something you want to tell me?"

"Marrin, there is *so* much I want to tell you—"

Marrin's great, furred arms caught Kaylin and drew her close. Heart-close. "I'll tell the children," she said softly, her voice a sensation along the top of Kaylin's skull. "You go and do whatever it is you need to do."

"Am I off report?" Kaylin stood in front of Marcus's desk. Marcus, for once in his life, seemed to find paperwork of interest. Either that, or he was considering some new way to shred it.

"I didn't put you on report. Take it upstairs."

"He wants to talk to me?"

Marcus met her eyes. His paw pads were moist; she knew this because he placed one over her hand. "Good work," he said quietly. "And yes."

"The Arcanists?"

"Apparently they were suddenly concerned with something that came up in idle conversation."

Kaylin winced.

"You *must* learn not to let arrogance goad you."

"Yes, sir."

"You're still on report."

"Yes, Marcus."

"Good. Go on." He lifted his hand; she still felt the tips of his claws against her skin as she started her way toward the Tower stairs.

Lord Grammayre had done her the kindness of leaving the door open. She approached him with the grovelling diffidence of a criminal as he gestured them shut behind her, half-expecting that she'd once again end up in that damn circle.

"Rise," he said, his tone of voice conveying an irritable *get up*. She didn't wait to be told twice. Usually, on the other hand, she didn't wait to be told once, which was often a bit of a problem.

To her great surprise, Tiamaris was in the tower, waiting. He was once again kitted out as a Hawk; the bronze armor was gone.

"You were supposed to go to the Palace."

"I went."

"But you—"

"Kaylin."

She looked back to the Hawklord.

"Lord Tiamaris's business is his own, and I trust you have learned enough today to understand why."

"Yes, sir."

His left wing flicked. "Lord Tiamaris?"

"I believe that we require her presence in this investigation."

"Clearly, if you seconded her *while* she was suspended." If he was annoyed, he was also amused. He could cross that line with little warning and less cause, so Kaylin decided to keep quiet. He turned to the mirror. "Records."

The mirror flared. The light was unusual, even for a mirror, and after a moment, the Hawklord spoke his name.

And she saw Catti, surrounded by robed men. From Catti's viewpoint. It was impossible for Kaylin to keep her hands from her daggers; she didn't even try.

"These are the men you saw?"

She nodded grimly, watching them.

"Records," Lord Grammayre said again. The scene shattered in an abrupt shift. She recognized the image that coalesced, although it wouldn't look that way again for some time: It was Catti's room, but it wasn't empty. There were men in it; they were also robed.

The walls tilted. Catti screamed. Red light filled the room.

"Magic?" She asked.

"Yes," Tiamaris replied. "Magic. Records, hold."

The image froze, the corner of the ceiling at the wrong angle. The Dragon pointed, and she could see—but barely— that one of the intruders held something crystalline in his hands. The source of the light. "Play." It was gone.

She wondered just how much useful information they could get from this; Catti was struggling wildly, and faces went in and out of the mirror's view. Catti was a foundling, and all grand dreams notwithstanding, she wasn't a Hawk; she couldn't see as a Hawk saw; couldn't expect that if she survived, anything that could be pulled out of her viewpoint might be useful.

The light grew intense. In the distance, Kaylin thought she heard growling. Marrin's.

"The same men?" she asked quietly.

"Possibly. There are fewer."

"If they had tried to kill her there—"

"The timing," Tiamaris said quietly, "was not right. They could kill her there, if her death was to be instant." He walked over to the mirror, held out his palm. It shifted again.

"Can you hear them?"

She nodded. "But I…don't understand what they're saying."

"No. It isn't Barrani."

She frowned. "It sounds like—"

"It is, to the best of my knowledge, a dead dialect. There will be similarities, however. If you heard the language spoken at length, you would probably understand half of what was said."

Dead dialect for dead Barrani. Made sense to Kaylin.

"Why aren't we allowed to speak about this?"

The Hawklord and the Dragon exchanged a glance.

"Look, it isn't like we haven't fought corpses before.

We've certainly had our run-ins with outcaste mages, and this wouldn't be the first time someone has used the dead."

"Did these strike you as the usual type of corpse?"

Given that the usual type of corpse was, all arguments aside, on a slab on its way to its family or the burner, Kaylin had to shake her head.

"Did they actually look dead?"

"With Barrani, it's probably hard to tell. They're perfect most of the time; I don't see why a little thing like death should get in the way of making the rest of us feel ephemeral and ugly."

He smiled.

Tiamaris did not. "How did you know that they were dead, Kaylin?"

She thought about it for a minute. Or longer. "They were slow," she said at last.

Tiamaris raised a brow. His eyes, however, were gold.

"For Barrani, they were slow. There were thirteen of them. I have a feeling that fifty wouldn't have stopped you—" She caught the Hawklord's expression and shifted direction rapidly. "But the four that had Catti should have been able to kill her well before Severn reached her."

"True. But not, I think, the answer."

"I don't know," she said defensively. "I've seen dead Barrani before—admittedly not often—and no, these ones didn't look like corpses. They just didn't look...alive."

"You see, Grammayre? Kaylin," he added, "have you ever healed Barrani before?"

She frowned. "No."

"Ah."

"What's that supposed to mean?"

"I am not certain. I think, however, that some part of the power that you use for healing has made you sensitive in ways that others would not be. If Severn had been asked, he would not have tendered your answer. To him, they might have been slow, but they wouldn't have been dead."

"But you knew."

"Yes," he said quietly. And grimly. "I knew."

"It has to be better news than live Barrani. For one, we'd probably all be dead if they had been."

Lord Grammayre said, "It is not better news."

"I kind of guessed that. I don't understand why."

"I am not entirely certain myself. Elantra is mere centuries old, and it is clear that the history of the times before its rise are now deliberately murky."

"Tiamaris?"

"The Barrani can die," he said quietly. "Of old age. It happens, but it happens seldom. Their age is not reflected physically—the death might go undetected by all save Barrani, otherwise. But when it happens—and I cannot think of a single such incident in the past three hundred years—the body is destroyed by its kin."

"So… what you're saying is they have no soul?"

He grimaced. "I am *not* going to ask you whether or not you studied religion when you were schooled here."

"I learned everything that was practical."

"Clearly your definition of what is practical needs some refinement."

She shrugged. He was obviously right, and love of argument only extended so far.

"That there was one such dead would be cause for concern among the Barrani."

"Why? Is it like a disease or something?"

"It is indeed exactly like that."

Her open mouth stayed that way, deprived of words.

"But I believe more insidious. There are stories, in human lore, of creatures who, while dead by any reasonable definition, create more dead. Records?"

"Vampire," the mirror answered, in a crisp and uninflected authoritarian tone.

"Ah. Yes, that is the word I was looking for. Unlike the corpses that walk—or shamble—these vampires were possessed of cunning."

"And strength, and speed, and the ability to, oh, turn into bats or wolves or rats." Kaylin snorted.

"The Barrani dead are not unlike that. While we do not believe they can reliably transform themselves into another form, they retain memory, and they offer something to the living in return for death."

"What? What could they *possibly* have to offer someone who's already going to live forever anyway?"

"That, Kaylin, we do not know. And there is not a single Barrani who would willingly answer the question, if they even know the answer. From your impertinent comment, Lord Evarrim knows that at least one such creature exists. It would not be a stretch to assume that there are more."

"There *were* more."

"And that they might indeed be old, if they are dabbling in the magics of the Old Ones."

She was silent. After a moment, she said, "There's something you're not telling me."

"She wasn't a good classroom student," the Hawklord said drily, "but there was a reason we allowed her to graduate in spite of that."

"Yes," Tiamaris said, ignoring the Hawklord. "There is something I'm not telling you."

Which meant that he wasn't going to. She rolled her eyes, shoved her hands in her pockets, and looked at the two men. "We're going back to Nightshade," she told them.

"Given your success while you were suspended," the Hawklord replied, "I am inclined to put you back on the duty roster. Yes," he added softly. "If there are answers, it is in Nightshade they will be found.

"Before you leave, however," Lord Grammayre continued, "there is one thing that I wish to ask you both."

Kaylin looked up. In fact, looked at anything but the circle at the Tower's center.

"Lord Grammayre?"

"The Tha'alani reading was, of course, expertly handled. It gave us details that we would never otherwise have—in particular the making of those marks—and the method of travel from the foundling hall."

"That is not, from the fire left in its wake, a suitable method of travel, Grammayre."

"No, it is not. That is not the pertinent question. Catti was aware of your arrival because it made a good deal of... noise."

Tiamaris nodded.

"She was not, however, aware of *how* you made that arrival."

"No."

"Kaylin, the Lords of Law have sealed the watchtower, and at the moment, the Imperial aides are examining it closely. It appears that a large hole was made in the external bearing wall."

She cringed.

"You were under strict orders. Where is the bracer?"

"I'm not sure."

"I see."

"Lord Grammayre, I will take responsibility for my intervention. She could not locate Catti while wearing the bracer."

"Nor could she destroy the outer wall."

Silence. Kaylin looked at the perfectly stiff Dragon face, and she was surprised. Tiamaris hadn't mentioned the destruction of the wall.

But Lord Grammayre *was* the Hawklord. "Kaylin."

"I'm fine."

"That in and of itself is cause for concern. I have seen the wall," he added quietly, "and the power it would take to destroy that wall resides in the hands of very, very few."

She said nothing. But in a contest of silence, she was always going to lose. "I wasn't out of control."

"No." He hesitated. "But even had you been, you would have felt its effects even a year ago."

"I do feel them, I just don't—"

He lifted a hand. "There is power in you," he said softly, "and it is growing. Be cautious, Kaylin. If you find the bracer, put it on. You are too emotionally involved in this." His wings stretched out. "If time were not of the essence, I would keep you here. But that, I think, would be costly. Go. Take Severn with you, if you can get Moran to release him."

She hesitated; something Tiamaris had said had taken a few minutes to work its way up to her conscious thoughts. "Tiamaris?"

His gaze was lidded, opaque.

"You said they couldn't kill her there because of the timing?"

He said nothing.

"And the timing's *today*."

It was the Hawklord who nodded, his eyes dark with something like sympathy. And rage. "Fly," he told her softly.

CHAPTER 18

Moran looked up when Kaylin entered the infirmary. Her brows gathered, and her forehead creased in its most frequent expression. "Which part of two days rest was unclear?"

Severn sat up, which deepened the lines around Moran's pursed lips. He started to speak a name, and stopped; it wasn't Kaylin.

"We don't have two days," Kaylin told the medic. "If we're lucky, we have two hours." And she'd wasted hours already.

Severn sat up, swinging both legs off the bed.

"He won't be at his best," Moran said, her voice shifting slightly, her oddly speckled wings flicking at her back. From Moran, this was almost miraculous.

"How much off his best will he be?"

The medic's wings flicked again. Kaylin winced. But she couldn't quite bring herself to tell him to lie down. And one short day ago? She probably wouldn't be here at all.

"Nightshade?" Severn asked, retrieving what remained of his clothing. It wasn't pretty. "Where are my weapons?"

Moran's left wing rose toward the far corner, and Kaylin retrieved Severn's sword, chain, four daggers and belt. They weren't exactly light.

"The quartermaster is swearing his head off," she added, "but not at you."

"I wasn't there."

She laughed.

He frowned. "Kaylin?" Apparently it was the wrong sort of laugh.

"I wasn't *thinking*," she told him, the words spilling out before she could—yes—think of stopping them. "We rescued Catti. But it isn't over. Tiamaris thinks—"

"They have to sacrifice someone else."

She nodded bitterly. "Today."

"There's not much of today left."

"There's sun."

"Do they need it?"

"Sun? How the hell should I know?" She took a deep breath, and added, "Tiamaris is waiting for us."

"Where in Nightshade are we going?"

"I *don't know*. I—what I did to find Catti I can't do for anyone else. And there's going to be *someone*, Severn. I—"

Moran's pursed lips parted. She stepped over to Severn, helped him kit up. From her cupboard of poisons, she brought out a small jar; liquid sloshed within the ceramic container. She glared at Severn until he opened his mouth, lifted the lid, grimaced at the smell and poured a large amount of what was causing that grimace into Severn.

Who gagged, but swallowed.

She put the lid back on, her frown etched around her eyes. "Kaylin."

"Moran?"

"Bring what's left of him back here, got it?"

Tiamaris met them on the steps of the Halls. She saw his back first; he was gazing fiefward, his hand across his eyes. The sun was heading toward the horizon.

He started to move when they reached him, and neither Severn nor Kaylin had much to say; they hit the streets in a slow jog, rattling like tin cans. Well, Severn did. Luckily, stealth was not an issue.

They all wore the emblem of the Hawks. Had they been thinking, they'd have ditched that—but they weren't about to turn around for something as trivial as dress. And it was a sign of the day that it *was* a triviality. Kaylin paused at the foot of the bridge, staring at the moving waters of the Ablayne as if she could read them. She freed her hair, pulled it back more tightly, twisting it into an almost uncomfortable knot, and exposing as much of her face as she could in the process. She shoved the stick back through its center.

"If mages were actually useful," she said, as she turned from the water and toward the fief, "they'd make hair things that actually keep the hair *in*."

Severn said nothing; he wasn't fooled by much. He stared at the symbol of Nightshade on her upturned cheek.

"Let's go," she said softly.

"Anywhere in particular?"

"Castle Nightshade."

He grimaced. But Tiamaris, still silent, nodded.

There were, as always, guards at the gate. Kaylin walked right past them, and they allowed this—but they intercepted Severn and Tiamaris. Almost grinding her teeth in frustration, Kaylin spun on her heel.

"We *do not* have time for this," she snarled. All in all, it was a damn good impression of a pissed off Leontine. "I am going to see Lord Nightshade, and they are coming with me. *Now.*"

One of the guards raised a black brow in almost sardonic reply. The other stepped back, toward the portal that only happened to look like a portcullis. He vanished.

Kaylin suppressed the urge to stab the remaining guard, mostly because it wouldn't do any good. Only because of that. And he knew, and it amused him. But Tiamaris held most of his attention; she was an afterthought. Severn didn't touch his weapons.

The guard reappeared, and gestured to his companion, who lowered his sword.

"By our Lord's leave," he said, with emphasis on every word, "we bid you welcome to Castle Nightshade."

Kaylin burst through the blackness as if it were gauze. It was the first time that passage into the castle hadn't disoriented her, and in some ways, she regretted it; she was almost shaking, torn now between fear and rage. It was a bad place to be.

Lord Nightshade was waiting for her, and everything she felt—too complicated to put into words of her own—must have been clearly written on her face; his expression shifted slightly.

"Lord Tiamaris," he said. "Severn." Niceties out of the way—and those were the extent that he offered—he turned to Kaylin. "There was a disturbance in the fief this afternoon."

"Yes."

"On several levels."

"Yes."

"You have come about them?"

"No."

"Ah. And you are dressed as a Hawk."

"Overlook it."

"I have." He inclined his head slightly. "What would you have of me, Kaylin Neya?"

Sarcasm had deserted her, and without it, she felt defenseless. Exposed in a way that being underdressed failed to achieve. "The Long Hall," she told him. And then, voice lower, "The seal of the Old Ones."

His brows rose slightly. "Tell me."

"Tell you what?"

Tiamaris touched her shoulder. "Kaylin, we have little time. Waste it in defiance, and it is still wasted. In the end, Lord Nightshade is Barrani. He gives nothing away. Pay this price, or pay a dearer one later, but decide now."

She met the fieflord's gaze, squared her shoulders, lifted her chin, and broke Imperial law. "There are dead Barrani wandering around your fief."

Nothing about him changed, and everything did; Kaylin wished the Records were recording the meeting, because she'd have time to peruse them later; to study, to learn and to understand. Now, she had instinct.

It was a poor substitute for time.

"Dead?" he said softly.

"Not in the normal way. But yes, dead. One of the disturbances."

"They were… in possession of the child."

She nodded. It didn't surprise her that he wasn't surprised.

"They did not complete their ritual."

She shook her head.

"Very well. That is enough, Kaylin. I need not caution you not to speak openly of this."

"No. I've already broken Imperial command to do it here."

"Here," he said, with the first faint hint of a smile, "there is no Imperial law." He turned and began to walk.

It was the first time in her life she could honestly say that she appreciated the lack of law in the fiefs—the lack of any law but the fieflord's. Kaylin followed, and after a moment, so did Severn and Tiamaris.

"Not the Dragon," Nightshade said, without looking back.

"There's nothing there he doesn't know about—"

"Not the Dragon."

"Tiamaris?"

"I am content to wait." It was more or less true. He stopped in the hall before the big slab of runed stone and folded his arms across his broad chest.

Lord Nightshade lifted his hands and placed them against the wall. The runes began to glow; this much, Kaylin expected. But beneath her uniform, she could feel the symbols across her skin begin to burn, and this, she hadn't.

She bit back surprise; it came out as a grunt, no more. Severn's hand touched her shoulder. She looked up and shook her head; the pain hadn't gotten worse. It hadn't gotten any better, but she could live with that.

Lord Nightshade, however, frowned. "Do you understand that there *is* a danger in what you propose?"

"I've been there before," she told him quietly. "I understand."

"It is a greater danger."

"Figures."

The doors opened, the wall sliding in on itself and evaporating, as if it were liquid. Just beyond them, sitting as she had first seen them, were the two Barrani. Their eyes were closed, their flawless lashes glinting with reflected light. This time, she took a long look at them before she walked through.

"They're not—"

"Like the ones who took your child?"

She nodded.

"What do you think, Kaylin?"

It was a long time before she found an answer. "No." It sounded like a yes.

This time, neither of the living statues moved.

"You are not bleeding," he said quietly, as if she had asked why.

She had never particularly liked the stiff poker face that Barrani of power habitually employed—but she found herself leaning toward learning it, and soon. If she could learn the language, anything was possible. Well, except for the grace.

Severn settled in by her right side. She kept herself from reaching for his arm as she walked, her eyes upon the heights.

"What would have happened if I had stayed in the seal's circle, that first time?" Her words echoed. They sounded thin and forlorn, and she hated that.

"I don't know," Lord Nightshade replied. "It was not, at the time, a risk that I was willing to take."

"And now?"

"There are greater risks." His steps, unlike her voice, were heavy, authoritative. This was his territory, and she was—barely—a guest.

"You could be more," he said softly.

"I think I'd rather be less." There was no defiance in the phrase; it was muted, and shorn of defiance, it was that most contemptible of things, to the Barrani: honest.

But he chuckled, which surprised her. "Not even vulnerability," he replied, "is outside of the game."

"She is not yours," Severn said coolly. He managed to keep all threat from the words; they sounded, to Kaylin's ears, like a statement of fact. Weather fact. Geography fact.

"And where," Lord Nightshade answered, "would the game be in that?" And he stopped in front of the doors. Kaylin would have sworn it took vastly less time to traverse the Long Hall than it had before.

"You must open the doors," he told her.

She winced. But she looked at the doors, and this time, Hawk's eye made them slightly different. Granted, she hadn't spent a lot of time looking at their faces before; she didn't have eyes in the back of her head.

"Why?" Severn said.

"Because speed is of the essence" was the cool reply. "Severn, you *are* a guest, and you are granted the hospitality of my Halls. Do not, however, confuse hospitality with tolerance."

The scar across his jaw stood out, but Severn nodded grimly. Kaylin, standing between them, noticed it all. She said, to Severn, "The marks on the door. Look at them."

"They're like the marks on you."

She nodded. "I…don't think they were here. Not the last time I saw them. The marks were different." She lifted the palms of her hands, clenched her jaw and touched the paneled surface.

Felt not prickling, but fire, and almost pulled her hands away. But the fire felt was not real; it was the effect of magic's summoning.

"Kaylin?"

She shook her head. "I'm—it's fine." But her hands were numb as the doors rolled slowly open; she had the momentum to push them because she had weight behind her.

The doors opened into the runed room. There were no trees, no captive forest, no gloomy arboreal sky beneath which they must pass; there was stone. Stone and light.

Severn caught her right arm in almost the same way that Lord Nightshade caught her left; they held her fast between them. And in spite of this, she was three steps over the threshold before she realized she was walking. "Kaylin," Severn said, speaking directly into her ear, his lips touching the edge of her lobe. There was warning in the word, and fear. None of it was for himself.

She could hear the voice of blue fire, and wondered if, were she mage-trained, she would ever hear fire's voice in any other color. Dim thought. She tried to pull free of her anchors, and almost succeeded.

The ceiling was alight; the foreign, ancient words seemed to swirl in a motion that made them look like burning water. Like a whirlpool, whose center was not yet visible. Things on the edge were crumbling, the letter forms dissolving in a slow rush of burning rain.

The floor was no different, and it was upon the floor that she struggled, dreaming of flight. Dreading the fall.

Severn's grip was stronger. She could almost look away from the light to see his face, its network of scars, the lines that had been cut there by weapon, the ones that had been worn there by age. His eyes were dark, and narrow; he looked like a hunter. Seven years had changed them both in ways that neither of them could have foreseen when they had been children in the fiefs.

Seven years.

And he *had* come after her, as she'd feared, but not, in the end, for the reasons she'd been half-certain he would. He had watched her, as the wolf watches; he had given her time and space in which to hide, in which to tell herself stories and lies. Had she healed at all?

Jade.

Steffi.

She was moving. One step after another, dragging with her men who were larger and stronger. The patterns on the floor lit the way, and as she passed them, she guttered their light. Or absorbed it. Her vision was not clear; it was clouded by brilliance that she could not raise hand to relieve.

"Kaylin Neya," Lord Nightshade said, his lips also close to her ear, teasing hair. Command in the name; she would have obeyed it if she understood it clearly. She had always feared the fieflord. But she had never known him. Did not know him now.

Light erupted from the center of the floor; the floor itself seemed to slant, to tilt toward that center. The seal was there, but she couldn't see it; fire had consumed its edges, the definition stone gave. She turned, blind, to Severn, and shouted, "My hand, take my hand!"

His grip shifted, warmth leaving her upper arm, fingers crushing her palm. He said her name, again, but this time it was a different name; different syllables. For just that second, she could see him clearly.

Lord Nightshade shifted his grip in like fashion, without need for words; she swayed between them, the whole of her upper body tilting forward, and forward again, in a long, dangerous lean that seemed to go on forever.

This, this was falling.

And the fire waited to catch and devour her.

It did burn.

But what burned? Not cloth. Not flesh. Words, perhaps. All the words she had. And as she lost them, the fire coalesced, but what had been hazy and indistinct was now bright, clear—more so than she'd ever been to herself. A man stood, robed in living, liquid flame; taller than Lord Nightshade. Taller than any man she had met, except in dream. His skin was shining, his arms, burning. Eyes that were bluer than flame opened, met her gaze. Hands that trailed flame reached out to touch her. To touch her arms. To touch her thighs.

She could feel neither of her hands, although she could see his as if at a remove. The pain, however, was real. It always was.

She bit her lip, tasted blood.

The man spoke a name, and although she had never heard it before, it was hers. She looked up, and up again; there was no stone here, no sky; there was a sense of nothing that went on forever. For perhaps the first time, she wondered about the downside of immortality.

"Kaylin."

"Elianne."

Distant words. The man stared at her, and she stared back, trying to remember how to speak.

He was frowning; she could see that clearly. "Chosen," he said, at last, although the two syllables were broken and stretched, as if they were spoken in a different language entirely, and had a different weight, a different meaning. "The portals are opening. You bring shadow with you."

She couldn't see herself clearly. Not as clearly as she could see him.

"You are a flawed vessel," he continued. "And you cannot be made whole."

Judgment, then. She almost bowed her head. Almost.

"What are you?"

It was a ludicrous question. She framed an answer, shorn of words, and offered it. Speech left her like light stained by color.

"What is a Hawk?"

A Hawk. Is that what she'd said? *An officer of the Lords of Law.* But that wasn't an answer. It was something said to a stubborn door-warden, a pompous merchant, a petty thief. She had never really asked the question herself, except when she was sick and tired of basic training; the Hawks were home, and home was something she didn't question too closely because she might lose it.

"What," he asked again, "is a Hawk?"

Hawks were birds of prey. With good vision. They circled the city; were, in fact, contained by it. They flew at the command of Lord Grammayre, and returned the same way. But no, no, this was wrong.

Wrong, because she didn't have *time*.

"Why?"

Because, she thought, irritation slowly overriding pain, Catti was safe—but Catti was one child.

Kaylin had become a Hawk. Yes, she'd failed almost every class she'd been forced to take. She'd learned to read, to write and to speak Barrani, because the Hawklord made absolutely clear that without these, she would never fly in his service. She learned the Laws, and learned how to maneuver around them without being outflanked, if it came to that. She'd spent more time than she cared to remember arguing with merchants, and bureaucrats, oh, hell, and everyone, about the subtleties of that law.

And at the end of the day, it didn't matter.

Because at the end of *this day,* a different child would be dead, a different child would become part of Records, his or her body covered in wards and disembowelled in some horrible act of ritual that she was powerless to stop.

You can't save them all. Who had said that? Marcus?

Then what's the point?

You want to live in a world where no one *even tries?*

No. And there was only one way *not* to live in that world. To try. To live through the horror of failure; to endure the guilt. To try again. To make that choice.

She lifted her chin, met his gaze. Her vision was clearer now.

"You are tainted," he said again, but this time, there was

resignation in the words, not judgment. "You are mortal. This, we had not foreseen. What knows age, what knows death, knows change…it cannot know perfection. The taint was in you before the mark was laid upon you. The taint was in you before the mark was changed. But you were Chosen," he added. She could hear the crackle in the words. Timber being consumed. Or time.

"You cannot open the way," he told her. "And you cannot close it. You are a key." But he lifted his hands. "The world changes, is changed. You were Chosen. You *are* Chosen. What you are must be enough even if you are too fragile for what you bear. To cleanse you would destroy you."

He laid those hands upon her brow.

"Something calls us." He paused, and then added, "Something has called our brethren. What wakes one, wakes all. Silence the call, before it is too late, and we will sleep."

How? How could she silence something she couldn't even hear? How could she stop someone from calling if she couldn't find them?

His eyes became so wide they took up half his face. "I cannot teach you," he said. "You would age and perish before you learned to hear. Look within yourself, and only there. You bear their taint now. If that is not *all* you are to bear, learn to see."

Her eyes began to burn. She could see his fingers moving, deliberately and slowly, as if they were brushes, and she were parchment. She wondered what he was writing there before she was in too much pain to wonder anything at all.

* * *

She was screaming as they pulled her from the pillar, although later, pain aside, she could *not* remember why. Severn had one hand in her hand—fingers pale from lack of circulation—and one on her upper arm; it was bleeding.

"He was unwise enough," Lord Nightshade said with a grimace, "to touch your forearm while you were…in conversation with the Old One."

Severn laughed. "Then there are two fools here, Lord Nightshade." Kaylin, foggy, thought it was the first time she had ever heard him use Barrani in that tone of voice. As if it were his natural language, and not something to be endured.

"I am protected against many things while I rule this domain," the fieflord replied, but there was a tightness in his voice.

Kaylin blinked. The room was dark. "Are the marks gone?" she whispered. Actually, to her embarrassment, she croaked. Kind of like the proverbial frog, but worse.

"They are not gone," Lord Nightshade replied. He lifted her to her feet, and his motion made her realize that the whole of her weight was carried between them. "But they are…lessened. Kaylin, what happened?"

"I…don't know." She shook her head. "But we can figure it out later. I want to—" She stopped. Looked at her arms. Flinched, and looked at the rest of her. She was completely unclothed, and covered, in places, by fine ash. Trying to cover herself with her hands was a lost cause; they were anchored, and neither of the men who anchored them seemed to be in a hurry to let go.

But before she could retreat into embarrassment—worse embarrassment—her skin caught the whole of her attention. From the underside of her breasts down, she was covered in writing.

And it was glowing, faintly, each thick stroke like the work of a master calligrapher. The center of each letter form was a crystalline blue; the edge of each, a black that she had seen only on Catti, and only when Catti had been beneath the blades.

Severn was the first to release her. Nightshade's hand lingered a moment longer, as if he did not trust her.

"Severn," she said, in the same croaking voice, "is my back like this too?"

"Right up the nape," he replied.

"What does it look like, to you?"

"Ash. It's gray," he added. "And different from the arm markings." He paused. "What does it mean?"

"How the hell should I know? He said I was tainted," she told them, her eyes drawn to the patterns, absorbed by the trace of their curves, the way they moved at the rise and fall of her chest. "But that I was all they had anyway." Her arms were shaky; her fingers were also white. She massaged them; apparently blushing did not extend to her hands.

"We almost couldn't hold you," Severn told her. His voice was low. Low enough that she had to listen to catch all the words.

"I saw you," she whispered. "I heard you call my name. Both of my names," she added, turning to catch Nightshade as well. "It was…enough. Lord Nightshade, I need a big room."

"Not this one."

"No. *Not* this one."

"And clothing?"

She swore. "That, too. Do you have *anything* practical?"

The answer was a big, fat, "sort of." Which he didn't say, of course. He didn't speak mortal tongues, at least not in her presence, and his Barrani was a bit on the stilted, high-caste side for her liking; it didn't contain colloquialism. He brought her a shirt, and pants—but they were silk-soft, thin and clingy. The Hawk was also absent, and she missed it.

Her hair was still bound, her face mercifully free of any mark but his. She avoided the mirrors in the room to which he led them, but it took a bit of work; there were a lot of them, all taller than she was, and all—of course—very fine.

"How long?" she asked them both.

"Less than ten minutes."

Plus another fifteen to get here and dress. "What time is it?"

Lord Nightshade gestured, and one of the mirrors shifted in the peculiar way that mirrors—enchanted ones—did. It became a window; she could see the streets of the fief beyond the castle, although it took her a moment to orient her vision.

"What do Barrani want?" she asked him, as she stared

at the falling shadows, the lengthened shadows, of the fief's buildings.

"Many things. But the dead? I cannot say."

"Power?"

"Power, perhaps. Life. For the Barrani, the two are not easily separable."

"I don't understand how they die," she said.

It was a question. He didn't answer.

She undid a button or two, rolled up her sleeves. She would have stripped, but there were witnesses. Witnesses who had already seen her butt-naked, but she still felt self-conscious. The Seal room had receded, and she was returning to herself. Whoever that was.

Her arms were still glowing, and the blue fire trapped there was like a written promise. In a language that she didn't understand.

She looked at the mirrors. "Are they all magic?"

"They are."

"Can they—do you have a map of the fief?"

A dark brow rose. It was an expression that was almost familiar. A Dragon's expression. A Hawklord's.

"Records," she said softly.

He smiled. "That is not the word that activates them, Kaylin. Ask, however, and I will grant you access."

"Where's Tiamaris?"

"He will be here soon."

"Good."

"How?"

"He's used your mirrors before. I haven't."

"He cannot pay the price of their use, now."

"What price?" She met his eyes. Her voice was almost normal. Almost. "I'm tired of games."

"That is because you are young, and you have not yet realized that that is *all* you have."

"No," she snapped. "It's all *you* have."

"A challenge?"

"A fact."

"Kaylin," Severn said. She looked at him; she had almost forgotten he was here. This was not his realm. But it wasn't hers either.

"The dead Barrani are in your fief," she told the fieflord. "They're gathered somewhere in Nightshade. You can't find them. Not in time."

"The death that they will offer today is not the death it would have been had they killed your foundling."

She didn't ask him how he knew what he knew. It would have been a waste of a question, had he answered. "So you think you have time?"

"I think *you* have time, Kaylin."

"I don't."

"Oh?"

"They know. They know that we know."

"It is…possible."

She waited. Realized that he could outwait her, in any number of ways. He probably had more people killed in a year than she could save. Certainly more than she intended to save today.

"What do you want from me?"

"Ah. Now that *is* an interesting question." He stepped away from her as he spoke, and toward the bank of mirrors; each one reflected his expressionless, flawless face. "What do you think I want, Kaylin?"

"I don't know. But I'm betting it has something to do with these." She lifted her arms; the sleeves, unbuttoned, fell immediately to her elbow in a fine drape of dark cloth.

"Betting is a mortal pastime."

"It's just another game."

"But mortals seldom gamble with anything of value."

Had he been standing closer, she might have hit him. The anger was sudden and sharp. Severn caught her eye, held it a moment; his jaw was clenched, but it stayed shut. For better or worse, this was her conversation.

"When Severn came to you," she said, her voice low, "you knew."

"No, Kaylin. I suspected."

"You let the killings happen?"

"I did not understand the purpose of the killings." His eyes narrowed. "And in truth, I did search. I understand some of the power inherent in death magic, but it was not a power that expressed itself within my fief. That, I would have known." He turned away; she saw, in multiple reflections, the length of his hair. "But when I met with Severn, when he spoke of you, I began to understand. I did not realize, at the time, how dangerous you were.

"How dangerous you would have been, had he not come to speak with me at all. Do you? Do you understand what you might have meant to Elantra? I think even the Dragon Emperor would have felt your threat, had he assembled the whole of his Court and taken to the streets against you. What," he added softly, "might have remained of those streets.

"But now? You were marked by one force. You have been slowly marked by another. I think of you as something fragile, balancing on a thin line that you cannot even *see*. And in that balance, should you manage to hold it, there is something of value."

"Power."

"Perhaps. But I will say this—if there is power, it will be yours."

"And not yours?" She lifted a hand to her cheek.

His smile was subtle. "Were I capable of taking what you might possess, perhaps. But others have played that game in our long history, and it is a dangerous game."

"You like games."

"Indeed. But I feel that a game is something that is played only when there is a chance of winning." He paused, and then he lifted his hand to the surface of one stretch of mirror. "The Dragon comes," he said, almost bored.

And the mirrors sprang to life, in concert. Not even the mirrors in the morgue could boast such a wealth of instant detail, such a depth of color, of vision.

"Lord Nightshade." Tiamaris tendered him a bow. A real bow.

"Lord Tiamaris. I believe that your part in this is almost at an end. I could, however, be mistaken. Come, Kaylin. This is my fief."

Kaylin stared. After a minute, she remembered to close her mouth.

* * *

The fief was not seen at a distance; not from a height greater than the tallest part of Castle Nightshade. But no matter how far away the farthest of the streets were, she could see them, could make out the details. She could also see the people in the stretching shadows; they were few. Night would fall soon, and although it was not yet upon them, they gathered their belongings, closed up their carts, made their way to their homes.

She could see the Four Corners, and she could see, as she followed their stretch, the building that she had once called home. Could see windows, and wondered who lived there now. There wasn't much space in the fief, and new occupants often didn't care what had become of the old ones.

But in all of this, she could see no answer, just the passage of time.

Severn came to stand by her side, and Tiamaris also joined her. The two men bore the crest of the Hawk that fire had burned from her. But she held its truth closer than that, now; it wasn't a simple adornment. It wasn't even a statement meant to convey authority to outsiders. It was what she *was*. Or what she hoped she could live up to being. She had to try.

Lifting her arms, exposing what she had always hidden, she stared at the blue and the black that adorned her arms until one melded into the other.

"Tiamaris," she said.

"Kaylin."

"This is the language of the Old Ones?"

She saw the shadow of his nod from the corner of her eye. "What were the Old Ones?"

"We are not entirely certain. Fragments of history exist, but not one living creature remembers them." His tone suggested that this was the reason there *were* living creatures. "Some believe that they gifted the races with language," he added. "With sentience."

"Why? Why would they do that?"

"Who can say? Why do painters paint? Why do singers sing? Why do writers write? There is an impulse to create."

"And to destroy."

"Yes."

"Are they so different?"

"That is a Barrani question." The Dragon's response was cool. Sort of like fire was cool.

"Why did they need language?"

"Pardon?"

She shook her head. "These," she said, lifting her arms, "are words. You said that. These are their words. But—but they sound so powerful. You said that it isn't even safe to study the words. That mages have died."

"Yes," His eyes narrowed. He reached out, his palm hovering above her skin, as if she were an artifact as dangerous as the ones that had killed those mages.

"Why did they need them?"

"Why does any thinking being need language?" He withdrew the hand. "You were not, perhaps, the best of students, Kaylin. But you *learned* to speak Barrani. You learned the

Leontine that would draw you closer to Sergeant Kassan. You failed—"

"Almost everything else. I know."

"Then why could you learn the languages?"

Because she had no choice. She couldn't be a Hawk without learning them. And she *had* to be a Hawk. She started to say this, but it wasn't entirely true. She had some small gift for languages. At least compared to her gift for any other academic subject. Memory intruded, as it so often did. "It was…something the Hawklord said. When I told him I hated Barrani."

"What was that?"

"That language was both a window and a wall, and that if I knew the words, I could choose which it would be. Without them, I had nothing—no way to—"

Understand.

"Words are power," she said softly, repeating Lord Grammayre's distant words as if she had just heard them, would always hear them. And she closed her hands, fault lines, life lines, disappearing in the clench. She stared at her arms. "You could read some of this."

"Some. But Kaylin, I cannot speak it. No one living can. We do not know the sounds, if they even had them, that those shapes represent. We guess at the meaning, but even that is like walking in the dark."

In the dark.

"I learned Leontine," she said. "You're right. I learned it for Marcus, because it was part of him. And Aerian. I learned that. Not for the Hawklord. For Clint. Because he loved it when I *tried*." These memories intruded as well, and she gripped them tight.

"I spoke with the Old One," she added softly.

They all froze.

"But I didn't use words. I couldn't. I spoke, and he understood, even though I didn't shove the meaning into containers."

Hesitantly, tracing sigils and their edges in the recess of memory, she, too, began to walk in the dark.

She heard Lord Nightshade's cutting breath, saw the light play against the motion of his hair as he moved, and moved again, standing in place, pivoting as the surface of silvered mirror, perfect map, shifted.

He turned suddenly to face her, and he held out his arms, mirroring her gesture, making the poverty of both her strength and her grace absolutely clear. Facing her, reflecting her, he waited, his eyes a shade that was exactly the heart of the darkest of emeralds.

And then he smiled, and gestured. "Kaylin Neya," he whispered. She felt every syllable. Without intent, her lips moved in reply, but she did not speak; didn't have to.

His name was in the air between them, window and wall, and the pattern of it—she could touch it without giving it voice, invoke it without descending into syllables. It was like, and unlike, the marks upon her arms, slender and intricate where they were bold, simple and stark where they twisted in upon themselves like snakes or vines, living things. It was like, and unlike, the symbols that adorned the ceiling and the floor of the seal room. Like, and unlike, the conversation with the Old One.

It was a part of her, the way the symbols were. It was a bridge, between what she had learned in the Tower of the Hawks and what she been given, in ignorance, as a child. A key.

A gift.

Her eyes widened.

Lord Nightshade's eyes were as wide as she had ever seen them, and they were blue, crystal blue, a color that was too pale for Barrani. She had feared him, had always feared him; he had been a shadow. The fieflord. Another death.

But she saw clearly, for a moment; he was death, yes, but he was not dead; he was more.

"You lied," she whispered.

He smiled. "Truth, like beauty, is in the eye of the beholder."

"I don't understand," she said, almost shaking her head, unable to keep expression from her face. "Your name—you *gave* it to me. It wasn't necessary."

"You see much," he said, "that I would have kept hidden from you. Yes, Kaylin. I could have pulled you from the seal, then, without offering you what I have offered none of my kin in centuries."

"But…but it's your *name*. I don't understand."

"Nor have you need," he replied. "Understanding is the end of the journey. Come, Kaylin. Find what I cannot find." He lifted a hand, brushed the mark he had placed upon her cheek. "You have paid. You bear my name, and you bear my mark. If I have given you something, I am Barrani—I have taken something in turn."

She could have pulled back; she didn't. The tips of his fingers were warm, and his expression was—almost—gentle.

"Time, Kaylin," he told her, and he lowered his hand.

She was left with his name in the silence.

With all the names of power that were written upon her, over and over, like bane and blessing.

"Yes," he said softly. "They are names. Some, I might have recognized once, had they been given to me. They are the names of the dead," he added, as her eyes widened. "But not the dead alone. Written there are also—I believe—the names of those who sleep—light and dark, law and chaos. Death magic," he added softly, and looked at Tiamaris. "Did you not tell her?"

"It was not necessary."

"Knowledge is power."

"If you can guard it, yes. Otherwise, it is simply death."

"Isn't it just power gained from killing?"

He laughed. "Then all power held in Elantra is death magic. No, Kaylin. It is…more than that. The names that are written, in a tongue that even I cannot read, have no power over the living. They once did. But they were uprooted. In our history, we struggled against the nature of names—they were our one weakness, our one vulnerability. What we learned in that ancient struggle we do not speak of openly, nor will you. But there are those who lost their names, and retained only the ability to invoke the power inherent in them."

She shook her head. Felt, for a moment, that she was stuck in a magic class again. Except *this* one wasn't theoretical.

"The dead ones do not know what they write upon their sacrifices," he said softly. "They know only that it brings them power for a brief time. They are lost to us. They have the cunning and the intelligence of our kind, but they are animals. And they are free. My name," he added, "is a binding. You can see it.

"See it. But understand that it is more—and less—than what your vision makes of it. Do not speak it."

She didn't need to. She knew she didn't really know who he was. But some part of her had thought she understood him, as much as she understood any Barrani who didn't wear the Hawk. She knew, now, that she didn't. He had given her something she couldn't have taken by threat or force. She didn't need to understand it; it was his name, but it was also hers.

"No one wrote these," she told him.

"Someone did."

"Who?"

"Say the Old Ones…perhaps it is true. Or say nothing. But time, Kaylin, will destroy you, in one way or the other. Choose."

Choice. She bit her lip and nodded.

Extending her arms, she stepped toward the mirror and touched the closest surface with the tips of her fingers. She stared at the symbols that were part of her skin, and drew them out, not speaking, no longer trying. They danced there, trapped and aging, and she caught them.

Tiamaris spoke. She didn't understand what he said.

But she didn't need to.

She could see the shadows seep from her skin into the mirror, part of her, and not part of her; could see them questing and struggling across a foreign landscape, flat and cold; could see them, at last, come to rest, to spread and deepen, gathering and dousing light, until only they remained.

She could almost feel their hunger; she could certainly feel their cold, their quest for warmth. Something sharp moved her; it was almost like pity. Except for the anger, the bitter, bitter anger, that followed.

"There," she said softly, and for just the space of that word, she could have been speaking her native tongue, Barrani or Leontine; they were equally alien.

"Kaylin." Severn's voice. Severn, not Barrani, not Dragon. She turned to look at him, then. Saw his expression, unguarded, the stillness in his face jarring.

She closed her eyes, pulled her hands away, lost the thread of words that were not her words, but part of her anyway, and *looked*.

The shadow covered a city block, and at its heart, waiting, something that spun that shadow, spreading it.

"What *is* it?" Severn asked her.

She shook her head. "I—I—"

"She doesn't know." Lord Nightshade looked beyond them both, and met the whirling red of unlidded Dragon gaze. "Lord Tiamaris?"

"It…is not possible."

"Tiamaris?"

He didn't answer. Kaylin hesitated for another heart-beat—and heartbeats had never seemed so long—before she touched the mirror with the flat of both palms and *twisted*.

"Lord Grammayre!"

In the flat of the surface of a single pane, the Hawklord looked back from the heights of the Aerie. "Kaylin?" It wasn't the first time she'd surprised him, but it was one of very, very few.

She could see, behind him, something on the wall; it was flat. He wasn't in the Tower.

"Records," she said, in a voice only slightly less intense. "Capture this image." She fed it the shadowed block.

"Records, display," the Hawklord said.

She had only once seen the Hawklord's wings snap up and out in the way they did now. It had almost killed her. "Yes," she said, seeing what he was seeing. "I need the Hawks. I need them there."

"Summoned," he told her, lifting both his hand and his voice. "Don't do anything foolish, Kaylin—"

She shattered the image, and turned to Severn.

"Do you need *all* of those daggers?"

CHAPTER 19

"The daggers," Lord Nightshade said softly, "are unlikely to be of use."

As she'd seen that for herself, she couldn't offer much of an argument, but she hated to be without a weapon.

Severn unbuckled the belt that held his daggers; he didn't wear arm sheaths. "Take them," he said. "I won't be using them." And he began to unwind the long chain.

Lord Nightshade watched the play of light against the links; it scattered, and the mirror returned the pieces, oddly contorted. Which, Kaylin thought, was about what you could expect from enchanted mirrors of a certain quality: they noticed things you couldn't. Well, that she couldn't, anyway. "You were not taught the use of that weapon by a mortal," the fieflord said, after a pause.

Severn shrugged.

"Nor was it made by one."

"I didn't ask."

The fieflord's lips thinned in frown. But he let it pass. "I am unused to allies," he told Kaylin. "And I work well alone. But I will meet you there." He paused, and then added, "Lord Tiamaris, I trust you know the way out?"

"I have found my way out of Castle Nightshade once before," the Dragon replied. "I trust that this time, my exit will be less contested?"

Barrani smiles were never warm. But the fieflord's was probably as close as they came; whatever past experience existed between them, Dragon and fieflord, amused him. "My men will be otherwise occupied." He reached out, and touched the surface of one silvered pane. It was not the pane that held the location of the shadows.

No image greeted that touch, or if one did, it was meant for the fieflord, and only the fieflord. "Ready my armor," he said. "And my sword. Gather in the courtyard, and do not tarry." He stepped toward the mirror, and passed through it, leaving them alone in the room.

"You know," Kaylin said, as the last of his cloak was swallowed, "I think I want one of those."

"No you don't," Severn replied, with the hint of a smile. "They're really not safe to use when you've been drinking. You have no idea where you'll end up."

Kaylin ran. The lack of armor, of anything confining, made her step lighter, her stride longer, than it usually was in an emergency. This meant that she wasn't left behind.

She had expected Barrani guards to be waiting around the corner, but the halls were cavernous in their emptiness.

Tiamaris did not lead; he followed Kaylin instead. "Kaylin," he told her, when she paused, "the fieflord has not yet finished with you."

She nodded, her thoughts elsewhere. "You can't go Dragon again, can you?"

"I can, as you so quaintly put it, 'go Dragon,'" he said, "but not without cost." From his tone, she didn't think the cost political. And because he was a Dragon, she didn't ask.

"How can we fight them, then?"

"Fire." He lifted an arm. "That hall."

"We don't have fire," she replied, as she caught sight of the light of candles, and the familiar curve of ceiling beneath which they burned. She made her way toward it.

"We don't," he agreed. "But the Hawks will not come unprepared." His smile was a momentary thing. "I have not seen Lord Grammayre in flight for some time."

"I'm not sure I've ever seen it."

"You will."

She would have replied, but the door swallowed her and spit her out before she could frame words.

She hit the ground swearing, rolled and came up unsteadily on her feet. The passage *into* the Castle had been so smooth, she'd expected the exit to go almost unnoticed.

Severn and Tiamaris fared better.

"He did that on purpose."

"I doubt it," Tiamaris replied. "And that was an impressive display of linguistic talent. It is unfortunate that it was so…limited in content."

"Sorry. I'd have added something in Dragon, but you're the only Dragon I know, and you don't swear much."

"If you are very lucky, that will continue to be the case." He lifted a brow. "Look," he said, and pointed.

She looked up. Even at this distance, she could see clearly that the sky was full of Aerians. The Hawklord had emptied the Aerie. She smiled. "Come on. We've got half a chance to beat them there."

Severn was already running.

They ran in the shadows of the fief's taller buildings; it was like a mininight of its own. If the fieflord's men had chosen the same route—and they knew the fief easily as well as Severn or Kaylin did—they moved quickly enough that they were far and away ahead. Kaylin had to remind herself that it wasn't a race.

But it *was*. She had to pause for breath, and Severn was half a block ahead before he noticed; he ran back, frowning.

She shook her head. "It's nothing." The exhaustion of using her power was beginning to make itself felt. She willed herself to ignore it.

"Kaylin, we're in Nightshade. Your body is now covered with writing that neither of us can read, and you just manipulated mirrors that are probably personally keyed to the fieflord in ways that neither of us can imagine. You've been bathed in magical fire, you've spent half the day running and you probably haven't eaten anything."

"And you did?"

"I was with Moran."

She grimaced. Unfortunately, her stomach agreed with Severn. "I'm not a wolf," she said at last. "I guess I'm not used to running."

He told her to do something that was anatomically impossible. In Aerian. She laughed out loud. "I don't even *have* wings," she said, as she straightened her shoulders.

"It's not lack of training," he said. He caught her by the shoulders, swung her around, and forced her chin up; his chain batted against her shirt, a reminder that she wore no armor.

He knew her almost better than she knew herself. Seven years, and none, passed between them. "I'm—" She shook her head. "I don't know what it is."

Tiamaris joined them quietly. "Severn?"

"Something's wrong."

"He means," Kaylin added, "*more* wrong." But the weakness in her limbs was almost a blessing—she should barely be conscious. Had the Old One somehow given her a reprieve?

The Dragon offered a rare smile. Without another word, he lifted Kaylin off her feet. She would have said something—and at that, something rude—but her arms and her legs were tingling, and that took the edge off her pride.

The streets passed beneath their feet as she rested against the broad chest of Dragon, her eyes on the sky.

* * *

The fire that lanced from ground to sky was a spectacle. It was hidden in part by the facade of old buildings, by the cramped quarters in which the poorer part of the fief huddled. But Kaylin could see the sudden orange glow, the tongues of leaping fire that sun didn't cast, and had she been running, well, she wouldn't be.

Tiamaris had nature's affinity for flame; either that, or as a Dragon, he was immune to it. He certainly wasn't bothered by it. Nothing about its presence gave him pause. Then again, neither had the dead Barrani, and he had known, before either Kaylin or Severn had, exactly what he faced.

"It appears," Tiamaris said, as the fires grew brighter, the orange melding into a sustained white, "that Lord Nightshade moves swiftly when he has cause." He stopped running and set Kaylin on her feet. "And it appears," he said, as she found those feet, and they rounded the corner onto Mayburn street, "that our enemies are not willing to be caught unprepared a second time."

"How do you know it's the fieflord?"

"Because it is his magic," the Dragon replied. "And the Hawks above have only just begun to circle. I do not think the ground Hawks have yet breached the fief." He drew his sword. It looked a lot like a dagger in his hand, straight and two-edged.

Not that she had time to really examine it; fire demanded most of her attention, partly because it was attached to moving people. And they didn't seem keen on burning.

In fact, to her dismay, they didn't seem to *be* burning. The fire followed them, clinging as it could to their surcoats, their hair; it was reflected in their eyes and by their swords. But it seemed to touch only those things; it didn't stop the swords from swinging.

Barrani, she thought, seeing them. It was possible to tell which were Nightshade's and which were not because of the fire; these Barrani were faster than the ones in the robes had been. There were similarities though; they didn't seem to notice the loss of a limb if it wasn't the one attached to their weapon.

She counted. It had been part of her basic training, this act of counting things in motion. She'd passed because it had been practical. And because she'd passed, she was here, in the streets of a fief she had promised herself she wouldn't return to, the numbers adding up to something she didn't like.

"Severn?" What Nightshade's Barrani couldn't do, they didn't have a hope in hell of doing themselves. And the enemy was in front of the only doors she could see. All four of them. The fighting had not yet spread to the doorways themselves. There were too many.

"Ahead of you," he said. "They can't occupy the whole block. Which building, Kaylin?" All of the words sharp, pointed.

She couldn't say. The map had seemed so damn clear at the time, the shadows so prominent, it hadn't even occurred to Kaylin that it was *possible* not to know the answer. She did what came naturally in the fiefs; she slipped back into the shadowed street they'd barely left.

Think, damn it. *Think*.

"Was Nightshade there?" she asked Tiamaris. The Dragon shook his head. "Okay. Let's go round the back."

"And hope that there is one."

Mayburn was long and narrow; it was, as most of the old roads were, punctuated by stone, rather than smoothed by it. There was a well along Mayburn, just a half block up from Triberry, the road they now followed. Behind Mayburn, parallel to it, was Culvert Road—which, like many of the fief's street names, had no meaning now.

Kaylin stopped at the well.

It was, as far as wells go, in decent repair, and it was obviously in use, given the season—but it wasn't thirst that stopped her. It was the woman; she was nestled in the lee of the rounded stone. Or she appeared to be. But Kaylin was a Hawk.

"Leave her," Tiamaris said quietly. "She's dead."

Kaylin heard him, but didn't take the time to argue. She changed her running stance, lowering herself almost to the ground, as if something as simple as a crossbow bolt could come out of any of the higher windows. She reached the woman at the same time Severn did, and she flinched.

He looked at her, aware of the motion, of what it might mean.

The woman *should* have been dead. But she wasn't.

Whoever had stabbed her—and it was a long, clean wound—had missed her heart. Not, from the blood that fled her lips, other vital organs. Her hands were red and wet, evenly gloved in red liquid.

Kaylin's arms *hurt*. But not as much as this stranger did, and the one pain overwhelmed the other. She slid her arms around the woman's shoulders, bent her head over the slack face, as if, for a moment, protecting it from witnesses. Spectators.

Severn touched her shoulder, but did not speak; Tiamaris, she was no longer aware of. "Can you do this?" Severn asked softly. She knew what he meant. Not the saving of the life, but the ability to do *anything* else afterward.

Before she could answer—if there was one—his fingers briefly tightened. It was his way of acknowledging the other question that he hadn't asked. *Can you walk away?*

This close to another person's face, vision blurred; Kaylin had no need to shut her eyes. She felt the power trickle down her arms, into her hands; those hands were pressed against shoulder and chest. The woman was larger than Kaylin, but curled in on herself as she was, the difference wasn't as significant as it would have been if they had tried to move her.

"She's lost a lot of blood." Her words. Clinical.

Severn said, "There are no medics here, but if you think you can hold on to her, there *are* a lot of Aerians."

She bit her lip, nodded, and let the power go. Unlike the healing with Catti, this was at least familiar. When the midwives called her, it was often because they thought they would lose mother—and child—to bleeding. They weren't always right, but they were right often enough.

That was harder than this. Blood from a bad birth came

from a jagged wound, several layers of torn flesh. It wasn't as clean. But her response was the same.

First, stop the bleeding.

Second, try to get the heart to work a little bit harder to replace the blood. Change something here, there, give something a little push.

She tried not to hear the screaming in the distance, because it *was* distant. The fieflord was in the streets. The Hawklord was above them. They could take care of things for *just* a little bit longer.

She finished the first; it wasn't actually hard, because, given life, time would do as good a job as she did now— messy, but functional. She just didn't have time of her own to do more.

But before she had finished the *real* work, the woman's face moved, her forehead jerking forward so suddenly, she clipped Kaylin's jaw. Kaylin caught the woman's hands as she tried to push herself up.

"My daughter," the woman said. Her voice wasn't strong, but it was low and intense; the words cut.

Severn knelt by her side. "We're here," he told the woman, in a much firmer voice than Kaylin could muster, "to save your child."

The woman had clearly lived in the fiefs for all of her life; suspicion and desperation wrestled for control of her features, and desperation won. It was close.

"We're Hawks," Severn continued, meeting and holding the wild gaze. "Look." And he pointed to the skies. To the Aerians that Kaylin had spent her adult life envying.

The woman's gaze was fleeting; it grazed sky, no more. But her hand rose, shaking, to touch the emblem emblazoned across Severn's surcoat.

Tiamaris came at last, and he bent, but did not kneel. "Tell us," he said, "where they took your daughter."

The woman lifted her hand and pointed.

Tiamaris lifted Kaylin by the arm. "Can you walk?"

She nodded.

"Can you run?"

Nodded again. Her hands were sticky, and she wiped them absently against the thighs of unfamiliar pants.

"It's the third building," Severn said quietly. He let the chain drop from one hand, shifting his grip. "There's fighting," he added.

"I can see that." It wasn't as bad as Mayburn. Two dozen Barrani, of either persuasion, were scattered along the relevant length of Culvert road. Most were wielding swords; some were wearing fire.

Something tugged at her—from the inside. "Nightshade's there," she said.

Tiamaris, looking every inch the grim Dragon Lord, Hawk or no Hawk across his chest, nodded.

"Tiamaris?"

"He is there."

"What's wrong?"

"Nothing."

Kaylin moved away from the well. Her eyes narrowed; they didn't have the depth of vision that Dragon eyes clearly had; she really had to look to find the fieflord. But when she did, she wondered why it had taken so long. He wore armor; he wore shin splints, his forearms were plated, and his hair was his only cape.

He also wielded a long sword. The Barrani Hawks had never favored blades, and given their reach and the ease with which they used staves, Kaylin hadn't much wondered why. She wondered now, but only briefly—because *his* sword seemed to stop the dead Barrani in their tracks.

"He'll cut a path through them," she said, half-gaping.

"With that sword." Tiamaris's voice was low and deep, constrained only by a throat too small for its full range. "Yes, he'll cut his path."

"He won't know where to go," Severn pointed out.

No, Kaylin thought. He wouldn't. "The Hawks?"

"They're not landing."

She grimaced. "How many?"

And Severn laughed. "Enough. Are you ready?"

She nodded again, although she had his daggers, and no other weapon. "Tiamaris?"

The Dragon frowned.

"What? What is it?"

"The Hawklord," he replied.

Fire began to fall, in a brilliant cascade of white and blue, from the heights. Where it touched building, it began to burn, and the building, unlike the Barrani, didn't put up much of a fight.

Kaylin swore.

Severn caught her arm as she leaped forward. "Kaylin!"

She turned, half-wild, to face him.

"There won't be anyone alive in that building. Anyone who could has already fled."

"The children are there!" She shouted back, her voice rising in pitch, her body shaking. She saw his hesitation, the marred decision in it, and she slapped him. He let her; her hand connected with the side of his face because he made no move at all to stop her, to deflect her.

"Severn," Tiamaris began, "there is a danger here—"

Severn nodded. He released Kaylin's arm; his fingers were white. His face, white as well, where her palm and fingers had marked him. "Tell the Hawklord to wait."

Dragon hesitations were marked by silence and stillness; there was nothing about them that resembled indecision.

"There is a risk," he said again. "If the children are killed before they can be sacrificed, the risk is greatly diminished."

Kaylin *hated* him then.

But Severn shook his head. "I've tried that safety before. I'm willing to take the risk."

"You won't bear the brunt of it."

"No," he said. "Kaylin, follow Nightshade."

She stared at him. At the palm print that was now turning red, changing the color of his skin.

"You're not a child anymore. Maybe you weren't one then. I don't know." His voice was low and intent, his gaze didn't waver. "But we'll try."

Tiamaris lifted his chin and *roared*.

Kaylin winced. "Well," she said, as every Barrani—dead or not—in the street seemed to shudder at the sound of that voice, "they know where we are now."

"Lord Nightshade knew where you were the moment you left his castle," the Dragon replied. "Go. I will…join the fieflord." And he leaped up, past them, his sword a flash of light, of something that resembled fire, as it left his sheath.

Only when Tiamaris was beyond them, only when they had reached the side of the first building, did Severn pause. "Children?"

She nodded.

"Not child?"

And shook her head. "I don't know," she asked, before he could ask her how she *did* know. "But…children."

He met her gaze, held it. Frowned. "Kaylin—your eyes—"

She knew, then. She could almost feel what she couldn't see. Tried not to talk much, because she would hear it as well. "What do the wolves know?"

"Not a lot, about you. Enough. You're marked," he added, "in our—in their—records." His chain was turning now; it flew in a barrier to their left. She was amazed that he could both keep it spinning and run; she would have tripped over it. Or cut her feet off. Hells, probably both.

Better to think about things like that. She tried very hard not to do anything else as she ran beside Severn.

But the children were being marked in a different way.

She didn't know them; she was certain of that. Not the way she had known Jade or Steffi. Not the way she knew Catti. Whoever their enemies were, they were desperate.

Should be desperate.

"Kaylin—"

She couldn't let Severn *touch* her. She moved. Tiamaris was by their side and gone, pacing them, lopping off limbs almost as casually as bureaucrats signed documents. The fires from above had ceased to fall; she wondered if they could be doused as easily as they had been set. A whole block could go up, in fire like that.

Think, Kaylin. Think.

Dagger in her hand. Dirt road beneath her feet. Beside her, for a moment, building. When the dead Barrani came toward her, in the tunnel concentration made of her vision, they were met not by Dragon, but by fieflord. She had always found it strange that Barrani blood could be so red; everything else about them was different. They lived forever. Surely they should have bled gold, or something similar.

"*Kaylin.*"

"I killed a man," she told Severn, speaking as if she were Records, and not Kaylin Neya. "I touched him." They were at the building's side now. The third building. She stepped over an arm, and ground her heel into the bend of its elbow when she saw it was still moving.

He shrugged, trying to make light of it. "You've killed more than one," he said. "If our records are accurate."

"He disintegrated. That was the word they used. I

touched him. He just…crumbled. From the inside. It was like black fire," she added. "I could feel it."

And she did.

"And the other three—I killed them too. Before Teela could. They—their skin just melted. Nothing else. Just their skin. Because the first one hadn't suffered *enough*."

He was by her side. He never left it. And she could barely see him, now; she could hear and feel and taste the blackness. No, she thought, *no*. She was going to lose it.

"That was the child prostitution ring," he said. His words were crystal clear, shorn of the darkness that enveloped hers. "They would have died anyway. They wouldn't have survived. It didn't make a difference."

It was true.

And it wasn't true. And the Hawks had accepted it, but only barely, and only because her touch wasn't always death. She had been afraid, after.

But not then. Not now.

No, that wasn't true. Now, she was afraid. Because the children were there, somewhere in there, and she wasn't with them yet. Some other darkness was, and she could almost feel it. Almost…touch it.

No.

But the word she spoke was different.

She had been with Teela and Tain that day, on what Teela had called a routine operation. She often wondered what would have happened to her if she had been with *anyone* else. Teela and Tain hadn't even flinched when the men had died screaming. And screaming. Teela had just sort of shrugged, as if she'd seen it all before; as if it were just another death.

Tain, at least, had said, "You'd better clean up—a lot—before we go back to the Halls."

"Kaylin?" Severn's voice brought her back. "You did it *once.*"

"Yeah."

"You didn't do it twice."

"No."

"Why?"

How to explain?

Because the children she had saved then had looked at her *as if she were worse.* As if she were more of an evil than the men she'd killed; more of a danger. And she realized, then, that some of the screams—most of them—hadn't been the screams of the dying. But when she'd been killing, she hadn't cared.

"You knew."

"The Wolf Lord knew," he said, grunting as the bars came down and the window—such as it was—waited.

"How?"

Severn's silence was his only answer.

"And he told you?"

Severn raised a brow. Answer enough.

"You don't care."

"No. I don't. But I was a shadow wolf, Kaylin."

"You want to trade dirty secrets?" She tried to smile as the bars came down.

He locked his fingers together and knelt; she put her foot in the stirrup his hands made. But he looked up, his smile pale, sharp, shorn of any mirth. "You already know the worst of mine," he whispered.

Before she could answer, he lifted her up, and she bent knees and weight into the jump as the glass and the thin strips of wood that held it in place shattered.

She rolled to her feet, grateful for boots; it was dark in the empty, small room. No sunlight penetrated the gaping hole she'd left; no light. She heard Severn land. Cursed him; he was lighter on his feet than she had been, and he weighed a lot more.

"There's a courtyard," he told her.

She frowned. "You saw it?"

He shook his head. "It's Culvert. The buildings are old enough."

"You think they're there?"

"Nowhere else they could be."

"Why?"

"The watchtower," he replied, looking past her to the closed door. He motioned her to the side, and positioned himself just behind its hinges. "They were on the ground floor, there."

"They could be in the basement—"

"Culvert Street doesn't have any basements. And the rooms here—too small."

Not to live in, just to die in.

She grunted because he couldn't see her nod; he was

looking at the edge of the door. For light, she thought. For movement.

The door flew open as he yanked it, hard.

She was in the hall, daggers in hand, before it had finished flapping. No one, here. Just a long hall that led toward fighting on one side, and toward another closed door on the other. She could see only that door; everything else was shadowed.

Severn couldn't swing that chain in this hall. But he shortened his grip on its length, pulling the blade into his hand. There was enough of a grip there, and just the hint of tang's lip. It wasn't a weapon she could have used in a fight without losing her own fingers.

She could see its edge more clearly than she could see Severn. He approached her, and she said, quietly, "Don't touch me." It wasn't a threat. Wasn't, at least, meant as one.

He accepted it as he accepted all warnings.

She began to run down the corridor, drawn to the closed door that ended it. She knew that this wasn't standard procedure. Knew it, couldn't stop herself. Her hands were shaking.

She shoved one dagger into a sheath as she reached the door. It was a wooden door—nothing in this building was made of anything but wood—maybe an inch thick. She put her hand flat against its surface. Felt it vibrating against her palm.

It dissolved against her skin in a whisper of black ash that started at the edges of the frame and blew inward. There should have been sunlight. There were steps—three flat steps—that led down to a barren common courtyard, ringed by the outer walls of each building's inner face. There were windows; had to be windows. She couldn't see them.

She could see night, moonless, dark, gathered in the heart of the courtyard. Within its folds, she could see men moving. Robed men, tall and graceful, utterly silent.

All but one.

He wore dark armor, a helm that hid his face, a sword that matched everything else about him: it was ornate, the blade's edge almost scalloped. Both edges, feet of it, almost a yard and a half. A great sword. It did not reflect light; there was none to reflect.

But he raised it, point toward the sky, as if in salute, and he turned his head to face her. His mailed hand rose and he lifted the face-plate of his ancient helm. The armor looked familiar to Kaylin, although she couldn't say why.

She had thought to see someone like Lord Nightshade in this elegant, powerful man. And there was some hint of the fieflord in the long contours of his face, but it was not a slender face, not a Barrani face.

Not a mortal face.

Golden eyes, unlidded and round, met hers as the stranger smiled. He lifted his free hand, as if in greeting, and lowered it, palm up. The joints of mail made no sound as his long fingers uncurled.

Daughter, he said, although his lips didn't move. *Daughter of darkness. We bid you welcome, to this, the first day of your birth. It has been long in coming.*

He was beautiful. Compelling. Age rolled off him without leaving a mark, as if it were majestic.

Her arms were tingling. Her legs. The skin along her back and her lower chest. All of the sigils, the marks that she knew, now, were like hidden names of power, undying and unchanged.

No, not unchanged. Almost against her will, she lifted her hand—the hand that held no dagger; the hand that was still black with the ashes of the door. Her nails were black, her fingers curved slowly inward, as if around a shape that she could only barely see.

The outer edge of night.

Severn drew himself up short just a step behind her; she heard his intake of breath as if it were the only breath drawn outside of that self-contained night. She heard him speak two words.

Had to struggle to understand them; they held no power, no compulsion, nothing of the beauty of the stranger she now faced.

"The children."

And vision twisted, her eyes watered, the marks upon most of her body shrinking inward and pulling at the edges of the skin on which they lay.

Hidden, insignificant, the children were scattered among the silent Barrani; they had no power. Would never have power. Thin, spindly, awkward, they flailed like—like cattle that understood that the slaughter was waiting.

Their small, pale mouths were open, their eyes wide;

they were covered in dirt, in bruises, smeared by tears; they were white, white with terror. And she *had not seen them* until Severn had spoken of their existence.

The shock must have transformed her expression, because the transformation was mirrored in the face of the armored stranger. *You are too early,* he said. *And far, far too late.* And he smiled, and the smile was beautiful; it was a promise.

You feel concern for these?

She couldn't answer. Her body was stiff now, tense; the story of action had yet to unfold her limbs.

They die anyway, daughter. They die every day. Give them the whole of your life, and you will waste only time; they are beyond your ability to save.

But they are not beyond the ability to save you. You were chosen by our ancient enemies. You were chosen without regard for any choice of your own. They are masters of Law, and as all masters of Law in this city, they serve their own interests.

We have given you choice, he added, and the whisper of his voice filled her, as if she were in truth just a vessel; the marks upon her body relaxed, the skin flattening. *We will give you power.*

With power, you can do as you desire.

It was true. It was *all* true.

You have been helpless all your life. He gestured. She saw a boy—a strange boy, dwarfed by Barrani in size, and by the utter lack of the strange, black beauty, that girded the rest. Mouth open, screaming in absolute silence, he was laid upon a slab of raised stone.

The marks upon her body were a part of her, and all of her watched in dull fascination, and she felt a warmth take her that she had *never* felt. Desire? Yes. The definition of desire. Her mouth was dry.

She ran her tongue across her lips.

Tasted blood.

Blood? She lifted fingers to her cheek, and felt the one mark upon her that was not affected by the dead and the dying, no part of their spell and their attraction.

It was bleeding.

The man in armor frowned.

Two things happened, then. Severn, rigid and silent, suddenly left her back exposed, leaping in beside her, the only light in the courtyard. His chain was at full extension, swinging, its links catching something that didn't exist in her vision: the fading of sunlight.

He didn't call her. But as he leaped past, she saw something else catch the light, and with it, her attention; the Hawk across his chest. Its brief flight.

The Barrani did not scatter; some lost limbs, one lost half his face. Blood spilled, red, living; she could see it pool, and it pooled in lines that were...words. Ancient symbols.

The man in armor slammed his face-plate down, changed the angle of his great sword. He *moved,* and if the Barrani were slowed by the strange hollowness that was their death, this creature, golden-eyed and bright in his darkness, was not.

He strode toward Severn, as Severn's feet landed upon the blood sigils, the old words. Severn would die here. At long last, he would die.

The thought came at a distance.

The blood-writ letters were closer; they were somehow more real. She looked at them, and her lips moved, and she felt the satisfaction of the armored man as his sword swung in a flat arc almost too fast for eyes to see.

She opened her lips.

And spoke.

But the word she spoke was not written there; it was written within her, beneath skin.

Calarnenne.

Kaylin.

She spoke his name again, subverting the strength of desire, twisting it, forcing it into the only channel that she could touch, bound as she was by too many words, none of them her own. And all of them.

And then Kaylin Neya found her wings, and she screamed a name, another name, as she at last leaped into the fight.

It was the Hawklord's name.

Kaylin Neya, weeping, claimed her Aerie, made her choice, and turned to join her Severn, the only ground Hawk here, as he faced death.

Death heard her, and lifted his head; his sword caught chain, or chain caught it, holding it in place. She cried out a warning to Severn, in the broken Elantran that the fieflings spoke as children, and Severn gave the chain a vicious tug.

The sword fell.

But it wasn't a triumph.

It was a castoff. It was unnecessary. The man in armor *roared*. And in the confined space of a large courtyard, he began to change, shedding the weakness of arms and legs.

Black wings rose out of his back, and claws extended from mailed fist—and only then, because she was still Kaylin—did she realize why the armor had looked so familiar: she had seen its like once before, but its color and shape were so different she hadn't recognized it for what it was.

The scales of a Dragon.

CHAPTER 20

Kaylin.

She didn't answer. Wouldn't have had time to process the sound had it come from outside of her, the way sound usually traveled. She had *just* enough time to slam into Severn, just enough weight to push him beyond the edge of the sudden eruption of Dragon's jaw. She trusted him to survive this, as she would have trusted no one but Teela or Tain; he was already on his feet, in command of the momentum, before she had come to a stop.

The Dragon's attention was still focused on her.

"Let them go," she told him, tense and low to the ground. Her voice, like the Dragon's, was a roar of sound, a personal storm. It should have surprised her.

His great eyes were orange, unlidded, the size of her fist. His breath was red, and traveled far beyond the reach of his tongue. She stood in the path of fire, and when it struck her, it parted as if it were water. Or ash. Where it passed, it left darkness, and only darkness, in its wake.

As she stepped forward, she did the same. It should have been hard to separate his darkness from hers. It wasn't. She crouched, bending her knees a few inches lower, and reached for the blood that Severn had spilled. Where she touched it, it, too, burned. These flames were black, with hearts of blue. Leather cracked beneath her feet; she tried her best not to step on that fire.

"So," the Dragon said. "You are still *mortal*." The word was a spit of contempt, a funereal wreath of smoke and ember. "Do you think you can *use* the power you contain? Fool. It will devour you."

She understood everything he said, and knew she couldn't. But she'd always been practical, and doubting her sanity wasn't all that pragmatic at a time like this.

"You speak of choice," she said. Severn was beyond the Dragon's jaws, just out of the reach of his claws. If the Dragon noticed Severn at all, he gave no sign of it, and Severn stepped…back. The darkness swallowed him, but she could hear the keening of his chain; what she couldn't see still existed.

"But the dead have none."

Eyes glittered, huge eyes, against the sheen of startling black. "You speak of my servants."

She said nothing.

He laughed softly. Laughter was fire and pain. "They surrendered their names," he told her softly, "in return for *power.* For freedom. They were given power," he added.

"And you?"

"I surrender nothing." He held out a hand; she could see fingers as if they were the soul of claws, small and ethereal, but somehow still present. If the Barrani were dead, the Dragon was not.

Not yet.

"You were a threat," the Dragon continued. "And a gift. But not yet. Not yet." And he leaped toward her suddenly, lunging, his wings rising and folding, their pinions bearing down on the stones that held her.

She leaped away as they came crashing groundward. Splinters broke the soles of her boots, cutting holes into the perfect fabric of her tunic, her pants. She grimaced. She'd done this before, and she hadn't enjoyed it the first time.

The Dragon reached out for the child who struggled across the altar, and she realized that Severn had—again—done his work, made his choice; he was upon that sacrificial stone, feet planted astride the young victim, his chain a wall against which the Barrani broke, again and again, as they sought the time in which to finish what they'd started.

Kaylin.

Nightshade's voice again. No command, no question, no warning marred her name; it was simply a word, a joining of two syllables. An anchor. She held it, held on to it, as she leaped forward, dreaming of darkness. The dream enfolded her. As the Dragon reared up, as his ebony claws extended, she leaped between Severn and death, her daggers forgotten as she raised both palms. Symbols came to life beneath their thin, torn shelter of black silk; they crawled up the backs of her hands, living things. She had never really thought of them as language before. Had never really thought of language as something that was living or dead; it was, like walking, something she rarely thought about at all, unless she was caught in the crossfire of legal Barrani, in which case the not thinking part took a lot more effort.

The Dragon was not so blessed.

As the symbols shifted, she felt their sudden weight across the mounds of her exposed palms. Fire was black, now; it would always be black. It enveloped her vision, and she let it, because the alternative was the unnatural gleam of Dragon teeth, Dragon scale, Dragon jaw. She had come all this way to do something.

But she forgot it, whatever it was: even the memory of Severn dimmed and faded as she at last gave in to inexplicable rage. There was glee in that rage, and malice, and—yes—a desire to cause pain and suffering. Or to share it.

She spoke the words. Her lips moved over syllables that made no sense to her ears, that contorted her throat, twisted her lips and changed the contour of her face, as if in the speaking, she had suddenly begun to grow jaws as lethal as the Dragon's.

Those jaws snapped shut on the resonant, lingering end of old syllables, and the gold of Dragon eyes, the red of Dragon eyes, gave way to a color that she had never seen: White, milk and ivory, an absence of slitted pupil. She heard the Dragon roar as scales began to peel away. Saw those scales fall, a glittering darkness, the weight a heavy rain of a type that make docks and city ports look like a fool's dream of safe harbor. They did not disintegrate; they did not turn into ash that even the slightest of breeze could obliterate. They hit broken stone with a clatter.

She noticed it, but barely; the Dragon had been exposed. Beneath the black scales lay something so pale it might have been skin. She lifted her hands again.

Teeth grazed her palms, slashing across the form and curve of thick sigils. Flesh left as well, and blood scattered across the scales that had fallen. Her blood. The pain was brief and sharp, and her fingers spasmed, as if they might follow.

But she was beyond pain. It might have been happening to someone else entirely; it might have been happening in a dream laced with dark fog and distance. She didn't bring her hands in, didn't try to protect them; who protected a sword, after all, when it had hit steel, a like weapon?

She heard the Dragon roar. *"Kill the children!"*

And his words made sense in a way that memory hadn't. Brought back memories older than the mere minutes of these ones, brought with it a pain and a terror that she thought she had faced down in the Hawklord's tower.

She'd been wrong. Would always be wrong. It was there, and *if* she moved quickly enough, if she gave over everything she had to the words that now adorned her, she might *finally* achieve her goal, and have peace.

She could save them. She could save them all.

He became her enemy, her only enemy. As if he were Severn, all along; as if he were the darkness that lurked in the hands that had done the inconceivable.

She leaped toward him, hands extended, and she hit him with the full force of her negligible weight. It wouldn't have moved Tiamaris, at a different time; Tiamaris would have stood there like a damn wall.

But this one? This Dragon *screamed*, and pain mingled with fury, drowning out all other sounds. Scales parted, again and again; some fell and some clung, sundered, useless armor. She saw the words in him, then, as they gave way. Saw, as she had seen Nightshade's gift, syllables as strong, as fine and as alien. She did not try to speak them; she made them her own.

Drew them in, as she had drawn words from the seal, the man of blue fire. Ate them.

He cried out in rage; pain was beyond him.

And then he began to shrink, to dwindle, to fall again into the casement of flesh that Dragons wore in Elantra. She could see the dark wash of blood that covered his chest, his arms, his shoulders, that trickled from the side of his mouth.

Not enough. Never enough.

She sent fire out in waves, in dark swirls and eddies, and he stood in their center, his own hands outstretched, the fire coming from them as dark as her own. They spoke the same grim, bitter language, in a silence broken by grunts, by heavy breaths.

All around them, fires burned, dark now, the red forgotten. Even the hearts of blue that had adorned the first fall of blood faded slowly from her vision. This was what she wanted. Only this. He had to suffer. He had to die.

Kaylin!

Not here. She heard and felt the tug of her name, and she struggled to relieve herself of its unwelcome weight. Not here, and not yet.

The Dragon shrivelled; he might not have been a Dragon at all; he might have been…a man. Just that; a man with odd eyes, his scales pulled in, his broken wings—and they were broken—pulled back into the shelter of shoulder blades and spine. She hardly noticed. The contest of language, the fight for conversational space, was all that mattered. Rock melted beneath her feet; she could feel it, but it didn't burn. Rock melted beneath his, to like effect. They were evenly matched.

She knew this.

And then she let go of even that much awareness, and let the blackness take her. Let herself be taken by darkness; it was the same, after all.

But into the darkness, light came, like a third sword, like an angle of conversation that she hadn't considered, another way of looking at death. It was a golden light, and it was broken by shining shards of different color, blinding in their contrast with the things that she had chosen to see.

She heard words, different words, thin and spoken; recognized—but barely—the voice that uttered them; she couldn't see the face, but she would have known Severn anywhere.

Kaylin, he said, at a great remove, his voice following this new light, *you're killing them. You're killing the children.*

No! She wanted to scream the words, but the language was wrong; she was mute. *You killed them! You, not me!*

She closed her hands; made fists of them. In the distance, she heard the breaking of a hundred bones, all at once. There were no screams, and she regretted their absence; she would do better next time.

But the voice spoke; whoever she had killed, it hadn't been Severn. Still. Always. How did you kill memory?

She struggled with it, with the darkness, with the words. Saw the Dragon recede, and made to follow, but only with power, with symbols, with words. She could do that, now.

But something held her back. Some words, something that Severn had said, now penetrated her awareness—as did the sense of the passing of rage.

It was almost over. The Hawklord would be angry.

Funny, that that was her first thought. Funny and humbling.

And then the light caught her extended arm, and she had enough time to recognize what it actually signified; she had abstracted it, somehow, forgetting.

It was the bracer. She couldn't see the hands that carried it, but *knew* they were Severn's. The bracer caught her wrist, and where it touched, she thought to feel fire. Felt instead a blessed coolness, a familiar weight. For just a moment she struggled against it, but there were things buried in memory that didn't need images to coalesce.

Lights danced. Blue, blue, red, blue, white, white.

She heard the click of the golden cage, and felt its invisible bars bearing down on her. Black shadows ebbed between those bars, seeking egress; they touched the light and cringed back, and back again, falling toward her skin as if from a great height.

She staggered as the ancient bracer that had been a gift and a burden given her by the Hawklord made its weight and presence known. Her vision cleared slowly, and with the passage of shadow and black night, her strength also fled. She sank to her knees—or would have—but Severn caught her before she could hit the ground.

Could hit what was left of it; it was shattered rock in places, and where the rock had been lifted or broken, the ground was red, almost liquid. Severn lifted her. She wanted to argue, but the movement of her lips made no sound at all.

He brought her up to his chest; she felt his chin against the top of her head. Felt the rise and fall of his chest, the breath that left his slightly open mouth as it pushed against her hair.

Her eyes cleared completely; reality returned, and with it, the words that she'd learned in the heart of the fief of Nightshade. Words that she couldn't speak. Worry followed, sudden and sharp, and behind it, much stronger, the metallic taste of fear. She grabbed at Severn's surcoat, saw the ragged Hawk beneath her fingers, and clenched.

"Severn—"

"They're safe," he told her quietly. His voice was thin. She wondered if it would always sound that way; the thunder in her ears was its own deafness. She looked at the courtyard in the fading of sundown, and saw that the bodies of Barrani were scattered across the stones.

And frowned. "The Dragon—"

"He's gone, Kaylin."

"You let him—"

"It was him, or the children," Severn replied.

"Where are they?" It was all she could think of to ask.

He gestured with his shoulder, and then, navigating broken ground, turned slowly to face them. They were huddled against the east wall of the courtyard, their bodies intertwined, their hands and arms around each other, their heads—different colors of hair blending in the scant light of evening—were bowed. But they were not terrified, and one boy looked up, his eyes passing over hers to meet someone's. Severn's, she thought.

The Barrani were not all dead.

But they would be. From above, fire began a gentle rain, and it was a red fire.

The Hawks were landing in the open courtyard in ones and twos. Where there was no safe place to stand, they hovered, pole-arms at ready, seeking the dead, or the soon to be deader.

"You…you saved them," she whispered.

He said nothing.

Reality bit her, hard. "You saved them from *me*." The shadows were better than reality; they caused less pain. To her. The gems on the bracer were glowing. She had never once seen them so bright.

"You didn't mean to threaten them," he told her. As if it were a comfort, or meant to be.

"I didn't even think of them," she whispered, and she

turned her face into his chest, into the threads of gold that had come unbound: the Hawk's symbol.

"You found them," he continued, although he couldn't see her face. "We would never have come in time if not for you."

"I would have done their work for them."

He said nothing, but his arms tightened. She felt them as an offer of protection. But how the hell did you protect someone from themselves?

"Severn—"

"Not now, Kaylin. Not now."

She heard the sound of wings, the sound of weapons striking flesh; the cry of the Aerians at war. Seven years ago she would have joined them.

And five minutes ago, she would have been their target. She knew it, and wondered how many of them did. Maybe none.

She knew Severn would never tell them.

"Corporal." Smooth, cold voice. It took her a minute to place it as Tiamaris's. She turned, then, but her hands still held on to Severn.

Severn's nod was bleak.

Tiamaris crossed the broken ground as if it was of no consequence. His step was heavy enough to dislodge already weakened flagstones. He stopped five feet from Kaylin, and met her eyes, holding them. Demanding, in silence, some answer that she was no longer certain she could give.

But after a moment, his shoulders relaxed, and the blade he carried fell slightly. "You saw," he said.

"The Dragon," she whispered.

"Makuron the Black," Tiamaris replied. "The only living outcaste."

The reason, Kaylin realized, when he fell silent, that there were no outcaste Dragons.

"Yes," a second voice said, and turning slightly, unwilling to relinquish her seat, she saw Lord Nightshade. His armor was rent, and his sword, crimson.

"You knew."

"No, Lord Tiamaris. But I suspected. Of those who have come to study the ancient ruins, only one has never been threatened by the power contained in the sigils." The fieflord met the Dragon's glance, and raised his sword.

The Dragon's golden eyes rounded, shifting into a deep orange, something just shy of red. The length of the fieflord's sword was reflected in his unlidded stare.

"Yes," Nightshade said, although his gaze fell upon Kaylin and remained there. "One of the three. *Meliannos*, the second."

Kaylin looked confused.

And Tiamaris smiled grimly. "Three weapons were crafted by the Barrani in a time when war was more…common. They had the power to withstand Dragon fire," he added softly, "and the strength to pierce Dragon armor. It has been… many years since I have seen one such. The Emperor does not favor them."

"It has been long in my keeping," the Barrani fieflord replied gravely, "and only against such need."

"The Emperor will know," Tiamaris said, eyes still upon the unsheathed blade.

The fieflord shrugged. "If he is wise, he already suspects. And I fear that the blade will not be his only concern, nor even his greatest."

"Makuron is not dead."

"No." The fieflord hesitated for a moment, and then met Kaylin's eyes. "You do not understand what transpired here."

She shook her head. Because she didn't. And because she did. She was shuddering now, as power fled. Consciousness would soon flee with it, but not yet. She struggled to keep her eyes open.

"Makuron is old," Nightshade said. "And you weakened him greatly. More, I fear, than either I or Lord Tiamaris might have, had we been present." He reached out; she stilled. His hand brushed the mark on her cheek, and almost without volition, she leaned into his fingers; they were cool and soft.

"I did not kill him," he told her, and she thought the words were meant only for her, although he spoke them carelessly in front of witnesses.

"You could have." As the words left her, she knew it was true.

"Yes. In his weakened state, I could."

"But you didn't."

"No."

"Why?"

"Because," he told her quietly, "I owed you a debt, and you would not consider it well repaid had I killed him. Having seen one who had the strength to pay that price, I chose to forego it, for your sake."

She frowned.

Lord Nightshade looked up then, and met Severn's gaze—or what she presumed was Severn's gaze.

Lord Tiamaris echoed that frown. But when it became clear that the fieflord was finished, he spoke. "You almost killed him yourself, Kaylin. Had you, I think you would have survived. But the children would not. And when the fires left you—if they ever did—you would bear the weight of their deaths."

The fieflord began to walk away.

"Lord Nightshade!"

He turned, his eyes a deep, deep green, with fragments of a cold blue at their heart.

"Thank you."

He bowed. "It is not over," he told her quietly. "Between us. Between the Old Ones. You are here, and you live, and you have used their power."

"Then he—"

"Makuron has lost much. But until he is dead?" He shook his head. "He is best not forgotten. It is not the first time that he has almost died."

"What did he—what was he trying to do?"

The fieflord's eyes widened a moment, and then he chuckled. It was the Barrani equivalent of an open laugh. "You don't understand," he said, shaking his head. "And I will not be the one to explain it. Not yet, Kaylin Neya, not even to one whom I've graced with my name." He turned away then, leaving them.

"Makuron could read the old writing," Tiamaris said

quietly. He looked again at Kaylin. "And he could summon…the dead."

"The Barrani?"

He nodded. His expression was about as warm as quarried stone.

"Why did they serve him?"

"He offered them power," Tiamaris said. "And yes, this is why Lord Nightshade cannot answer you. Makuron offered them the power for which they surrendered their names."

"But—"

"Power is strange and fickle. What they thought they surrendered was the vulnerability with which all immortals are afflicted—the weakness of name. What they surrendered instead was much, much more than that. Like all such bindings, it serves two purposes."

"I don't understand."

"No. You don't." He hesitated for another minute, and then said, "History is not our guide, it is not our friend. It is a passing stranger, one which shadows legend, sprinkling it with the seeds of truth. It is said that the Old Ones—which ones, we do not know—created the races. The first, the immortals, were their greatest creations. But they could not give them life without giving them names. The words had power," he added, "but I think you understand this one fact better than even I.

"Regardless, the Old Ones made our forms, but our forms were *not* living. Into the heart of these, they carved runes and sigils, each unique, and when they had finished, they *spoke* those names for the first, and the only, time. And the power of those words is said to have wakened each—Dragon, and Barrani. We were few, then.

"But the names were the source of our existence, and we were bound to those who knew them." He paused. "Not a one of us likes to be ruled, Kaylin. You could not understand that, no matter how much you might think otherwise. You are mortal."

"But immortals—they have children. Do they name them?"

"No." His lower lids rose.

She knew him well enough to change the subject. "And the rest of us?"

"How you were created, we do not know. There is some argument. Some scholars believe that you came to this world by some method of travel denied those of us bound to it by the ancient laws." His shrug was about as expressive as his face.

"From another world? There's more than one?"

She saw from the look on his face that he had no intention of answering that question. If he could. Dragon pride, she was discovering, was as tricky as legal Barrani to negotiate. Still, this was more than she'd ever gotten him to say, and she didn't want this subdued openness to end before she'd managed to get everything she could. "But… the dead ones?"

"When it became clear that the names themselves were a leash, it is said that some of the living rebelled. Those who had names attempted to divest themselves of that one weakness. They studied the tongue of the ancients. They even felt, in their hubris, that they understood it. They sought to replace what was written at their creation with words over which they had control. And at least one succeeded.

"They now bear a greater weakness because of it. The power that took the place of their names hollowed them. They are not what they were."

"Do they even remember what they were?"

His smile was thin, like a knife's edge. A honed knife. "Very few of us know, very few have had reason to speak at length with the dead. It is...dangerous," he added quietly. "They can take the names we bear, if we are not cautious, and if they cannot become those names, they can take power from them, replacing it slowly with the lingering state that is their endless death."

"Then what are *these*?" She held out an arm. It was a bad idea; her hands were trembling.

"Older still," he whispered. "And a sign that old powers are waking. The...scholars believe they are the words upon which the names were founded. Those sages," he added, "who survived their study. And perhaps it is true. I will not say what I think. I will say only this—let them sleep, Kaylin, if you can." He paused. "The Hawklord's trust in you was not ill-founded. I do not know why you were chosen, if that is what you meant to ask—and it was, even if you do not know it."

"But the marks changed—"

"Yes. They changed. Had Severn not intervened the first time—" He paused. Saw her grim expression, the pain in it that she was too damn tired to conceal. "I am sorry," he said softly, "but you are strong enough to bear this. You already know it. Had Severn not intervened the first time, you would have been lost, both to him and to us. You would *be*, in form and shape, Kaylin Neya—but you would be only a vessel, and at that, a vessel whose neck is held by the only outcaste Dragon in the history of my kind.

"And Elantra would not, now, be a city. What it might become, I do not know, but the dead would be beyond number—some of them, Barrani, some, Dragon. Mortals simply falter, and they, too, would litter the streets like cattle.

"What Severn did, I will not justify—it was not my action. But I will say this…. He saved not only Elantra, but the Empire, for the Dragon Lord that would have arisen in the aftermath of your power would *be* Emperor, and his reign unlike anything you can imagine, even in nightmare." He bowed his head. "We had hoped, with the death of those children seven years ago, and your absence from the fief, that it was over."

"It is now."

"Yes," he said softly. "It is. Tonight, in this place, and by your own will. You wondered why the deaths came so quickly, this time—but the answer must surely be clear, now—you are no longer a mortal on the threshold of adulthood…you *are* adult. Coming into your power without his intervention," he added, "would mean that that power *would be* yours. It was a gamble. He could end his long exile in a handful of mortal deaths, had he but found you, as a child on the brink. He could sense your waking. He must have known how short his time was. Time is a constraint that seldom binds the immortal.

"Had you been allowed to pay the price, to stand for moments longer against Makuron with the full force of that ancient power as your only guide, you would better understand what each mark *is*. I can only…guess."

"Guess, then. Tell *me*."

"The new marks, the changed marks are, in part, the names of the dead, taken from them centuries before you were born. I think—and I once again offer conjecture from the uncomfortable vantage of ignorance—that he hoped to use those names to bind you, to mark you in a way that Nightshade himself has not, to make your power subservient to his own. He could not use the writing that was originally placed there, but if he could change it, corrupting it, until it was something he could speak, he could take that power into himself."

"But he *has* a name."

The Dragon was utterly silent. After a moment, he offered a weary smile and lifted his gaze. She couldn't see where it ended, but she could guess.

"She's Kaylin," Severn said. His voice held a shrug, but as he carried her, he didn't. "She sees what she sees."

"I have pitied her teachers in my study of her transcripts," the Dragon confessed. "But I have so rarely understood their complete astonishment at her inability to see."

But what she saw, as the sun's light guttered, was the glistening ebony of familiar Aerian skin. Clint alighted slowly. He was wounded; his forehead was an ugly gash, and he'd bled into his own eyes. Not pretty. But not life-threatening, either—at least not his own life. His pole-arm had been snapped in the middle, but he held it anyway; anyone who had served with the Barrani Hawks as long as he had knew the value of a good, long club.

"Kaylin?"

"Clint," she said. Her eyes widened as she saw bloody streaks across the even gray of his wings. "Your flight feathers—"

"They'll hold." He paused, his gaze slanting toward the east before his shoulders relaxed. "It's pretty much over," he told her. "The…other Barrani…are walking pyres now. They're a bit hard to kill," he added.

"They would be. They're already dead."

"They bleed a lot for dead people. And they make *us* bleed a lot." His smile was grim. He slid into Barrani. "The Hawklord will require your presence for debriefing."

She nodded; it was all the obedience he required. Had it been necessary, she would have danced or done somersaults, although not without pain. Then she looked to the east as well, to the knot of lost children who were waiting in silence, a stunned silence that would haunt dreams for decades. Hers. Their own.

"What will we do about the children?" She counted them as a Hawk counts. There were ten. One boy, naked, was covered in the marks; two girls had likewise been marked, and they covered themselves with shaking hands, attempting to hide the sigils that had also covered Catti. Catti and over forty dead children whose bodies had been left in the streets of the fief of Nightshade. She wanted to get up, to strip herself of the long, torn shirt she wore, to give it to one of the children. But she couldn't move.

And what she did not do, the Aerian Hawks began to do instead. The children were frightened, and she wanted to tell them not to be. They would be safe with these men, these winged beings, so much like Angelae in appearance they seemed—at this moment—to be gifts from a merciful god. If there were any.

"We will make every effort to find their parents," Severn told her. His voice was quiet, even subdued. She looked up at his face, saw it at an odd angle, the chin the widest thing in her field of vision. He'd lost blood, just as Clint had, and another scar might adorn him in a few weeks' time.

She hadn't the strength to remove it; the bracer saw to that. But she didn't ask him to remove the bracer, either. It was still glowing, still making its silent accusation.

"How many of them still have living parents?" Bitterness seeped into every word. She thought of the woman by the old well.

"At least one," he replied softly. "But Kaylin, those that don't, we will take to Marrin. And Marrin will make them hers."

She thought of the Leontine, and she was oddly comforted. "They're old, for foundlings," she told him, as he began to move. And they were; between ten and twelve years of age, and under the shadow of puberty.

"They're old," he agreed. The words were fading. She could feel their rumble in his chest. "But they'll survive to be older." If the words were bitter—and they might have been—she didn't cling to them.

She let him carry her away; away from the children for whom, as Severn had often said, she had a weakness.

Just not enough of a weakness not to kill them all. She closed her eyes; they were heavy anyway, and there wasn't much she wanted to see.

But closing her eyes wasn't much better; something trailed from each, tracing the curves of her cheeks. It wasn't a lot like peace. Luckily, she had an out: she faded into unconsciousness.

CHAPTER 21

She slept for three days.

Woke for hours at a stretch, and ate what she was given; it was mostly mush or broth. She lay abed in a familiar room; it was the one that she lived in. The mirror was silent; someone had covered it.

No, she thought, as she shook herself out of sleep for a moment. *Severn* had covered it.

He came and went from view. She was both afraid to see him and afraid that she would never see him again, depending on how awake she managed to be. She let him spoon feed her for the first two days, but on the third, she insisted on feeding herself, and he sat, crouched on the only chair she owned, staring out the window. Or staring at her reflection in it.

Severn wasn't the only person she saw. Teela and Tain

made their way across her threshold, and she woke once to see Teela draped across the bed like a slightly fussy cat. Clint came to visit, and he brought his baby with him, apologizing because the baby wasn't exactly quiet. She wanted to tell him that she didn't mind the tears—because she didn't—but he faded from view, and when she woke, he was gone.

Even Caitlin and Marcus came to see her; Caitlin brought flowers, and tsked about the condition of the room, picking up a piece of discarded clothing that she swore could almost stand up and walk out on its own. Her voice, when it came from the kitchen, was even more shocked, in that maternal way. It made Kaylin smile.

It made Kaylin weep.

Marcus spoke to her, holding her hand; she knew he did, because she had a distinct memory of the soft paw-pads against her palms. Against her forehead. Leontine breath was not exactly the most pleasant of sensory experiences, but she felt that as well; felt his tongue touch her forehead in benediction. Or gratitude.

"Get your butt out of bed," he growled in her ear. "Or I'll dock your pay."

She smiled wanly. "How long have I been out?"

"Three days. And counting. I'd throw you out of bed, but Caitlin would shred my fur. And my wives would make hunt-meat out of me."

She heard an agreeable growl, and saw Marcus roll his Leontine eyes. One of the wives—she couldn't quite focus to see which—was standing ten feet beyond his shoulder.

"I came," she said, in her slurry, perfect Leontine, "to keep him in line. The males never know their place."

"Now you know," Marcus told Kaylin, his paw-pads soft against her forehead as he pushed her gently, but inexorably, back into her pillows, "why I spend so much time at the office."

Marrin came to visit after she'd slept again, and Marcus and Caitlin, and the wife who had spoken with such certain affection, had been banished by sleep. Her fur, still white around the edges, was perfectly flat, and it had regained some of its luster. Her claws were completely sheathed.

"You look tired," Kaylin said.

Marrin hissed in Leontine laughter. "Someone should take the cover off the mirror," she said, "if *you* can tell *me* that." She paused, and then added, "I have seven new kits, and they all want to meet you." But her eyes flickered as she said it.

Kaylin closed her eyes. "I'm sorry," she whispered.

Leontine claws caught her chin just gently enough not to pierce skin. But not, in truth, by much. "Don't," Marrin said firmly.

"But I—"

"Don't feel sorry for yourself. Not while I'm here."

"But they don't want to—"

"Yes," she said quietly. "I'm their pride-mother. I know what they really want. If they haven't figured that out yet, they will. They're rough around the edges," she added "and they're so scrawny you couldn't make a meal out of the lot of them. But we'll change that." She paused. Her eyes glittered. "They're scared," she said quietly. "They think I mean to use them. But you came from the fiefs, and you can talk sense into them. One or two are already at home—but the others? When you can, Kaylin. Come."

She, too, touched Kaylin's forehead with her paw-pads. They were dry. But Marrin mothered, and she hated to *be* mothered. Kaylin said nothing.

"Severn's been in to see them."

The words didn't terrify Kaylin. They would have, once.

"I...like him, Kaylin. I don't know what he did to you. I won't ask. Whatever it was, he's paid. He's still paying. But he brought them to me, and he covered the expense of clothing them. He'll do."

Tiamaris came later, with, of all things, flowers. She stared at them as if they were withered branches. Or as if he were mad, and it wasn't safe to look at him that way. "The Emperor is in your debt, Private Neya."

She cringed.

He nodded. "Very wise. You are, of course, too weak to attend him. I think it would be very wise if you remained too weak to attend him. He is not a patient man."

"Meaning I'll embarrass the Hawks and he'll have to kill me?"

"Something very like that." He spoke, not in the Barrani that was his most frequently used language, but in Elantran. "What will you do now?"

"Now?"

"Now that it's over."

He held her gaze, his own golden, his lower lids hidden. "I will, I think, be a Hawk for some time yet. It is…an interesting life. The rhythm is mortal, the time is odd. But I find it satisfying in a way that I have seldom found my work satisfying." He reached out for her hand. No, she amended, not for her hand.

For the bracer. It was a steady, warm weight. "The gems are dull now," he told her.

"I know."

"I think it would be safe to remove it, if you felt the need."

She shook her head. Thinking of why it was on her wrist; of what might have happened had it never been placed there at all. "Not yet," she said softly.

"You are growing, Kaylin Neya. In wisdom."

"Is it always going to hurt so much?"

"The gaining of wisdom? Not always." His smile caught her by surprise; it was gentle. Almost human. "The Emperor has graciously allowed you to remain in the ranks of the Hawks."

Both of her brows rose.

"Yes," he said, although she hadn't asked. "He considered strongly seconding you to his service for the use of your healing gift alone. But arguments were made on the behalf of the Hawks, and he has chosen to relinquish your service." Tiamaris rose.

"Lord Grammayre?"

"He is waiting for you, Kaylin. When you are ready, he will still be waiting."

She felt a pang of disappointment.

"He is a Lord of Law," the Dragon told her gently. "And although you saved the city, the city still moves beneath him, and his duty is still clear."

She settled back into her bed, weary.

Severn came into view. "Tiamaris," he said firmly.

"I know. I have already tired her." The Dragon rose, but he stopped a moment and carefully arranged the flowers in the vase he had also had the foresight to bring, since she didn't own one. "But Corporal, I think you could also—what is the phrase? Ah. You could use some sleep."

"I've slept," was the cool reply. It didn't invite further commentary, and the Dragon gave a very Dragon-like shrug.

On the fourth day, Kaylin stood and walked around the confines of her cramped apartment. That she could, without slipping on laundry piles, was a testament to Caitlin's dislike of mess. The kitchen was also—in as much as it could be—spotless. Kaylin was torn between delight and chagrin.

"Let me guess," she said to Severn, who was never far from her side. "She cleaned the mirror, too."

"It's gleaming," was his reply. "She had something to say about the fingerprints all over it. I won't, however, repeat it."

"Have you even been home? I mean, to yours?"

He said nothing. Answer enough. She walked in circles until her legs hurt. This didn't take as long as she would have liked. Four days.

"This is the worst it's ever been," she said, almost to herself.

"Fighting Dragons will do that to you."

"Was I?" she asked him, as she sat heavily on the side of her bed.

"Were you?"

"Fighting Dragons."

He was silent.

On the fifth day, walking wasn't hard. She dressed herself, and she took the cloth down from the mirror, partly because it was one of her only two towels, and she was tired of feeling dirty. She washed herself while Severn stepped out of the apartment, dried her hair and then put her clothing back on. She chose the street uniform.

When Severn returned, she was ready for him. His brow rose slightly when he saw what she was wearing. "Are you strong enough?" he asked.

She nodded quietly. "If I don't look at something besides these damn walls, I'll go mad."

He nodded, and fell into step beside her, at least until she hit the door. She paused there.

"Severn?"

He nodded.

"Thank you." And then, because she didn't want him to misinterpret it, she added, voice low, "for the children."

His expression didn't shift, and that was a sign. He was waiting now, and guarded. But he surprised her; after a moment, he said, "Which ones?"

It hurt.

He flinched, because she must have. One of these years, she'd learn to control that.

Steffi, Jade. She wanted to cry. Didn't.

"You saved the world," she said, trying to keep her voice light. "Then. That's what Tiamaris said." She struggled with the rest of the words, because she had never *ever* thought she would say them. "I couldn't have. I would have let the world burn in black fire. I would have died first." Her eyes were a little too wide, but they had to be; they were filmed with water, and she *hated* tears.

He was cautious. Silence followed.

"Why didn't you kill me instead?" She had to whisper. She couldn't speak. "If I had died—no one's saying it, but I *know*—it would have been over."

"It might have been over," he replied, the words drawn out of him slowly, as if he didn't want to release them. "But Tiamaris thinks it unlikely; he said it was more likely that some other child would bear the marks instead, and it would have started all over."

But she shook her head. "You couldn't have known it, then. Why? Why them? Why not *me*?" The heart of the only question that remained for her. She had never thought she'd ask it; could almost believe she was still asleep, and in the grip of the worst of her nightmares. "They were *children*."

"We were all children," he told her. And then, because the discussion demanded more, he added, "Do you really not know?"

And she did. But she couldn't stop herself. She wanted him to lie. Realized it, and hated herself for the weakness. "You saved the world," she said again, but weakly. It sounded like pleading to her.

Because it was.

He said, "I've only ever lied to you once, and I can't lie to you now. I'm sorry." He started to walk away.

"Severn!"

The open door was between them; he stood on the other side of the frame, a third of a lifetime away.

"Don't. Don't tell me that you did this *for me*."

"If killing myself would have helped, I would have done it," he said, voice low, eyes narrowed. "I almost did. But I was *too old* to be a sacrifice. It was going to be Steffi or Jade, and either of them would have done to you what Catti's death would have done. They didn't suffer," he added, but he closed his eyes and turned his head as he said it. It was more of a prayer than a statement; as much of a plea as she had *ever* heard him make.

"I'm sorry," he added, in a bitter, bitter voice that aged him. Aged them both. "But the truth, Kaylin? I grew up in the same fief you did. I didn't give a damn about the rest of the gods-cursed city; they didn't give a damn about us.

"I did it for *me*. Because even then, I wasn't willing to lose you."

He stepped back, stepped toward the stairs. Turned to

meet her gaze briefly. Briefly was enough. He had sat by her side while she slept; he had watched her, stood guard over her, made her drink and eat and sleep.

And he knew, as he left, that that time was gone.

She stood, numb, in the door, her hand rising to grip the frame, as if without it, she would fall, the floor would swallow her, the blackness destroy her.

She would have welcomed it, and because she would have, it didn't happen.

Clint and Tanner were on duty at the front entrance. She wondered when the Swords would start their rotation; she didn't like them as much, but she wouldn't, being a Hawk.

"Kaylin," Clint said. But he didn't say more. Her expression was not the usual harried terror of someone about to be late for her own funeral, and he knew her pretty well; he knew what it meant. He shifted the pole-arm into his left hand, and he reached out with his right, touching her shoulder. Gripping it for a moment to offer what words wouldn't.

She forced a smile, and knew how bad it looked when he grimaced. "Don't even," he said, with a wry—and genuine—smile of his own. "You've missed a bit of work," he added. "And a bit of excitement."

"What kind of excitement?"

"Oh, the usual."

She thought about dates for a minute, and then her brows rose. "Festival duty," she said, as if the words were worms, and she had accidentally put them in her mouth.

"Smart girl," Tanner said, lifting his helm as if it were a hat. "And you missed sign-up."

She groaned. "Does the fact that I had a decent reason give me a bye?"

"Does it ever?" Clint's laugh was natural, rich and resonant. The laugh she loved. She straightened her shoulders, found that it wasn't as hard as she thought it would be, and shed a bit of gloom. "If I have to cover the tables," she said, adding a few choice Aerian words as decorative color, "someone is in *deep* trouble."

"You might have some say—the list isn't quite finalized."

"Isn't quite?"

"Caitlin has it, but it's not due up until the end of the day."

Given that day had already half-passed, she swore and sprinted up the steps. Stopped, turned back and buried her fingers in Clint's flight feathers.

His expletive was a joyful sound to her ears, although she wouldn't repeat it in polite company.

She burst into the office, and was ashamed to admit that the run up the stairs and down the halls had winded her. Which meant, of course, that she wasn't damn well *going* to admit it.

Marcus looked up as the doors swung behind her. His desk was a pile of paperwork, and he growled at her, his hair standing slightly on end. "You see *this?*" He said, his mock anger laced with real annoyance.

She nodded politely. Which was safest.

"This is the result of your little outing in the fiefs."

"*All* of it?"

"Every last damn bit." His claws bit desk as he pushed himself out of his chair.

"Well, you know what they say."

"No good deed goes unpunished."

"Exactly."

"The Leontines *don't* say that, Private."

She shrugged, but managed to grin. It wasn't even forced.

"Kaylin."

She didn't answer. The shift in his voice, the way his growl curled round the syllables of her name, was serious. "I'm sorry," she said, meaning it.

"For what?"

"For making you worry."

"Good. I have one favor to ask of you."

"Sure."

"Don't make me worry again."

"Yes, sir."

He reached out, his claws sheathed. But his hand stopped short of her face, and settled in her hair instead, ruffling it. Or, more accurately, pulling some of it free from its binding. "You did well," he told her. High praise, from Marcus. In fact, it was the only kind of praise he offered. Short.

"It wasn't just me—"

"But you're *late* again, and the Hawklord is waiting."

"You could have mirrored—"

"Someone keyed your mirror off. You might want to fix that."

Someone. Severn. She said, because it was safe, "Where's the Festival duty roster?"

"Caitlin has it. And bribes are illegal."

"Yes, sir."

"Good. Get out of my sight."

"Yes, sir."

She made her way to Caitlin's desk, got intercepted by Caitlin and hugged so tightly breathing was in question. But when Kaylin pulled back, she did what Marcus hadn't: caught Kaylin's face in her hands, and pulled it up. Tsked at the dark circles under the youngest of the Hawk's eyes. "You aren't sleeping," she said, making an accusation out of concern.

"I've done nothing *but* sleep for the last—what is it? Week?"

"Then take two."

"Ha. After I sign up."

Caitlin shrugged. "You're such a ground Hawk, dear," she said, with an affectionate smile. She held out a small sheaf of papers. Kaylin took them. Cursed when she saw what was left, and then fell silent when she saw her partner assignment.

Tain.

She hesitated, and Caitlin, old hand, could read the hesitation as if it were perfectly executed Barrani. But she waited in silence while Kaylin continued to flip through those papers, looking for a name. She looked up at last, when she couldn't find it.

"He's still a Hawk?" she asked.

"He's still a Hawk," Caitlin replied, not asking who Kaylin meant. "But the Wolf Lord has asked to speak with Lord Grammayre about his disposition. There's every chance—if office gossip is anything to go by—that Severn will be back with the Wolves before the week is out."

Kaylin nodded, as if the words made sense. And they did. Bitter sense.

"Kaylin, dear, don't crumple those. I don't have another copy."

"Sorry."

"I know. You always are." Caitlin hesitated, and then added, "The Hawklord is waiting for you."

"What have I done wrong this time?" But the words were uninflected. Severn. Wolves.

It was best. For both of them. The past was too damn much of a tangle, and it was a tangle of brambles, thorns without roses. She set the papers on the desk and turned at last toward the far door. Toward the Tower steps.

The climb was longer than it had ever been. She had to stop twice, and was glad that there was no one beside her; the guards at the doors on every landing didn't appear to notice her sad lack of endurance.

The Tower door was closed. The mark upon its center, ward against intruders, waited for her hand. She lifted her palm wearily, barely noticing magic's bracing slap. The doors slid open, and she crossed the threshold, looking up only after she had cleared them.

Lord Grammayre stood in the Tower's center, his arms

folded, his eyes narrowed. "You're late," he said. As if this were just another day.

And it was. She was a Hawk. She had made that choice. The world didn't stop for her tragedies; it didn't stop for her past. It didn't stop for anything, and that was a good thing.

"Sorry, Lord Grammayre."

He raised a pale brow. His wings unfolded beneath the domed ceiling slowly and deliberately. But his arms remained folded across his chest, like closed doors. She stood there, feeling seven years younger.

"The Lord of Wolves came to visit this morning," the Hawklord said, breaking her silence. Adding weight to it.

"Oh."

"He has requested the transfer of Corporal Severn Handred."

"Oh." Because her mouth was hanging half-open, she added, "Does he know?"

"Severn?"

She nodded.

"He was present."

"He's going back to the Wolves?"

"Kaylin Neya," the Hawklord frowned. "What have I told you about drawing conclusions?"

She stared at him blankly. This didn't change the direction his mouth was curving in.

"Very well. Since you did not disgrace the Hawks *this time*, I will excuse this almost intolerable display. I said that the Lord of Wolves requested the transfer. I said that Severn was present. Where, in those words, did I say that he had returned to the Wolves?"

"But—but..."

"I leave it up to you," the Hawklord told her, his voice strangely neutral.

"But it's not my life."

"No. It's not. It was, however, the Corporal's only request, and given the success of the mission, I acceded. You are considered to be on active duty," he added, his voice softening.

The words barely registered. She bit her lip. Wanted to be older, tougher, more resilient. It was the weakness, she thought. The backlash of using the power.

Lies.

She looked at the circle on the floor. Avoided it.

His wings were at their full extension, and he slowly lowered his arms. "Fledgling," he said, in Aerian.

And she looked up at him, wordless, unable to control her expression. Without another word she crossed the floor, closing the gap that separated them in the only way she knew how.

His arms caught her first, enfolding her; he bent over her, the difference in their height evident by the way his shoulders curved. Her hands came up to touch the Hawk emblazoned across his chest, and she bowed her head into her fingers, closing her eyes and welcoming this very different darkness.

His wings folded around her like a soft wall.

"I don't want him to leave," she whispered.

He could probably feel the words more clearly than he could hear them. But his lips were beside her ear as he bent, protective now, as if she were in truth not yet ready to fly without guidance.

"I know, Kaylin."

"But I don't—"

"Hush."

"I don't think I can just *forget*—"

"You can't, Kaylin. Don't try. You are not Barrani, and you are not Dragon. Because you are neither, time will help, and only time." He paused. "I will give you whatever time it is in my power to give. I will deny the request of the Wolf Lord."

She hated tears.

Hated them.

But the Hawklord didn't. He held her, in the height of his Tower, and for a moment, she pretended that she believed in the safety his arms offered.

* * * * *

But Kaylin must leave the Tower once more!
CAST IN COURTLIGHT
continues the story in
Summer 2006

LUNA™

On wings of fire she rises...

On Fire's Wings
CHRISTIE GOLDEN

Born without caste or position in Arukan, a country that prizes both, Kevla Bai-sha's life is about to change. Her feverish dreams reveal looming threats to her homeland and visions of the dragons that once watched over her people—and held the promise of truth. Now, Kevla, together with the rebel prince of the ruling household, must sacrifice everything and defy all law and tradition, to embark on a daring quest to save the world.

On sale July 25.
Visit your local bookseller.

**Hidden in the secrets of antiquity,
lies the unimagined truth...**

Introducing

a brand-new line filled with mystery
and suspense, action and adventure,
and a fascinating look into history.
And it all begins with DESTINY.

In a sealed crypt in
France, where the
terrifying legend of
the beast of Gevaudan
begins to unravel,
Annja Creed discovers
a stunning artifact
that will seal her destiny.

*Available every other
month starting
July 2006, wherever
you buy books.*

GRA1TR